FACE OFF

EDITED BY

DAVID BALDACCI

sphere

SPHERE

First published in the United States in 2014 by Simon & Schuster
First published in Great Britain in 2014 by Sphere
This paperback edition published in 2015 by Sphere

1 3 5 7 9 10 8 6 4 2

A CIP catalogue record for this book is available from the British Library.

ISBN 978-0-7515-5494-6

Printed and bound in Great Britain by Clays Ltd, St Ives plc

For Gayle Lynds and David Morrell

Writers, Dreamers
Extraordinaire

Contents

Introduction

In 2004 two accomplished thriller writers harbored a dream. Their names: Gayle Lynds and David Morrell. To that point both Gayle and David had enjoyed long and successful careers. But something was missing. The 'who-done-its' had Mystery Writers of America. Those who specialize in fear, the Horror Writers Association. And the Romance Writers Association had long numbered thousands of members.

Every genre seemed to have a trade group.

Except thriller writers.

So Gayle and David decided to start one.

It began in Toronto on October 9, 2004, and from that small beginning sprang International Thriller Writers. Today over 2,500 men and women, from forty-nine countries around the world, hold membership. Eighty percent are working thriller writers. The rest are industry specialists, agents, editors, and fans. Every July the genre gathers in New York City for Thrillerfest. It's quite literally summer camp for thriller writers and thriller enthusiasts. The Thriller, awarded every year in a variety of categories, is now *the* prize thriller writers covet, since it was both created and bestowed by their peers.

From its beginning ITW strived to innovate. Doing what everyone else had done was never in its business plan. So, in 2007, when board member (and superb British thriller writer) David Hewson suggested that the organization not charge dues the idea was immediately embraced. If a writer is published by an ITW-recognized house (of which there are hundreds), then membership is free.

So how would the organization sustain itself? Pay its bills?

The answer came in another innovative way.

The organization would create its own books that would be sold to publishing houses, the revenue from which would generate operating capital.

Risky? You bet. Gutsy? Definitely.

But an idea right up ITW's alley.

ITW's first publication, *Thriller* (2006), was the first anthology of thriller short stories ever compiled (remember that precept about never doing what others had done). Thirty-three ITW members donated stories. James Patterson (an ITW member) agreed to serve as editor, and the result became one of the most popular anthologies of all time—selling over 500,000 copies worldwide. The revenue from that groundbreaking book not only provided ITW with initial operating money, it also endowed the organization. *Thriller 2* (2009) and *Love Is Murder* (2012) followed. Keeping with this innovative theme ITW published the first audio book ever written only for the ear: *The Chopin Manuscript,* which became a resounding success. Edited by the incomparable Jeffery Deaver (an ITW member), *Chopin* was named the 2008 Audio Book of the Year. That was followed by another audio success, *The Copper*

Bracelet. A move into the world of nonfiction came with *Thrillers: 100 Must-Reads,* edited by David Morrell and Hank Wagner, which continues to garner widespread critical acclaim. Another ITW board member, the legendary R. L. Stine (creator of *Goosebumps*), led the organization into the world of young adult fiction with *Fear.* Annually, ITW shepherds a class of writers through their challenging inaugural year in what is known as the Debut Author Program. *First Thrills,* edited by ITW founding member Lee Child, became an anthology of stories from the 2011 class.

What an impressive résumé.

All created by author-editors who volunteer their time and writers who donate their stories. Nearly every single penny earned from ITW's publications has gone to the organization.

And that will be the case with this book.

I joined ITW early on. I agreed with Gayle and David. It was time for an organization of thriller writers. I've been waiting for a project where I could become more involved with the group, so when I was approached about editing *FaceOff* I immediately said yes.

The entire concept intrigued me.

Take iconic writers with iconic characters and face them off against each other. Normally, this could never happen. Each writer is under contract to his or her own respective publishing house. Teaming with another writer, from another house, and combining characters would contractually be impossible. Which house would publish the story? No way to make that call. And no way either house would allow the story to be published by a third company. Only with ITW's model—that the stories are donated and the money goes to the organization—would this work.

So this volume is truly a once-in-a-lifetime event.

All of the contributors are ITW members. All eagerly agreed

to participate. When I was told that ITW founding member Steve Berry, who worked with James Patterson on *Thriller*, would offer assistance as managing editor, I was thrilled. He's the glue that held this project together. Thanks, Steve, for all you did.

And thanks to all of the contributors.

Where else will you be able to see Jeffery Deaver's Lincoln Rhyme meet John Sandford's Lucas Davenport? Or Patrick Kenzie entering the world of Harry Bosch? Fans of Steve Berry's Cotton Malone and James Rollins's Gray Pierce have clamored for years to see those characters together. Then there's Lee Child's Jack Reacher meeting up with Joseph Finder's Nick Heller in a bar in Boston—and doing what Reacher does best. Plus Steve Martini's Paul Madriani becoming entangled with Linda Fairstein's Alex Cooper. And the ever-odd Aloysius Pendergast coming face-to-face with the scary world of R. L. Stine.

These are just a few examples of what lies in the pages ahead. All of the stories come with an introduction that describes the writers, their characters, and a bit about the story's gestation. At the end of the book are contributor biographies—a way to learn more about each of these amazing talents.

You're in for a real treat.

So let the face-offs begin.

David Baldacci
June 2014

DENNIS LEHANE
VS. MICHAEL CONNELLY

Red Eye

On paper it seemed like a cool idea. Bring Patrick Kenzie and Harry Bosch together in a short story for a good cause. But Dennis Lehane and Michael Connelly quickly realized that it was easier said than done. Both characters are rooted in the verisimilitude of the places they live and the jobs they carry out. They're fictional, sure, but their creators had worked hard to ensure that neither ever made a false move. In short, Harry Bosch and Patrick Kenzie live or die with readers on the basis of their believability. No gimmick short story—good cause or not—could be allowed to mess with that.

So how would these two iconic characters come together?

Most important, who would come to whom?

Would Bosch go east to Kenzie's Boston, or would Boston come to LA?

It seemed from the start the natural thing would be to send Bosch east. In the most recent Bosch books Harry works for the LAPD's Open-Unsolved Unit, a cold case squad that, by its nature, involves travel. When people think they've gotten away with murder, part of that getaway is moving away. Since many of Bosch's investigations have led him out of town, it was decided. Bosch would go to Boston and, while on a case, would cross paths with Kenzie.

Michael started the story in Los Angeles, formulating a crime and a case that Bosch would work several years after it occurred. He would trace a suspect to Boston, travel there to observe, and surreptitiously gather a DNA sample from a discarded coffee cup or a tossed cigarette butt. Once there, he'd cross the radar of Patrick Kenzie, who was working his own investigation, only for different reasons.

Michael wrote the first six pages of the story and a few more containing potential angles of exploration. He e-mailed the package to Dennis, suggesting he add another six pages or so and finish the story. Quick and easy. They'd be done, then back to work on their own stuff in a few days.

Michael waited for a reply.

Then, he waited some more.

A few days turned into a few weeks.

He finally dummied up an e-mail saying he'd had Internet issues and just wanted to see if his start of the story had been received. When Dennis responded it was with a finished tale, adding twenty more pages, evolving the plot from the shorthand to the complex and humorous.

So here it is, the first face-off.

Red Eye

As a practice, Harry Bosch did his best to stay out of tunnels but as he came out of Logan Airport, a tunnel was unavoidable—either the Ted Williams or the Sumner, take your pick. The rental car's GPS chose the Williams, so Harry drove down and deep under Boston Harbor. The traffic backed up at the bottom and then completely stopped as Bosch realized that the timing of his red-eye flight from LA had landed him in the heart of morning rush hour.

Of course, the tunnel was much bigger and wider and was well lit in comparison to the tunnels of his past and those of his dreams. He was also not alone in his predicament. The passage was wall to wall with cars and trucks—a river of steel under the river of water, only one of them flowing at the moment. But a tunnel is a tunnel and soon the chest-tightening feeling of claustrophobia took hold. Bosch started to sweat and impatiently honked the horn of his rental in impotent protest. This apparently only served to identify him as an outsider. The locals didn't honk, they did not rail against that which they could not change.

Eventually, traffic started moving and he finally emerged, lowering his window to let in the fresh air. He made a mental note to find a map and then chart a way back to the airport that did not include going through a tunnel. Too bad the car's GPS didn't have a NO TUNNELS setting. He would have to find his way back to the airport on his own.

The LAPD's Open-Unsolved Unit's travel protocol called for Bosch to check in with the local authorities immediately upon arrival in another city. In this case that would be the District E-13 offices of the Boston Police Department in Jamaica Plain. This was the district that included the address Bosch had for Edward Paisley, the man whose DNA Bosch had come to take—surreptitiously or not.

Bosch, however, often trampled on the official cold case protocol. He usually followed his own protocol, which involved getting the lay of the land first and maybe putting an eye on his quarry— then going in to meet and greet the local constabulary.

Bosch planned to check out Paisley's address, maybe get a first look at him, and then check into the room at Courtyard by Marriott he had reserved on Expedia. He might even take a short nap after check-in, to make up for the lost sleep on the flight out. In the early afternoon he would go to District E-13 and tell the captain or major in charge that he was in from LA on a fifteen-year-old cold case murder. He would then most likely be paired with a division detective who had fallen from favor with command staff. Squiring around a visiting detective following a lead on a 1990 cold case was not a choice assignment.

Two nights before, at a bar on Warren Street in Roxbury, Dontelle Howe had asked Patrick Kenzie, "You got kids?"

Patrick half nodded, a bit confused on how to answer. "One on the way."

"When?"

"Any day now."

Dontelle Howe smiled. He was a trim black man in his early thirties, with close-cropped dreads and clothes so crisp you could smell the starch from two rooms away. "First?"

Patrick nodded.

"Ain't you a little old?" Dontelle took another dainty sip from the one brandy he allowed himself every weeknight. Weekends, he'd assured Patrick, he could drink his weight in Henney, but weeknights and Sundays he kept his limit at one because every morning he drove a bus full of forty-five children from their homes all over the city to Dearborn Middle School in Roxbury, about two blocks from the bar where he'd agreed to meet Patrick after work.

"A little old?" Patrick checked himself in the bar mirror—a little grayer, okay, a little heavier, fine, a little less on top than he would have hoped, sure, but not bad for forty. Particularly forty years lived as hard as he'd lived his. Either that, or he was bullshitting himself, which was just as likely. "You don't look like you'll be auditioning for any boy bands yourself, Dontelle."

"But I already got two in grade school. Time they're in college and me and the woman are kicking it somewhere in Florida, I'll *be* your age."

Patrick chuckled and drank some beer.

Dontelle Howe's voice grew deeper, more somber. "So no one's looking for her? *Still?*"

Patrick made a metza-metza motion with his hand. "Police think it's a custody thing. Father's a real piece of shit, and no one can find him. No one can find her, either, so they think it's a case of one-plus-one equals she'll turn up."

"But she's twelve, man."

"She" was Chiffon Henderson, a seventh-grader Dontelle Howe picked up every morning from the Bromley-Heath housing projects in Jamaica Plain and dropped off nine hours later in the same spot. Three nights ago, Chiffon had left her bedroom in the back of the unit she shared with two sisters and her mother. The leaving wasn't in dispute; the question of whether it had been voluntary was. She'd exited through a window. No signs of struggle or forced entry, though her mother had told police that Chiffon often left her window open on a mild night even though she'd been warned a thousand times not to. The police were focusing on Chiffon's father, Lonnie Cullen, a deadbeat dad four times over to four different households, who hadn't checked in with his parole officer this past weekend and couldn't be found at his last known address. There was also some talk that Chiffon may have started seeing a boy who lived in one of the other buildings in the projects, though no one knew his name or much about him.

Chiffon's mother, Ella Henderson, worked two jobs. By day, she checked in patients for four OBGYN partners at Beth Israel; nights she cleaned offices. She was a poster child for the burdens of the working poor—so much time spent trying to feed your kids and keep the lights on that you never spent any time with them until the day they told you it was too late to start trying.

Two days ago, she'd checked in Patrick's wife, Angie, for her final appointment before their child, expected to enter the world a week from today, would be delivered. As Ella Henderson double-checked the insurance info and verified the parents' dates of birth, she began to weep. It was weeping without drama or noise, just a steady stream even as her polite smile remained in place and her eyes remained fixed on her computer screen.

Half an hour later, Patrick had agreed to ask around about her daughter. The lead cop on the case, Detective Emily Zebrowski, had a current caseload of twelve investigations. She told Patrick she welcomed his help, but she saw no evidence of an abduction. She admitted that if it were an abduction, Chiffon's bedroom was the place to do it, though—a tall elm towered over her window and those above her; her building was at the rear of the Heath Street complex and the city was five months behind replacing bulbs in the lamps back there that had been shot out by drunken persons unknown on New Year's. Emily Zebrowski told Patrick, however, that no one heard a peep that night from Chiffon Henderson's bedroom. People rarely vanished involuntarily, the detective said; that was more something you saw on TV than encountered in the real world.

"So your operating theory?" he'd asked.

"Her father," Detective Zebrowski said. "Guy's got priors the way other guys have nose hair."

"To what end?"

"Excuse me?"

"He's a scumbag," Patrick said, "I get it. But his scumbaggedness makes sense usually, right? There's motive behind it. He steals one of his kids, he wants to get paid or get the mother off his back for something. But here the mother's got no money, she's never sued him for child support or alimony, and what guy with his psychological makeup wants to bring his twelve-year-old daughter back to his spot, have her ragging on him from dawn to dusk?"

Detective Zebrowski shrugged. "You think d-bags like Lonnie Cullen think things through before they do them? If they did, they wouldn't know the number on their orange jumpsuits better than their own birthdays. He did it because he's a criminal and he's an idiot and he has less impulse control than a flea at a livestock auction."

"And the boyfriend angle?"

"Looking into it."

Two nights ago Dontelle said to Patrick, "But you don't believe it?"

Patrick shrugged. "Deadbeat dads dodge their kids, they don't kidnap 'em, not the ones who've been out of the picture as long as Lonnie has. As for the boyfriend theory, she's, what, shacked up with him for three days, they never go out to grab a bite, call a friend?"

"All I know," Dontelle said, "is she seemed like a sweet kid. Not one of them typical project girls who's always frontin', talkin' shit. She was quiet but . . . considerate, you know?"

Patrick took another drink of beer. "No. Tell me."

"Well, you get a job like mine, you got to do a probation period—ninety days during which they can shitcan you without cause. After that, you with the city, man, gotta fuck up huge *and* be named Bin Laden for the city be able to get rid of your ass. I hit my ninety a couple weeks ago and not only did Chiffon congratulate me, she gave me a cupcake."

"No shit?" Patrick smiled.

"Store bought," Dontelle said, "but still. How sweet is that?"

"Pretty sweet." Patrick nodded.

"You'll see in about twelve years with your kid, they ain't too into thinking about others at that age. It's all about what's going on up here"—he tapped his head—"and down there"—he pointed at his groin.

They drank in silence for a minute.

"Nothing else you remember about that day? Nothing out of the ordinary?"

He shook his head. "Just a day like any other—'See you tomorrow, Chiffon,' and she say, 'See you tomorrow, Dontelle.' And off she walk."

Patrick thanked him and paid for the drinks. He was scooping his change off the bar when he said, "You had a probationary period?"

Dontelle nodded. "Yeah, it's standard."

"No, I know, but I guess I was wondering why you started so late in the school year. I mean, it's May. Means you started in, what, February?"

Another nod. "End of January, yeah."

"What'd you do before that?"

"Drove a tour bus. Drove from here to Florida, here to Montreal, here to P-Town, all depended on the season. Hours were killing me. Shit, the *road* was killing me. This job opened up, I jumped."

"Why'd it open up?"

"Paisley got a duey."

"Paisley?"

"Guy I replaced. Other drivers told me he was a piece of work, man. Show up with forty kids in his charge, eyes all glassy. Even the union wouldn't protect him after the last time. Drove the bus off the side of the American Legion Highway, right?" Dontelle was laughing in disbelief. "Damn near tipped it. Gets out to take a piss. This is at six thirty in the ante meridiem, feel me? He gets back in, tries to pull back off the shoulder, but now the bus *does* tip. That's Lawsuit City there, man. Forty times over."

"Paisley," Patrick said.

"Edward Paisley," Dontelle said, "like the ties."

Paisley lived on Wyman Street in a gray row house with fading white trim. There was a front porch with an old couch on it. Bosch drove by the place and then circled the block and went by again before finding a parking space at the curb a half block away. By adjusting his side-view mirror he had a bead on the front door and porch. He liked doing one-man surveillances this way. If somebody was looking for a watcher they usually checked windshields. Parking with his back to his target made him harder to see. Edward Paisley may have had nothing to do with the murder of Letitia Williams all those years ago. But if he did, he hadn't survived the last fifteen years without checking windshields and being cautious.

All Bosch was hoping for, and that he'd be happy with, was to see some activity at the home to confirm that Paisley was at the address. If he got lucky, Paisley would go out and grab a cup of coffee or a bite to eat at lunch. Bosch would be able to get all the DNA he'd need off a discarded cup or a pizza crust. Maybe Paisley was a smoker. A cigarette butt would do the trick as well.

Harry pulled a file out of the locking briefcase he took on trips and opened it to look at the enlargement of the photo he'd pulled the day before from the Massachusetts DMV. It was taken three years earlier. Paisley was white, balding, and then fifty-three years old. He no longer had the driver's license, thanks to the suspension that followed the DUI arrest four months ago. Paisley tipped a school bus and then blew a point-oh-two on the machine and with it blew his job with the school district and possibly his freedom. The arrest put his fingerprints into the system where they were waiting for Bosch. Sometimes Harry got lucky that way. If he had pulled the Williams case eleven months earlier and submitted the prints collected at the crime scene for electronic comparison there

11

would have been no resulting match. But Bosch pulled the case four months ago and here he was in Boston.

Two hours into his surveillance Bosch had seen no sign of Paisley and was growing restless. Perhaps Paisley had left the house for the day before Bosch could set up on the street. Bosch could be wasting his time, watching an empty house. He decided to get out and do a walk-by. He'd seen a convenience store a block past the target address. He could walk by Paisley's address, eyeball the place up close, then go down and pick up a newspaper and a gallon of milk. Back at the car he would pour the milk into the gutter and keep the jug handy if he had to urinate. It could be a long day watching the house.

The paper would come in handy as well. He'd be able to check the late baseball scores. The Dodgers had gone into extra innings the night before against the hated Giants and Bosch had gotten on the plane not knowing the game's outcome.

But at the last moment Bosch decided to stay put. He watched a dinged-up Jeep Cherokee pull into a curbside slot directly across the street from his own position. There was a lone man in the car and what made Bosch curious was that he never got out. He stayed slumped a bit in his seat and appeared to be keeping an eye on the same address as Bosch.

Bosch could see he was on a cell phone when he first arrived but then for the next hour the man remained behind the wheel of his Jeep, simply watching the goings-on on the street. He was too young to be Paisley. Late thirties or early forties, wearing a baseball cap and a thin gray hoodie over a dark-blue graphic tee. Something about the cap gave Bosch pause until he realized it was the first one he'd seen in a city filled with them that didn't have a B on it. Instead, it had what appeared to be a crooked smiley face on it, though Bosch couldn't be positive from the other side of the street. It looked to Bosch like the guy was waiting for somebody, possibly the same somebody Bosch was waiting for.

Eventually, Bosch realized he had become a similar object of curiosity for the man across the street, who was now surreptitiously watching Bosch as Bosch was surreptitiously watching him.

They kept at this careful cross-surveillance until a siren split the air and a fire truck trundled down the road between them. Bosch tracked the truck in the side mirror and when he looked back across the street he saw that the Jeep was empty. The man had either used the distraction of the passing fire truck to slip out, or he was lying down inside.

Bosch assumed it was the former. He sat up straight and checked the street and the sidewalk across from him. No sign of anyone on foot. He turned to check the sidewalk on his own side and there at the passenger's window was the guy in the baseball hat. He'd turned the hat backward, the way gang squad guys often did when they were on the move. Bosch could see a silver chain descending from the sides of his neck into his graphic tee, figured there was a badge hanging from it. Definitely a gun riding the back of the guy's right hip, something boxy and bigger than a Glock. The man bent down to put himself at eye level with Bosch. He twirled his finger at Bosch, a request to roll the window down.

●—◆—●

The guy with the Hertz NeverLost GPS jutting off his dashboard looked at Patrick for a long moment, but then lowered his window. He looked like he was mid-fifties and in good shape. Wiry. Something about him said cop. The wariness in his eyes for one; cop's eyes—you could never believe they truly closed. Then there was the way he kept one hand down in his lap so he could go inside the sport coat for the Glock or the Smith if it turned out Patrick was a bad guy. His left hand.

"Nice move," he said.

"Yeah?" Patrick said.

The guy nodded over his shoulder. "Sending the fire truck down the street. Good distraction. You with District Thirteen?"

A true Bostonian always sounded like he was just getting over a cold. This guy's voice was clean air; not light exactly but smooth. An out-of-towner. Not a trace of Beantown in that voice. Probably a fed. Minted in Kansas or somewhere, trained down in Quantico and then sent up here. Patrick decided to play along as long as he could. He tried to open the door but it was locked. The guy unlocked it, moved his briefcase to the backseat, and Patrick got in.

"You're a bit away from Center Plaza, aren't you?" Patrick said.

"Maybe," he said. "Except I don't know where or what Center Plaza is."

"So you're not with the bureau. Who are you with?"

The man hesitated again, kept that left hand in his lap, then nodded like he'd decided to take a flier.

"LAPD," he said. "I was going to check in with you guys later today."

"And what brings the LAPD out to JP?"

"JP?"

"Jamaica Plain. Can I see some ID?"

He pulled a badge wallet out and flipped it open so Patrick could study the detective's badge and the ID. His name was Hieronymus Bosch.

"Some name you've got. How do you say that?"

"Harry's good."

"Okay. What are you doing here, Harry?"

"How about you? That chain around your neck isn't attached to a badge."

"No?"

Bosch shook his head. "I'd have seen the outline of it through your shirt. Crucifix?"

Patrick stared at him for a moment and then nodded. "Wife likes me to wear it." He held out his hand. "Patrick Kenzie. I'm not a cop. I'm an independent contractor."

Bosch shook his hand. "You like baseball, Pat?"

"Patrick."

"You like baseball, Patrick?"

"Big-time. Why?"

"You're the first guy I've seen in this town not wearing a Sox hat."

Patrick pulled off his hat and considered the front of it as he ran a hand through his hair. "Imagine that. I didn't even look when I left the house."

"Is that a rule around here? You've all got to represent Red Sox Nation or something?"

"It's not a rule, per se, more like a guideline."

Bosch looked at the hat again. "Who's the crooked smiley-faced guy?"

"Toothface," Patrick said. "He's, like, the logo, I guess, of a record store I like."

"You still buy records?"

"CDs. You?"

"Yeah. Jazz mostly. I hear it's all going to go away. Records, CDs, the whole way we buy music. MP3s and iPods are the future."

"Heard that, too." Patrick looked over his shoulder at the street. "We looking at the same guy here, Harry?"

"Don't know," Bosch said. "I'm looking at a guy for a murder back in nineteen-ninety. I need to get some DNA."

"What guy?"

"Tell you what, why don't I go over to District Thirteen and check in with the captain and make this all legit? I'll identify myself, you identify yourself. A cop and a private eye working together to ease the burden of the Boston PD. Because I don't want *my* captain back in LA catching a call from—"

"Is it Paisley? Are you watching Edward Paisley?"

He looked at Patrick for a long moment. "Who is Edward Paisley?"

"Bullshit. Tell me about the case from nineteen-ninety."

"Look, you're a private dick with no 'need to know' that I can see and I'm a cop—"

"Who didn't follow protocol and check in with the local PD." He craned his head around the car. "Unless there's a D-thirteen liaison on this street who's really fucking good at keeping his head down. I got a girl missing right now and Edward Paisley's name popped up in connection to her. Girl's twelve, Bosch, and she's been out there three days. So I'd love to hear what happened back in nineteen-ninety. You tell me, I'll be your best friend and everything."

"Why is no one looking for your missing girl?"

"Who's to say they're not?"

"Because you're looking and you're private."

Patrick got a whiff of something sad coming off the LA cop. Not the kind of sad that came from bad news yesterday but from bad news most days. Still, his eyes weren't dead; they pulsed instead with appetite—maybe even addiction—for the hunt. This wasn't a house cat who'd checked out, who kept his head down, took his paycheck, and counted the days till his twenty. This was a cop who kicked in doors if he had to, whether he knew what was on the other side or not, and had stayed on after twenty.

Patrick said, "She's the wrong color, wrong caste, and there's enough plausible anecdotal shit swirling around her situation to make anyone question whether she was abducted or just walked off."

"But you think Paisley could be involved."

Patrick nodded.

"Why?"

"He's got two priors for sexual abuse of minors."

Bosch shook his head. "No. I checked."

"You checked domestic. You didn't know to check Costa Rica and Cuba. Both places where he was arrested, charged, had the shit beat out of him, and ultimately bought his way out. But the arrests are on record over there."

"How'd you find them?"

"I didn't. Principal of Dearborn Middle School was getting a bad feeling about Paisley when he drove a bus for them. One girl said this, one boy said that, another girl said such and such. Nothing you could build a case on but enough for the principal to call Paisley into her office a couple times to discuss it." Patrick pulled a reporter's notebook from his back pocket, flipped it open. "Principal told me Paisley would have passed both interviews with flying colors but he mentioned milk one time too many."

"Milk?"

"Milk." Patrick looked up from his notes and nodded. "He told the principal during their first meeting—he'd already been working there a year; the principal doesn't have shit to do with hiring bus drivers, that's HR downtown—that she should smile more because it made him think of milk. He told her in the second meeting that the sun in Cuba was whiter than milk, which is why he liked Cuba, the white lording over everything and all. It stuck with her."

"Clearly."

"But so did the Cuba reference. It takes work to get to Cuba. You gotta fly to Canada or the Caribbean, pretend you banged around there when in fact you hopped a flight to Havana. So when her least favorite bus driver got a DUI while driving her students, she eighty-sixed his ass straightaway, but then started wondering about Cuba. She pulled his résumé and found gaps—six-month unexplained absence in eighty-nine, ten-month absence in ninety-six. Our friendly principal—and remember, Bosch, your principal *is* your pal—kept digging. Didn't take long to find out that the six months in eighty-nine were spent in a Costa Rican jail, the ten months in ninety-six were spent in a cell in Havana. Plus, he moved around a lot in general—Phoenix, LA, Chicago, Philly, and, finally, Boston. Always drives a bus, and only has one known relative—a sister, Tasha. Both times he was released from foreign jails he was released into her custody. And I'm willing to bet she walked a bag of cash onto her flight that she didn't have with her on the flight back home. So now, now he's here and Chiffon Henderson is not. And you know everything I know, Detective Bosch, but I bet you can't say the same."

Bosch leaned back against his seat hard enough to make the leather crackle. He looked over at Patrick Kenzie and told the story of Letitia Williams. She was fourteen years old and stolen from her bedroom in the night. No leads, few clues. The abductor had cut out the screen on her bedroom window. Didn't remove the screen, frame and all. Cut the screen out of the frame with a razor and then climbed in.

The cut screen put immediate suspicion on the disappearance. The case was not shunted aside as a presumed runaway situation the way Chiffon Henderson's would be fifteen years later. Detectives from the major crimes unit rolled that morning after the girl was discovered gone. But the abduction scene was clean. No trace evidence of any kind recovered from the girl's bedroom. The presumption was the abductor or abductors had worn gloves, entered, and quickly incapacitated the girl, and just as quickly removed her through the window.

However, there was one piece of presumed evidence gathered outside the house on the morning of the initial investigation. In the alley that ran behind the home where Letitia Williams lived investigators found a flashlight. The first guess was that it had belonged to the abductor and it had inadvertently been dropped while the victim was carried to a waiting vehicle. There were no fingerprints on the flashlight as it was assumed the perpetrator had worn gloves. But an examination of the inside of the flashlight found two viable latent fingerprints on one of the batteries.

It was thought to be the one mistake that would prove the abductor's undoing. But the thumb and forefinger prints were compared to those on file with the city and state and no match was found. The prints were then sent on to the FBI for comparison with prints in the bureau's vast data banks, but again there was no hit and the lead died on the vine.

In the meantime, the body of Letitia Williams was found exactly one week after her abduction on a hillside in Griffith Park, right below the observatory. It appeared as though the killer had specifically chosen the location because the body would be spotted quickly in daylight hours by someone looking down from the observatory.

The autopsy on the victim determined that she had been repeatedly sexually assaulted and then strangled. The case drew heavy attention from the media and the major crimes unit but eventually it was shelved. No clues, no evidence, no leads. In 1992 Los Angeles was ripped apart by race riots, and cases like the murder of Letitia Williams dropped off the public radar. The file went to archives until the Open-Unsolved Unit was formed after the start of the new century and eventually Bosch came to the archived case files and the fingerprints that were matched to Edward Paisley in Boston.

"That's why I'm here," Bosch said.

"Did you come with a warrant?"

Bosch shook his head. "No, no warrant. The prints match is not enough. The flashlight was found in the alley, not in Letitia's bedroom. There is no direct tie to the crime. I came to get DNA. I was going to follow him and collect it. Wait for him to toss a cup of coffee or a pizza crust or something. I'd take it back with me and see if it matches semen collected from the body. Then I'd be in business. Then I'd come back with a warrant and take him down."

They sat in the car and stared out at the street and Bosch could feel Kenzie stewing on something. He wasn't a big man and he had a friendly, boyish face; he dressed in the street clothes of a neighborhood guy, kind of guy would pour your beer or fix your car. On first glance and even on a second, he seemed harmless and sweet, kind of guy you'd be happy for your sister to bring home. But Bosch had spent enough time in his company now to feel a hot wire running in the guy's blood. Most people probably never tripped it. But God help the ones who did.

Kenzie's right knee started to jackhammer up and down in such a way that Bosch doubted he was aware of it. He turned on the seat, looked at Harry. "You said in your case the girl's body was found a week after the abduction."

"That's right."

"But she was dumped there because she would be found almost right away by the people at the observatory."

"Yeah, the body was left at night and noticed the next morning after daylight."

"How long had she been dead?"

Bosch reached to the backseat and opened the briefcase. He brought back a thick blue binder full of records from the case. He spoke as he looked through the pages. He had the answers in his head already. He was just looking at the autopsy report for confirmation.

"She had been dead seventy-two hours when found."

"That's three days. That meant the guy kept her alive for four days."

"Right. The indications were that she was repeatedly—"

"This is the fourth day. If this asshole follows any sort of pattern, well, shit, Chiffon Henderson was taken Monday afternoon." He pointed back down the sidewalk at the gray row house. "We need to get in that house."

• ◆ •

Patrick took the front door while Bosch went around back. Patrick had told the LA cop he was reasonably proficient picking a lock, but Paisley's front door sported a lock Patrick had never seen before. New, too. And expensive by the looks of it—a five-hundred-dollar lock on a forty-dollar door. Patrick tried a series of picks but none of them could get to first base with the cylinders. It was like trying to pass a plastic stirrer through a rock.

The second time he dropped a pick, he bent to retrieve it and the door opened in front of him.

He looked up at Harry Bosch standing on the threshold, a

Glock dangling from his left hand. "I thought you said you could pick a lock."

"I clearly overestimated my prowess." He straightened. "How'd you get in?"

"He left a window unlocked." Bosch shrugged. "People, right?"

Patrick had expected a dump inside but the house was quite clean and mostly bare. The furniture was modern Scandinavian—lots of bright white and brighter chrome that clashed with the older wainscoting and dark wallpaper. Paisley was renting; the landlord probably had no idea about the lock.

"Something in here he doesn't want people to see," Patrick said.

"Gotta be in the basement, then," Bosch said. He jerked a thumb back at the shotgun layout of the apartment—foyer and living room and then a long corridor that went straight back to the kitchen, all the other rooms branching off it. "I cleared this floor."

"You cleared this floor? How long were you planning to leave me out on the front porch?"

"I figured another half an hour before you snapped and kicked in the door. I didn't have that kinda time."

"LA sarcasm," Patrick said as they headed down the hallway. "Who knew?"

Halfway down the hall, on the right, was a door the same dark brown as the wainscoting. Patrick exchanged a look with Bosch and the cop nodded—now would be the time.

Patrick drew the .45 Colt Commander off his hip and flicked the safety off. "You see a bulkhead around back?"

Bosch looked puzzled. "A bulkhead?"

"You know, an entrance to the basement. Double doors, steps down."

Bosch nodded. "Locked from the inside." And then, as though

further explanation were needed, he said, "We generally don't have basements in LA."

"You don't have snow or a wind chill factor, either, so, you know, fuck you." He tossed Bosch a bright, tight smile. "Any basement windows out back?"

Another nod. "Black curtains over them."

"Well that's bad," Patrick said.

"Why?"

"No one puts curtains over their basement windows around here unless they got a home theater or they're playing Dead Hooker Storage." He looked around the apartment. "Edward does not strike me as the home theater type."

Bosch nodded, his pupils adrenalized to twice their size. "Let's go back out, call it in legit."

"What if he's down there with her right now?"

That was the dilemma, wasn't it?

Bosch exhaled a long breath. Patrick did the same. Bosch held his hand over the doorknob and said, "On three?"

Patrick nodded. He wiped his right palm on his jeans and readjusted a two-handed grip on his gun.

"One. Two. Three."

Bosch opened the door.

The first thing they noticed was the padding on the inside of the door—at least six inches of premium leather soundproofing. The kind one found only in recording studios. The next thing they noticed was the dark. The scant light to find the stairs came from the hall behind them. The rest of the cellar was pitch black. Patrick pointed at the light switch just past Bosch's ear, raised his eyebrows.

Bosch shrugged.

Patrick shrugged.

Six of one, half a dozen of the other.

Bosch flicked on the lights.

The staircase split the cellar like a spine, straight down the center, and they went down it fast. A black heating-oil tank stood at the bottom, quite old, rust fringing the bottom of it.

Without a word, Bosch went left and Patrick went right.

The element of surprise was no longer an option for them.

Only for him.

On the side of the cellar that Patrick chose—the front—the framing was old and mostly unfinished. The first "room" he came upon contained a washer, a dryer, and a sink with a cake of grimy brown soap stuck to the top of it. The next room had once been a workshop. A long wood table abutted the wall, an old vise still fastened to the table. Nothing else in there but dust and mice droppings. The last room along the wall was finished, however. The framing was filled in with drywall on one side and brick on the other, a door in the middle. Heavy door. And thick. The frame around it was solid, too. Try and kick in a door like that and you'd finish your day getting fitted for an ankle cast.

Patrick removed his left hand from his .45 and rubbed it on his jeans. He flexed the fingers and reached for the doorknob, holding the .45 cocked awkwardly at about mid-chest level. It didn't look pretty, he was sure, but if he had to pull the trigger, he had a fair chance of hitting center mass on anyone but a dwarf or a giant.

The doorknob squeaked when it turned, proving something a cop had told him years ago—you always made the most noise when you were trying to be quiet. He threw open the door and dropped to his knees at the same time, gun pointing up a bit now, left hand coming back on the grip, sweeping the room from left to right, sweeping back right to left even as he processed what he saw—

Edward Paisley's man cave.

Patrick edged his way through the doorway onto an Arizona Cardinals rug, drew a bead on a BarcaLounger trimmed in Sun Devils colors. A Phoenix Suns pennant shared space with one from the Phoenix Coyotes and Patrick had to peer at the latter to realize the Coyotes played in the NHL.

If he learned nothing else from this day, he now knew Arizona had a professional hockey team.

He found baseball bats signed by Troy Glaus, Carlos Baerga, and Tony Womack. Baseballs signed by Curt Schilling and Randy Johnson, framed photos of Larry Fitzgerald and Kurt Warner, Shawn Marion and Joe Johnson, Plexiglas-encased footballs, basketballs, and pucks, Patrick again thinking, They have a *hockey* team?

He picked up a bat signed by Shea Hillenbrand, who'd broken into the Bigs with the Sox back in 2001, but got shipped to Arizona before the Sox won the Series last year. He wondered if that stung or if being able to lie out in the Arizona sun in January made up for it.

He'd guess it didn't.

He was putting the bat back against the wall when he heard someone moving through the cellar. Moving fast. Running actually.

And not away from something, but toward it.

•—◆—•

Harry had worked his way along the back of the cellar finding nothing but wall and rocky, jagged flooring until he reached a tight space where an ancient water heater met a prehistoric oil heater. The space reeked of oil and mold and fossilized vermin. Had Bosch not been searching for an adolescent in possible mortal danger, he might have missed the corridor on the other side of the heaters. But his penlight picked up the hole in the darkness on the other side of a series of pipes and ducts that were half hanging, half falling from the ceiling.

Bosch worked his way past the heaters and entered a long thin space barely wide enough to accommodate any mammal with shoulders, never mind a full-grown adult male.

As soon as you entered a tunnel, the first problem you noticed was that there was no left, no right, and no place to hide. You went into an entrance and you headed toward an exit. And should anyone who wished you ill pop up at either point Alpha or point Zeta, while you were passing between those points, your fate was in their hands.

When Bosch reached the end of the passageway, he was bathed in sweat. He stepped out into a wide unlit room of dark brick and a stone floor with a drain in the center. He swept the room with his penlight and saw nothing but a metal crate. It was the kind used to house large dogs on family trips. A blue painter's tarp partially covered it, held to the frame by nine bungee cords.

And it was moving.

Bosch got down on his knees and pulled at the tarp but the bungee cords were wrapped tight—three of them crossing the crate lengthwise and six crossing it widthwise. The cords were clasped down at the base of the crate and stretched taut so that separating the clasps with one hand was not an option. Bosch placed his Glock by his foot as the crate continued to rock and he picked up the sound of someone mewling desperately from under all that tarp.

He pulled apart the clasps on the first of the three lengthwise cords and still couldn't get a clear view inside. He put the penlight in his mouth and went to work on the second and that's when the room turned white.

It was as if someone had hung the sun a foot above his head or lit up a ballpark.

He was blind. He got his hand on his Glock, but all he could see was white. He couldn't tell where the wall was. He couldn't even see the crate anymore and he was kneeling in front of it.

He heard something scrabble to his left and he turned his gun that way and then the scrabbling broke right, coming around his weak side, and he turned with the Glock crossing his body, his eyes adjusting enough to pick up a shadow. Then he heard the thump of something very hard turn something less hard into something soft.

Someone let out a dull yelp and fell to the floor in all that blinding light.

"Bosch," Patrick said, "it's me. Close your eyes a sec."

Bosch closed his eyes and heard the sound of glass breaking—popping actually—and the heat left his face in degrees.

"I think we're good," Patrick said.

When Bosch opened his eyes, he blinked several times and saw the lights high on the wall, all the bulbs shattered. Had to be in the seven-hundred-watt range, if not higher. Huge black cones behind them. Eight lights total. Patrick had pulled back the curtain on the small window at the top of the wall, and the soft early-afternoon light entered the room like an answered prayer.

Bosch looked at Paisley lying on the floor to his right, gurgling, the back of his head sporting a fresh dent, pink blood leaking from his nose, red blood streaming from his mouth, a carving knife lying beneath his twitching right hand.

Patrick Kenzie brandished a baseball bat. He raised his eyebrows up and down and twirled it. "Signed by Shea Hillenbrand."

"I don't even know who that is."

"Right," Patrick said. "Dodgers fan."

Bosch went to work on the bungee cords and Patrick joined

him and they pulled back the tarp and there she was, Chiffon Henderson. She was curled fetal in the crate because there was no room to stretch into any other position. Patrick struggled with the door until Bosch just took the roof off the crate.

Chiffon Henderson had electrical tape wrapped around her mouth, wrists, and ankles. They could tell it hurt her to stretch her limbs, but Bosch took that as a good sign—Paisley had kept her caged but possibly unmolested. Bosch guessed that was supposed to commence today, an appetizer to the murder.

They bickered as they removed the tape from her mouth, Bosch telling Patrick to be careful of her hair, Patrick telling him to watch he didn't tear at her lips.

When the tape came free and they went to work on her wrists, Bosch asked, "What's your name?"

"Chiffon Henderson. Who're you?"

"I'm Patrick Kenzie. And this other guy? He was never here, okay, Chiffon?"

Bosch cocked his head.

Patrick said, "You're a cop. From out of town. I can barely get away with this shit, but you? They'll take your badge, man. Unless you got a no-knock warrant in your pocket I can't see."

Bosch worked through it in his head.

"He touch you, Chiffon?"

She was weeping, shaking, and she gave that a half nod, half head shake. "A little, but not, you know. He said that was coming. He told me all sorts of things were coming."

Patrick looked at Paisley huffing into the cement, eyes rolled back into his head, blood beginning to pool.

"Only thing coming for this shithead is the strokes that follow the coma."

When her hands were free, Patrick knelt to get at the tape on her ankles and Bosch was surprised when the girl hugged him tight, her tears finding his shirt. He surprised himself when he kissed the top of her head.

"No more monster," he said. "Not tonight."

Patrick finished with the tape. He tossed the wad of it behind him and produced his cell. "I gotta call this in. I'd rather be bullshitting my way free of an attempted murder charge than an actual homicide rap, if you know what I mean, and he's turning a funny shade."

Bosch looked at the man lying at his feet. Looked like an aging nerd. Kinda guy did your taxes out of a strip mall storefront. Another little man with soiled desires and furious nightmares. Funny how the monsters always turned out to be little more than men. But Patrick was right—he'd die soon without attention.

Patrick dialed 911 but didn't hit SEND. Instead he held out his hand to Bosch. "If I'm ever in LA."

Bosch shook his hand. "Funny. I can't picture you in LA."

Patrick said, "And I can't picture you out of it, even though you're standing right here. Take care, Harry."

"You, too. And thanks"—Bosch looked down at Paisley, on his way to critical care, minimum—"for, um, that."

"Pleasure."

Bosch headed toward the door, a door only accessible from the front of the cellar, not the back. Beat the hell out of the way he'd entered the room. He was reaching for the doorknob when he turned back.

"One last thing."

Patrick had the phone to his ear and his free arm wrapped tight around Chiffon's shoulders. "What's that?"

"Is there a way to get back to the airport without going through that tunnel?"

IAN RANKIN
VS. PETER JAMES

In the Nick of Time

Combing characters from different fictional universes into the same story is something writers often contemplate, usually after one drink too many late in the evening at a conference or convention. The technical difficulties of that endeavor quickly intrude, and the "good idea of the night before" ends up in a drawer, never to see the light of day. So Peter James and Ian Rankin knew the challenges that lay in arranging a meeting between their two respective heroes.

For one thing Roy Grace and John Rebus are of different

generations and backgrounds. They have vastly different ideas about law enforcement. For another, they operate five hundred miles apart—Grace in Brighton, a resort city on the south coast of England—Rebus in Edinburgh, the capital of Scotland. Both countries, while constituents of the United Kingdom, have different legal systems, different rules and regulations.

Night and day to each other actually.

So how, realistically, could these two men meet and do business together?

Fans of John Rebus know he's a big music fan, growing up in the early 1960s with The Who as his heroes. One of The Who's best-known albums, *Quadrophenia,* is set partially in Brighton, at a time when rival gangs (the Mods and the Rockers) would battle on its waterfront. For many people in the United Kingdom the pitched and brutal wars between the clean-cut, smartly dressed Mods and the long-haired, leather-jacketed Rockers are what Brighton is all about.

So here was the germ of an idea.

A crime from that era, brought to light decades later on a deathbed in Edinburgh. Rebus has to decide if it is worth investigating such ancient history and eventually asks Roy Grace for help. Along the way both men journey into the other's universe, coming to appreciate the differences and gaining an understanding of how the other views the criminal world.

Like I said.

It's night and day.

There was also room for both of the characters' sidekick/colleague to make an appearance and engage in some gentle sparring, too. The result is a story that adds to the mythology of both Peter's and Ian's series, while staying true to the spirit of all their books.

In the Nick of Time

His name was James King and he had something to confess.

His wife was waiting for Rebus in the hospital corridor. She led him to the bedside without saying much, other than that her husband had "only a week or two, maybe less."

King was prone on the bed, an oxygen mask strapped to his gaunt, unshaven face. His eyes were dark-ringed, his chest rising and falling with what seemed painful effort. He nodded at his wife and she took it for an instruction, drawing the curtains around the bed so that King and Rebus were shielded from the other patients. The man pulled the mask down so it rested against his chin.

"ID?" he demanded. Rebus dug out his warrant card and King peered at the photograph before offering an explanation. "Wouldn't put it past Ella to rope some poor sod into pretending. She thinks the drugs must have done it."

"Done what?" Rebus was lowering himself onto a chair.

"Got me imagining things." King paused, studying his visitor. "You don't look much younger than me."

"Thanks for that."

"But it means you'll remember the Mods? Early sixties?"

"I'm not sure they made it this far north. We had the music, though . . ."

"I grew up in London. Had the Lambretta and the clothes. My wages either went on one or the other. Weekend trips—Brighton and Margate. I liked Brighton better . . ." King drifted off, his eyes becoming unfocused. There was a tumor in him that had grown too large to be dealt with. Rebus wondered what painkillers the doctors were giving him. He had a headache of his own—maybe they had a few pills to spare. There was loud wheezing from somewhere beyond the curtain—another patient jolted into life by a coughing fit. King blinked away whatever memories he'd been replaying.

"Your wife," Rebus said. "When she called us she said there was something you wanted to say."

"That's what I'm doing," King retorted, sounding irritated. "I'm telling you the story."

"About your days as a Mod?"

"My last time in Brighton."

"You and your scooter?"

"And a hundred others like me. It was a religion to us, something we were going to take to the grave." He paused. "And we hated those Rockers almost as much as they hated us."

"Rockers were bikers?" Rebus checked, receiving a slow nod of agreement from King. "Pitched battles on the seafront," he went on. "I remember it from *Quadrophenia*."

"Anything and everything became your weapon. I always had

33

a blade with me, taken from my mum's cutlery drawer. But there were bottles, planks of wood, bricks . . ."

Rebus knew now what was coming, and leaned in a little closer toward the bed.

"So what happened?" he prompted.

King was thoughtful for a moment, then took a hit of oxygen before saying what needed to be said. "One of them—jeans stained with oil, three-inch turn-ups, leather jacket, and T-shirt—he starts running the wrong way, gets separated from the pack. A few of us peel off and go after him. He knows he's not going to outrun us, so dives into a hotel just off the esplanade. Far as I remember we were laughing, like it was a game. But it wasn't, not once we'd cornered him in one of the storerooms off the kitchen. Fists and feet to start with, but then he's got a blade out and so have I, and I'm faster than him. The knife—my mum's knife—was still sticking out of his chest when we ran." King looked up at Rebus, eyes widening a little. "I left him there to die. That's why I need you to arrest me." His eyes were filling with liquid. "Because all the years since, I've never gone a day without remembering, waiting for your lot's knock at the door. And you never came, did you? You never came . . ."

Back in his second-floor tenement flat, Rebus smoked a couple of cigarettes and dug out his vinyl copy of The Who's *Quadrophenia*. He flicked through the booklet of photos and the little short story that accompanied them. Then he lifted his phone and called DI Siobhan Clarke.

"Well?" she asked.

"It's archaeology," he told her. "Summer of sixty-four. I'm assuming it landed on my lap because someone mistook me for Old Father Time. Didn't even happen in Edinburgh."

"Where, then?"

"Brighton. Mods and Rockers. Blood in the nostrils and amphetamines in the blood." He exhaled cigarette smoke. "Nearly fifty years ago and a confession from a man with days left to live—always supposing he did it. Stuff the hospital is giving him, he could be telling us next he's Keith Moon's long-lost brother."

"So what do you think?"

"I just wish he'd asked for a priest instead."

"Worth bouncing it south?"

"You mean to Brighton?"

"Want me to see if I can find a CID contact for you?"

Rebus stubbed out the cigarette. "King did give me a couple of names, guys who were there when he stabbed the victim."

"The victim being?"

"Johnny Greene. The murder was in the papers. Frightened the life out of King and that was the end of his Mod days."

"And the others who were with him?"

"He never saw them again. Part of the deal he seems to have made with himself."

"Fifty years he's been living with this . . ."

"Living *and* dying with it."

"If he'd confessed at the time, he'd have served his sentence and been rid of it."

"I thought it best not to bring that up with him."

He heard her sigh. "I'll find you someone in Brighton," she eventually said. "A burden shared and all that."

He thanked her and ended the call, then slipped the first of *Quadrophenia*'s two discs out of its sleeve and placed it on the deck. He'd never been a Mod, couldn't recall ever *seeing* a Mod, but at one time he'd known this record well. He poured himself a malt and turned up the volume.

For the first time in several months, after an unusually high spate of murders in the city of Brighton this spring, Roy Grace finally had some time to concentrate on cold case reviews, which was part of his remit in the recent merger of the Sussex and Surrey Major Crime branches. He had just settled at a desk in the cold case office when DS Norman Potting entered without knocking, as usual, his bad comb-over looking thinner than ever and reeking, as normal, of pipe tobacco smoke. He was holding an open notepad.

"Had an interesting call earlier this morning from a DI in Scotland, Chief, name of Siobhan Clarke. Pity is, she had an English accent. I've always fancied a bit of Scottish tottie."

Grace raised his eyes. "And?"

"One of her colleagues went to see a bloke in hospital in Edinburgh—apparently terminally ill, wanted to make a deathbed confession about killing a Rocker in Brighton in the summer of sixty-four."

"Nineteen sixty-four? That far back, and he's dying—why couldn't he keep his trap shut?"

"Maybe he reckons he'll avoid hell this way."

Grace shook his head. He'd never really got this religious thing about confession and forgiveness. "Just your era, wasn't it, Norman?"

"Ha!"

Potting was fifty-five but with his shapeless frame and flaccid face could have passed for someone a good decade older.

"I've had dealings with Edinburgh. Don't know anyone called Clarke, though."

Potting looked down at his notebook. "Colleague's name is Rebus."

"Now *that* name I do know. He worked the Wolfman killings in London. Thought he'd be retired by now."

"That was definitely the name she gave."

"So what else did she say?"

"The deathbed confession belongs to one James Ronald King. He was a Mod back then. The bloke he killed is Johnny Greene."

A phone rang at one of the three unoccupied desks in the office. Grace ignored it. The walls all around were stickered in photographs of victims of murders that had never been solved, crime scene photographs, and yellowing newspaper cuttings. "How did he kill him?"

"Stabbed him with a kitchen knife—says he took it with him for protection."

"A real little soldier," Grace said sarcastically. "Have you checked back to see if there's any truth in it?"

"I have, Chief!" Potting said proudly. "It's one of the things DI Clarke asked me to find out. A Johnny Earl Greene died during the Mods versus Rocker clashes on May 19, 1964. It was one of the worst weekends of violence of that whole era."

Grace turned to a fresh page in his policy book and made some notes. "First thing is to get the postmortem records on Greene and a mugshot and send them up to Scotland so Mr. King can make a positive ID of his victim—if he wasn't too wasted at the time to remember."

"I've already requested them from the coroner's office, Chief," Potting responded. "I've also put a request in to the Royal Sussex County Hospital for their records at the time. He might have been brought in there if he wasn't dead at the scene."

"Good man." Roy Grace thought for a moment. "My dad was a frontline PC during that era. He used to tell me about it—how on some bank holidays back then Brighton became a war zone."

"Perhaps you could ask him if he remembers anything about this incident?"

"Good idea. But we'd need to find a medium first."

It took a moment for this to register. Potting stood, frowning for a moment, then said, "I'm sorry, guv. I didn't realize."

"No reason why you should."

Two days later, Norman Potting came back into the cold case office, clutching an armful of manila folders, which he dumped on Roy Grace's desk, then opened the top one. It was the pathologist's report on Johnny Earl Greene.

"It's not right, guv," the old sweat said. "Take a look at the cause of death."

Grace studied the document carefully. The list of the man's injuries did not make good reading:

Multiple skull fractures resulting in subdural and extradural hemorrhage together with direct brain tissue injury from fragments of skull displaced into the brain.

Rib fractures causing flail chest, and laceration by broken ribs of the liver, spleen, and lungs.

Extensive fractures of the maxilla and mandible with hemorrhage causing direct upper airway obstruction and fatal inhalation of blood, combined with stamping injury to the trachea causing cervical vertebral dislocation.

Stamping injuries to the ribs, again lacerating the major thoracic and abdominal organs.

Multiple defensive injury fractures to the small bones of the hands and wrist indicative of fetal position adopted by the victim. Traumatic testicular and scrotal rupture.

Grace looked up at the detective sergeant with a frown. "There's nothing here about any stab wounds. This James King, in Edinburgh, is certain he stabbed his victim?"

"I spoke to John Rebus twenty minutes ago. No question, according to him, King stabbed him in the chest with the kitchen knife. Left it in the body when he fled the scene."

"A knife's unlikely to have been overlooked, even back in the day," Grace said wryly.

"Agreed."

"Which would indicate Johnny Greene was not the victim, or am I missing something?"

"No, guv." Potting grinned and opened another folder. "I got this from the hospital. We're lucky. One more year and the records would have been destroyed. Saturday, May nineteen, nineteen sixty-four, they treated a stab assault casualty. Sabatier bread knife still in his chest. Name of Ollie Starr. He was an art student and member of an Essex biker gang. The blade damaged his spinal cord and he was transferred to the Spinal Injuries Unit at Stoke Mandeville Hospital up in Bucks."

"Do the records say what happened to him?"

"No, but I have the name of the officer who attended the scene and accompanied him to the county hospital. PC Jim Hopper."

Grace did some quick mental arithmetic. It was now 2013. Forty-nine years ago. Many police officers started in their teens. "This PC Hopper, he might still be around, Norman. He'd be in his sixties or perhaps seventies. If you contact Sandra Leader who runs the Retired Brighton and Hove Police Officers Association, or David Rowland, who runs the local branch of NARPO, they might know his whereabouts." NARPO was the National Association of Retired Police Officers.

"I already have. And, guv, I think you are going to be very

interested in this. PC Hopper retired as an inspector, but is still with us. What's more, he's kept in touch with Ollie Starr. The man lives right here in Brighton, apparently, and is mightily pissed off that his assailant has never been brought to justice."

"Did he give you an address?"

"He's getting it. He also invited us to a reunion."

Grace narrowed his eyes. "Reunion?"

"The retired officers of Brighton and Hove. It's this Saturday at the Sportsman Pub at Withdean Stadium."

"From what I've heard tell of Rebus, he wouldn't say no to a drink."

Potting perked up. "Reckon DI Clarke might be tempted, too?"

"She might." Grace studied his calendar. It was Wednesday. The rest of his week, including the weekend, was clear. He'd promised to spend time with his beloved Cleo and their baby, Noah. If this could be cleared up on Saturday, he'd have all day Sunday. Then again, how would Rebus and Clarke feel about working a weekend? "Give me their number in Edinburgh," he said.

At ten thirty AM Saturday morning, after collecting John Rebus and Siobhan Clarke from an early Gatwick flight, Grace and Potting drove them into Brighton, with just the one detour so they could sightsee the beach and pavilion.

"Been here before?" Potting asked Clarke, turning his head to study her more closely.

"No," she said, eyes on the scenery.

"Gets busy on the weekend," Grace explained. "Day-trippers from London."

"Just like nineteen sixty-four," Rebus commented.

"Just like," Grace echoed, meeting the older man's eyes in the rearview mirror.

"You work cold cases?" Rebus asked him.

"On top of my other duties," Grace confirmed.

"I did that, too, until Siobhan here rescued me." The way he said it made it sound as if he disliked being beholden.

"Much crime in your neck of the woods?" Potting was asking Clarke.

"Enough to keep us busy."

"Stuff we get here—"

But Grace broke in, cutting Potting off. "It's not a competition."

But of course it was, and always would be, and when Grace next met Rebus's gaze in the mirror, the two men shared a thin smile of acknowledgment.

In a conference room at Sussex House CID HQ, coffee was made before they sat to watch a video compiled by Amy Hannah of media relations. She had put together a selection of clips from Saturday, May 19, 1964, accompanied by a soundtrack from the era: The Dave Clark Five, Kinks, Rolling Stones, Beatles, and others.

"Nice touch," Rebus commented as "The Kids Are Alright" played.

With the blinds down they watched the massed ranks of Mods, between the Palace and West Piers, many of them on scooters, wearing slim ties, tab-collared shirts, sharp suits, and fur-collared parka jackets, wielding knives, and the Rockers, in studded leather jackets, some of them swinging heavy chains and other implements. The Rockers looked little different to modern-day Hells Angels, apart from the pompadour hairstyles.

Battle raged, battalions of Brighton police officers in white helmets on foot and on horseback, flailing their batons while being belted with stones and bottles.

Siobhan Clarke sucked air in through her mouth. "I had no idea," she said.

"Oh, it was bad," Grace told her. "My mum said my dad used to come home regularly with a black eye, bloodied nose, or fat lip."

"Tribal," Potting added. "Just two tribes at war."

"Nearest we'd have up north," Rebus commented, "would be the pitched battles at Celtic-Rangers games."

"But this was different," Grace said. "And I'll tell you my theory if you like."

"Go ahead."

Grace leaned forward in his seat. "They were the first generation ever in our country that didn't have to go and fight a war. They had to get their aggression out on something, including each other."

"You still see it on a Saturday night," Rebus added with a slow nod. "Young men sizing each other up, fueled, and wanting some attention."

"Stick around a few hours," Potting said, making show of checking his watch.

When the video was over, Rebus told the room that he needed a smoke.

"I'll join you," Grace said.

"Me, too," added Potting, pulling his pipe from his pocket.

Siobhan Clarke shook her head. "You lads run along." Then she aimed the remote at the DVD player, ready to watch the clips all over again.

●◆●

After fish and chips at the Palm Court on Brighton Pier, they headed to Withdean Stadium and entered the pub, where the reunion was in full swing.

"Retired?" Rebus snorted. "Most of them are younger than me." He looked around at the hundred or so faces.

"Full pension after thirty years," Grace commented.

"It's the same in Scotland," Clarke explained. "But John isn't having it."

"Why not?" Grace sounded genuinely curious.

Clarke was watching Rebus head to the bar, Potting hot on his heels. "It's gone beyond being a job to him," she offered. "If you can understand that."

Grace thought for a moment, then nodded. "Completely."

By the time they got to the bar, Potting was explaining to Rebus that Harveys was the best local pint.

"Just so long as it's not the sherry," Rebus joked.

Once they had their drinks, Potting led them over to the retired inspector Jim Hopper, who had attended the badly injured Ollie Starr on that Saturday afternoon in 1964. Hopper was a giant of a man, with a shaven head rising from apparently neckless shoulders, giving him the appearance of an American football player. But his eyes were sympathetic, his demeanor gentle. Potting handed him a drink. He took a sip before speaking.

"I told Ollie you might be coming to speak to him. He seemed hellish relieved. Ever since that assault, his life's turned to a bucket of turds."

"You've kept in touch with him?" Rebus nudged.

"I have, yes. To tell the truth, I've always felt partways responsible. If we'd had more men on the ground that day, or we'd spotted him being chased." Hopper winced at the memory. "I was with him in the ambulance. He thought he was dying, poured out his whole story to me, as if I was the last friend he'd ever have."

"Do you think he'd be able to identify the assailant after all this time?" Clarke asked quietly.

"No doubt about it. Couldn't happen now, of course, with CCTV and DNA. Nobody'd get away with it."

"It was half a century back," Rebus reminded Hopper. "You sure his memory's up to it?"

A grim smile broke across the retired officer's face. "You need to see for yourselves."

"See what?"

"Visit him and you'll find out."

"Is he married?" Clarke asked.

Hopper shook his head. "Far as he's concerned, his life ended that day. Stabbed in the chest, then the cowards just walked away."

There was silence for a moment. They were in a bubble, far from the chatter and gossip around them.

"Give us his address," Rebus ordered, breaking the spell.

Roy Grace had been in some shitholes in his time, and Ollie Starr's ground-floor flat, on the other side of the wall from the Brighton and Hove refuse tip, was down there with the worst of them. It was dank, with dark mold blotches on one wall of the tiny hall. As they strode through into the sitting room, there were empty beer bottles littering the place, an ashtray overflowing with butts, soiled clothing strewn haphazardly on the floor, and an ancient, fuzzy television screen displaying a football match.

But none of the detectives looked at the football. All of them stared, with puzzled faces, at the pencil sketches that papered almost every inch of the otherwise bare walls. From each of them an expressionless man stared out. He was the same man in every drawing, Grace realized, but he was aged progressively, from late teens to mid-sixties. At every stage he was portrayed with different hairstyles, with and without beard or moustache. They reminded Roy Grace of police Identi-Kit drawings.

"Bloody hell," Rebus muttered, stepping farther into the room. "It's James King." He turned to Ollie Starr. "Where did these—?"

"My memory," Starr said, flatly.

"You've not seen him?"

"Not since the day he stuck a knife in me."

"The likeness is amazing."

"Meaning you've got the bastard." The muscles in Starr's face seemed to relax a fraction. "Never forgot his face," he continued. "And I was a student at Hornsey School of Art. Promising future, they said, maybe doing adverts and stuff. Instead of which, I've just been drawing him, year after year, hoping one day I'd see him."

Siobhan Clarke cleared her throat. "We think the man who at-tacked you is critically ill in hospital."

"Good."

"That answers my first question."

Starr's eyes narrowed. "What's that, then?"

"Whether you'd want to go ahead with a prosecution after all this time." She paused. "Against a man with not long to live."

"I want to see him," Starr growled. "I *need* to see him, face-to-face, the closer the better. He has to be shown what he did. Ru-ined my life, and the only thing that kept me going was the dream."

"What dream?" Grace asked.

"The dream of you lot coming here, delivering the news." Starr blinked back a tear. We all have our dreams, eh?" His voice cracked a little. "But a man's reach should exceed his grasp / Or what's a heaven for?"

Grace was moved that the man had read Browning. He lived in a tip, yet clutched at beauty. How different might his life have been if . . . ?

If.

He caught John Rebus's eye, and then Siobhan Clarke's, and knew they were thinking the same thing—while Potting tried to examine Clarke's legs without her noticing.

"We'd need to bring you to Edinburgh quickly," Rebus was saying. "Could you fly up Monday?"

"Train might be less hassle," Starr said. "Give me time to decide whether to spit in his face first or go straight for a punch."

Hospitals always made Roy Grace feel uncomfortable. Too many memories of visiting his dying father and, later, his dying mother. Late on Monday afternoon he followed Rebus and Clarke along the corridor of the Royal Infirmary. It looked new, no smells of boiled cabbage or disinfectant. Transport had been awaiting the group at Waverley Station, Clarke making sure the visitors glimpsed the famous castle before they headed to the outskirts of the city. As Rebus pushed open the doors to the ward, Grace glanced back in the direction of Potting and Starr. Neither man showed any emotion.

"Okay?" Grace checked, receiving two separate nods in reply.

Rebus, however, had come to a sudden stop, Grace almost colliding with him. The bed in the corner was empty, the table next to it bare.

"Shit," Rebus muttered, eyes scanning the room. Plenty of patients, but no sign of the only one that mattered.

"Can I help?" a nurse asked, her face arranged into a professional smile.

"James King," Rebus informed her. "Looks like we're too late."

"Oh dear, yes."

"How long ago did he die?"

The smile was replaced with something more quizzical. "He's not dead," she explained. "He went into remission. It happens sometimes, and if I were the religious sort . . ." She shrugged. "Spontaneous and inexplicable, but there you are. Mr. King's back home in the bosom of his family, happy as the proverbial Larry!"

•◆•

Twenty minutes later, Rebus knocked on the door of the bungalow on Liberton Brae. Ella King answered, then stared stonily at the small entourage outside.

"My husband's changed his mind," she blurted out. "It was the drugs he was taking. They got him hallucinating."

"Fine, then," Rebus said, holding up his hands as if in surrender. "But could we come in a minute?"

She didn't seem at all sure, but Rebus was already barging past her, stalking down the hall toward the living room, Grace and Clarke right behind him. James King was seated in a large armchair, horse-racing on the television. He was dressed in slacks and a polo shirt, a newspaper on his lap and a mug of tea by his side.

"You've heard the news?" he boomed. "They're calling it a miracle, for want of any better explanation. And has Ella explained about the drugs? I must have been rambling, the time I talked to you."

"Is that a fact, sir? Well, is there any chance you could ramble your way to the front door? There's an old friend of yours waiting to see you."

King's face creased in confusion, but Rebus was gesturing for him to get up, and get up he did, shuffling toward the front door.

Norman Potting stood on the path outside, hands resting against the handles of Ollie Starr's wheelchair.

"James King," Rebus said, "meet Oliver Starr."

"But we've never met. I . . . I don't know him. What's this all about?"

"You know me, all right," Starr snarled, his whole body writhing as if a current were passing through it. "Your bread knife's still in an evidence locker in Brighton. Did your mum never ask you what happened to it?"

Grace watched King's face. It was as if the man had been slapped.

"What's going on?" his wife asked, voice trembling.

"A man did die that day," Clarke explained. "But not the man your husband attacked. When he saw it reported, he jumped to conclusions."

"Is this the man who stabbed you, Mr. Starr?" Grace asked.

"I'd know him anywhere," Ollie Starr replied, eyes burning into King's.

"You old fool," Ella King yelped at her husband. "I told you to leave it alone, take it to the grave with you. Why did you have to bring it all up?"

"James Ronald King," Grace was intoning, "I have a warrant issued for your arrest. I'm arresting you on suspicion of the attempted murder of Oliver Starr. You do not have to say anything, but it may harm your defense if you do not mention when questioned something which you later rely on in court. Anything you do say may be given in evidence. Is that clear?"

"I'm in remission," King gasped. "The rest of my life ahead of me . . ."

"Had a good life so far, have you?" Starr snarled. "Better than mine, at any rate. All the years I've spent in a bloody wheelchair! No wife, no kids!"

"You can't do this," Ella King was pleading. "He's a very sick man." Her hand was gripping her husband's arm.

Rebus shook his head. "He's not ill, Mrs. King. We heard it from his own mouth."

"But he *is* sick," Potting interjected. "Takes a sick mind to shove a knife so deep into someone it breaks their spine."

"So far in the past, though," Ella King persisted. "Everything's different now."

"Not so different," Rebus replied, looking toward Clarke and Grace. "Besides which, I'd say we got here just in the nick of time."

Roy Grace nodded his agreement.

Different cities, different cultures, different generations, even, but he knew he shared one thing above all else with John Rebus—pleasure in each and every result.

R. L. STINE

VS. DOUGLAS PRESTON AND LINCOLN CHILD

Gaslighted

D ouglas Preston and Lincoln Child created their character, FBI agent A. X. L. Pendergast, almost by accident. Lincoln was an editor at St. Martin's Press and had just edited Doug's first nonfiction book, *Dinosaurs in the Attic,* a history of the American Museum of Natural History. After that experience, the two decided to write a thriller set in a museum. Doug wrote the first few chapters—involving the investigation of a double murder—and sent them to Lincoln for his opinion. Lincoln read the pages and had one objection. He felt the two cops on the investigation were essentially identical. So he suggested they fold both into the same character (who became Lieutenant Vincent D'Agosta). But then he added, "We need a new kind of detective for the second investigator. A person who's unusual—and who'll be like a fish out of water in New York City."

Doug, already irritated at this criticism of his prose, responded sarcastically, "Yeah, right. You mean, like an albino FBI agent from New Orleans?"

Silence passed for a few moments between them.

Then Lincoln said, "I think that could work."

Over the next fifteen minutes Special Agent Pendergast was formed, like Athena from the forehead of Zeus.

And the rest, they say, is history.

Over the course of many books Agent Pendergast has faced some unusual adversaries, including cannibalistic serial killers, arsonists, a murderous surgeon, a mutant assassin, and even his own mad-genius brother. But never has he confronted an adversary like Slappy the Ventriloquist Dummy.

Slappy is one of R. L. Stine's creepiest creations. Bob is one of the best-selling authors of all time, with over 400 million books sold around the world. He is the creator of the amazing *Goosebumps* series of novels. Millions of kids began reading thanks to Bob's imagination. Within the *Goosebumps* series Bob introduced Slappy, through such memorable tales as *Night of the Living Dummy, Bride of the Living Dummy,* and *Son of Slappy.* Carved from coffin wood, when brought to life by a certain spoken phrase, Slappy is sarcastic, rude, sadistic, and threatening, with a raspy voice and enormous physical strength. He usually seeks to enslave the luckless child who brought him back to life. He's so popular that he's the model for an actual ventriloquist's dummy sold by many retailers to this day.

Bob tells the story of how Slappy was inspired by a 1945 anthology film called *Dead of Night*. One segment of the movie told the story of a terrifying and murderous ventriloquist's dummy that eventually took possession of his owner's mind. Bob saw the film when he was young and it scared the daylights out of him. Interestingly, as a child, Bob owned a Jerry Mahoney dummy of his own. Eventually, he became fascinated by the idea that something so human-looking and seemingly harmless could turn so completely evil.

The idea of pairing the elegant, urbane FBI agent Pendergast against an evil dummy seemed so incongruous—so impossible—that Doug, Lincoln, and Bob were immediately captivated by the challenge. The result is a psychological thriller where both the dummy and Agent Pendergast play against form, assuming roles that familiar readers may find strange and unsettling.

One thing is certain—this story is not intended for children.

Gaslighted

There was a tap-tapping sound. That was all. Was it a clock? No: it was too loud, too irregular. Was it the creaking of an old house? The ticking of a radiator?

The man listened to the sound. Gradually he became aware of certain things—or rather, the absence of things. The absence of light. Of sensation. Of a name.

That was unusual, was it not? He was a man with no name. He had no memory. He was a tabula rasa, an empty vessel. And yet he sensed that he knew many things. This was a paradox.

The ticking sound grew louder. The man struggled to understand. Sensation began to return. He was blind—hooded. His hands and feet were immobilized. Not bound, but strapped. He was lying on a bed. He tried to move. The restraints were soft, comfortable, and effective.

He was not hungry. He was not tired. He was neither hot nor cold. He was not frightened; he felt calm.

Tap, tap, tap-tap. He listened. A thought came into his head: if he could understand what made that sound, perhaps all else would come back.

He tried to speak, and a sound emerged. The hiss of breath.

The tap-tapping stopped. Silence.

Then he heard a creaking sound. This he recognized: footfalls on a wooden floor. They were growing closer. A hand grasped the hood, and he heard the sound of Velcro parting. The hood was gently removed and he saw a face drawing toward him. He realized, from the movement of air over his scalp, that his own head had been shaved. He had once had hair—at least he knew that much about himself.

And then the face moved into his field of view. The light was dim but he could make out the face quite distinctly. It was a man in his forties, wearing a gray flannel suit. The face was sharp. It had high cheekbones, an aquiline nose. Bony ridges around the eyes gave it a skull-like, asymmetric quality. His hair was ginger-colored and he sported a thick, neatly trimmed beard. But the most startling effect was in his eyes: one was a rich hazel-green, clear and deep, the pupil dilated. The other was a milky blue, opaque, dead, the pupil contracted to a tiny black point.

The sight of the eyes triggered something—something massive. A Niagara of memory came thundering back, all at once, leaving the man on the bed almost paralyzed with the crushing weight of it. He stared at the man bending over him.

"Diogenes," he whispered.

"Aloysius," the man said, his brow furrowed with concern. "Thank God you're awake."

Aloysius. Aloysius Pendergast. That was his name: Special Agent Aloysius Pendergast.

"You're dead," he said. "This is a dream."

"No," said Diogenes, almost tenderly. "You've awakened from a dream. Now you're on the road to healing—at long last." As he said this, he leaned over and unstrapped his brother's wrists from their leather restraints. He leaned over to fluff and adjust Pendergast's pillow, smooth the sheets. "You can sit up if you feel able."

"You've done this to me. This is one of your schemes."

"Come now, please. Not this again."

Out of the corner of his eye, Aloysius saw movement. He turned his head. The door to his room had opened and a woman was walking in. It was a woman he recognized instantly: Helen Esterhazy, his wife.

His dead wife.

He stared in horror as she approached. She reached out to take his hand and he pulled it away. "This is a hallucination," he said.

"This is very real," she said gently.

"Impossible."

She sat down on the edge of the bed. "We're alive—both of us. We're here to assist in your recovery."

Aloysius Pendergast mutely shook his head. If this wasn't a dream, then he must be under the influence of drugs. He would not cooperate in whatever was happening to him, whatever they were doing. He closed his eyes and tried to remember how he had gotten to this place; what events led up to this . . . imprisonment. But his short-term memory was a blank. What, then, was his last memory? He struggled to find it. But there was nothing—just a long, black road going back as far as his memory would travel.

"We're here to help you," Diogenes added.

Pendergast opened his eyes and stared into the heterochromic

55

eyes of his brother. "You? Help me? You're my worst enemy. And besides, you're not here. You're dead."

How did he know his brother was dead? If he couldn't remember, how could he be sure? And yet, he was sure . . . wasn't he?

"No, Aloysius," Diogenes said with a smile. "That's all part of your fantasy. Your illness. Think back on your life, or what you believe has been your life. What is your profession?"

Pendergast hesitated. "I'm . . . an FBI agent."

Another gentle smile. "Okay. Now think about that. We know all about this 'life' of yours. You've spent the last months talking about it with Dr. Augustine. We've heard all about the insane exploits, the wild encounters. We've heard about all the people you've supposedly killed, about your narrow escapes. We've heard about genetic monsters eating people's brains and infantile serial killers living in caves. We've heard about underground mutant armies and Nazi breeding programs. We've heard about a certain young lady who is a hundred and forty years old . . . That, Aloysius, is the fantasy world you're finally awakening from. We're real; that crazy world is not."

As Diogenes rattled these items off, each one suddenly resonated in Pendergast's memory, bursting like a firework. "No," he said. "It's exactly the opposite. You're twisting everything. You're not real; that other world is real."

Helen leaned over, her violet eyes looking into his. "Do you really think the FBI, the buttoned-down FBI, would allow one of its agents to run amok, killing people willy-nilly?" She spoke calmly, her voice cool and rational. "How could all that be real? Think back on these so-called adventures of yours. Could one man, one person, really experience all that and live through it?"

Diogenes spoke again, his buttery Southern accent like a balm. "You simply couldn't have survived all the adventures you've told

Dr. Augustine about. Don't you see? Your memories are lying to you. Not us."

"Then why am I restrained? Why the hood?"

"When the breakthrough came," said Diogenes, "when Dr. Augustine finally breached the hard shell of your fantasies, you became . . . disturbed. We had no choice but to have you restrained, for your own safety. They hooded you because the light was bothering you. You've always had an aversion to light, ever since you were a child."

"And why the shaved head?"

"That's necessary for the treatment, the placement of electrodes. Electrical stimulation of the brain."

"Electrodes? What in God's name is being done to me?"

"Try to relax, Aloysius," Helen said soothingly. "We know how difficult this must be. You're awakening from a long, long nightmare. We're here to help you back to reality. Try to sit up. Have a drink of water."

Pendergast sat up and Helen adjusted the pillows behind him. He now took a closer look at the room. It was elegant, paneled in oak, with leaded glass windows opening to a sweep of green lawn and flowering dogwood trees. He noted that the windows were discreetly barred. A Persian rug covered much of the gleaming parquet floor. The only indication that this was a hospital room was an odd-looking medical instrument, set into the wall by the head of his bed, with dials, tiny lights, and a series of electrodes dangling on long, colored leads.

His gaze was arrested by a strange sight: in a satin wing chair in the far corner sat a ventriloquist's dummy. The dummy had brown hair and scarlet lips. It was wearing a doctor's white coat with a stethoscope draped around its neck. Its mouth hung open, revealing a dark hole. Its glassy blue eyes underneath arched eyebrows stared directly at him, unblinking. It sat up very straight, its legs sticking straight out, its polished brown shoes decorated with painted orange laces.

At that moment, the door opened and a man strode in, a big, cheerful fellow with a fringe of hair around a bald pate. He was dressed in a blue serge suit with a red bow tie, a red carnation in his boutonniere. He carried a clipboard.

Diogenes rose and extended his hand. "Hello, Doctor. We're so glad you're here. He's awake and, I daresay, a lot more lucid than before."

"Excellent!" said the doctor, turning to Pendergast. "I think we've achieved a real breakthrough here."

"Breakthrough? Not at all. This is some sort of induced hallucination, some scheme to affect my sanity."

"That," said the doctor, "is the last gasp of your delusion talking. But that's quite all right. May I?" He indicated a seat next to the ventriloquist's dummy.

"I am perfectly indifferent to your comfort," said Pendergast. "Do as you wish."

The doctor sat down, unperturbed. "I'm so glad to see you able to recognize Helen and Diogenes. That in itself is a huge step. Before, you couldn't even see them, so powerful were your fantasies of their being dead. Now, if I may, I'd like to explain all this to you while you're lucid."

Pendergast waved a hand.

"Yours is a deep and complex case—perhaps the most complex in my experience. What I am now summarizing is the result of months of painstaking reconstruction. During your time in the Special Forces, twenty years ago, you suffered an unbearably traumatic experience. We've covered that thoroughly and don't need to touch on it again. Suffice it to say, the experience was so dreadful it presented a threat to your sanity, indeed to your very existence. You left the Special Forces. But the trauma produced in you an extreme form of PTSD, which lay deeply buried and untreated. Like a cancer, it worked away on you over the years. Being a man of means, you could afford not to work—and enforced idleness may have been the worst thing for you. You became delusional. Your primary way of dealing with this untreated PTSD was to become, in your own mind, an all-powerful FBI agent, who rights wrongs, kills without mercy, and rids the world of evil. This fantasy took over your very existence."

Pendergast stared at the doctor. As much as he wanted to disbelieve, there was a disturbing logic to it. As proof, here were Diogenes and Helen, two people he'd believed dead, in the room, living, breathing, and to all his senses absolutely real. He couldn't deny the reality of his own eyes. And yet . . . his memories of his FBI days, which the earlier litany of Diogenes had opened to him as if by a floodgate, were just as strong.

"You've been in a dark place," the doctor said, tapping his pen on the clipboard. "But you're making real progress at last, thanks to my course of treatment. In fact, things were looking so promising that, last week, I brought in the two people who care about you the most—your brother and your ex-wife—to be by your side. It's always darkest just before you emerge from the tunnel."

"What is this place?"

"This is the Stony Mountain Sanatorium, outside of Saranac Lake in Upstate New York."

"And how did I get here?"

"Your housekeeper found you barricaded in your Dakota apartment, raving about Nazis. The police were called, your brother was notified, and he and your ex-wife arranged to bring you here. That was almost six months ago. It was slow, difficult going at first, but

the progress you've made recently is most encouraging. Now—
after what I've just explained, how do you feel?"

Pendergast turned to Diogenes and was once again struck by
the look of brotherly concern on his face. "But you made it your
life's work to destroy me."

An expression of distress crossed Diogenes's face. "That, Aloysius, is the most painful part of your delusions. I've never been
anything to you but a loving brother. Sure, we had our differences
as kids. What brothers don't? But to see those childish tiffs grow
into this adult paranoia was really painful. But I love you, brother,
and I long ago realized it was an illness—not a choice."

Pendergast turned to Helen. "And you?"

She lowered her eyes. "First, it was your fantasy about me
being killed by a lion in Africa. And then your delusion morphed
into something even more bizarre—that I hadn't been killed by
a lion at all, but by Nazis in Mexico. There came a time when
I just couldn't take it. That's why I divorced you. I'm so sorry.
Maybe I should have been stronger. But the fact is I never stopped
loving you."

There was a silence. Pendergast looked around the room. It
was all so real, so vivid, and so calming. Despite himself, he felt a
sense of release, as if a long nightmare was finally ending. What
if they were telling the truth? If so, the horror of Helen's death
hadn't happened. It was all in his mind. And how wonderful to
be released from those dreadful memories, that crushing sense
of guilt, pain, and remorse, free of all the horrible things he had
witnessed as an FBI agent. And he could let go of the pain of Diogenes's insanity and implacable hatred. "How do you feel?" Dr. Augustine had asked. He felt at peace. He could forget everything
now. It was as if all the shackles of his old, false memories, his old,

imagined actions, were dropping away, and he was being given a second chance in life.

"I think I would like to sleep now," he said.

He awoke in the dark. It was night. He sat up and saw Helen, sitting in a chair near the bed, dozing. She awoke, her eyes opening, and smiled. She glanced at her watch. The moonlight was lighting up the lace curtains in the window, casting an ethereal glow over the polished oak walls. The chair with the dummy was now empty.

"What time is it?"

"One o'clock."

He felt strangely refreshed, alert.

"Would you like me to turn on a light?" she asked.

"No, please. I like the moonlight. Do you remember the full moon?"

"Oh, yes," she said. "Of course. The moon."

Pendergast was shaken. He felt a sudden sense of gratitude that she was alive, that she had not died—that he was not responsible.

"What I mean, if I haven't been in the FBI, what have I been doing?"

"Well, we met after you had left the Special Forces. You never talked about it and I never wanted to pry. You were living a life of leisure and intellectual pursuit at the old family estate down in Louisiana, and we spent quite a few idyllic years there, as well as traveling the world. Tibet, Nepal, Brazil, Africa."

"Africa?"

"Big game hunting. I was never killed by a lion, however." She smiled thinly. "Let me just say this, Aloysius. Let me get this off my chest. I'm not proud of myself for leaving you—but I began to fear for my safety. Living with you became increasingly dangerous. Through it all, Diogenes was a saint. He learned of this experimental treatment here at Stony Mountain. It was our last option."

Pendergast nodded slowly. "What will become of me now?"

"I'm told the recovery will take time. You'll have to stay here until the doctor feels it's complete. It might be another six months."

"You mean, I can't leave?"

Helen hesitated. "You'll have to face the fact that you've been legally committed. But it's for your own good. After all, it took you years and years to develop these delusions. You can't expect to get well overnight. In time, you'll be able to return to Penumbra and pick up your old life of leisure." She took both his hands in hers. "After that, who knows what might happen? Maybe there's even hope for us."

She squeezed his hands. He returned the pressure.

She smiled, stood up. "I'll come see you tomorrow, around noon."

Pendergast watched her go. A long moment passed as he fell deep into thought. For a very long time the room was utterly silent. A strip of moonlight marched slowly across the floor.

Finally, perhaps two hours later, he rose from the bed. On the far side of the room was a heavy metal locker, no doubt added at the time the space was converted into a hospital room. It was secured with a padlock. He looked about. On a table in one corner sat some papers. He flipped through them, but they were only newsletters and hospital menus. Slipping two paper clips off the documents, he went to the locker and—with a movement that was almost automatic—unbent both clips, inserted first one and then the other into the padlock, and with a single deft movement sprung it open.

He paused. How did he know how to do that? From his Special Forces days? His memory of that time was still so damnably miasmic.

He peered into the cabinet. It held a black suit, a white shirt, a tie, shoes, and socks. He touched the material of the suit, soft and elegant, as familiar as his own skin. He felt a prickling sensation at the base of his neck. He searched the suit and pants, going first to the pocket that—he supposedly remembered—held his FBI wallet. Nothing. The other pockets, all the little custom-made slots and pouches, were there. And all were empty. No ID, nothing.

He slipped off his hospital gown and put on the shirt, stroking the fine pinpoint cotton. Then came the pants, the Zegna tie, the jacket, the socks. As he picked up the John Lobb shoes, he thought of something, flipped over the left shoe, and detached the heel. There, nestled in a carved hollow, was a razor blade, a set of lock picks, two sealed ampoules of chemicals, and a tightly folded hundred-dollar bill.

He stared. Could this, too, be a product of his delusional FBI period?

Refastening the heel, he put on the shoes. He walked to the window, unlatched it, and swung it open. A breeze scented with hemlocks flowed through the vertical iron bars. He tried again to summon his last memory. They said he had been in there six months. Had it been winter, then? He tried desperately to remember, to see the landscape in front of him covered with snow, but could not.

Flexing his arms, he reached out and grasped two adjoining metal bars. They were wrought iron, of poor quality, and corroded. With all his force, he pushed outward with each hand. Slowly but surely, the wrought iron deformed under his immense strength until an opening large enough for him to slip through had been made. He let go, breathing hard. But now was not the time to leave. No—he needed answers first.

He fastened the window shut and drew the curtains. Moving cautiously, he went to the door of his room, tested the knob. Locked, of course. In ten seconds he had picked it with the aid of the paper clips, again marveling at his instinctual skill.

He cracked the door and peered out. The lights were on in the hall, and at the far end he could see a nurse's station attended by a nurse and two orderlies. All were alert and busy. He waited, timing his exit until their attention was elsewhere, then ducked out of the door and pressed himself into the darkness of the next doorway. Another patient? With a deft twist of the paper clips, the lock opened, and he found himself in a room like his own, only much smaller. A man lay in the single bed. He, too, had a shaved head, but he looked thin and wasted, and his bare arm sported the old tracks of a heroin addict. His bed had been outfitted with the same medical device Pendergast had noticed in his own room.

With extreme caution, Pendergast exited the dark space and moved down the long hall. Each room he peered into was similar: a sleeping patient with a shaved head, frequently gaunt and wasted-looking.

This was getting him nowhere.

He paused to consider the possibilities. Either his version of reality was correct, or theirs was correct. Either way, unfortunately, seemed to indicate that he was crazy. He needed more information to choose which of the two insanities was real.

Stepping out of the last patient's room, he stuck his hands in his pockets and—not sure, exactly, what he was doing, and yet strangely certain of his actions—strolled back down the hall toward the nurse's station. The two orderlies—big strapping blond men, six-feet-four inches, a matched set—watched him approach, first with incomprehension on their faces and then with alarm. He saw that both men were armed.

"Hey . . . hey!" one of them cried, flummoxed at his appearance. "Who the hell are you?"

He strolled up to them. "Pendergast, at your service. The patient from room 113."

In a practiced move, they parted and took up positions on either side of him. "Okay," the first said, speaking calmly, "we're going to take you back to your room, nice and easy. Understood?"

Pendergast did not move. "I'm afraid that's not acceptable."

They both moved a little closer. "Nobody wants any trouble."

"Incorrect. I do want trouble. In fact, I positively welcome it."

The first orderly reached out and gently grasped his arm. "Enough with the tough talk, friend, and let's go back to bed."

"I do hate being touched."

The second orderly had now moved in, crowding him.

The orderly's grip tightened. "Let's go, Mr. Pendergast."

There was a flicker of movement; the sound of a fist hitting a gut; the sudden wheeze of expelled air—and then the orderly buckled over and collapsed to the floor, grasping his diaphragm. The second orderly swung to grab Pendergast and a moment later was doubled up on the floor as well.

The nurse at the station turned toward an alarm, pulled it, and a siren began to wail. Red lights went on and Pendergast could hear automatic bolts shooting in various door locks. Almost instantly, half a dozen monster orderlies appeared out of nowhere and converged on the nurse's station, where Pendergast stood calmly with crossed arms. They surrounded him, weapons drawn. The two orderlies on the floor continued to lie in a fetal position, gasping and sucking in air, unable to speak.

"Gentlemen, I am ready to go back to my room," said

Pendergast. "But please don't touch me. I have a 'thing' about it, you might say."

"Just get the hell going," said one of the orderlies, apparently the leader. "Move."

Pendergast strolled down the hallway, orderlies before and after. They entered the room and one turned on the light, the last one shutting and locking the door. The lead orderly gestured toward the open metal cabinet, at the foot of which lay Pendergast's hospital gown.

"Strip off your clothes and get back in your gown," he said.

Meanwhile, another orderly was speaking on a walkie-talkie, and Pendergast could hear him assuring someone that all was under control. The siren stopped and silence descended once again.

"I said, strip."

Pendergast turned his back on the orderly, facing the locker, but made no move to take off his clothes. A moment passed and then the lead orderly stepped forward and grabbed him by the shoulder, pulling him around.

"I said—"

He fell silent as the barrel of a Smith & Wesson .38—removed from one of the disabled orderlies—was pressed against his head.

"All the radios on the floor," Pendergast said in a calm, firm voice. "Then the weapons. And all your keys."

Unnerved at the sight of a gun in a patient's hand, the orderlies quickly complied, the radios and pistols piling up on the Persian carpet. Pendergast, still covering the head orderly, sorted through the pile, pulling out one of the radios. He removed the batteries from the others and ejected the rounds from the revolvers, stuffing batteries and bullets into the pocket of his jacket. Sorting through the keys, he found a master, stuck it into the keyhole of his room door, and snapped it off. He turned the working radio over in his hands, found the panic button, and pressed it. The alarm shrieked back to life.

"Elopement!" he cried into the radio. "Room 113! He's got a gun! He went out the window. He's running toward the woods!" Then he turned off the radio, plucked out its batteries in turn, and tossed it on the floor.

"Good evening, gentlemen." He nodded at them gravely, then unlatched the window again, and leaped out into the night.

As he pressed himself against the dark side of the mansion, the lawn and grounds suddenly blazed with floodlights. He could hear shouts over the sound of the alarms. Moving alongside the edge of the building, keeping behind the shrubbery, he worked his way along the bulk of the great mansion turned insane asylum. As he had hoped, security officers and orderlies were running across the lawn, flashlight beams dancing about, all operating on the assumption he had fled into the woods.

Instead, Pendergast remained against the building, an almost invisible shadow, moving slowly and carefully. In a few minutes he had worked his way around to the front. Here, he stopped to reconnoiter. A sweeping driveway curved through a vast lawn to a porte cochere at the building's entrance, tastefully planted with arborvitae. Flitting across the graveled drive, Pendergast secreted himself in the dense shrubbery beside the porte cochere.

It took just under five minutes for a late-model Lexus to come tearing down the driveway, scattering gravel, and slow to a stop under the porte cochere.

Excellent. Most excellent.

As the door was flung open, Pendergast dashed forward and rammed the driver—it was, as he'd expected, Dr. Augustine—back into the automobile, forcing him into his seat. Keeping the doctor covered with the gun, he quickly slipped into the passenger's seat.

"Do keep driving," he said as he closed the door.

The car continued down the driveway and back out toward what was evidently a manned guardhouse and gate. Pendergast slid off the seat and crouched under the dashboard.

"Tell them you forgot something and will be right back. Deviate from the script and you will be shot."

The doctor complied. The gate opened. Pendergast rose back onto the seat as the vehicle accelerated.

"Turn right."

The car turned right onto a lonely country road.

Pendergast turned on the vehicle's GPS and studied it briefly. "Ah. I see we're nowhere near Saranac Lake, but quite a lot closer to the Canadian border." He looked over at Dr. Augustine and removed the cell phone from his coat pocket. Keeping his eye on the GPS, he gave the doctor a series of directions. Half an hour later, the car was proceeding down a dirt track, which dead-ended at a lonely pond.

"Stop here."

The doctor stopped. His lips were set in a thin line, and he was white-faced.

"Dr. Augustine, do you realize the consequences of kidnapping a federal agent? I could kill you right now and get a medal for it. Unless, of course, I'm as crazy as you claim, in which case I'll be locked up. But either way, my dear doctor, you will be dead."

No answer.

"And I will kill you. I want to kill you. The only thing that will stop me is a full, immediate, and complete explanation of this setup."

"What makes you think this is a setup?" came the doctor's quavering voice. "That's your delusion talking."

"Because I knew how to pick a lock. I took this revolver away from an orderly as easily as taking candy from a baby."

"Of course you did. That's your standard Special Forces training."

"I'm too strong to have been locked in a mental hospital for six months. I bent the bars in my window."

"For God's sake, you spent half your time working out in our gym! Don't you remember?"

A silence. Then Pendergast said: "It was a masterful job. You almost had me believing you. But I grew suspicious again when Helen did not rise to my comment about the moon—sharing the full moonrise was always our private signal. That put me on my guard. And then I knew for certain it was a setup when Helen took my hands in hers."

"And how in God's name did you know that?"

"Because she still had her left hand. There's one memory in my life that's so powerful that I know it can't be a delusion. It occurred during the African hunting expedition in which Helen was attacked by a lion. My memory of the moment when I found her severed hand, still bearing its wedding ring, is seared too deep in my memory to be anything but real."

The doctor was silent. The moon shone off the small lake. A loon called from some distant shore.

Pendergast cocked the Smith & Wesson. "I've endured enough prevarication. Tell me the truth. One more lie and you're dead."

"How will you know it's a lie?" asked the doctor quietly.

"It becomes a lie when I don't believe it."

"I see. And what's in it for me if I cooperate?"

"You'll be permitted to live."

The doctor took a deep, shuddering breath. "Let's start

with my name. It's not Augustine. It's Grundman. Dr. William Grundman."

"Keep going."

"For the past decade, I've been experimenting with memory neurons. I discovered a gene known as Npas4."

"Which is?"

"It controls the neurons of your memory. Memory, you see, is physical. It's stored through a combination of neurochemicals and trapped electrical potentials. By controlling Npas4, I learned how to locate the neural networks that store specific memories. I learned how to manipulate those neurons. I learned how to erase them. Not delete—that would cause brain damage. But erase. A far more delicate operation."

He paused. "Do you believe me so far?"

"You're still alive, aren't you?"

"I discovered that this technique could be very lucrative. I started a clinic—under the cover of the Stony Mountain Sanatorium. While the sanatorium is visible, naturally, what goes on there is quite underground."

"Continue."

"People come to my underground clinic to be rid of memories they no longer want. I'm sure you can imagine all sorts of situations in which that would be desirable. I make those memories go away for a price. And for a time, that was satisfactory. But then my research led me to a discovery that was even more extraordinary. I theorized that I could do more than erase memories. I could also create them. I could program new memories. Imagine the potential market for that: for the right price, you could be given the memory of having spent a weekend at Cap d'Antibes with the Hollywood starlet of your choice, or of scaling Everest with Mallory, or of conducting the New York Philharmonic in Mahler's Ninth."

As he spoke, the doctor's eyes shone with a kind of inner light. But then the eyes glanced at the gun again, and they became veiled and anxious once more. "Can't you lower that gun?"

Pendergast shook his head. "Just keep talking."

"Okay. Okay. I needed guinea pigs in order to perfect the memory insertion procedure. You can imagine the results of programming the wrong memories. So I arranged to have indigent people, drug addicts, the homeless, secretly transferred up to my clinic from New York City hospitals."

"Those are the gaunt patients I saw around me."

"Yes."

"People nobody would miss."

"That is correct."

"And how did I get there?"

"Ah. What a lot of trouble you were. It seems that, as part of some case you were working on, you became suspicious of Stony Mountain. You managed to check yourself into Bellevue, posing as a homeless tubercular, and you were duly transferred up here. But there was an accident, a miscommunication, and your clothes ended up being transferred with you. Those were not the clothes of a homeless drifter. I became suspicious, made inquiries, and ultimately learned who you really were. I couldn't just kill you—as you pointed out, killing a federal agent is never the best solution. Much better would be to reprogram you with new memories. To gaslight you, as it were: erase from your memory the real reasons for your coming here, and to add new memories that would, in the end, convince your superiors and loved ones that you had become mentally ill. After that, no one listens to a crazy person. No matter what you said, it would be chalked up to your illness."

"Diogenes and Helen were not real."

"No. They were phantoms, reconstructed out of your memory

71

by manipulating Npas4." Grundman paused. "It appears my research into Helen could have been a little more thorough."

"And the dummy?" Pendergast asked.

"Ah. The dummy. I call him Dr. Augustine. He's a crucial part of the treatment. He doesn't exist, either. The dummy isn't real. He's the conduit, the vehicle—the Trojan Horse, as it were—which I first insinuate into the patient's mind. If I can plant Dr. Augustine in your mind, I can use him to leverage any other memory I wish to insert."

There was a long silence, interrupted by the calling of the loons. The full moon cast a buttery light over the water. Pendergast said nothing.

The doctor stirred nervously in his seat. "I assume that, since you haven't killed me, you accept my story?"

Pendergast did not answer directly. Instead, he said: "Step out of the car."

"You're going to leave me here?"

"It's a lovely summer evening for a walk. The main road is about ten miles back. The local police will probably pick you up before you have to trek the whole distance." He waved the doctor's cell phone meaningfully. "You'll miss the SWAT team raid on your clinic, of course . . . lucky you."

Grundman opened the door and stepped out into the night. Pendergast slid over to the driver's seat, turned the car around, and headed slowly back down the dirt road. Behind him he could see Grundman, standing at the verge of the lake, silhouetted in the moonlit water.

With Grundman's phone in his hand, he began to dial the number of the New York field office of the FBI—the first step toward raiding and shutting down Stony Mountain. But he didn't complete the call. Slowly, he let the phone drop into his lap.

He knew who he was—knew without a shred of doubt. He was Special Agent Aloysius Pendergast of the FBI. This episode at Stony Mountain had been a nightmare, a waking delusion. But now it was over. Dr. Grundman's treatment had been fiendishly effective—but it had failed in the end, as it must. His mind, his memories, were simply too strong to erase or manipulate for long. Now he knew, with utter conviction, who he really was. He knew his true history—it was coming back to him at last. He could put all this behind him, get on with his life. His real life.

And yet—

He looked down at the phone in his lap. As he did so, he glimpsed something in the rearview mirror—something he unaccountably had not noticed before.

There, sitting in the backseat of the car, staring back at him with blue, unblinking eyes, painted red lips, and dressed in a white lab coat with the polished brown shoes, was Dr. Augustine.

M. J. ROSE
VS. LISA GARDNER

The Laughing Buddha

Old world versus young gun. Pragmatic versus the occult. Actual versus the surely impossible. That's the premise M. J. Rose and Lisa Gardner started with. The end result?

A cunningly clever tale.

M. J. Rose doesn't believe she invented Malachai Samuels any more than he may have invented her. But certainly Samuels changed her writing career when he first showed up in *The Reincarnationist* (2007). Samuels became the impetus for M.J. to take her first foray into metaphysical and historical fiction, and she hasn't turned back from that course since. Samuels is, without question, unique. He's an enigmatic Jungian therapist, entrenched in research into past life regressions—a journey he's never actually been able to take himself.

Which is partly why that's become his obsession.

The other reason is that, like M.J., his ancestors, going back to the nineteenth century, have been invested in questioning the mystical lines between past and present. Bringing law enforcement face-to-face with Malachai Samuels, a man who's managed to evade them at every turn for years, intrigued M.J. Especially when the cop in question would be one of her favorites.

Detective D.D. Warren.

Here's an interesting fact. Lisa Gardner's D.D. Warren actually exists in real life. Gardner named her hardened Boston detective after her neighbor, a beautiful blonde best known for her baking and gardening skills. In the beginning, Lisa intended for D.D. to only appear in one chapter of Gardner's sniper novel *Alone*. But D.D.'s brash Boston attitude and relentless determination quickly captured readers' imaginations. Before she knew it, Lisa ended up writing half a dozen novels featuring her neighbor's namesake. The decision to use D.D. for this story was an easy one. Who better to take on the charming, enigmatic Dr. Malachai Samuels, a man suspected of multiple murders but proved guilty of none, than a young, street-smart homicide cop?

Add in the spice of Boston's Chinatown and the legend of a rare artifact and you have the perfect recipe for a thriller.

Or maybe something else entirely?

Something unexpected.

The Laughing Buddha

New York City—1884

Twilight settled over the city, shrouding it in a grayish haze. He hated this time of day, the hour lost between darkness and light, when everything became indistinct. Standing in the shadows he watched the mansion from across the street. Linden trees partially hid the Queen Anne–style villa but he could see light glowing through the glass sunburst below the curved-top window. The lugubrious strains of Beethoven's *Moonlight Sonata* wafted from the open balcony door, appropriate accompaniment to the gloomy dusk.

Even in this murkiness, the elaborate building with its gables, scrolled wrought iron railing, and dozens of gargoyles tucked under the eaves was an impressive sight; a symbol of wealth.

But not his wealth.

Unconsciously, he clenched his jaw, felt the tightness, then forced those muscles to relax.

The front door—with its bas-relief coat of arms of a giant bird rising from a pyre—opened and a finely dressed woman stepped out. She didn't have any idea what she might be coming home to later that evening, but he did and thought about how, if the worst happened, she'd accept his sympathy, come to rely on it, and never guess he'd been the one to orchestrate her grief.

"Percy? Esme? Hurry now, we can't be late for your cousin's birthday party," she called.

The children ran past her; the ten-year-old boy and his eight-year-old sister scampering down the steps and preceding their mother into the waiting carriage.

Once the sound of the children's laughter and the hoofs clomping on cobblestones was far in the distance, the man crept across the street and silently let himself into the house. Quietly as he could, he traversed the black-and-white marble squares in the imposing foyer and walked down a hallway to the library's open doorway where Trevor Talmage worked at his desk, bent over his papers, reading and making notes, oblivious to the intruder.

"Well aren't you the busy boy."

Momentarily startled, Trevor looked up, then smiled indulgently. "When did you get here? Why didn't Peter announce you?"

"I let myself in."

"I didn't know you still had a key," he said, sounding more tired than surprised at the news.

"Would you like it back?"

A moment's hesitation. Trevor was considering it but would the bastard have the nerve to say yes?

"No, of course not. Would you like a glass of port? I just got a new shipment from Madeira." Trevor motioned toward the crystal decanters and glasses on the sideboard.

"That sweet stuff? I'll take a brandy."

Trevor rose to get him the libation and refill his own glass at the same time and Davenport eyed the papers overflowing the desk. "So at last I see the famed text. Out of the vault for an evening. How are the translations going?"

"Amazingly well." Now there was palpable excitement in Trevor's voice. "According to the scribe who wrote this, the lost Memory Tools were absolutely not a legend. They existed. He saw them and gives a full description of each of the amulets, ornaments, and stones. He writes that they were all smuggled out of India and brought into Egypt well before 1500 BC which, you realize, suggests present-day historians are incorrect about when the trade routes opened. This is going to create a lot of controversy when I publish."

"You're still planning on publishing?"

Trevor handed his brother a glass filled with amber that shimmered like gold in the lamplight. "Of course. And please, don't try to argue me out of it again. Our father created the Talmage Trust because he believed history was important. He who controls the past controls the future. I firmly agree and—"

"Control is exactly why you can't publish. Don't you understand just how much control you'd be giving up," Davenport interrupted, pleading, really hoping—now that he was there—that Trevor would not force his hand.

"If these tools exist and if they can aid people in rediscovering their past lives, we—you, me, and every member of the Phoenix Club—need to ensure this power is used for the good of all men, not selfishly exploited," Trevor argued.

"That document was found at an excavation by a man who was paid with our father's money. I won't let you do this."

"*You* won't let me do this? *You* can't stop me." Trevor laughed derisively. "Don't you understand how meaningful this is? How spiritually significant? It's not a cache of gold and silver coins we're arguing over, this could be the key to finding proof that we return in new incarnations. We can't own information like this, it has to be available to everyone, how else will the actual Memory Tools be found? This discussion is closed."

"The decision to publish is not yours alone," Davenport said.

"I can say that same sentence back to you," Trevor retorted.

"Damn you!"

Davenport slammed down his glass of brandy so hard that it shattered, spilled liquor quickly threatening to ruin the papers.

Annoyed with his brother—no, with himself, for letting Davenport get to him, Trevor cursed as he scooped up the ancient text and placed it out of harm's way on top of the books on a shelf behind him. But there were still his notes to salvage. As fast as he could he grabbed pile after pile of his papers and put them on top of other books on other shelves.

He was turned away from his brother so he didn't see him draw the small silver revolver from his jacket pocket or see the competitive grimace on his brother's face, as if they were children playing a game that Davenport was determined to win.

The force of the bullet slammed Trevor forward into the shelves, the impact of his body pushing one pile of his notes behind a row of books. He reached out to steady himself, grabbed hold of a leather volume that ironically turned out to be the Tibetan Book of the Dead.

It fell with him onto the floor.

Blood spilling out of him as quickly as the brandy spilled out of the broken glass, Trevor lay dying, watching his brother steal out of the library, pistol back in his pocket, spoils under his arm, fearing—until he stopped thinking completely—what would become of the precious knowledge he tried but failed so miserably to protect.

The book didn't save him in the end.

The old volume, leather bound with faded gold embossing and frayed edges, remained partially grasped in the dead man's right hand where he'd collapsed onto the floor behind his massive desk, felled by a single gunshot wound to the chest. Now, Boston sergeant detective D. D. Warren stood within an inch of the victim's well-dressed body, one of the only spaces available in the cluttered office, and did her best to interpret the scene.

"He held it up," she mused out loud, to her partners, Neil and Phil. She gestured to the fallen tome. "Saw the gun, responded instinctively to block the shot."

Neil, the youngest member of their squad and a former EMT, immediately shook his head. "Nah. No sign of gunpowder, no damage from a slug. Victim grabbed the book on the way down." Neil pointed to a fanned-out pile of papers that teetered dangerously close to the edge of the marble-topped desk. "Bet the book was on top. Impact of the bullet spun the victim to his left, he reached for the desk, but caught the book instead. Took it with him to the floor."

"Book would've been knocked to the side," D.D. countered. This kind of crime scene back-and-forth was one of her favorite games. As far as she was concerned, dead men did tell tales. "Collateral damage. Whereas our guy has the novel halfway in his hand."

"You want to know how many miscellaneous objects I've had to pry from dead men's hands?" Neil shrugged. "People see the end coming, and reflexively hold tight. I don't know. Maybe they think if they cling hard enough to this world, they won't have to pass to the next."

"No way to prove it," Phil muttered from the doorway. The

senior member of their squad, he was mid-fifties with a devoted wife, four kids, and rapidly thinning hair. Being a family man didn't mean he was too squeamish to view the victim up close and personal. Two hulking Fu Lions, however, carved from solid stone and standing five feet high, currently kept him in place. Or maybe it was the brightly painted ceramic dragon that roared across the front edge of the marble desk. Or the plethora of jade statuary that sprouted like oversized leaves from cluttered rows of shelves, crammed with more leather-bound novels.

Phil held a mask up to his mouth. Not for the smell, but because sneezing would absolutely, positively ruin their crime scene and in a space this cramped and dusty it was almost impossible not to.

D.D. straightened, pinching the bridge of her nose as she worked to avert her own reaction to the musty air.

"All right. Let's start with victimology. What do we got?"

Phil did the honors. "Victim is Mr. John Wen. Fifty-eight, widowed, no record, no outstanding warrants. According to his shop clerk, Judy Chan, who found the body first thing this morning, Mr. Wen was a quiet soul, devoted to his work, which, as you can probably guess by looking around, involved importing ancient Chinese artifacts. And not the cheap kind. He was the real deal. Background in antiquities, elite roster of clients, handled custom orders, that kind of thing. He liked the hunt and authenticating the pieces. Her job was to deal with the public."

D.D. nodded. It would explain the location of Wen's shop, tucked away from the hustle and bustle of Beach Street, which formed the brightly decorated main artery running through the heart of Chinatown. Also, in contrast to Wen's neighbors, whose store windows offered colorful arrays of silk dresses, or specialty foods, or a chaotic jumble of cheap imports, Wen's storefront showcased only a trio of intricately carved dark wood panelings. Once inside, a discreet bronze plate identified the panelings as belonging to such-and-such a dynasty, but they could now be yours for a mere $150,000. Come to think of it, such price points also explained the fine cut of Mr. Wen's elegant navy-blue suit. A man who moved in elite circles and carried himself accordingly. Interesting.

"So businessman," D.D. filled in. "Educated, obviously. Respected? Trusted?"

Phil nodded.

"Probably not about theft," she continued, eyeing the small fortune in jade left around the tiny office. "But maybe a business deal gone bad? Mr. Wen identified the piece as Third Dynasty, when really it was built last week in the finest factory in Hong Kong then aged by six-year-olds beating it with heavy chains."

"Not possible." A new voice spoke up from behind Phil.

He made way as best he could in the cramped doorway, and a beautiful, if solemn, Asian woman appeared.

"You are?" D.D. prompted.

"Judy Chan. I have worked with Mr. Wen for five years now. He was a good man. He wouldn't cheat. And he didn't make mistakes."

"How'd you meet Mr. Wen?"

"He ran an ad in the paper, looking for a store clerk. I answered."

D.D. eyed the assistant, taking in the girl's petite frame, elegantly sculpted cheekbones, glossy waterfall of jet-black hair. She asked the next logical question: "Please describe your relationship."

The assistant gave her an exasperated look. "I *worked* with Mr. Wen, Wednesdays through Sundays, nine to five. Occasionally, I would come in off hours to help him prepare for meetings with some of his more special clients. You know, the kind of people who want a three-thousand-year-old armoire as a signature piece in their foyer, and are willing to pay for it."

"Got a list of said clients?"

"Yes."

"And his calendar. We'll want to see that."

"I understand."

"Was he meeting with someone last night?"

"Not that I knew of."

"Would he tell you?"

"Most of the time. His projects were not secret. More and more, he would even ask for my help. He appreciated my computer skills."

"When did you last see him?"

"Yesterday, five PM, when I locked up the store."

"Where was he?"

"Back here, in his office. He generally stayed after the store was closed, catching up on paperwork, researching pieces. He didn't have a family. This," Judy gestured around the cramped office, "this was his life."

"Was he working on anything special?" Phil asked from beside her.

"Not that he had mentioned."

"Missing anything special?" He gestured to the crowded space.

For the first time, the girl hesitated. "I don't . . . know." All three Boston detectives studied her. "His office," she said at last, "he kept it busy."

D.D. raised a brow, considering that the understatement of the month.

"Mr. Wen always said he thought better when surrounded by the past. Most of the items in this room were things he'd collected along the way, gifts from colleagues, clients, friends. And the books . . . he loved them. Called them his children. I used to beg him to let me at least dust, attempt to tidy up. But he would never let me. He liked things just this way, even the piles of paper covering his desk. The horizontal filing system, he called it. It never failed him."

The girl's voice faded out. She wasn't looking at them, but staring at the desk intently. "It's wrong," she said flatly. "I can't tell you how exactly. But it's wrong."

D.D. obediently turned her attention to the desk. She noted mounds of paper, a scatter of miscellaneous notebooks, a rounded wooden bowl filled with yet more office detritus, then beside it a heavily gilded female figurine whose curves were definitely more robust than D.D.'s own, not to mention multiple haphazard piles of obviously old and dusty books.

"I don't see a computer," she ventured at last.

"He worked by hand. Thought best that way. When he needed to look something up, he used the computer in the front of the store."

D.D. went about this another way. "Was the store locked this morning?"

"Yes."

"Security system?"

"No. We had been talking about one, but Mr. Wen always argued, what kind of thieves stole antique furniture? The truly valuable pieces here . . . they are large and heavy, as you can see."

"But all the jade figurines—"

"His private collection. Not for sale."

Phil picked up the thought. "But the door was locked. So whoever entered, Mr. Wen let him or her in."

"I would assume."

"Would he meet people in his office?" D.D. asked, gesturing to a space that was clearly standing room only.

"No," the assistant filled in. "Generally, he met with them in the showroom. Sitting at one of the tables, that sort of thing. He believed in the power of history not just to survive, but to retain its usefulness. Don't just buy an antique, he liked to say. Live with it."

D.D.'s gaze zeroed in once more on the book still resting on Mr. Wen's open hand. "Did he have books in the showroom?"

"No, his—"

"Personal collection. I get it. So, if he was meeting someone who was interested in a volume, per se—"

D.D. knelt back down, trying to get a better look at the leather-bound novel. The gilded titling was faded, hard to read. Then she realized it wasn't even in English, but in a language she couldn't recognize.

"The Buddha," Judy suddenly gasped.

"What?"

"The Buddha. That's what's missing. Here, the left corner of Mr. Wen's desk. He had a solid-jade Buddha. From the eighth-century Tang Dynasty. The Buddha always sat here. Mr. Wen got the piece just after his wife died. It was very special to him."

"Size?" Phil already had his notebook out.

"Ummm, the Buddha himself eight inches tall. Very round, solid, the sitting Buddha, you know, with his round belly and laughing face. The statue was placed on a square wooden base with gold seams and inlaid abalone. A substantial piece."

"Value?" D.D. asked.

"I'm not sure. I would need to do more research. But given that ounce for ounce, fine jade is currently more valuable than gold, a piece of that size . . . yes, it is valuable."

D.D. pursed her lips, liking the idea of the theft gone awry for their murder motive except, of course, for the number of remaining jade pieces that still littered the victim's bookshelves.

"Why the Buddha statue?" she murmured out loud, more to herself than anyone.

Judy, the beautiful assistant, shook her head, clearly at a loss for an explanation.

"One piece. That's all you think is gone?"

"I will keep looking, but for now, yes, that one piece."

"So Buddha, something about Buddha."

D.D. was still thinking, as Neil said, "Hello. Got something."

He had lifted the book from Mr. Wen's outstretched fingers. Now, they all watched as something fluttered to the floor. Obviously not old, but a recent addition to the office. Something worth clutching in a dead man's hand?

"What is it?" D.D. asked.

"Business card." Neil flipped it over. "From the Phoenix Foundation. For one Malachai Samuels."

D.D. parked her rental car on New York's Upper West Side, then turned her attention to the mansion across the street. She wasn't a huge architecture buff but had lived in a historic city long enough to recognize the Queen Anne style of the villa, including the glass sunburst below the curved-top window. Personally, she liked the gargoyles peeking out from under the eaves.

Of course, she wasn't here for the architecture. She was here about a murder. She made her way up the front walk, pausing long enough to inspect the bas-relief coat of arms that decorated the mansion's front door. Took her a second, then she got it—the image was the mystical phoenix that granted the office its name.

Buzzz.

The front door finally opened, and D.D. entered the Phoenix Foundation.

She presented her credentials to the waiting receptionist. The front desk, D.D. noticed, was very old and most likely very valuable. It also held hints of Chinese design. The kind of desk John Wen might have imported into his shop and sold to a client, such as Malachai Samuels.

"Sergeant Detective D.D. Warren," she introduced herself. "I'm here to see Dr. Samuels."

"Do you have an appointment?"

"No, but I think he'll see me."

The young woman looked down at D.D.'s detective shields, then pursed her lips and made a phone call.

"If you'll have a seat, the doctor is with a patient but he'll be free in fifteen minutes."

Fair enough. D. D. retreated to the camel-back sofa provided for visitors. She'd been warned this interview would not be easy. Dr. Samuels was not without some experience when it came to answering questions involving homicide.

For now, she occupied her time on her laptop, reading more of the articles she'd pulled about the esteemed therapist.

Malachai Samuels was a Jungian therapist who'd devoted his life to working with children with past-life issues. He and his aunt, who was the codirector of the foundation, had documented over three thousand children's journeys and presented remarkable proof of the lives they'd discovered in their regressions. So fastidious was their research and methodology, they were actually accepted by the scientific community and often spoke at psychiatric conventions.

In the last seven years, however, Malachai had been named a

"person of interest" in several different criminal cases involving stolen artifacts, resulting in the deaths of at least four people. The reincarnationist had never been charged with any wrongdoing. But the FBI special crimes detective D.D. had contacted, Lucian Glass, was disturbed when he heard Malachai's name was connected to yet another murder.

Glass still believed Malachai was complicit in several of the cases and that he should be in prison. "But we've never been able to find any actual evidence of his participation. I hope you do, Detective Warren. I hope you do."

"Detective Warren?" A rich, mellifluous voice cut through her thoughts. D.D. looked up to find the man in question now standing directly before her.

"Dr. Malachai Samuels. How may I be of assistance?"

Samuels was wearing a well-cut navy suit, carefully knotted silk tie, and a crisp white shirt with a monogram on the right cuff. Everything about him, from his clothing to his manner of speaking, suggested a gentleman of an earlier time. Which already got D.D. to thinking. Was the good doctor merely collecting valuable old artifacts, or did he include himself among them?

"I'm here about an incident in Boston," she said. "Could we talk someplace more private?"

"Of course, this way."

He led her down a hallway lit by stained-glass sconces and lined with turn-of-the-century wallpaper. Silk would be her guess. With a faded floral pattern and hints of what was probably real gold.

"Would you like any coffee or tea? Perhaps bottled water?" he asked as he opened the door to what D.D. surmised was his personal office. In keeping with the theme of the rest of the place, the space was lined with old books and lushly appointed with a fine Persian rug, an antique desk, and a comfortable leather couch and chairs. It faced an inner courtyard planted with trees and flowers, as befitting someone with a doctor's fine sensibilities.

D.D. said she'd like some water, then took a seat, still cataloguing the plethora of antiques and works of art scattered about. A tingle of excitement shot up her spine when she noticed a Chinese jade horse on Samuels's desk.

Malachai handed D.D. a crystal glass filled with ice water. He took a seat opposite her on the other side of the glass coffee table.

"Now, how can I help you?"

"We found your business card at the scene of a murder."

"That's terrible. Who was killed?"

"Mr. John Wen."

Malachai's face showed no emotion. In fact, he remained so unruffled that D.D. was instantly suspicious.

"Did you know him, Doctor?"

"I'm a therapist, Detective. Even if I did I couldn't tell you. Everything that goes on in my office is confidential. Surely you understand that."

"The man is dead, Dr. Samuels. His confidentiality is on the floor in a pool of blood."

Malachai remained silent.

"Surely you understand that by not talking to me you are as good as admitting he was a patient."

"If that's the conclusion you want to draw, so be it. But I'm neither saying he was or wasn't. I'm not at liberty to discuss your case with you."

"Your business card was there when he died."

"How unfortunate, then, for us both."

D.D. frowned, feeling the first tinge of annoyance. Samuels was within his rights but it was going to make the case more complicated if she had to wait to get a court order.

"Last time you saw him alive?" she fished.

"Who said I ever saw him?"

Special Agent Lucian Glass had been right: Samuels was good.

D.D. went about it another way. "Hypothetically speaking, if you were a detective investigating the homicide of man who imported ancient Chinese artifacts, who would you question?"

Samuels merely arched a brow. Then, almost imperceptibly, he tilted his head in the direction of the decorative mirror hanging over his left shoulder.

A Freudian slip, D.D. thought, or just the incredible arrogance of a well-respected gentleman who may or may not have gotten away with murder?

"I am sorry, Detective," Dr. Samuels informed her, "but I cannot assist you in this matter. Now, if you don't mind, I have another patient waiting."

He stood up, and she had no choice but to follow. Show over, meeting adjourned. D.D. had wasted an entire day, not to mention a decent portion of her department's budget, on a trip to New York that had yielded her absolutely nothing.

"Nice horse," she said, pointing at the jade piece as she rose to stand.

"Thank you."

"Where'd you buy it?"

"I didn't; like many objects in this building, I inherited it. I moved it into my office, however, because I find it particularly compelling. Do you know why people collect antiques, Detective Warren?"

Aha, finally a little conversation. "They like old things?"

"Perhaps. More accurately, they identify with old things."

D.D. couldn't help herself. She gazed around his clearly

nineteenth-century office. The good doctor didn't appear offended, more like amused by her unspoken point.

"Mr. John Wen," she tried one last time, "didn't just collect antiques. By all accounts, he believed people should live with them. Such as you do."

"Exactly."

"What does that mean?"

"That means you're spending too much time in the present, Detective Warren, given that you are investigating a man who was all about the past."

Dr. Samuels granted her one last, knowing smile. Then graciously but firmly, he escorted her out the door.

•◆•

After the Boston detective departed, Malachai returned to his office where he poured himself an inch of forty-year-old Macallan. Lifting the heavy crystal tumbler he took a sip. Savored it. Then, drink in hand, he sat down heavily in the chair at his desk. Opening his top drawer he withdrew his Symthson notebook.

This was a private journal that he kept to record his musings on "The Search," as he had been referring to it for the last thirty-five years, ever since he'd opened a nineteenth-century book on mesmerism that he'd come across in the library and a scrap of old, yellowed paper had fallen out. The handwriting had been spidery and appeared to have been written with a pen dipped in ink, which, along with what it said, helped Malachai date the note to the mid-to-late 1800s.

Meeting with Mr. T at two PM regarding place to secure the papers. Wednesday, at his establishment, 259 Broadway.

According to family legend, Malachai's ancestor, Davenport Talmage, had been in possession of papers that detailed all the amulets, ornaments, and stones that made up the lost cache of Memory Tools. Smuggled out of India and brought into Egypt before 1500 BC, these items were said to be able to stimulate past-life memories.

Had Davenport written the note? Did it refer to the list of lost tools?

Without too much trouble, by matching the handwriting to letters in the archives, Malachai had been able to ascertain the note had been written by Davenport Talmage, one of the original founders of the Phoenix Club. Knowing who'd written it had enabled Malachai to further narrow the note's provenance to sometime between 1884 and 1901. No earlier than 1884 as that was when Davenport had inherited his brother's estate and taken over running the club. And no later than 1901 as that had been the year Davenport had died.

The address, 259 Broadway, was where the jewelry, stationery, and design firm of Tiffany & Company had been located during that era.

Was "Mr. T" Tiffany himself? Probably. Davenport had been immensely wealthy. What objet d'art had Tiffany made at Davenport's request in order to hide the papers? Had the item been sold? Or did it still exist here in the mansion, where nearly every room boasted numerous Tiffany lamps and windows? Not to mention all the mansion's fireplaces, which were fronted with iridescent tiles fashioned by the famous glassmaker and jeweler. Meaning the papers could very well be hidden in plain sight. An aggravating idea, that they could be so close and yet remain invisible to him.

Now Malachai turned the pages to his notes from the last few weeks. The section where he'd recorded his sessions with Mr. John Wen.

There had been eight sessions in all. Each one going over and over the same territory. An antiques dealer, Wen had come to Malachai for help in understanding why he was drawn to certain objects and places. He was haunted by them. Obsessed. For years he'd been trying to get clarity on the feelings that gripped him upon seeing certain items. Twice he'd almost gone bankrupt buying up estates that were not worth what he paid, just to ensure that he could get a certain piece. Desperate, he'd finally allowed for the possibility that past-life memories were driving him. In searching for someone to help him, he'd heard about Dr. Samuels and claimed that somehow he felt the same way about coming here that he did about the antiques. He just knew the Phoenix Foundation was the place he'd find help.

But what Wen didn't know, at least not consciously, but that he'd revealed to Malachai under hypnosis, was that in the past— over a hundred and thirty years ago—he'd been one of the Talmage brothers who'd founded this very institution.

And if he was the incarnation of Davenport or Trevor, then maybe, Malachai had theorized, Wen could lead him to the fabled papers.

To anyone else it would have been a story to scoff at. But Malachai had worked with thousands of children whose past-life memories he and his aunt had verified. Malachai had seen his patients make connections that defied logic and what others called reason. Malachai had never had a past-life memory of his own. No amount of hypnosis or meditation worked for him. But he'd seen his patients cured of their fears, phobias, and neuroses once they were able to identify them and understand they belonged to previous incarnations. He'd witnessed the healing power of regained memories. The astounding relief his patients felt once freed from their karmic nightmares.

All Malachai wanted was to know his own past lives. But to do that he needed a functioning Memory Tool, and in order to find one of the few fabled tools he needed to know which item he was searching for. Davenport's papers would be his map, a complete list of all the known Memory Tools. And he'd thought that perhaps John Wen, a Chinese art and antiques dealer from Boston, had possessed the clue to finally unearthing Davenport's long-lost papers.

Which meant John Wen's murder wasn't just a shame.

It was downright inconvenient.

•◆•

Dr. Malachai Samuels had bested her.

There was no way around it.

In the three days following her day trip to New York, back in Boston, D.D. had turned the conversation around and around in her mind. She shared the discussion—or rather, the lack of it—with her squadmates Phil and Neil. She even called and reported her lack of interviewing prowess to Special Agent Lucian Glass.

She'd gone up against a person of interest in four potential murders, and she'd gleaned . . . nothing. Not a single shred of information or insinuation. Just the rather prosaic observation that antiques dealers identified with the past. Which clearly explained her current need for dim sum. When dealing with an extremely troubling murder in Chinatown, dim sum was the way to go.

But if John Wen imported antiques because he identified with the past, what did his killer care about? All of those priceless items in the shop, and the murderer had taken just one thing: a jade Buddha.

Why that?

D.D. spotted the proprietor of the popular restaurant waiting patiently next to the door. An older Asian gentleman in an impeccably cut suit, he'd already greeted most of his customers by name. It occurred to her he might be able to help her out.

She raised a hand to catch his attention, and he promptly walked over.

"Excuse me," she said, "could you tell me where the closest Buddhist temple is in Chinatown?"

"There are several, Detective. Which one are you looking for?"

"How'd you know I was a detective?"

"You are investigating the murder of John Wen. We all know."

"Did you know Mr. Wen?"

"Yes, a very fine man. He helped me find the four silk screens hanging in the banquet room. In fact, if you are interested in Buddhist temples, may I suggest you consult Mr. Wen's assistant, Miss Chan?"

D.D. regarded him blankly. "Why Judy Chan?"

The proprietor's turn to appear flustered. "Because of her pendant, of course. The small jade Buddha she always wears around her neck. A symbol of her own religious calling, I would assume."

D.D. thanked the man for his time. Then she paid her bill and got on the phone to her partner Phil. Because they'd interviewed Judy several times and on none of those occasions was Mr. Wen's beautiful assistant wearing a jade Buddha pendant.

Which made her wonder what else Judy Chan had to hide.

According to Phil, Judy Chan's home address was a fourth-floor walk-up just around the corner from the restaurant in Chinatown. D.D. found the brick building easily enough. Unfortunately, no one answered Judy's buzzer. A quick ring of the second-floor unit, however, earned her an elderly Chinese woman in a pink floral housecoat.

D.D. flashed her shield, providing a quick impression of official public servant.

"Fire department," D.D. announced. One of the first things she'd learned in community policing: most inner-city populations didn't trust cops. Firemen, on the other hand, who could save their homes and businesses from burning down, were treated with respect.

The old woman studied her critically.

"I need to conduct a test of the fire escapes. Just making sure everything is in working order."

A frown. Growing uncertainty. The older woman's natural suspicion of such an odd request warring with her desire to feel her apartment building was fire safe.

D.D. pressed ahead. "Just need quick access so I can take a walk up and a walk down. I'll be in and out in five minutes, and your building will be cleared for another five years. Otherwise, I gotta bring the fire marshal down, maybe a whole inspection crew . . ."

The promise—threat?—of more city officials got the job done. The aging tenant gestured for D.D. to follow her into her apartment, and three minutes later, D.D. was climbing up the fire escape to Judy's fourth-floor unit.

She didn't have probable cause to enter the unit, of course. Just a growing suspicion that Judy Chan hadn't been fully forthcoming. But a quick glimpse of the woman's living space wouldn't hurt. And if D.D. happened to spy something such as an eight-inch-tall stolen jade Buddha statue or even better, a smoking gun, then voila, D.D. would be within her rights to access the woman's apartment and maybe even close a murder case.

With a bit of effort, D.D. heaved herself onto the fourth-floor platform, staggering to her feet. Her hands hurt from gripping the rusty metal fire escape, not to mention her heart was pounding painfully in her chest.

Then she looked up.

"Holy crap!"

Buddhas. Everywhere. Judy Chan's fourth-floor unit was covered in images of the Laughing Buddha. Buddha paintings, Buddha statues, Buddha-embroidered pillows, even tiny gold and jade and silver Buddha figurines. Everywhere D.D. looked, for as far as the eye could see, was yet another image of the Buddha.

Then, as she stood there still openmouthed, the front door of Chan's apartment opened. John Wen's former assistant entered her home.

Accompanied by Dr. Malachai Samuels.

•◆•

Malachai felt good about his day.

Indeed, after learning that Mr. John Wen had been killed, taking with him any clues the man might have possessed regarding the location of the legendary list of lost Memory Tools, Malachai had been forced to reconsider his strategy.

The police, including that blond Boston detective D.D. Warren, would be watching him, which ruled out any overt acts, such as searching Wen's antiquities shop or personal residence. Then it had occurred to Malachai that he didn't need to engage in such base acts, when a simple gesture of courtesy would suffice.

He had called Wen's assistant, a beautiful woman he'd met once when she'd accompanied Wen to the Phoenix Foundation in New York, and extended his deepest condolences. If there was anything he could do to help Miss Chan during this time of sadness, he was available. In fact, he'd be in Boston by the end of the week.

Perhaps they could meet for a cup of tea, share reminiscences of a man they had both respected and admired.

Malachai's father had long ago taught him the value of a well-cut suit, impeccable social standing, and a cultured voice. Miss Judy Chan had agreed nearly immediately. The morning tea progressed to a casual stroll around Boston's Chinatown—an amazing cultural center, third largest in the country—and then, finally, to Malachai's delicate request to visit Wen's store one last time.

Miss Chan had been happy to comply. If they could simply stop by her apartment first, in order to retrieve the key . . .

Malachai had followed her up the four flights of stairs without complaining despite the discomfort in his leg. An incident in Vienna years before had left a permanent disability that he did his best to ignore. Standing beside her, he waited as the young woman opened the door to her residence. And then he received his first shock of the day. Buddhas. Figurines, carvings, paintings, embroideries, silk washings. Images of a kind, benevolent Buddha everywhere one looked.

Miss Chan, her tailored knee-length camel-colored coat still buttoned to her chin, paused, glanced at him self-consciously.

"I am a collector," she said.

"Indeed." Malachai raised his hands to assist the lady with her coat. Suddenly, he was not in a hurry to continue on to Wen's shop. The truth, he realized, the key to the secret he had sought for so long, was here. One modern-day woman's obsession. A trained therapist's insight into a reincarnated soul.

"Could I trouble you for a glass of water?" he suggested now. "I'm afraid the walk up the stairs has left me parched."

"Of course." Freed of her coat, Judy headed smartly toward the modest galley kitchen. Alone in the room, Malachai started in on the buttons of his own immense black wool greatcoat, while taking a quick inventory of the room.

Was it his imagination, or did he just see a shadow flash behind the window? No matter. He could already feel his blood quicken, a familiar thrumming in his veins.

All these years later, the Buddha, with his enigmatic smile and numerous teachings on karma and reincarnation, held the key.

"When did you first start collecting Buddhas?" he asked, as Judy reentered the room. She handed him a tumbler of water, and he could detect a faint tremor in her fingers as the glass passed from her to him.

"I'm not really sure. All my life, I suppose."

"Did Mr. Wen know?"

"Of course." She flushed, her hand resting self-consciously on her chest. "He even gifted me with a jade Buddha medallion. A talisman of sorts."

"Did Mr. Wen ever speak of his sessions with me?"

"I know he was seeing you about his own . . . collecting issues. His terrible need at times to acquire items whether they made sound business sense or not. He said you believed he was a reincarnated soul, still looking for something he had lost many lives ago."

"And you?"

The young woman stilled, then twisted her head slightly to take in the full surroundings of her apartment. Her hair moved with her, a black silk curtain that obscured her face from him. "I do not know why I do what I do," she whispered finally. "A born-again soul, still searching to right a wrong? It makes as much sense to me as anything."

"Might I suggest a short hypnosis session?" Malachai offered quietly. "It won't take more than thirty, forty minutes of your time, and might very well provide you with some of the answers you seek. In fact, I could do it right here, in the comfort of your home."

She didn't answer him, so much as she moved closer to the couch, then, after another moment of hesitation, took a seat.

Malachai didn't wait for a second invitation. He slipped off his coat, eased into a dainty bamboo-framed chair across from her, and incredibly aware of the Buddhas' watching eyes, he began, by using a simple backward-counting technique, to slowly lead his patient through the curling ribbons of time.

"Where are you?" he asked five minutes later.

Judy described a mansion, partially hidden behind linden trees.

What? Malachai leaned forward, not sure he could yet make the assumption he was yearning to make.

"Tell me, what do you see? What do you hear?"

"A carriage driving by. Horses' hooves. It's twilight and people are arriving home from their day's work. I hear strains of Beethoven's *Moonlight Sonata.*"

"Do you know the street where this mansion is?"

"Of course. Eighty-third Street off of Central Park West."

She was describing his ancestral home, Malachai realized, his excitement growing as he sought to maintain an even composure, a soothing, rhythmic voice. Judy Chan had returned to what was now the Phoenix Foundation, in New York City, sometime in the late nineteenth century.

This was truly fascinating because the first time he'd put John Wen under, the antiques dealer had returned to the exact same place and time. To anyone else it would have been a coincidence but not to Malachai. There were no coincidences when you were dealing with reincarnation. Every act had repercussions, every encounter a purpose. We return to be with the same people in similar circumstances to complete the karmic circle, to right our wrongs, to be given another chance. Souls whose fates were forever intertwined, finding each other, again and again and again. Following a repeating pattern of doom.

Every time Malachai witnessed a patient travel he felt privileged to be part of the journey. But this time he also felt ebullient. His own family history—complicated and mysterious—might finally be resolved.

John Wen had been shot and killed by an intruder in his study, just as Malachai's ancestor Trevor Talmage had been shot and killed over one hundred years ago. Murdered in his own study by an intruder, according to family lore.

Or had he been?

Upon Trevor's death, his brother Davenport had inherited the house and everything in it, including Malachai's longed-for treasure, the list of lost Memory Tools.

And now, as Malachai listened to Judy Chan describe every detail of a study she couldn't know in a time period she shouldn't be able to recall, Malachai felt another piece of the puzzle slide into place.

"What are you doing there?" Malachai asked.

"My brother is wrong," Judy Chan said, answering a different question, her voice stronger than it had been a moment ago. She was sitting up straighter, too, Malachai noticed, her demeanor becoming more agitated.

"What is your name?" Malachai asked.

She didn't answer his question. Instead, she continued arguing with a ghost Malachai couldn't see or hear.

"The decision to publish is not your choice."

"Publish what?" Malachai asked. "Who are you talking to?"

"My brother," Judy Chan hissed. "He is wrong."

And then Malachai knew. Trevor had not been shot by a stranger. His brother, Davenport, had done the deed.

"Do you know Mr. Tiffany?" Malachai asked, breaking one of the rules of hypnosis and interrupting the moment to interject a question that might bring the patient out of the episode.

But his hunch was correct.

"Yes," Judy said. "He designed the lamps in the house. The tile work. Jewels for the family."

Malachai pictured the note he had found, written in Davenport's hand about the visit to Tiffany's studio so soon after Trevor's death. Had Davenport killed his own brother in order to seize the ancient text describing each lost Memory Tool? He must have. Then, he'd sought to hide the evidence of his crime in a treasure chest created by Tiffany. To keep secret that which he never meant to share. Not in that life, or beyond.

And now Judy, in the present, had shot her boss, John Wen, in order to steal the papers back once again.

Instantly, Malachai realized the answer to everything he'd been looking for wasn't in the past. It was in this room, staring him right in the face.

The Laughing Buddhas.

"Judy," Malachai said, his voice urgent. "You can hear me now. You need to leave the house in New York. You need to come forward. To the present."

Judy remained in her seat, returning slowly.

"You are in John Wen's office," he informed her, his rich voice deep and compelling. "It is five days ago, you have come to see your boss. Then, you see a Buddha. Tell me about the Buddha."

"It is an eight-inch, solid-jade Buddha," she whispered. "Sitting on a square wooden base with gold-seamed corners and inlaid abalone. Mr. Wen has had it for months now. Months when I have implored him to give it to me."

"He won't listen to you."

"The Buddha must be shared, I begged him. It is wrong to keep it secret, hidden from the world. True power is sharing knowledge in order to help others, not hoarding it for yourself."

Malachai blinked, puzzled. "So you decided to take back what belonged to you. You shot Mr. Wen. You removed the Buddha from his office. Where is the Buddha now, Miss Chan? Tell me, and I will help you share it with the world."

The woman's dark, slitted eyes held a strange, spectral gleam. She was not yet in this existence, Malachai realized. But nor was she in the other.

"Violence," she murmured. "It always ends in violence. Brother against brother, spouse against spouse, friend betraying friend. I loved him and I have felt his bullet. I loved him and I struck the mortal blow. Is there truly no other way?"

Malachai realized belatedly that Miss Chan was holding a gun, a small antique pistol she'd pulled from the folds of her dress and now had pointed directly at his sternum.

He had made a mistake. A terrible, terrible mistake.

"You are not Davenport," he whispered. No, of course not. John Wen had been Davenport, a man who'd shot his own brother in order to keep the legendary text a secret. "You are Trevor," Malachai continued to Judy Chan. She was the reincarnation of the brother who'd wanted to share the list of lost Memory Tools with the world, and paid with his life.

One hundred and thirty years ago, Trevor had been the victim. This time around, to judge by the pistol held so steadily in Judy Chan's hand, that would not be the case.

The secret of the Laughing Buddha had to be shared. And Trevor/Judy was willing to do it, no matter the price.

"I can help you," Malachai heard himself whisper, his voice hoarse with uncommon desperation. "Show me the Buddha. I think I know its secret. I'll show you and we can share it with the world."

But Judy's finger was already tightening on the trigger.

Lives tumbling over lives. An endless procession of old injustices and fresh pains. Lessons still unlearned, cycles yet unbroken.

The list of lost Memory Tools forever out of his reach.

Malachai lunged forward.

The antique pistol exploded to life once again.

•—◆—•

The moment D.D. saw Judy Chan sit down on her sofa, the detective had known the woman was in trouble. The glazed look that had come over her eyes, the sudden slackness of her features.

Malachai was doing something to her. Drugging her, tampering with a witness, interfering with a murder investigation. It all sounded like probable cause to D.D. She started backpedaling as quietly as one could down a rusty fire escape, then dropped to the ground and picked up her cell.

She requested uniformed officers, division detectives, and her squadmates and she wanted them now.

She buzzed the second-story apartment again, frantically seeking entrance. This time, the elderly woman didn't come down, but stuck her graying head out the window above.

D.D. didn't bother with pretenses anymore. "I'm a cop, and the tenant on the fourth floor is in trouble. Open up! Quick!"

The woman appeared to consider the matter. Then slowly, but surely, the front door opened and D.D. sprang ahead.

Four flights of stairs. Minute this case was done, she was booking more time with the StairMaster. But for now, around, around, around.

She burst onto the fourth-floor landing just in time to hear a gunshot. Crap. She threw herself at the door, and it flew open, apparently unlocked.

Her own firearm drawn, she dropped to the floor and scrambled into the unit, gaze already seeking an injured, possibly even murdered, Judy Chan.

Instead, she discovered the woman in question standing quietly before her, smoke still pouring from some ancient-looking derringer.

"He lied. He would've kept the Buddha for himself," Judy said calmly. "The Buddha is meant to be shared."

Then she handed the strange little pistol to D.D., just as Malachai moaned from behind the sofa, "If you could be of some assistance, Detective. I believe I have just been shot."

◆—●

Malachai shifted in his chair with some discomfort. Being shot in the leg that had been hurt in the stampede in Vienna years before had been an unlucky break. This time around, however, at least he'd fared better. It turned out Judy Chan wasn't a very good shot when partially hypnotized. While she'd murdered her boss with a single bullet to the heart, her woozy state—the very state Malachai had put her in—had saved his life.

Eight months had passed and now she was in prison having been found guilty despite an aggressive effort on her attorney's part to prove that she was criminally insane, deluded by visions from a so-called past life.

Malachai had sat in the back of the courthouse every day. If

Miss Chan's attorney proved that believing what you remembered from a past life meant you were insane, Malachai's own life's work would have been held in question, his passion turned into a joke used against him. But the prosecutor had won. With over 25 percent of the country believing in reincarnation and several world religions based on its precepts, the defendant's case didn't pass muster. The jury hadn't accepted the murder was Chan's attempt to right a centuries-long feud. But they did convict her on a charge of second-degree murder stemming from armed robbery.

Reincarnation had not lost that day, Judy Chan had.

"And now we have Lot 121," the auctioneer called out in his singsong voice.

Malachai watched as the jade turtle that belonged to the estate of John Wen soared past its estimate of $10,000. The antiques dealer had indeed amassed a very valuable collection of fine antique Chinese treasures. It was a shame he'd had to die protecting one of them.

The turtle was removed by a young man in a dark-brown uniform and a similarly dressed man brought out the next item for sale and placed it on the podium.

"And now," said the auctioneer in his Boston accent, "we have the Laughing Buddha. Lot 122. A fine example of eighth-century Tang Dynasty carving."

The wait for the estate to come to auction had seemed interminable to Malachai, but the police wouldn't release the items in Wen's office until after Chan's trial and arraignment were complete.

"Do I hear ten thousand?" the auctioneer called.

Malachai had needed to be careful when he'd come to Skinner's to inspect the Buddha before this sale. If he'd shown too much interest in it someone might have noticed and wondered why. The private viewing room in the auction house where he'd looked it over had a camera in plain sight. Malachai hadn't dared risk trying to take the statue apart to determine if the base might actually be the secret receptacle used by Davenport to hide the list of lost Memory Tools. But closer examination had revealed such a thing might be possible. The approximate size and shape of the wooden base. The classic Tiffany artistry showcased by the gold-seamed corners and intricately inlaid abalone. In Malachai's mind, the statue's base could very well be the piece commissioned by Davenport from Tiffany himself after that first murder, over a century ago.

"Fifteen thousand on my right. Do I hear—yes, twenty to the gentleman in the back. Do I hear twenty-five? Twenty-five thousand, thank you, ma'am."

For the next few moments Malachai waited for a lull in the bidding. He didn't want to help drive up the price. Expecting a slowing in bidding to come at $50,000, he was unhappy when it didn't arrive till the price hit $75,000.

But what difference did money make now, with his quest nearly over, the list of lost Memory Tools about to be his? He had been waiting for decades.

"I have seventy-five thousand from the gentleman in the back. Going once. Twice."

Malachai raised his paddle.

"Thank you, sir," the auctioneer said, acknowledging the new bidder. "I have eighty thousand in the front . . . and . . . eighty-five in the rear. Now to you, sir, ninety thousand in the front."

Finally, after another five minutes, the bid was again with Malachai at one hundred fifty and there it stopped. Malachai's head was spinning. Was it his?

"Going once. Twice." The bang of the gavel. "Thank you, sir. One hundred and fifty thousand in the front."

Malachai had won his prize.

After paying for the jade statue, Malachai took the objet d'art back to his hotel room at the Ritz Carlton where he'd booked a suite.

Carefully and with ceremony, he unwrapped the carved sculpture that rested on a fine base with hammered gold-seamed corners inlaid with abalone. The Tiffany signature had been verified by the auction house. The catalogue gave the base alone an estimated value of $10,000.

But that did not even come close to what it was worth.

Malachai enjoyed pomp and appreciated ritual. He believed in savoring the moments that mark one's life. This was such a pinnacle. He'd reached the end of a long, long road today.

Leaving the Buddha sitting regally on the table by the window, Malachai removed the bottle of Cristal champagne he'd put on ice before leaving for the auction house. Opening it with a pop, he poured himself a flute of the pale yellow ambrosia.

Raising his glass, he toasted the silent statue and then took a sip. Thinking, as he did, of John Wen who had died for this moment. Of Judy Chan, who was going to rot in prison for her efforts to prevent it.

"The time has come, my friend," Malachai said as he walked to the table. He'd done his research. He wouldn't have to remove the jade piece from the pedestal. All he had to do was manipulate the seams on the underside of the base. By pressing them in a certain way, he would, the experts had assured him, reveal a carefully concealed cleft.

It was easier than he'd imagined. And as promising as he'd dreamed. The base gave way, a fine sprinkling of dust falling onto the table, indicating it had not been opened in many years. As he'd hoped, no one at Skinner's had discovered this compartment.

Malachai didn't look into the hidden compartment. Not yet. The anticipation after so very long was too delicious.

He took a long, slow sip of the cold bubbly.

This was his moment. After almost 150 years, the past and the present had come full circle. Malachai reached into the narrow enclosure. His fingertips felt . . . smooth wood . . . and . . . more smooth wood . . . satiny.

He tipped the piece over. Stared into the narrow coffinlike space where he was certain the treasure he sought had once been stashed. Where now there was nothing.

Malachai Samuels held the statue in his hands and stared into the abyss. For a moment, even though it was nigh on impossible, he thought he heard the Buddha laughing. Or maybe it was merely Davenport Talmage, still hoarding his list of lost Memory Tools from beyond the grave. Forever his to hide, and Malachai's to seek.

STEVE MARTINI
VS. LINDA FAIRSTEIN

Surfing the Panther

act: In 1922, Howard Carter, then an itinerant archaeologist who had been combing the Valley of the Kings, discovered one of the largest treasure troves in history. Carter, on a single-minded quest for nearly two decades, unearthed the tomb of the boy king, the pharaoh Tutankhamen. He found subterranean caverns filled with priceless artifacts, hundreds of items of hammered gold, precious gems, and entire chariots crafted from exotic woods. Among those objects was a priceless figurine, a statuette of the boy king perched on the back of a black panther. The cat, carved from ebony, was molded from exotic resins, its formula known only to the ancient Egyptians.

Fact: For nearly ninety years the priceless artifacts from Carter's find, including the panther and its golden king, resided in the Egyptian Museum at Cairo. Then, in early February 2011, in what became known as the Arab Spring, civil unrest gave way to looting. The museum was breeched and among the items taken was the statuette of the boy king atop the black cat.

Fact: On September 11, 2012, a marauding band of terrorists attacked the U.S. consulate in Benghazi, Libya, torching the structure and killing four Americans including the U.S. ambassador. For weeks the burned-out structure languished, largely unguarded, with documents, some of them highly classified, strewn about in the abandoned wreckage.

Got your interest?

For two talented writers like Steve Martini and Linda Fairstein, this was all they needed to start a story.

Paul Madriani is the protagonist of twelve best-selling novels by Steve Martini, a former journalist and California lawyer. Linda Fairstein was a lawyer, too, a prosecutor for thirty years, and the head of the Sex Crimes Unit of the New York County District Attorney's Office. Wily prosecutor Alexandra Cooper is her creation. So far there have been fifteen novels featuring Cooper.

Crossing swords at a lawyers' conference seemed the easiest way for these two characters to connect. Next, an enterprising young reporter returns from Benghazi and files a story about what she may have found in the burned-out consulate building. When that reporter turns up dead, Madriani and Cooper find themselves launched on a mad chase in search of the killer and the golden boy king.

It's a legal thriller for the twenty-first century.

From two masters.

Surfing the Panther

So what you're saying is that you have no sympathy for the victim?"

"As I explained previously, I can't discuss a pending case," said Madriani.

"Well, then, let's go back to the hypothetical," said Cooper, flashing a smile at him. "I just tried to get you to tip your hand about that big case you're trying in LA. Give the locals here some pointers. The situation we've been given to discuss today has a few similar issues. I'd like to know what you gain by being so vicious about a dead woman."

"There's no lack of sympathy, not on my part."

Cooper ignored his denial. "Why is it so many litigators show no empathy for the female victim? In our hypo, she was a woman excelling in a male-dominated vocation. Or maybe you saw her as someone who was socially undesirable—a parasite, perhaps?"

"Your choice of words, not mine," said Madriani. He didn't

like being cross-examined. Alexandra Cooper made him feel like a witness on the stand.

"But you agree with that assessment, don't you? You like blaming the victim." She knew she had him over a barrel and was pressing hard.

Paul Madriani, a criminal defense lawyer, knew that he'd be making a mistake if he allowed her to mention the case he currently had on trial in LA. Like stepping on the trigger of a land mine. He tried to figure some way to ease off and keep her focused on this exercise.

"Let's just say that a jury is not likely to view the activities of your hypothetical victim as rising to the level of a holy calling. Can we just agree on that? Fair game?"

"The hypothetical deceased ran a top-tier advertising agency, Paul—a start-up she created with her own guts and brain."

"She started up more male body parts than one could count, Alex. I'll give you that," Madriani said. "She also ran an escort service out of her Park Avenue offices."

Some laughter from the audience, but none from Alex Cooper whose gaze at the moment consisted of two slits, both directed like lasers at Madriani's Adam's apple. To Cooper, a thirty-eight-year-old career prosecutor, head of a pioneering sex crimes unit in New York City, these were fighting words.

"So you think she deserved to die, Paul?"

"As I said earlier, you have to admit that the woman's death may well have had to do with some of the lowlifes she encountered in the sex trade and nothing to do with my hypothetical client's business strategies."

"We have a question from the audience." The moderator tried to break up the gender brawl with some Q & A.

"What you're saying," said Cooper, not quite ready to give up the fight, "is that a woman operating a legitimate portion of her company, perhaps more aggressively than her male competitors, deserves to be sexually assaulted, then bludgeoned—"

"That is not what I said."

"She deserved the end she got, is that it? Is that the takeaway for the young lawyers here in the audience?"

Cooper and Madriani found themselves pitted against each other as speakers on a criminal-law panel of the New York State Bar Association, debating tactics in capital cases. In today's session, they were using the example of a businesswoman in both legitimate and illegitimate realms, who'd been brutally sexually assaulted in her Manhattan office. As the defense attorney, Madriani was representing the hypothetical accused—a rival businessman—and his argument was that the deceased had many more unsavory enemies in her secondary "career" who may have killed her. In other words, he was casting aspersions on the dead victim's character in order to create reasonable doubt for his client. And Alexandra Cooper wasn't having any of it. Madriani had committed to the engagement months earlier, long before he had a trial date in a similarly high-profile case—*People v. Mustaffa*—which was supposed to be off-limits for the panel's discussion since this matter was now pending, though Cooper was doing her best to rile him on it. He had taken the weekend off to fly to New York, and was now beginning to rue the day.

"Is that your pathetic attempt at a defense?" Cooper asked, before he could answer her last question.

"That's not what I'm saying at all."

"Then perhaps you should explain yourself," said Cooper.

"Paul Madriani never needs to explain himself," the moderator said. "He's a master in the well of the courtroom. In fact, Alex, since we're almost out of time, I suggest you take our visiting dignitary down to the bar and buy the first round. Isn't that your tradition during jury deliberations?"

"It was nothing personal, Alex," Madriani added. "It has nothing to do with the victim's gender."

Alex was used to having the last word. She tried to interject another comment, but could see that some of the attendees were closing their notebooks, hoping to snag an introduction to the two lawyers before they could escape the conference ballroom.

Madriani was having none of it. "What I mean is that you don't have the most sympathetic victim in this kind of a situation."

"Really? You think anyone deserves to die in such a horrific way? Would it be better for you if it was a male victim who had his genitals mutilated?"

"No!" he said. "Well, maybe!"

Laughter from the audience. Right now Madriani was beginning to sense what that might feel like. Cooper offered up a smile, the gender card dropped on the table by a skilled prosecutor, showing him how it's done. "Can I ask you a question, Ms. Cooper?"

"Be my guest," said Alex.

"I take it you're not on special assignment here, undercover so to speak, with the LA District Attorney's Office, are you?" Lawyers in the audience laughed again.

Cooper just smiled. "Touché! I tried to get you off-mark, Paul, but I couldn't budge you. Better to have met you here than in the courtroom. And thanks for coming to do this."

Litigators started moving to the podium in the front of the room. Paul leaned over to Alex as she stuffed her notes into a folder. "The hotel bar in fifteen?"

"No."

"Don't be a bad sport."

"I'm just being a good hostess, Paul. Lose your acolytes and I'll take you to the best bar in Manhattan. Best steaks, too, knowing how you like to devour red meat."

Madriani smiled and nodded to accept the invitation.

"I made a seven o'clock reservation at Patroon. It's a few blocks away. I'll meet you in the lobby and we can walk over."

Alex recognized the first man—four or five years with the Legal Aid Society doing defense work—who had lined up in front of Madriani's place at the table.

"Mr. Madriani," he said, introducing himself and reaching up to shake hands. "You're off the record now. I'm just curious to know how you plan to walk the tightrope in your trial, in the Mustaffa case. I've got something like that coming up in the fall."

"Like what?"

"You know. The victim in your case. Carla Spinova."

Madriani glanced at Cooper as if to say, *You started this.*

Anyone who saw the news on television knew that Spinova was part of the international paparazzi.

"The victim here probed people's secrets with her camera. She rooted through their trash for a living, a provocative career to say the least. A good lawyer has got to use that against the prosecution, don't you think?" said Paul.

"Oh, really?" Alex asked, resisting the wiser choice of walking away from the discussion. "According to the medical examiner, if I recall correctly, Spinova's vagina was ripped in four places by a weapon with a sharp serrated edge."

"Stick to the hypothetical," Madriani said. "I'm in front of a judge in LA who'd sooner drop the hammer on me for violating a gag order than parse words after reading my comments in the newspaper."

"Either way," Cooper said, "a woman who lived on the margins is dead, and you're the one representing her killer."

"If there was a global ranking for those who invaded other people's privacy with a camera, Carla Spinova surely would have been seeded no lower than one or two on that list," Madriani said, lowering his head so that only Alex and the young man in front of him could hear him. "It's not like there's a shortage of potential suspects, people who harbored a great deal of ill will toward her. Other dudes who might have done it."

"So you're not just blaming the victim. You're throwing up some red herrings?"

Madriani nodded and thanked the lawyer for his question, then turned to Alex. "I'm ready for that cocktail, before I get myself in trouble talking about Mustaffa."

"You deserve it. And if I were prosecuting your case, Paul, I'd make do with the photographs from the ME's postmortem and take my chances with your high-profile client," Cooper said.

Ibid Mustaffa was indeed Madriani's client, and at the moment the skilled attorney figured that God might be on his side. He only had a thousand or so prosecutors in the LA County DA's Office to worry about. The fates had saved him from Alexandra Cooper.

On their way out, Madriani greeted a few acquaintances and answered some generic questions about trial strategy. The last straggler asked whether his Southern California firm was hiring. Madriani laughed and waved the young woman off. "Try me again in a year."

Cooper was waiting near the exit. Before Madriani could reach her, he was intercepted by a man who'd been seated in the rear of the audience.

"Excuse me, Mr. Madriani, but I was wondering whether you

think the victim's death might have had anything to do with her recent trip to North Africa?"

The man spoke with a slight British accent, as if he might have been schooled in the UK, but was not born there. He wore a white linen suit and held a Panama hat in one hand, something out of a Bogart movie—*Casablanca*—a throwback to the forties. And the victim he was referencing was not the hypothetical ad maven/madam of the mock trial.

"I'm sure you heard me say I'm not here to comment on Mr. Mustaffa's case." Madriani knew about Carla Spinova's trip. He and his investigators had checked it out and found nothing significant to tie it to her death.

"But you know she was killed on the eve of her return to Africa," the man said, running a hand around the brim of his hat.

"And your point is?" said the lawyer.

"Whether that could have anything to do with her murder."

"Not that we're aware of," Madriani said, assuming the man with whom he was speaking was also a lawyer. "Unless you know something I don't."

The man shrugged a shoulder and sat down in the near-empty room.

Madriani felt an ice-cold finger on the back of his neck. He turned around to face Alex Cooper.

"I'm getting thirsty, Paul."

"I hear you."

"I see why you're so formidable in the courtroom. And I hope I didn't come down too heavily, but they told me they wanted the program to have a little heat."

"Heat is one thing. Hell is another."

She laughed.

"Just make sure the judge in Mustaffa doesn't get a transcript."

"Not to worry. I can always call the DA out there if he puts up a stink. He's a good friend, and I'm the one who tried to make you go rogue. It's the least I can do after taking advantage like that."

They headed down the escalator and walked out onto Lexington Avenue, with Alex leading the way to the upscale eatery on Forty-sixth Street.

"Thanks."

"Of course," she countered with a grin, "it would help if I knew what you were up to as well."

"Damn. Are you always on the meter, Alex?"

"Totally off the record. It will all be on the airwaves after you open on Monday. What's the story?"

Paul Madriani was too smart to tip his hand to a prosecutor—a smart one—whom he'd just met hours ago.

"Ibid Mustaffa's a taxi driver in West Los Angeles. Out of work. And Carla Spinova was a Russian émigré who carved notches in her camera case by taking titillating pictures of notables, often in scant attire and at times in compromising situations. She was raped and murdered. That's the People's case."

"And that's the part I know, Paul. Everyone does."

Spinova had invaded the private grounds of numerous palaces and royal abodes in the UK so many times that security forces were beginning to think she had a complete set of the Beefeaters' keys. She was known as the woman who always got her shot. That was, until the night she got her throat slit.

"That's all I've got to say about it, Alex."

"So we're reduced to war stories for the entirety of an elegant dinner? I'll be a total bore."

"I'll take my chances with that," Madriani said. "I've got all the excitement I need once I hit the ground in LA this week."

The maître d' greeted Alex warmly and took her leather folio as she introduced him to Paul Madriani.

"The usual, Ms. Cooper?" Stephane asked, guiding her to a table at the front of the smartly decorated room.

"Double-down on the Dewar's. It's been a long day."

"And for you, Mr. Madriani?"

"I'd like a vodka martini, straight up."

"Certainly." Stephane handed them each a menu, which they put aside, making small talk about each other's personal life and backstory till the cocktails arrived.

"Cheers, Paul. The committee asked me to thank you again for taking the time to do the panel. You put on a good show."

"A pleasure to work with you. Hypothetically, that is," Madriani said. "What do you recommend for dinner?"

Before Alex could answer, a shadow descended on the table, and they both looked up. The man in the white linen suit—the one who had asked Madriani the question about Carla Spinova's trip to North Africa—hovered in front of them. He held a satchel under one arm, his hat in the other hand.

"Sorry, I don't mean to interrupt, but if I might have a moment." He was looking at Madriani. "I apologize for following you over here, but it's rather important."

"Perhaps I should leave," said Alex. Her prosecutorial instincts were on high alert because of the man's unexpected intrusion at the chic restaurant.

"No. No," said the man. "Don't get up."

"Draw up a chair," said Madriani, who was intrigued by the man's persistence. "Join us."

The man did so and sat down. "My name is Samir Rashid. Those who know me call me Sam." He handed each of them a business card. It bore the emblem of the United Nations, UNESCO printed in embossed type across the face. His name, address, and phone number were in small bold type across the bottom.

"What can I do for you?" said Madriani.

"Perhaps it's what I can do for you," said Rashid. "You are lead counsel for Mr. Ibid Mustaffa?"

Madriani nodded. "Yes."

"I believe I have valuable information that will prove, beyond any question or doubt, reasonable or otherwise, that your client did not murder Carla Spinova."

"I think I should leave," said Cooper.

"No. No," said Rashid. He placed his hand on her wrist as if to insist that she stay. "What I have to say is in no way privileged. You are a prosecutor here in New York, correct?"

"Yes."

"Then you should hear me out as well. I don't have much time right now as I have an engagement I must keep, but I will tell you this: Carla Spinova went to North Africa to take pictures that she thought would earn her a considerable amount of money. Instead that trip got her killed."

"Go on," said Madriani.

"On September 11, 2012, the U.S. consulate in Benghazi was attacked and burned. The U.S. ambassador and other Americans were killed."

"Yes." Paul remembered the tragedy well, as it made headlines with widespread political accusations that were still ongoing.

"For nearly three weeks following those events, the consulate building—what was still standing—was left unguarded and largely open," said Rashid. "There is also information that confidential and classified documents remained in the rubble. I have it on good authority that Spinova traveled to Benghazi to obtain photographs of the building and its charred interior. She found something when she was there, a document that would have given her what you call a juicy story, which she intended to sell to the news media with her photographs. But before she could do so she was murdered, and not by your client."

"How do you know all this?" asked Madriani.

"Trust me. I don't have much time to talk right now, but perhaps we can meet tonight at my office at the UN Plaza."

"It's Saturday. The UN building is closed," said Alex. Her initial skepticism was butting up against details about the horrific tragedy in Benghazi, and the fact that the Spinova murder might have had international consequences rather than simply prurient ones.

"I will make arrangements for you to get in. Can you meet me there, say, nine o'clock?"

Madriani had a plane back to LA the following morning but his evening was free after this dinner, and to say that his curiosity was piqued was an understatement. "I'll be there, just as soon as we've finished our meal."

"And you, madam?" Rashid looked at Alex.

"I don't have a stake in the Mustaffa case," she said. "And I'm not sure that Mr. Madriani would want me . . ."

"You are a public prosecutor. You made a big deal in our discussion an hour ago about the court system not being a game, Alex. That's your mantra, I think," Madriani said. "You have a stake in doing justice, do you not?"

She nodded.

"Then please. You've been very outspoken about criticizing prosecutors who won't consider exculpatory evidence right up till the time of a verdict."

Alex hesitated as Madriani pressed the invitation. "Okay. Okay, I'll go with you."

Rashid gave them instructions to an underground parking facility at the UN building. He pulled a parking pass from his leather folio and gave it to Alex. "You have a car? Put this on your dash, it will get you past the guard." He got up, bade them farewell. "Until tonight."

Nine o'clock behind the UN building, Alex and Paul walked toward the monolithic tower, home of the United Nations Secretariat. Before they had gone fifty yards, a figure stepped out of the shadows and raised his arm waving toward them. He was still wearing the wrinkled white linen suit from earlier in the day.

"I trust you had no difficulty parking?" said Rashid.

"None," said Alex. "You keep long hours."

"No rest for the weary," he replied. He led them toward a side entrance to the main building. Before they got there Rashid hailed a janitor who had the door open and was just going inside. "Can you hold the door for us? Thank you." Rashid slid his keys back into his pocket and led the way toward a service elevator at the back of the building. He turned, smiled, and said: "I cheat. I'm not supposed to use it but it's so much closer to my office than the main elevators."

Two minutes later they were in his office, a spacious corner room on the seventh floor with large windows on two sides, overlooking the East River. Rashid's nameplate was on the desk, a university diploma on the wall and a photograph—Rashid with his family, wife and, Paul counted them, five children. Two of them appeared to be adults.

Rashid took the chair behind the desk. "Please have a seat."

He gestured toward the two chairs across from him. "Unless, of course, you'd rather sit on the couch."

"This is fine," said Madriani. Paul was anxious to cut to the chase. He wanted to know what Rashid had and whether, in fact, it might have any impact on his case. And he didn't have much time.

For the defense, the Mustaffa trial was going nowhere fast. Police had evidence that Mustaffa's taxi was in the area of the murder scene the night that Spinova was killed. GPS data from the car's tracking system placed the vehicle close to the vicinity where the body was found. But what was most damaging was the eyewitness testimony of the State's principal witness. Madriani was still trying to figure out how to deal with it. He knew something bad was coming from documents he received during discovery. Perhaps the man would equivocate, but Paul doubted it. And the testimony could prove to be a killer depending on precisely what the witness said he saw.

"Can I offer you anything to drink? Coke? Water?"

Both lawyers shook their heads.

"Then let's not waste time. As I told you, Spinova went to Libya about two weeks after the Benghazi raid on the consulate. But the story begins before that. Late January 2011, the so-called Arab Spring. There were deadly riots all over Egypt. People were dying in the central square in Cairo. You may have seen pictures," said Rashid. "Camels trampling some, others being shot."

Madriani and Alex nodded.

"Much of this, including fires, buildings torched, took place within a stone's throw of the Museum of Cairo. Have either of you ever been there?"

"I have," said Alex.

"Then you are familiar with some of the artifacts on display. In particular, I am talking about Howard Carter's collection, the treasures from the tomb of Tutankhamen."

"Yes," said Alex.

"What does any of this have to do with Spinova's murder?" asked Paul.

"Bear with me," said Rashid. "On the night of January 29, 2011, under cover of the riots and fires raging outside the museum, thieves broke in and stole items from the Tut collection. What they couldn't carry off, they vandalized. Included among the objects that were taken was a priceless gold figurine of the boy king standing on the back of a panther carved from black ebony. It was one of the premier items recovered by Carter from the tomb in 1922."

"Of course," Alex said. "It's a spectacular piece."

"There is no way to put a dollar value on the object other than to say that it is priceless. The thieves damaged the base of the statue, the ebony panther. They broke off the gold figurine and took it. We have reason to believe it is still missing."

"Yes, but what does this have to do with Spinova?" said Paul.

"I'm getting to that. When Spinova went to the burned-out consulate building in Benghazi, she was intending to take pictures and perhaps write an article about what she saw there. She was hoping to be one of the first to visit the site with a camera and she assumed that she could benefit financially from the information. However, this all changed after she climbed through one of the open windows of the building because of something she found."

"What was that?" Alex asked. She was all in now.

"A document," Rashid said. "It was a classified memorandum from your CIA referencing items stolen from the museum in Cairo."

"Did you know any of this, Paul?"

Madriani shook his head from side to side.

"Go on." By now Alex Cooper was all ears.

Madriani had taken out a small notepad from his suit coat pocket and appropriated a corner of the desk to jot down notes.

"The document in question, we are told, reveals the names, the identities, of the thieves involved, including the mastermind behind it. Also, an inventory of what was taken, as well as what was damaged, which the museum has been loath to offer up and which we believe is considerable."

"What exactly is your role in all of this?" asked Alex.

"We are part of UNESCO," said Rashid. "The United Nations Educational, Scientific and Cultural Organization. Specifically my office is charged with enforcing the Convention for the Fight Against the Illicit Trafficking in Cultural Property. It is why we are so concerned about the contents of this memorandum, the one that Spinova found at the consulate and which her killer presumably was after. You see, there is a far more sinister element to all of this." He paused and looked meaningfully at them.

"According to our sources, the items stolen, and in particular the gold figurine of the boy king, the figure of Tut code-named Surfing the Panther in the memorandum, were transported to Libya shortly after the theft."

Madriani stopped writing when he heard about the gold statue and its code name.

"They were placed in the care of an artisan whose job it was to craft a number of identical replicas," Rashid said. "The people at the Museum of Cairo would tell you that the damaged figurine was left behind by the looters. Of course, they had to say this. They even show pictures of it being restored. To say otherwise, given the political upheaval at the time, the change in government . . . well, heads would have rolled, quite literally, of those who were in charge of the museum.

"You see, the gold content of the figurine is minimal. It is its historic provenance that gives it vast monetary value. It is too recognizable to be sold to a legitimate museum, but private collectors would pay a fortune to obtain it for their own personal gratification. Because a buyer could not advertise its possession, the thieves would be free to make multiple copies and sell them to unwary but corrupt collectors at exorbitant prices, each one believing that they had the original item. Those buyers would never be able to disclose the fact that they paid tens of millions of dollars, perhaps more, for false replicas. They would be defrauded without recourse."

"Makes good sense," Madriani said.

"But here is the important part. It is the reason U.S. intelligence got involved in the first place. They uncovered the identity of one of the potential buyers who was bargaining for the original figurine. He was willing to pay a huge sum to acquire it."

"Who is that?" said Alex.

"According to our information, the former supreme leader of North Korea, Kim Jong-il," Rashid said. "The reason for the memorandum, and again we have not seen the document, but we have sources who tell us that Kim and the mastermind behind the theft had, as you say, struck a deal, an agreed-upon sum for delivery of the figurine. The price, if our information is correct, was half a billion dollars, U.S."

Madriani whistled as he looked up. "We're in the wrong business. Still, that's a considerable inducement for murder. Kill Spinova to keep her from taking her story and the CIA memo to the media."

"Precisely," said Rashid.

"How do you know all of this?" Madriani needed evidence.

"It is my job," said Rashid.

"Perhaps you can obtain a copy of the memorandum, the CIA memo, from the State Department?" said Alex.

Rashid shook his head. "They will not share information with us. Not on this. I suspect it is because of the national security implications surrounding the North Korean involvement. We are aware that the United States is engaged in highly sensitive negotiations with Kim's son and successor Kim Jong-un, baby Kim, over nuclear weapons in North Korea. They are not going to jeopardize those negotiations over something like this."

Madriani looked up from his notes. This was dynamite that could turn the tide in his defense of Mustaffa. The problem was there was no way to ignite it. He needed proof, solid evidence. Otherwise there was no way the trial judge would allow him to even mention it in front of the jury.

•◆•

Nine thirty Monday morning and the intercom buzzed on Alex Cooper's desk. The office outside her door at One Hogan Place in Manhattan, the headquarters for the New York District Attorney's Office, hummed with activity.

The voice on the intercom was Cooper's secretary. "Call for you on line one. A Mr. Rashid from UNESCO. Do you want me to take a message, tell him you're busy?"

"No. I'll talk." Alex picked up the phone. "Hello."

"Ms. Cooper. I hope I did not catch you at a bad time."

"Mr. Rashid. I have a meeting in twenty minutes but I can spare a moment."

"I was wondering if you could tell me whether Mr. Madriani is still in town?"

"No, he left yesterday morning. Why do you ask?"

"Because I called his office in San Diego. They said he was

out of the area, unavailable for several days. That he could not be reached. I didn't want to leave a message. What I have to tell him is highly confidential."

"He was supposed to give his opening statement today."

"That's what I was afraid of. Is there any way you can reach him?"

"I don't know. Is it urgent?"

"If he wants to save his client it is vital."

"What is it?" Alex Cooper already knew more than she should have.

It took Alex almost two hours to track Madriani down through his office in Coronado and from there to his cell phone in LA where she left a message. Just after three East Coast time, noon in LA, he called her back during a break in the trial.

"I hope it's important," said Madriani.

"Pressed for time, are you?"

"Just a couple of sharks from the DA's office working their way up my leg from the ankle to the knee. Nothing to worry about."

"Rashid has been trying to get a hold of you since yesterday," said Alex. "He says the DA's office is about to lower the boom on your client."

"I thought they already had," said Paul.

"A witness by the name of Terry Mirza. Do you know the name?" asked Alex.

"I do," said Paul. "But how does Rashid know—?"

"Be quiet and listen. You don't have much time. Rashid claims this guy Mirza saw your man dump Spinova's body in an alley in West LA the night of the murder."

Mirza's name was on the state's witness list but the information had not been released to the press or made public. Even Paul did not yet know the precise details of Mirza's testimony, only that he was a percipient witness to the body dump, only sketchy notes from police reports that the cops had left intentionally vague. They had closeted Mirza away since before the trial to keep him out of the clutches of Paul's investigators, not that Mirza would have talked to any of them.

"Why are you telling me this, Alex?"

"Because I trust you. I trust your reputation. And there are two ways to go at this. I happen to believe that a DA's job is to do justice."

"What two ways do you have in mind?"

"Like I said, the DA out there is a good friend of mine. I'll call him. Maybe he'll listen to me. Take a hard look at what we give him about Cairo. Let him know he may be sitting on exculpatory evidence."

"I hope your second idea makes more sense. He's been stonewalling me on this."

"Look, Paul. I can't go rogue here, much as I might like to. But one of my best friends just left the office. Jenny Corcoran. She's waiting for a background check for an appointment she just got at Justice in DC. She's a pit bull in the courtroom. She might work with you on this."

"And you're telling me I can—?"

"Trust her? Completely. You have my word."

"So what will you say to the DA?" Paul asked.

"According to Rashid, this guy Mirza is going to tell the jury that he saw your man pull a large plastic bundle from the backseat of his cab in an alley off Lankershim Boulevard the night Spinova was killed. Presumably the reason there was no blood in the backseat of your man's cab is because she was killed somewhere else and dumped there."

"That's their theory," said Paul. "Lemme get this straight, Mirza can positively identify Mustaffa as the man driving the cab and dumping the body?"

"Rock solid, according to Rashid," said Alex.

"You're sure? I need to know how confident he is, whether I can shake him on cross."

Mirza had ID'd Mustaffa from a photo array. Paul already knew that. He was hoping beyond hope that he could get the witness to equivocate on the identification, just a slight crack in the wall. After all, presumably, he was a disinterested witness with no stake in the case. Was he absolutely, positively one thousand percent certain it was Mustaffa that he saw? No one was ever one thousand percent sure of anything. "It might have been him, I can't be entirely sure." This was all Paul needed. Something he could play with and stretch like a rubber band in front of the jury on closing, and hope that it snapped.

"According to Rashid, Mirza will positively identify your client at the scene, and he won't be burdened by any doubts."

Paul's heart climbed into his throat. "Don't tell me that Mirza has photographs of the body being dumped. And how does Rashid know all of this?"

"No, there are no photos," said Alex. "Rashid says Mirza will be lying through his teeth."

"What?"

"Listen carefully. Do you have a notepad? Here're the details on what Rashid told me. We're both going to have to move quickly."

•◆•

The criminal courts building on Temple Street in downtown Los Angeles had an ominous feel for Madriani ever since the start of the Mustaffa case. Even the courtroom was foreboding, Department 123 on the thirteenth floor. Had Madriani been superstitious, the only thing worse might have been the number of the Beast—666.

Bad news, too, that the DA had been off-put by Alex Cooper's attempt to intervene in one of his biggest cases. But Alex had surprised Madriani by taking the week off from her own job and flying out to be at the trial, sitting discreetly in the rear of the courtroom—one spectator among many—after her friend Jenny Corcoran confirmed that her presence might help Madriani get at the truth.

This morning, on direct examination, the testimony of Terry Mirza was presented to the jury as if it were written, produced, and directed for a Broadway production with an audience of twelve. It came on smooth as silk as the nine women and three men in the jury box took notes and listened intently. There was not the slightest equivocation as Mirza identified the defendant, Ibid Mustaffa, as the man he saw in the alley that night, the one who dragged the plastic-shrouded and bloodied body of Carla Spinova from the backseat of his yellow cab.

Mirza even identified the cab number as well as the license plate number of the vehicle. He had everything but the VIN number off the engine block. When asked if he was absolutely certain that it was Mustaffa that he saw that night, he said he had no doubt whatsoever. He told the jury that he observed the defendant clearly from several different angles as Mustaffa struggled under the bright lights of a streetlamp to drag the body over to the edge of the alley, against the side of a building, where he left her and drove off.

The witness also testified that the defendant was wearing gloves. This would explain the lack of fingerprints on the plastic tarp used to wrap the body.

When the prosecutor had hammered the last nail in Mustaffa's coffin and turned the witness over to Paul, the jurors were looking at Madriani as if to say, *Try and get out of that one.*

Paul introduced himself to the witness. "Mr. Mirza, let me ask you, what is your first name, your given name? It's not Terry, is it?"

"No. It's Tariq."

"What is the origin of the name? I mean, it's not English or Irish or German."

"Objection, Your Honor. What's the relevance?"

"I think the jury has a right to know a little bit about the witness and where he's from," said Paul.

"I'll allow it," said the judge. "But keep it short, Mr. Madriani."

"Mr. Mirza, where is your family from?"

"My parents were Bedu, Bedouins. From the desert, originally Saudi Arabia."

"Do you have family in Saudi Arabia at the present time?"

"I have an uncle who lives there."

"Were you born here in this country?"

"No. I came here when I was three with my mother and father and two brothers."

"Do you have any other relatives living in the Middle East, say, outside of Saudi Arabia, at the present time?"

"Objection as to relevance, Your Honor." The prosecutor was on his feet once more.

"May we approach the bench?" said Madriani.

The judge waved them on. Off to the side, away from the witness, Paul told the judge that the questions were intended to lay a foundation for the issue of credibility, which was always relevant. After all, it was the prosecution who put the witness on the stand.

"I will give you a little latitude, Mr. Madriani, but let's try and tie it to something in the case." The judge eased back in his chair.

Paul picked up where he left off.

"Yes," said Mirza. "I have one brother and my grandparents who live in Shubra al-Khaymah."

"And where is that?" said Paul.

"It's a town just outside Cairo in Egypt."

"So your family lives in the same country my client is from?"

"If you say so," said Mirza.

"When is the last time you spoke to your family in Egypt?" said Paul.

"I don't know. I don't remember."

"A month ago?"

"Longer."

"Two months?"

"I don't know. As I said, I can't remember."

"Mr. Mirza, isn't it a fact that the testimony you have offered before this jury here today is false? Is it not true that you never saw anything that night and that, in fact, the information you have testified to here today was provided to you by outside parties who have threatened your family in Egypt unless you testify in accordance with their instructions?"

"No, that's not true," said Mirza.

"Isn't it a fact, Mr. Mirza, that you received a letter, typed correspondence, hand-delivered to your home, instructing you to incriminate my client, telling you what to say, giving you details including the defendant's taxi number, the license number of the vehicle, the location of the alley, and other specifics like the time of your supposed observations, and telling you that unless you did as the letter instructed your family members in Egypt would be killed? Is that not a fact?"

"No. I don't know what you're talking about." The discomfort level of the witness was obvious.

Madriani lifted a sheaf of papers from the table in front of him.

Beneath the papers were several large glossy photographs as well as photocopies of a letter and its envelope. Madriani handed one set to the bailiff who delivered it to the judge and another to the prosecutor.

"May I approach the witness, Your Honor?" The judge nodded as he read from his copy of the letter.

"Mr. Mirza, this is not the original but a copy of the letter in question. The original has already been examined by a laboratory employed by the defense. It was turned over to the police for their examination less than an hour ago. I should tell you that our experts have already identified your fingerprints on the original letter and its envelope. You should be advised that perjury is a serious crime. I remind you that you are under oath."

Mirza looked at the document.

"Your Honor, we've never seen this before." The prosecutor was on his feet waving his copy of the letter at the judge.

"Neither had I, Your Honor, until late yesterday morning," said Madriani, "when, subject to a subpoena, the letter was found in a safe-deposit box belonging to Mr. Mirza at Fontana Bank in the city. It was tucked inside a large manila envelope containing some insurance documents."

"I've never seen this before," said Mirza, his hands shaking.

"We would ask for a continuance," said the prosecutor.

Madriani ignored him. "Then perhaps you can explain to the jury and the judge how it came to find its way into your safe-deposit box with your fingerprints on it?"

"The witness will answer the question." One thing judges don't like is perjury.

Mirza looked up at the judge, then toward the prosecutor, and finally at Madriani. A bewildered expression spread across his face. "I don't know! I really don't know!"

•◆•

Six days later, after the police crime lab verified Mirza's fingerprints on the letter and its envelope, both sides made their closing arguments to the jury.

In the courtroom, crowded to overflowing, Alex Cooper sat just beyond the railing behind Madriani at the counsel table. In closing, it took little more than an hour for Madriani to shred the State's case given that the testimony and evidence of the prosecution's chief witness had turned to dust. Other than the bleak GPS data putting Mustaffa's taxi in the vicinity of the body dump, Mirza's testimony was the only real evidence tying him to the crime. Worse, it now appeared as if there was an active conspiracy afoot to frame Mustaffa.

Paul explained to the jury that while he could not defend Mirza's conduct on the stand, he understood the unwillingness on the part of the witness to own up to his perjury. After all, his family was in jeopardy and he had reason to be afraid for them.

Mirza, to the last breath, denied ever having seen the letter in question. He claimed that, to his knowledge, no one had ever threatened his family and no one had told him what to say on the stand. He was adamant. No doubt the DA's office would take him to its own version of the woodshed for a thrashing on the issue of perjury if the jury failed to believe him. Still, there was no way to explain the fingerprints and the letter in the safe-deposit box, all belonging to Mirza.

After retiring to the jury room for deliberations, it seemed that the headiest item on the jury's agenda was the election of a foreman. Before the noon break they were back with a verdict. "On the count of violation of Penal Code Section 187, first-degree murder, we, the jury, find the defendant, Ibid Mustaffa, not guilty."

There was a veritable uproar in the courtroom as Mustaffa was discharged by the judge. Madriani made plans to meet with him the following Monday at his office in San Diego. Mustaffa left to get his personal belongings that had been taken from him the night of his arrest.

Paul, Alex, and Jenny Corcoran retreated through the phalanx of reporters to a restaurant for lunch and a glass of wine. It was Friday afternoon. Alex had to fly back to New York, but Jenny was able to stay on. She made plans to get together with Paul and his girlfriend, Joselyn Cole, as well as his law partner, Harry Hinds, in San Diego for a quick visit.

After lunch, some local sightseeing, and a heavy dinner, the lawyers parted as Paul dropped Alex at the airport. She was still conflicted, she told him, about how it felt to hear that Mustaffa was acquitted when her first assumptions about his guilt in this heinous crime were so strong.

Paul headed back to his own room. He would spend one more night in the City of Angels before collecting his luggage, picking Jenny up the following morning, and heading south to San Diego and home.

As for Jenny, she was exhausted. As soon as she got to her room and showered, her head hit the pillow and she tried to sleep. But still the subconscious was at work. Something troubled her. It was the testimony of Terry Mirza.

In the true-to-form trials of the real world, *Perry Mason* endings with witnesses crumbling on the stand and admitting their guilt do not occur, except in one narrow band of cases. People who commit perjury and who are confronted on the stand with irrefutable evidence of their lies often do recant their testimony, particularly when admonished by counsel and the judge in stern language that perjury is a serious crime for which they could pay a stiff penalty, including time behind bars, if convicted. Mirza had been told this several times and still he stuck to his testimony. He insisted that he had never seen the letter threatening his family or directing him how to testify.

The letter had still another quality to it, like a rabbit pulled from a hat. Samir Rashid somehow had acquired information about Mirza and his family in Egypt. According to Rashid, they were under a severe threat of death from the people who had raided the Cairo Museum and stolen the golden figurine, Surfing the Panther. These people had already killed Carla Spinova to get their hands on the memorandum left behind in the charred U.S. consulate building in Benghazi, the memo that identified the mastermind behind the museum theft, as well as the deal for the sale to the North Korean dictator. Rashid's same sources had told him about the letter delivered to Mirza and the threat to his family. The Cairo thieves were desperate to convict Mustaffa for Spinova's murder—to make her death appear to be a brutal sexual assault, staged to seem so—because it would put an end to the controversy and leave them free to do their deals with their stolen booty. Case solved. Story over. It all made sense. Sort of.

Slowly her subconscious released her and Jenny drifted off to sleep. She couldn't tell how long the slumber lasted, minutes or hours, disoriented as she was in the dark room. But she was awakened with a start by the noise next to her head. She opened her eyes in the dark, little blinking lights in unfamiliar places and the sound of the electronic ringtone blaring next to the bed. She grabbed for the receiver and found it on the second stab.

"Hello."

"Hello, Jenny. Paul Madriani here. I'm sorry to wake you."

"What is it?" She looked at the clock on the nightstand. It was four thirty in the morning.

"We need to talk. The police called me ten minutes ago. Ibid Mustaffa is dead."

"What?"

"He was killed by a hit-and-run driver at an intersection in West Los Angeles two hours ago. The police found my business card with the hotel phone number in Mustaffa's pocket. They said he was drunk, stumbled into the street, and got nailed. According to witnesses, the driver sped off."

Jenny's mind, still half asleep, raced trying to absorb it all.

"Corcoran, are you there?"

"Yes. I'm here."

"Mustaffa was Islamic, devout. He prayed five times a day. More to the point, he didn't drink."

An hour later, the two lawyers sat bleary-eyed hunched over the table in Paul's hotel room gulping coffee from Styrofoam cups, something from an all-night café on the corner.

"I don't believe in coincidence," said Jenny. "You want to know what I think?"

"What?" said Paul.

"I think Mirza was telling the truth. I don't think he'd ever seen that letter before. I mean, you had him in a vise right there on the stand, squeezing him with hard evidence. Why not own up? After all, if your family is in jeopardy, it's no longer a secret."

"Then how did his prints get on the letter and the envelope?"

"Blank paper," said Jenny. "Maybe somebody got into his house. We all stack paper in our printers. Somebody could have taken the bottom page from the feeder. Or better, somebody hands Mirza a blank piece of paper in an envelope. He opens it, looks at it. Whoever gives it to him says, "Oops, wrong envelope," takes it back, and gives him something else. Mirza never thinks twice about it. The contents of the letter are then typed or printed on the blank page and suddenly the witness is confronted with it in court."

"You're forgetting something. How did the letter get into Mirza's safe-deposit box?" said Madriani.

"Where there's a will, there's a way. You said it was found inside an envelope with some insurance documents."

"Right."

"Where did the insurance papers come from?"

"I don't know. I assume an insurance agency."

"Yes and we, as well as the court, all assumed that Mirza either hid the letter or misfiled it with his insurance papers. Now let me ask you, who reads insurance documents?" said Jenny.

Paul looked at her. "Nobody."

"Exactly. You receive them and you file them away somewhere safe. Anybody could have gotten to that manila envelope with the insurance documents and slipped whatever they wanted in it before it was delivered to Mirza. Look again and you might find pictures of Mirza shooting from the grassy knoll in Dealey Plaza."

Paul thought for a moment. "And who knew exactly where to look for the letter?"

"Rashid," said Jenny. She looked at her watch, picked up the receiver on the nightstand, and started dialing, first an outside line.

"Who are you calling?"

"Alex. I need to pick her brain, but it's going right to voice mail."

"She may still be airborne," Paul said.

Jenny tried again and asked for information this time.

"I would like the phone number for New York, the United Nations, UNESCO, if there is a separate listing."

"What about his business card?" said Paul.

Jenny shook her head. "If I'm right, that's probably an answering service. They'll answer with any name a client gives them."

Ten minutes later they had the news. The good part was that UNESCO had its own main number; the bad news was that no one by the name of Samir Rashid worked there. There was no listing under that name for any employee.

Jenny slammed the receiver into the cradle. "He played you and Alex like a piano. How the hell did he get into the building? His office?"

"After hours. On a Saturday night," said Paul. "And the janitor who just happened to be going in through the side door. The man is just full of coincidences. He used the service elevator instead of the bank of elevators near the main entrance. I should have known it was way too smooth."

"No going through security," said Jenny.

"Exactly. He probably paid the janitor at the door to let Alex and me in. You hang a few pictures and certificates on the wall, put a holder with business cards on the desk, slip a plastic plaque with your name on the office door and you're in business. What we saw is what he wanted us to see. It's all about confidence," said Paul. "Put yourself in the right setting, surround yourself with a cloak of authority, and you can peddle anything."

"To two gullible lawyers, searching for the truth," said Jenny. "And all you got was smoke and mirrors. Alex will go ballistic."

"Don't be so hard on us. We were the perfect marks. I've got a loser of a case. He's got the answer, the solution to all my problems. He plays on the interests of justice. We both wanted the fair result, especially when we figured out that Mustaffa was being set up."

"Why does he want to get Mustaffa off?" said Jenny.

"Mustaffa killed Spinova," said Paul. "He had something Rashid wanted and he was holding it over Rashid's head unless Rashid helped him beat the charges."

"What?"

"The CIA memorandum," said Paul.

"What? You think that was real?" said Jenny.

"The best con is one that includes a kernel of truth. Mustaffa killed Spinova to get the memo—and he got it. But in the process he got nailed. Mirza saw him dump the body. Cops caught up with him and Mustaffa used the memo which, unless I'm wrong, identifies Rashid as the mastermind behind the Cairo Museum theft. Mustaffa used the memo to extort Rashid. 'Help me or else.' If Mustaffa goes down for the count, he uses the memo and the evidence in it to cut a deal for himself come sentencing."

"Enter two overanxious lawyers," said Jenny. "And Alex, trying to do the right thing by the dead woman. Make sure the wrong guy isn't convicted unfairly. Those autopsy pictures haunted her."

"Now Mustaffa's dead. The memo's gone," said Paul, "and God knows where Rashid is, assuming that's even his name, which you and I both know it is not. He may be a lot of things, but stupid is not one of them."

"I hate being used like this," said Jenny.

"You think I like it? I had an obligation to defend Mustaffa to the best of my ability. But suborning perjury was not included among my services."

"So what do we do?" said Jenny.

"You got me," said Paul. "We could go to the trial judge and the DA and explain what happened. Of course, what good is that? Even if Mustaffa were alive he would be beyond the reach of the court, double jeopardy being what it is, which is redundant in this case since he's dead."

"Rashid is a coconspirator," said Jenny. "He's still liable."

"Try and find him," said Paul. "He's busy peddling his wares, little golden statues, remember?"

"Yes, I heard about them," said Jenny. She thought for a moment. There was a twinkle in her eye. "That's it!"

"What?"

"The answer."

"The answer to what?" said Paul.

"A woman scorned. Alex will want a hand in this. Maybe the DA will listen to her now."

•◆•

Eight days later a sleek Gulfstream G650 touched down on the runway at the heavily guarded airport just outside Pyongyang, the capital of North Korea. It taxied to a stop in front of a large hangar as the stairway was wheeled up next to the door. It swung open and a man stepped out onto the platform. He was carrying a small wooden box under one arm.

The man who called himself Samir Rashid looked down at the official entourage waiting for him at the foot of the steps, behind them the line of shiny black limousines and security cars waiting to escort him to the government house, what is called the Grand People's Study House.

Rashid walked briskly down the steps until he reached the tarmac, where he extended his right hand in greeting toward the general who was first in line. Before the officer could take it, a guard stepped around him and quickly slapped the cold, hard metal of handcuffs around Rashid's right wrist. Another guard took possession of the wooden box while they manacled Rashid's other hand.

"What is this? What are you doing?"

"Silence," said the general. "You will come with me. Is this the statue?" He gestured toward the box.

"It is, and your leader will be very angry with you for the manner in which I am being treated. There is no excuse for this. I had an arrangement with his father and have an understanding with your Dear Leader. I assure you he will be very upset when I speak to him about this."

"Yes," said the general. "Perhaps you can explain the meaning of this to him." The officer reached for something handed to him by one of his subordinates standing next to him. It was a newspaper, two of them actually, copies of the *New York Times* and the *Los Angeles Times,* each of them one day old. Blaring headlines just below the fold from New York:

AUDACIOUS THEFT FROM CAIRO MUSEUM
ATTEMPT TO SELL BOGUS TUT STATUES

From Los Angeles the revelation:

PROSECUTOR UNVEILS ELABORATE FRAUD IN
SPINOVA MURDER TRIAL, COCONSPIRATOR ON THE LAM

Rashid's eyes raced over the newsprint trying to absorb the full impact of the words. Adrenaline flooded his heart as glimpses of his fate revealed themselves here and there in the words on the page—"golden knockoffs"—"North Korean dictator"—"unsuspecting buyers"—"fraud"—"murder," the last of which seemed to be the least of Rashid's worries. In that instant, the man who had called himself Samir Rashid knew that he would never leave North Korea alive.

It is true what they say: justice is a funny thing. It comes in many different forms.

JEFFERY DEAVER
VS. JOHN SANDFORD

Rhymes with Prey

ombining Lincoln Rhyme and Lucas Davenport in a single adventure seemed an insurmountable problem. Rhyme, the hero of Jeffery Deaver's series that began with *The Bone Collector* (1997), is a quadriplegic and, of necessity, sticks close to home in New York City. Davenport, the star of John Sandford's *Prey* series, is an ace investigator living in Minnesota—working presently for that state's Bureau of Criminal Apprehension.

How could the two ever meet?

Fortunately, Davenport's talents as a no-nonsense, take-no-prisoners cop have transported him to the Big Apple before. In *Silent Prey* (1992), NYPD Detective Lily Rothenburg enlisted Davenport's aid in nailing the psychotic killer Dr. Michael Bekker, who was prowling the streets of Manhattan. Rhyme, too, has a partner, Detective Amelia Sachs, so Jeff and John decided it was a natural fit for this foursome to join forces to tackle the case of a murderous sculptor for whom art and death are inextricably—and gruesomely—intertwined.

The combination of these four was particularly harmonious since Lucas Davenport and Lily Rothenburg are known for their streetwise policing and skill at psychological profiling—while Lincoln Rhyme and Amelia Sachs ply the complementary skill of forensic science. Together, they take on the task of figuring out who's doing what and why to victims in Lower Manhattan's chic art scene.

The process of writing this story was seamless. Both John and Jeff are experienced at this sort of thing. Together, they developed an outline, comprising about eight scenes, then divided up the task of writing each one. Jeff handled the crime scene and forensics-oriented portions, John the undercover and street investigations. Rather than writing serially—one section after the other, sending the finished portions to each other—amazingly, they worked simultaneously. When the rough story was finished, they each polished the completed manuscript, combined edits, and, voila, they had a story.

It's a chilling tale, one filled with each author's trademark reversals and twists. You'll think twice about ever walking into an art gallery again.

And heaven help you if you ever strike up a conversation with a stranger in a bar.

Rhymes with Prey

The night was hot, and close, and the midsummer perfume of Central Park West—the odor of melted bubble gum, mixed with discarded cheese pretzels and rotten bananas, or something just like that—seeped into the backseat of the taxi as it cleared Fifty-seventh Street and headed north.

The taxi driver was Pakistani, from Karachi, he said, a slender, mild-mannered man who smelled lightly of cumin with an overlay of Drakkar Noir cologne. He listened to what might have been Pakistani jazz, or Afghani rap, or something even more exotic; the couple in the backseat wouldn't have known the difference, if there was any difference. When the male passenger asked how big Karachi was, the driver said, "More big than New York City, but more small than New York City if includes the suburgers."

The woman said, "Really," with an edge of skepticism.

The Pakistani picked up the skepticism and said, "I look in Wiki, and this is what Wiki say."

The male passenger was from Minnesota and, not knowing any better, or because he was rich and didn't care, overtipped the driver as he and the woman got out of the cab. As it moved away, he said to her, "I could use a suburger right now. With catsup and fries."

"You just don't want to deal with Rhyme," she said. "He makes you nervous."

Lucas Davenport looked up at Lincoln Rhyme's town house, a Victorian pile facing the park, with a weak, old-fashioned light over the doorway. "I'm getting over it. When I first went in there, I had a hard time looking at him. That pissed him off. I could feel it, and I feel kinda bad about it."

"Didn't have any trouble looking at Amelia," said Lily Rothenburg.

"Be nice," Lucas said, as they walked toward the front steps. "I'm happily married."

"Doesn't keep you from checking out the market," Lily said.

"I don't think she's on the market," Lucas said. He made a circling motion with an index finger. "I mean, can they—?"

"I don't know," Lily said. "Why don't you ask? Just wait until I'm out of there."

"Maybe not," Lucas said. "I'm getting over it, but I'm not that far over it. And he's not exactly Mr. Warmth."

"Somebody might say that about you, too," Lily observed.

"Hey. Nobody said that to me while getting busy in my Porsche."

Lily laughed and turned a little pink. Way back, back before their respective marriages, they'd dallied. In fact, Lucas had dallied her brains loose in a Porsche 911, a feat that not everyone thought possible, especially for people their size. "A long time ago, when we were young," she said, as they climbed the steps to Lincoln's front door. "I was slender as a fairy then."

Lucas was a tall man, heavy in the shoulders, with a hawk nose and blue eyes. His black hair was touched with a bit of silver at the temples and a long thin scar ran from his forehead across his brow ridge and down onto his cheek, the product of a fishing accident. Another scar, on his throat, was not quite as outdoorsy, though it happened outdoors, when a young girl shot him with a piece-of-crap .22 and he almost died.

Lily was dark-haired and full-figured, constantly dieting and constantly finding more interesting things to eat. She never gained enough to be fat, couldn't lose enough to be thin. She'd never been a fairy. She was paid as a captain in the NYPD, but she was more than that: one of the plainclothes influentials who floated around the top of the department, doing things meant to be invisible to the media. As someone said of her, she was the nut cutter they called when nuts *seriously* needed to be cut.

Like now. She'd brought Lucas in as a "consultant" from the Minnesota Bureau of Criminal Apprehension, because she didn't know who she could trust in her own department. They might have a serial-killer cop on the loose—or even worse, a bunch of cops. And if that was right, the cops wouldn't be out-of-control dumbass flatfoots, but serious guys, narcotics detectives who'd become fed up with the pointlessness and ineffectiveness of the war on drugs.

The four dead were all female, all illegal Mexicans, all had been tortured, and all had some connection to drug sales—although with two of them, Lucas thought, the connection was fairly thin. Still, if they were dealing with the cartels, and if there was a turf war going on, they could have been killed simply as warnings. And torture was something the cartels did as other people might play cards.

On the other hand, the women may have been tortured not as

punishment, or to make a point, but for information. Somebody, the commissioner feared, had decided to take direct action to eliminate the drug problem, with the emphasis on *eliminate*. The bodies were piling up: so he called his nut cutter and the nut cutter called Lucas. The duo had just been downtown checking out and talking with the honchos that made up the department's famous Narcotics Unit Four. Or infamous, some said. The trio of shields—two men and a woman—had earned the highest drug-conviction rate in the city with, the rumors went, less than kosher tactics. Lately they'd been running ops in the area where the women had been killed.

Lily pushed the doorbell.

Amelia Sachs came to the door, chewing on a celery stalk, and let them in. She was a tall woman, slender and redheaded, a former model, which pushed several of Lucas's buttons. Given all of that, their relationship had been testy, maybe because of Lucas's initial attitude toward Lincoln and his disability.

Lincoln was in his Storm-Arrow wheelchair, peering at a high-def video screen. Without looking at them, he said, "You got nothing."

"Not entirely true," Lucas said. "All three of them were dressed carelessly."

Lincoln turned his head and squinted at him. "Why is that important?"

Lucas shrugged. "Anyone who dresses carelessly bears watching, in my estimation," he said. He was wearing a Ralph Lauren Purple Label summer-weight wool suit in medium blue, a white dress shirt with one of the more muted Hermès ties, and bespoke shoes from a London shoemaker.

Amelia made a rude noise, and Lucas grinned at her, or at least showed his teeth.

"Easy," Lily said. To Lincoln: "You're basically right. We got nothing. We weren't exactly stonewalled, we were know-nothinged. Like it was all a big puzzle, and why were we there?"

"Were they acting?" Lincoln asked.

"Hard to tell," Lucas said. "Most detectives are good liars. But if somebody put a gun to my head, I'd say no, they weren't acting. They didn't know what we were talking about."

"Mmm, I like that concept," Amelia said.

"What?" Lucas asked. "Lying?"

"No. Putting a gun to your head."

Lily rolled her eyes. "Amelia."

"Just having fun, Lily," Amelia said. "You know I love Lucas like a brother."

"And I hope it stays that way," Lincoln grumped. "Anyway . . . while you were out touring the city, we've made some significant progress here. There were some anomalies in the autopsy photos that I thought worth revisiting. The bodies were found nude, of course, and so dirt and sand had been comprehensively impressed in the victims' skins, along with grains of concrete. However, in examining the photos, I noticed that in several of these flecks, we were getting more light return than you might expect from grains of sand or soil or concrete. The photos were taken with flash, of course, a very intense light. The enhanced light return would not have been especially noticeable under the lights of an autopsy table. I sent Amelia to investigate."

"I found that all four victims had tiny bits of metal ingrained in their skin. The cut surfaces were shiny, which is why Lincoln was able to see them in the high-res photos," Amelia said. "There weren't many of them, but some in each. I recovered them—"

"And brought them here," Lincoln said. "They were uniform in size, and smaller than the average brown sugar ant. We ran them through the GDS 400A Glow Discharge Spectrometer, a Hewlett

Packard Gas Chromatograph, and a JEOL SEM-scanning electron microscope. Those're instruments for determining the composition of a liquid, gas, or solid—"

"I know what they are; I'm a cop, not a fucking moron," Lucas said.

Lincoln continued without acknowledging the interruption. "And found that they were flecks of bronze."

Lily said, "Bronze. That's good, right? We need a bronze-working shop."

Amelia said, "It's good in a way. The fact is, bronze has become pretty much a specialty metal—it's used to make bells, cymbals, some ship propellers, Olympic medals, and bronze wool replaces steel wool for some woodworking applications. It's used in high-end weather stripping for doors."

Lincoln, impatient, said, "Yes, yes, yes. But the flecks are not bronze wool, and they are rounded, with no flat sides, as you would get from weather stripping, and so on. Nor do they appear to be millings, which you would get with propellers and cymbals and such, because the grain size is too consistent."

"How about sculpture?" Lucas asked.

Lincoln was momentarily disconcerted, then said, "I concluded that since the grains were so uniformly sized, and so sharply cut, they most likely came from a hand-filing process. The most common hand-filing process used with bronze involves . . . sculpture casting."

Lucas said to Lily, "That was apparent to me as soon as they mentioned bronze."

"Quite," Lincoln said.

Lily: "So we're looking for a foundry."

"Perhaps not," Lincoln said. "There is another aspect worth mentioning. There weren't many of these bronze filings. I surmise that the murders may have taken place not in the foundry area, where you would expect a variety of returns from the casting process—and we have no bronze-related returns other than these flecks—and probably not even in the filing or grinding area. It appears to me that the grains were tracked into the area where the murders took place. Still, the kill site was near the filing area, or there would have been even fewer grains."

Lucas said, "So, what, we're looking for a room off a studio? Maybe even living quarters?"

"Not living quarters. I think we're looking for a loft of some kind. A loft with a concrete floor. All four victims had flecks of concrete buried in their skin, but two of them were found lying on blacktop, not concrete. And it's an empty building. Probably an abandoned warehouse."

"Where do you get that?" Lucas asked.

Lincoln twitched his shoulders, which Lucas had learned was a shrug. "The women weren't gagged. Whoever killed them let them scream. Either because it didn't bother them, or because they enjoyed it. And they felt safe in letting them scream."

Lucas nodded at him: "Interesting," he said.

Lily ticked it off on her fingers. "We're looking for a male, probably, because they're the ones who do this kind of thing; either a sculptor, or somebody who works with a sculptor, who has a studio or a workshop in an empty warehouse."

"Either that, or somebody picked the building without knowing about the bronze filings," Amelia said. "They have nothing to do with bronze, except that they happened to pick a place with bronze filings on the floor. Could have been there forever."

"I doubt that," Lincoln said.

"It's a logical possibility, though," Lily said.

Lucas: "I'm with Lincoln on this."

Lily asked, "Why?"

Lincoln looked at Lucas and said, "You tell them."

"Because the particles are still shiny enough that Lincoln picked them up on the bodies. They're new."

Lily nodded and Amelia said, "Okay."

"And he's a freak. He's a sadomasochist who knows what he's doing. He's got a record," Lucas said. He turned to Lily. "Time to fire up the computers."

And the computers were fired up, not by Lucas, Lily, Amelia, or Lincoln, but by a clerk in the basement of the FBI building in Washington. Lily spoke quietly into the shell-like ear of the chief of detectives, Stan Markowitz, who spoke to a pal in the upper strata of the FBI, who wrote a memo that drifted down through several layers of the bureaucracy, and wound up on the desk of an inveterate war-game player named Barry.

Barry read the note, and punched in a bunch of keywords, and found, oddly enough, that there were four bronze sculptors in the United States who had been arrested for sex crimes involving some level of violence, and two of them had had studios in New York.

One of them was dead.

But James Robert Verlaine wasn't.

•◆•

"James Robert Verlaine," Lily read the next morning. They were in Lincoln's crime lab, once a parlor.

"Or as we know him, 'Jim Bob,'" Lucas said.

"Has a fondness for cocaine, has been arrested twice for possession of small amounts, did no time. Also arrested years ago for possession of LSD, did two months. Four years ago, he was charged with possession of thirty hits of ecstasy, but he'd wiped the Ziploc bag they were in and he'd thrown it into the next toilet stall, where it landed in the toilet and wasn't fished out for a while. Quite a while—somebody hadn't flushed. The prosecutor dumped it for faulty chain of evidence. Last year he was arrested in an apartment over on skid row in a raid on a meth cooker, but he was released when it turned out the actual cooker was the woman who was renting the apartment. Verlaine said he was just an innocent visitor. The prosecutor dumped it again, insufficient evidence."

"Get to the sex," Lucas said.

"He's never been arrested for a sex crime, but he's been investigated," Lily said, reading from the FBI report. "He's known for sculptures with slave themes involving bondage, whipping, various kinds of subjugation of women. A woman named Tina Martinez—note the last names here—complained to police that he'd injured a friend of hers named Maria Corso, who was supposedly modeling for one of these bondage sculptures. Corso refused to prosecute, said there'd been a misunderstanding with her friend. The investigators say they believe she was paid off."

"He's a bad man," Amelia said.

"Bad," Lincoln agreed. "With a substantial interest in drugs."

"And probably with the kind of brain rot you get from meth," Lucas said.

"Do you have a plan?" Lincoln asked.

"I plan to spend some time with him today. Just watching. Amelia and Lily can help out. See what he does, who he talks to, where he hangs out."

"Do we know where he lives?" Lincoln asked.

"We do," Lily said.

Lincoln said to Lucas, "I wonder if the women could handle the surveillance and keep you informed, of course."

Lucas said, "No reason they couldn't, I guess. Easier with three of us. Why?"

"I have an idea, but I want to speak to you privately about it. Just to avoid the inevitable question of conspiracy."

"Oh, shit," Lily said.

•◆•

Well, now, here's a pretty.

Tasty, this one.

Oh, he could picture her on her back, arms outstretched, yeah, yeah, lying on something rough—concrete or wood. Or metal.

Metal's always good.

Sweat on her forehead, sweat on her tits, sweat everywhere. Mewing, gasping, pleading.

For a luscious moment, every other person in the club vanished from James Robert Verlaine's consciousness as his eyes, his *artist's* eyes, lapped up the brunette in black at the end of the bar.

Tasty . . .

Raven hair, tinting from red to blue to green to violet in the spotlights. Disco décor, punk music. Rasta's could never make up its mind.

Hair. That aspect of the human form fascinated him. A sculptor of hard materials, he could reproduce flesh and organ, but hair remained ever elusive.

She glanced toward him once, no message in the gaze, but then a second time, which was, possibly, a message in itself.

Studying her more closely now, the oval face, the sensuous figure, the provocative way she leaned against the bar as she carried on a conversation on her cell phone.

It irritated him that her attention was now on some asshole a mile or ten miles or a hundred miles away. A smile. But not at Verlaine.

Mona Lisa, he reflected. That's who she reminded him of. Not a compliment, of course. Da Vinci's babe was a smirky bitch. And, Lord knew, the painting was way overrated.

Hey, look over here, Mona.

But she didn't.

Verlaine flagged down the bartender and ordered. Like always, here or at one of the other clubs where he hung out, Verlaine drank bourbon, straight, because girls liked it when men drank liquor that wasn't ruined with fruit juice. Beer was for kids, wine for the bedroom after fucking.

Mona looked in his direction once again. But didn't lock eyes.

He was getting angry now. Who the hell was she talking to?

Another scan. Little black dresses were a coward's choice—worn by women afraid to make a statement. But in Mona's case, he forgave her. The silk plunged and hovered just where it ought to and the cloth clung like latex paint to her voluptuous figure.

And what hands! Long fingers, tipped in black nails.

Hair was tough to duplicate, but hands were the most arduous of sculptors' challenges. Michelangelo was a genius at them, finding perfect palms and digits and nails in the heart of marble.

And James Robert Verlaine, who knew he was an artistic, if not blood, descendant of the great master, created the same magic, though with metal, not stone.

Which was much, much tougher to accomplish.

The crowd in Rasta's, Midtown, was typical for this time of night—artsy sorts who were really ad agency account managers, nerds who were really artists, hipsters pathetically clinging to their fading youth like a life preserver, players from Wall Street. Packed already. Soon to be more packed.

Finally, he caught Mona's eye. Her gaze flickered. Could be flirt, could be fuck off.

But Verlaine doubted the latter. He believed she liked what she saw. Why wouldn't she? He had a lean, wolfish face, which looked younger than his forty years. His hair, a mop, thick and inky. He worked hard to keep the do in a state of controlled unruliness. His eyes were as focused as lasers. Thin hips, encased in his trademark black jeans, tight. His work shirt was DKNY, but suitably flecked and worn. The garment was two-buttons undone with the pecs just slightly visible. Verlaine humped ingots and bars of metal around his studio and the junkyards where he bought his raw materials. Carried oxygen and propane and acetylene tanks, too.

Another glance at Mona. He was losing control, as that familiar feeling rippled through him from chest to crotch.

Picking up his Basil Hayden's, he pushed away from the bar to circle Mona's way. He tried to get past a knot of young businessmen in suits. They ignored him. Verlaine hated people like this. He detested their conformity, their smugness, their utter ignorance of culture. They'd judge art by the price tag; Verlaine bet he could wipe his ass with a canvas, spray some varnish on it, and set a reserve price of a hundred thousand bucks—and philistines like this'd fight to outbid themselves at Christie's.

L'art du merde.

He pushed through the young men.

"Hey," one muttered. "Asshole, you spilled my—"

Verlaine turned fast, firing off a searing gaze, like a spurt of pepper spray. The businessman, though taller and heavier, went still. His friends stirred, but chose not to come to his defense, returning quickly to a stilted conversation about the game.

When it was clear Mr. Brooks Brothers wasn't going to do something stupid and get a finger or face broken, or worse, Verlaine gave him a condescending smile and moved on.

Easing up to Mona, Verlaine hovered. He wasn't going to play the let's-ignore-each-other game. He was too worked up for that.

He whispered, "I've got one advantage over who you're talking to." A nod at the phone.

She stopped speaking and turned to him.

Verlaine grinned. "I can buy you a drink and he can't."

Tense. Would she balk?

Mona looked him over. Slow. Not smiling now. She said into the phone, "Gotta go."

Click.

His index finger crooked for the bartender.

"So, I'm James."

Playing it coy, of course. She said something. He couldn't hear. The music at Rasta's was a one-hundred-decibel remix of groups from twenty years ago, the worst of CBGBs.

He leaned closer and smelled a luscious floral scent rising from her skin.

Man, he wanted her. Wanted her tied down. Wanted her sweating. Wanted her crying.

"What's that?" he called.

Mona shouted, "I said, so what do you do, James?"

Of course. This was Manhattan. That was always question number one.

"I'm a sculptor."

"Yeah?" A faint Brooklyn lilt. He could tolerate that. The skepticism in her eyes, no.

His iPhone appeared and, shoving it her way, he flipped through the pictures.

"Jesus, you really are."

Then Mona looked past him. He followed her gaze and saw a tall redhead, smiling as she made her way through the crowd. A stunner. His eyes did the triplet glance: face, tits, ass. And he didn't care that she saw him doing it.

As tasty as Mona.

And no LBD for her. Leather miniskirt, fishnets, low-cut dark-blue sequined top, strapless.

The arrivee tossed her beautiful hair off her shoulders, glistening with sweat. She cheek-kissed Mona. Then pitched a smile Verlaine's way.

Mona said, "This is James. He's a real sculptor. He's famous."

"Cool," the redhead said, eyes wide and impressed—just the way he liked the pretties to be.

He shook their hands.

"And you are?" he asked the redhead.

"I'm Amelia."

Mona turned out to be Lily.

Verlaine got Amelia a Pinot gris and a refill of his bourbon.

Conversation wandered. Protocol demanded that, and Verlaine had to play the game a little longer before he could bring up the subject. You had to be careful. You could ruin an evening if you moved too fast. A girl by herself? You got her drunk enough, you could usually get her to "try something different" back at your place without too much effort.

But two together? That took a lot more work.

In fact, he wasn't sure he could pull this one off. They seemed, fuck it, smart, savvy. They weren't going to fall for lines like, "I can open up a whole new world for you."

No, may have to write this evening off. Hell.

But just then Lily leaned forward and whispered, "So what're you into, James?"

"Hobbies, you mean?" he asked.

The women regarded each other and broke out in laughs. "Yeah, hobbies. You have any hobbies?"

"Sure. Who doesn't?"

"If we tell you about our hobby, will you tell us about yours?"

When a sultry raven-haired pretty in a tight LBD asks you that question, there's only one answer: "You bet."

The redhead reached into her tiny purse and displayed a pair of handcuffs.

Okay, maybe the night was going to be easier than he thought.

• ◆ •

James Robert Verlaine had a certain charm, Amelia Sachs gave him that.

The clothes were weird—*Midnight Cowboy* meets Versace—and he probably owned more hair products than she did. But, despite that, his witty attention was completely on her and Lily.

With Lincoln Rhyme as a romantic as well as professional partner, Amelia had been freed from the madness of the dating world. But before him there'd been innumerable evenings in restaurants and bars with men who were anything but present. Their thoughts kept zipping back to Nokias or BlackBerrys in jacket pockets, to business deals sitting on office desktops, to girlfriends or wives they'd forgotten to mention.

A woman knows right away when a man's with her or not.

And Jim Bob—she loved Lucas Davenport's nic for him—definitely was. His sniper eyes bored into theirs, he touched arms, he asked questions, made jokes. He *inquired*.

Of course, this wasn't typical bar meeting talk—about family and exes, about the Mets, the Knicks, politics, and the latest retreads from Hollywood. No, the theme for tonight was such esoterica as describing the type of rope he enjoyed tying "girls" up with, where to get the best mouth gags, and what kind of whips and canes caused the most pain but left the fewest marks.

Back at Lincoln's loft, the four investigators had decided the way to Verlaine's psyche was through his fly. His sado-sexual history would give them entry. Lily had gone to the bar first—strategizing that a single bulb might draw the moth less suspiciously. Yep on that one. Then Amelia—in an outfit she'd had to purchase an hour earlier—had arrived to seal the deal. And it had taken a whole sixty seconds to find out that Verlaine usually came to Rasta's before heading to his fave S&M dives.

Thank you, Facebook.

Verlaine's phone appeared again and he punched in a passcode. A private photo album opened. And he leaned forward to show off his prize shots.

Amelia struggled not to show her disgust. She heard Lily inhale fast, but the senior detective turned the sound into a whisper of admiration. Verlaine missed her dismay.

The first image was of a naked woman, wearing only a necklace, blindfolded, with her hands taped or tied behind her. She was kneeling on a slab of concrete. Interesting, Amelia thought, and caught Lily's eye. Concrete, just like the victims.

The woman in the picture had been crying—her makeup had run to her chin—and her breasts were streaked with ugly welts.

Verlaine, obviously aroused, eagerly scrolled through more images, which Amelia found increasingly hard to look at. It took all her willpower to appear aroused by the images of cruelty.

He gave a running narrative of the "partners." Amelia only heard the word "victims."

Ten minutes.

Fifteen.

At that point Verlaine said, "Excuse me, ladies. I need to run to the little boy's room. Behave while I'm away. Or not!" He laughed. "Back in a sec."

"Wait," Lily said.

Verlaine turned.

"Always wondered something."

He lifted an eyebrow.

"What's the plural of sec?"

"That son of a bitch," Lily said. She wasn't smiling.

"God, that was awful," Amelia added. "What do you think?" She was nodding back toward the toilets where Jim Bob might be emptying his bladder but was sure to be filling his nostrils.

"Sleazy, scummy, I want to take a shower in hand sanitizer."

"Agreed. But is he a killer?"

"Those pictures," Lily whispered. "I've worked sex crimes but that's about the worst I've seen. From some of those wounds, I guarantee he put one or two of them in the hospital." She considered the question. "Yeah, I could see him taking it a step further and killing somebody. You?"

"I think so."

Lily continued, "I *hope* so. Man, I really do. I don't want the crew from Narcotics Four to be behind this."

Amelia didn't much care for the detectives running the elite unit—Martin Glover, Danny Vincenzo, and Candy Preston all had egos like runaway stallions—but no cop wants to think that colleagues are torturing and killing wits just to up their conviction rate, however noble their cause.

Amelia looked over her friend. "So. You and Lucas, you had a thing, right?"

"A while ago, yeah. In Minnesota and when he came here. Really clicked between us. Still does. But not that way. We've moved on. And you and Lincoln seem like a good fit."

"Just like you were saying. It clicks. Can't explain it, don't think about it."

"Lucas has some problems with him. You know, being in the chair."

"Happens some." Amelia laughed. "Of course, Lincoln rides people hard and then they get fed up and go, 'You're such an asshole.' Or, 'Fuck you.' They forget he's a quad. That breaks the ice and it's all good."

"With Lucas, I think it's something more. He won't talk about it." Lily lowered her voice. "For me, I have to say, when Lucas and I met, it was, a lot of it was physical. I need that. You and Lincoln?"

"Oh, yeah. Believe it or not, it's good. Different obviously. But good . . . Ah, here comes our lord and master."

Wiping his nose with his fingers, Verlaine was oozing his way through the crowd. Amelia was sure he turned sideways intentionally to rub against an ass or two.

One of his "accidental" victims—a petite redhead in a leather skirt and black blouse—turned fast and, eyes dark angry disks, shouted words they couldn't hear. Fast as a gun hammer falling on a primer, he wheeled and shoved his face into hers.

"Christ," Amelia muttered, reaching toward her purse, where a baby Glock rested. "He's going to hurt her."

"Wait. We move in, that fucks up the whole op."

They watched closely. A cold smile blossomed on Verlaine's face as the woman looked at him warily. She was attractive and her figure was perfect, though it was clear she'd had acne in her youth or some illness that left scarring.

In the space of a few seconds, as he spoke to her, still smiling coolly, her expression morphed from confused to shocked to devastated; Amelia knew he was commenting on her complexion. He kept leaning forward, taunting, taunting, until she picked up her purse and fled into the bathroom, sobbing.

Amelia said to Lily, "His expression. What's it look like to you?"

"Like he just fucked somebody and wants a cigarette."

Verlaine eased through the crowd back to the bar.

"Hey, there, ladies. Miss me?"

•—◆—•

The thing about burglary was, the careful burglar was rarely disturbed by the homeowner. It was always some snoopy neighbor who did him in.

Lucas sat on a darkened stoop across the street from Verlaine's building, just watching and listening. The neighborhood was a tough one, not far from the East River, and not yet gentrifying; the buildings might be a little too rotten, a little too undistinguished, a little too far upriver. Verlaine's building was a bit of a puzzle—only two stories tall, but wide and deep. Too large for a single inhabitant, Lucas thought. It had a shallow entrance above a wide one-step stoop, with bricked-up spaces on the bottom floor that were once windows. The place could have been a hardware store at one time, with walk-up apartments above it; in another neighborhood, farther downtown, it would have become a nightclub, or a restaurant. Here, it was just a derelict building, without a single light showing, either through the barred windows on the main door, or from the windows on the second floor. Was there somebody else in there? Verlaine himself, Lucas knew, was at a Midtown bar.

Nothing moving. And still Lucas waited.

He'd had a little heart-to-heart with Lincoln. When the women were gone, Lincoln said, "If you go to the black cabinet by the window, in the bottom section, the left side, there's a drawer."

Lucas went to the cabinet, opened a lower-level door, pulled out the drawer, and found an electric lock rake.

He took it out and pulled the trigger. Dead.

"An artifact from my former life. It'll still work, but you'll have to put some double-A batteries in it."

"You want me to crack Verlaine's apartment?"

"Lily said you occasionally used unconventional tactics."

Lucas said, "I'll take a look at it. Even if this thing works, there could be other problems. Might be other people around, locks have gotten better."

"So then you don't go in," Lincoln said. "I just feel it would be useful if somebody could take a preliminary look. Can't use it as evidence, of course."

Lucas nodded. "Yeah. Once you *know*, everything else gets easier."

Then he said, "Look, I know I pissed you off because I was having trouble dealing with your disability."

"You did. Piss me off," Lincoln said.

"Yeah, well," Lucas scratched his neck. "It doesn't have anything to do with you. It's purely out of fear. This scar"—he touched his neck again—"a little girl shot me in the throat with a .22. Went through a coat collar, through my windpipe, got to my spine, but not into it. The kid should have killed me—she would have, but there was a doc right there, and she did a tracheotomy, and kept me breathing until we got to the hospital. But if the kid had had any other kind of gun, or if the slug hadn't gone through the collar first, she would have either blown my spine out, and I would have been dead on the spot, or I would have been like you. It was a matter of a quarter inch or so, or any other caliber. I look at you and I see me."

"Interesting," Lincoln said.

"After the accident, did you think about suicide?"

"Yes. Quite considerably," Lincoln said. "Sometimes, I'm not sure I made the right choice, staying alive. But my curiosity keeps me going; I always seem to have work." He smiled. "God bless all the little criminals."

"And then there's Amelia," Lucas said.

"Yes. Then there's Amelia."

"You're a lucky man, Lincoln," Lucas said.

Lincoln laughed and said, "It's been a while since anyone told me that."

After an hour on the stoop, Lucas decided that he'd either have to make a move on the building, or go away. He stood up, dusted off the seat of his jeans, and saw a man walking along the sidewalk toward him, alone. The man spit in the gutter and came on. When he got to Lucas, he stopped and said, "You got an extra twenty?"

"No."

"I'm not really asking," the man said.

"Take a close look at me," Lucas said.

The man took a closer look, then said, "Fuck you," and went on down the street. He looked back once, then turned the corner and was gone. Lucas waited another few minutes, to see if the man came back, then crossed the street and, using his cell phone as a flashlight, looked at the lock. An old one—a good one, when it was made, but now old. With a last look around, Lucas took the rake out of his pocket, slipped the pick-arm into the lock. The rake chattered for a moment, as Lucas kept the turning pressure on, and then the lock went.

He stepped inside, closed the door, and called, "Anybody home?"

He listened, got no response, except a scrabbling sound in the ceiling—a rat.

"Hey, anybody? Anybody here?"

Nobody answered. He took a flashlight from his pocket, turned it on. He was in a wide hallway, with steps going up to his right, and with a double door to the left. The hallway smelled of burned metal, as though somebody had been working with a welding torch. He was in the right place.

He tried the double door and found it open, with a bank of light switches on the wall to the left. He closed the door behind him and turned on the lights. He was in a wide-open studio with several two-foot-tall bronze sculptures sitting on heavy wooden tables, with a variety of metalworking tools—files, electric grinders, polishers, hand scribes. The air inside smelled of burned metal and polishing compound.

The sculptures were all on sadomasochistic themes: nude women being whipped, bound, beaten. Just what you need to add that extra spark to your living room, Lucas thought.

At the far edge of the studio was a low, wooden wall, perhaps ten feet high, which was two or three feet short of the ceiling. Behind it, Lucas found a queen-sized bed, a chest of drawers, a large closet stuffed with clothing, a bathroom, a second closet with an apartment-sized washer and dryer stacked one on top of the other, a kitchenette, and a small breakfast table with two chairs. A television was mounted on a swing arm at the foot of the bed. He poked through the living area for a moment, found nothing of particular interest, and continued his tour of the studio. And found, at the back, an internal door, sheathed in metal, that was set in a frame a step below the rest of the floor—a door that most likely led to a basement, Lucas thought. He looked at the lock, and realized that the rake wouldn't work: the thing was probably a year old, a Medeco.

After the quick tour of the lower floor, he turned out the lights, stepped back in the hallway, and used the flashlight to climb the stairs to the second floor. The second floor was a trash heap: a line of single rooms that had apparently last been used as a flophouse, each with a wrecked cot or a stained mattress, various pieces of mostly broken furniture. More rats: he never saw one, but he could hear them.

Nothing for him there.

He went back down to the studio, closed the door, turned the lights on, went to look at the cellar door again. No way to open it: it was impossible. He pounded on it a few times and listened, heard nothing. What they really needed, he thought, was behind that door, and he had no way to get there.

He'd been inside for five or six minutes, and time was wearing on him.

He took a plastic bag out of his pocket, and from the bag, several more Ziploc-style bags, each with a white spongelike pad in it. Lincoln's instructions had been simple enough: press the pad into anything you'd like to pick up, then put the pad back in the plastic bag, and seal it. Lucas worked his way through the studio, doing just that: sampling bronze filings from the floor, off a workbench, and out of the teeth of a metal file. Moving to the welding area, he found a selection of welding rods, and stuck one of each kind in his pocket, and, from a trash bin, several used rods.

He sampled several stains that might possibly have been blood, but there were enough stains around the place, oil and lubricants, that he had his doubts. He was taking a sample when he saw, in a small niche off the main working space, a half dozen crucifixes on neck chains, along with a necklace of cheap aqua-colored stones, a thin string of seed pearls, a ring on a chain, and three sets of earrings, all pinned to the wall with tacks. And he thought, *Trophies?* If they were, there were twelve of them. There was nothing else like them in the room: he took a half dozen photos with his cell phone.

Time to leave. On his way out, he looked at each of the bronze sculptures, and a clay maquette for another, and noticed that each of the women portrayed in the sculptures was wearing a single piece of jewelry of some kind, apparently to emphasize her nakedness. Was it possible that the jewelry collection did not represent trophies, but was for use with models?

He was thinking about that when Lily called. "He's moving."

"And I'm gone," Lucas said. And he thought, *Not for models. They were trophies, and there were twelve of them.*

"You believe it?" Lucas Davenport said, walking into the town house. He held up the plastic bags. "This shit fell out the window when I was walking by Verlaine's apartment."

Lincoln spun the motorized wheelchair around, noting eagerly—almost hungrily—the evidence in the Minnesotan's hand.

"Sometimes you catch a break. Anything obvious?"

"No piles of bones or bloody shackles. There's a steel door leads somewhere—the cellar, I think. Love to see what's behind that." He explained that the lock rake wasn't up to the task, though. They'd need a warrant and a sledgehammer.

Lincoln turned his attention to the evidence.

Lucas dropped down into one of the wicker chairs near one of the large high-definition monitors that glowed like a billboard in Times Square.

"Lucas?" Thom Reston, Lincoln's aide, stood in the doorway. He was a slim, young man, dressed in a lavender shirt, dark tie, and beige slacks. "Tempt you? Beer? Anything else?"

"Later, thanks."

Lincoln said, "Whiskey for me."

"You've had two already," Thom countered.

"I'm so pleased at your sterling memory. Could I have a whiskey? Please and thank you?"

"No."

"Get me—" But he was speaking to an empty doorway. He grimaced. "All right. Let's get to work. Mel, what's in the haul?"

Mel Cooper looked like a geek, which he probably was since he was the Mr. Wizard of forensic science on the East Coast, if not the country. The man was pale and trim and had thin hair and Harry Potter glasses that invariably slid down his nose.

Pulling on gloves, a surgeon's cap, and a disposable jacket, Cooper took the bag and set the contents out on an examination pad—large sheets of sterile newsprint.

"Good job," he mused, looking at the carefully sealed bags. "You worked crime scene before?"

"Naw," Lucas said. "But I lost a rape-murder conviction once 'cause some rookie tripped and dropped the perp's shoe into Medicine Lake. It was the only evidence we had that would've nailed the prick and I had a very uncircumstantial-minded jury. The prick walked."

"That hurts," Lincoln said.

"Course, he went after another vic a month later. He didn't pick well. She kept a five-five Redhawk under her mattress. Just a three fifty-seven, not a forty-four. But it did the trick."

"Was there anything left of the guy?"

"Not much above the neck. Justice got done, but it would've been a whole lot cleaner if the CS kid had held on to the evidence. Taught me to treat it like gold."

First, Cooper and Lincoln did a visual of the splinters and curlicues of bronze and other metals.

Using an optical microscope on low power, Lincoln compared them with the scraps found in the backs of the women victims. He was looking at the shape of the scraps, along with the indentations from the tools that had trimmed them off a large piece of metal—presumably one of the sculptures. "Tool marks look real close to me," Lincoln said.

Lucas walked over to the high-def monitor plugged into the microscope via an HDMI cable. "Yeah, I agree."

They next had to compare the chemical composition of the metal from the crime scenes with that of the scraps Lucas had found at the studio. Cooper went to work analyzing each one, using the glow discharge spectrometer, the gas chromatograph, and the scanning electron microscope.

"While we're waiting," Lucas said, pointing to a bag. "Possible blood stains. From the floor near his bedroom."

Cooper tested with luminol and alternative light sources.

"Yep, we've got blood."

A reagent test confirmed it was human, and the tech typed it. The sample, however, didn't match the types of the women victims from the earlier scenes.

They tested concrete samples that Lucas had collected, too, and compared them with the concrete particles found in the women's backs. "Close," Cooper assessed. "No cigar."

"Hell." Lincoln then glanced at the doorway; he'd heard the nearly undetectable sound of the key in the lock. A moment later the female detectives walked into the parlor.

"How'd it go?" Lily asked Lucas.

He shrugged. "Some evidence fell off the truck." He nodded to the equipment, merrily analyzing away. He glanced at Amelia's outfit. "Damn, you need to go undercover more often."

Lily hit him on the arm. "Behave."

Lucas then asked the women, "What was Verlaine like?"

"Dangerous," Amelia said.

Lily filled in, "He looks at you like you're naked and he can't decide what to lick first."

"And then what to whip."

"So the S&M hunch paid off?"

"Big-time. He's the *S* all the way. Wants to be the hurter, not the hurtee."

Lily explained about his personal Pinterest album. "Jesus, took all my willpower not to kick him in the balls. You should've seen what he did to some of those women."

"He pressure you two lovely ladies to go home with him?" Lucas asked.

"Sure, but we had to postpone our threesome. Somehow his glass kept getting refilled. He was in no shape to tie anybody up after that much bourbon. I was tempted to let the asshole stagger home and hope some mugger beat the crap out of him. But Amelia was the mature one and we got him into a cab."

Sachs glanced at the plastic bags. "What does the evidence say?"

"Just getting it now," Lincoln told her, and grumbled, "Right, Mel? It seems to be taking forever."

Mel Cooper, hunched over a computer monitor, didn't respond. He shoved his glasses higher on his nose and said, "Interesting."

"That's not a useful term, Mel," Lincoln snapped.

"I'm getting there. Lucas collected five different kinds of bronze from Verlaine's. One is typical modern formula: eighty-eight percent copper and twelve percent tin. Then alpha bronze, with about four to five percent tin.

"Some other samples have a higher concentration of copper and zinc and some lead—that's architectural bronze. Others are bismuth bronze—an alloy that's got a lot of nickel, and traces of bismuth. One sample surprised me—it had a Vickers hardness value of two hundred."

"That's the bronze used in swords," Lucas said.

They all looked at him. "For the role-playing games I write. Helps to know about old-time weapons. Roman officers had bronze swords; foot soldiers had iron."

Amelia asked, "You think he uses bronze as a weapon?"

Lucas shook his head. "No, I think what it means is that he gets his materials wherever he can find them. Probably from dozens of junkyards and construction sites."

"I agree," Lincoln said.

Cooper added, "And there's triethanolamine, fluoroboric acid, and cadmium fluoroborate."

"That's flux—used in brazing and soldering," Lincoln said absently.

"Okay, the big question: any associations, Mel?" Lucas asked.

In crime scene work, very few samples of evidence actually "matched," meaning they were literally the same. DNA and fingerprints established true identity but little else did. However, samples of evidence from two scenes could be "associated," meaning they were similar. If close enough, the jury could deduce that they came from the same source. Here, the team had to show that the shavings found in the first victims' bodies could be closely associated with those Lucas had collected from Verlaine's studio.

Cooper finally pushed back from the screen. He didn't seem happy. "Like the concrete, the flux and welding rods are close to the trace from the earlier crime scenes."

Lincoln's face tightened into a frown. "But those are used by *anyone* brazing, welding, or working with bronze. I want to establish identity with the bronze scraps themselves."

"Understood. But that's more of a problem." He explained that

175

four of the bronze samples at the first crime scene were completely different from any of the metal collected by Lucas. One sample Lucas had collected that night had the same composition as several fragments in the first scenes. The others were similar but had "some compositional differences."

"*How* similar?" Lincoln snapped.

"I'd feel comfortable testifying that it was *possible* the scraps embedded in the victims came from Verlaine's loft. But I couldn't do better than that."

The evidence *suggested* but didn't prove that Verlaine was the killer.

"Same with his behavioral profile and his history of sex offenses," Lily added. "The S&M. It's *likely* he's antisocial enough to kill. But that ain't enough to swing the jury."

That irritating little "beyond a reasonable doubt" requirement.

Lucas told the women about the mysterious door to the basement. "I'm betting there's something incriminating down there, but without a warrant, we're not getting in."

Cooper now put the pictures of the necklaces up on the high-def TV. "Trophies, I'm betting," Lucas said.

"Crosses mostly," Lincoln observed. "Hell, that means there are seven or eight more victims out there. Nobody's found the bodies yet."

"Or," Lucas said, "that those are for vics he's got coming up?"

Lily said angrily, "We've gotta stop this fucker. I mean now!"

"Trophies, *some* evidence, a behavioral profile that's in the ball-park," Amelia summarized. "He's gotta be the one, even if we can't make a case just yet. But the good news is if he's the one, nobody from the department is involved. Verlaine's just some lone psycho."

"Wouldn't be too sure about that," Lucas said. "There's another possibility."

Lincoln understood. "Could be that Narcotics Four has been *using* Verlaine to torture and kill the women to get leads they could use."

"Exactly."

Amelia scowled. "Sure. Verlaine's been a bad boy. Maybe somebody from the drug detail's been extorting him to get information from the women. That way the cops'll keep their hands clean."

Lily sighed. "I'll take the hit on this one."

They looked at her.

"We've got to tell Markowitz the news: A, we don't have enough evidence to collar our favorite suspect. And B, his world-famous drug detail isn't in the clear, either." She looked over her teammates. "Unless, of course, somebody else'd rather have that little chat."

They all smiled her way.

•◆•

"We've caught another one, Sir. Woman, twenties."

It was eight thirty the next morning and COD Stan Markowitz was sipping his first coffee of the day, in one of the old-time containers, blue with Greek athletes on it. But hearing this news he lost all taste for java. And for the bagel sitting in front of him, too.

It took a fuck of a lot for him to sour on walnut cream cheese.

The chief of detectives snapped, "In *her* twenties? Or in *the* twenties?"

The young detective, a skinny Italian American, said, "She was twenty-nine. Latina. Found the body in a vacant lot in NoHo." He was standing in the doorway, not in or out, as if Markowitz might decide to fling a stapler at him. It'd happened before.

"I don't like the name NoHo. It's not a real place. I can live with SoHo but even TriBeCa's pushing it."

The kid didn't respond but there was really nothing to respond to.

"Crime Scene's on it now," he said.

Markowitz stroked his round belly through the striped white shirt the wife had laid out for him that morning. He wadded up the oozing bagel and pitched it emphatically into the wastebasket. It landed with a surprisingly loud thud; this was the first entry of the morning.

"TOD?"

"Examiner's saying about midnight," the detective said. "No specific leads yet. No wits. Same as the others: she was a user, crack and smack. Found in a lot known for drug activity."

"He's a psycho, that's what he is. It has nothing to do with the drugs. Don't get that rumor started."

"Sure. Only—"

"Only what?"

A hesitation at this. "All right."

Markowitz glanced down at a file on his desk.

RED HOOK OPERATION. CLASSIFIED.

The NYPD had top-secret files, too. Langley has nothing on us, he thought.

"That's all," Markowitz said. "I want the crime scene report before the ink's dry. Got it?"

"Sure." The young detective remained standing.

With a glare, the COD sent him scurrying.

His landline had started ringing. Six buttons, lighting up like Christmas trees.

One reporter, two reporters, three reporters, four.

He glanced at the empty doorway and sent a text, then hit the intercom switch.

"Yes, sir?"

"Hold all calls."

"Yes, sir, except the—"

"I said hold—"

"The commissioner's on two."

Naturally.

"Stan. There's *another* one?" The man didn't have a brogue, but Markowitz often imagined that Commissioner of Police Patrick O'Brien sounded like he just came off the boat from the old country.

"Afraid so, Pat."

"This is a nightmare. I'm getting calls from Gracie Mansion. I'm getting calls from Albany." His voice lowered and delivered the most devastating news. "I'm getting calls from the *Daily News* and the *Times*. The *Huffington Post,* for heaven's sake."

One reporter, two reporters.

The commissioner continued, "The vics are *minorities*, Stan. The killings are bad for everyone."

Especially them, Markowitz thought.

Then finally the commish wasn't wailing anymore, but asking a question. "What do you have, Stan?" A grave tone in his voice, then: "It's pretty important that you have something. You hear me, Stan? I mean, really important."

You have something.

Not we. Not the department. Not the city.

Markowitz said quickly, "We've got a suspect."

"Why didn't anybody tell me?" But his voice was balmed with relief.

"It happened fast."

"You've got him in custody?"

"No, but he's more than a person of interest."

The pause said that wasn't what the commissioner wanted to hear. "Is he the perp or not?"

"Has to be. Just a few loose ends on the case before we can collar him."

"Who is he?"

"Sculptor. Lives downtown. And the evidence is solid."

"Listen, Stan," the commissioner said, back to whining, "there is way too much flak hitting the fan." Patrick O'Brien would rather butcher a figure of speech than utter an expletive. "Make it work."

"Uhm, what, Pat?"

"Wouldn't the citizens of New York love to read that we have a suspect?"

"Well, Pat, we *do* have a suspect. Just not enough for a warrant. Or an announcement in the press."

"You said the evidence was solid. I heard you say that. The citizens of the city'd feel so much better knowing that we're on top of it. It'd be great if they could read that by the time the *Times* online got updated in the next cycle."

Which was about every half hour.

"And I'd feel better too, Stan."

Despite the COD's dozen-year track record, the commissioner could drop him to a low-level spot in public affairs in the time it took to microwave a Stouffer's lasagna. "All right, Pat."

After organizing his thoughts, Markowitz picked up his cell phone. Hit a number.

"Rothenburg."

"I just heard, Detective. Another one."

"That's right, Stan. We're at the scene. Amelia's running it now. The vic was tortured first, just like the other ones."

"I wanted to let you know you're going to hear in the press that we have a suspect."

After a dense pause, Lily said, "Who?"

"Well, the sculptor, Verlaine."

"He's *our* suspect, Stan. He's not the press's suspect. There's a big difference. Verlaine's not for public consumption at this point."

"What does your gut tell you, Lily?"

"He's an asshole, he's a sadist. And he's the doer."

"What's the percentage?"

"Percentage? Christ, I don't know. How does ninety-six and three-tenths percent sound?"

The COD let the irrelevance pass.

"It's going to put people at ease, Lily."

Silence, presumably as she tried to process why they needed to put people at ease. "That's not in my job description, Stan. My job is catching assholes and putting them in jail."

He looked up. He noted a woman in a suit, standing in his outer office, waiting. She was the one he'd texted fifteen minutes ago.

Markowitz said, "And I've looked into your other theory."

"What's that?" she asked, an edge to her voice.

"What you told me last night. That somebody, maybe from Narcotics Four or someplace else in the department, was using Verlaine to kill the women. Don't waste time pursuing that."

"Why not?"

Now his voice was hard as a metal file. "Because, Detective, I was profiling perps when you were getting your knuckles rapped for mouthing off in class. Verlaine's a single operator. His psych profile is as obvious as the front page of the *Post*. Now make the case against him. STAT."

"What part are you missing, Stan? If you announce, he burns his fucking apartment down, there's no evidence left, and the case goes to shit. He gets off . . . and goes on to kill somebody else."

The thing about nut cutters is they sometimes cut any nuts in their path, not just the ones you want them to.

"Detective," he snapped. "You're going to hear on the news in a half hour that we have a suspect in the serial killing of those women. If that means you've gotta get your ass in gear and work faster and harder—then do it!"

Click.

He looked into the outer office and nodded. The stocky woman was in her forties, blond, and with a dry complexion and eyes that suggested she'd never laughed in her life. Her clothes were dowdy.

She looked around to make sure they were alone. Markowitz nodded at the door. Detective Candy Preston swung it shut.

He whispered, "We've got some problems."

"I heard." The woman was a nut cutter, too. But she had the most melodious voice. He could hear her reading stories to children.

"I need you to move forward with what we talked about."

"Now? I thought we were taking things slow."

"We don't have the luxury of taking things slow." The chief of detectives unlocked the bottom drawer of his desk and handed her an envelope. It was thick but not as thick as you'd think. Fifty thousand dollars, in hundreds, really doesn't take up a lot of space.

"I'll do it now," said Preston. She was one of the senior members of the Narcotics Unit Four detail. She slipped the money into her purse and rose, walked to the door. Her feet, he noticed, were as delicate as her voice.

Just before she touched the knob, Markowitz said, "Oh, some advice, Detective?"

She frowned at the implication that she was green. Stiffly she said, "I've handled things like this in the past, Stan. I know—"

"That's not my advice. My advice is don't fuck up."

• ◆ •

Amelia was switching back and forth between WABC and WNBC and said, before anyone else did, "We're screwed."

"Maybe," Lucas said. He turned to Lincoln: "I understand from my BCA people that fires mess up DNA?"

"That's right," Lincoln said. "Theoretically, if he dumped a few gallons of gas down that basement—if the basement is the kill room—he could wipe out the most critical evidence. We wouldn't get DNA unless we found an actual body."

Lucas said to Lily, "You know what I think. If those are trophies hanging on his wall—"

"They are," Lincoln said.

"Then we're dealing with a lot more than four dead. Even if we don't have what we need for a search warrant, we need to go in there anyway."

Lily shook her head. "We need a warrant."

Lucas turned to Lincoln. "Help me out here."

Lincoln said, "We took samples from the poured concrete steps outside the building, for which we didn't need a search warrant, and we found that the concrete matched the flecks of concrete in the victims' backs. We also found flecks of bronze which are chemically identical to the bronze found in the victims' backs."

"But—" Amelia said.

Lincoln raised his hand. "Quiet."

"That's certainly enough for a warrant," Lily said. "At least, if I go to the right judge, and I will. If you'll write out the specs for the application, I can have it in an hour."

"I'll do that," Lincoln said. And to Lucas: "If you'll go back to the building with a couple of collection pads, get those samples for me. Backdate them to this morning. There may not be any bronze, but we've got a fair collection of it now. Take a few flecks with you. You know. Just in case."

They all looked round at each other, then Lucas said, "At least a dozen trophies."

"After you make the collection, just wait there," Lily said. "I won't be long behind you."

"I'll go with Lucas," Amelia said. "If we need to block the back of the building, or he needs backup while we're there."

"You might want to bring an entry team," Lucas said to Lily.

"Entry team? I'm bringing everybody. I'll make a courtesy call to the FBI, they'll want to have an observer."

"I'll be there," Lincoln said. "I don't want your entry team trashing my evidence."

They took Amelia's car, a maroon 1970 Ford Torino Cobra, heir to the Fairlane, kicking out nifty 405 horsepower, with 447 pounds of torque. They made the twenty-minute trip in twelve minutes. Eight minutes out, she looked at Lucas and said, "You're not holding on to anything."

"You know what you're doing," he said. "You're almost as good as I am."

She snorted: "What do you drive?"

"A 911."

"I always heard"—she paused in her comment to chop the nose off a town car as she took a left turn—"that 911 drivers—"

"Have small penises. I know. Every time I meet somebody who can't afford a 911, I get the 'small penis' line. So I ask them how large a sample they've looked at."

She grinned as she said, "I'll tell you what, though: in a fair run, I'd eat your 911 alive."

"I don't like the word 'fair,'" Lucas replied. "'Fair' always means, 'to my advantage.' If it's not to my advantage, it's 'unfair.' If you guys ever get to Minneapolis, bring your car. I've got a run just across the border, in Wisconsin. Narrow blacktop, blind hills, twenty miles long, maybe two hundred braking curves."

"That's not fair," she said, but she grinned again, and threw the Cobra down an alley, the walls whipping by, two feet away on each side, six inches from Lucas's window when she dodged a trash can. Lucas yawned and said, "Wake me up when we get there."

He tilted back in his seat and then said, "By the way, I'm one of the best action shooters around."

Amelia dropped off Lucas, who was dressed in jeans, a polo shirt, and running shoes, at Verlaine's apartment. He was carrying a backpack loaned to him by Amelia. There were four men on the long block, two on each side, each one by himself.

Amelia was headed around the block, where she could watch the back of the building. Lucas sat on Verlaine's stoop; he was too well fed to be a street person, but from a distance, with the pack by his feet, he could pass. They'd put a few bronze flakes in the bags with the sampling pads before they left, and now he took them out, one at a time, trying to look like he was shaking cigarettes out of a pack, and pressed them into the stoop. When he had five samples in place, he put them in the pack and zipped it up.

That done, he stood and ambled up the block, took out his cell phone, and called Lily, Lincoln, and Amelia, and said the same thing to all of them: "We're good to go."

Lily said, "Forty minutes."

"What's taking so long?"

"Nothing. You just got there quicker than you should have. I've got the application, I'm seeing the judge in about two minutes, and the entry team is gearing up. So, easy, boy."

Lucas continued up the block, and on to the next block, and then walked back, and finally, with nothing at all going on at

Verlaine's building, he turned the corner and walked around the block, where he found Amelia's car, parked, with Lincoln's Chrysler van right behind it. Amelia climbed out of the passenger's side: "Want to leave the pack?"

"Yeah." He looked at his watch. "Half an hour, yet. I'll find another place to sit."

"Stay in touch," Lincoln said, from the back.

Lincoln's aide, Thom, who was driving, said, "I brought some sandwiches along. These two can spend hours at a crime scene. If you want a ham-and-cheese—"

"I not only want one, it'll give me something to do while I'm watching," Lucas said. "Some reason to be sitting there."

Lucas ambled back around the block, carrying his brown-paper sandwich bag, and found a stoop fifty yards down the block from the entrance to Verlaine's studio. He sat down, took Thom's ham-and-cheese out of the sack, took a bite, and said, aloud, "That's a great ham-and-cheese."

He was thinking about the fact that you almost couldn't buy a great ham-and-cheese in the Twin Cities, and why that might be, but that you could get a great one in Des Moines or Chicago, and then thought about Chicago being the "hog butcher to the world," when a man stuck his head out of the door behind him and said, "This look like a fuckin' cafeteria? Hit the road, asshole."

Lucas chewed and swallowed, then shook his cell phone out of his pocket and dialed Lily, ostentatiously pushed the speakerphone button, and, when she answered, said, "I'm being hassled by a guy across the street from the target, at 219—how long would it take to get, say, a half dozen building inspectors here? The place doesn't look so sturdy."

"I could have them there in an hour," Lily said.

Lucas looked at the guy in the doorway. "An hour good for you?"

"Stay as long as you want," the guy said, and eased the door shut.

Five minutes after that, a white van drove by Verlaine's building, and the guy in the passenger's seat took a close look at Lucas, and then nodded to him. Lucas nodded back. The van reappeared another five minutes later, going in the opposite direction, and this time the driver nodded to him.

Ten minutes after that, Amelia called: "We got the blocking squad here. Lincoln and I are coming around."

And Lily: "One minute."

The entry team arrived in two white, unmarked vans, closely followed by Lily in an unmarked car, another unmarked car, Amelia's car, and two patrol cars. Behind them all, Lincoln's van turned the corner. Lucas jogged down the street toward them as the vans stopped directly in front of Verlaine's stoop and two guys carrying an entry ram hustled up to the door; four cops in armor were right behind them, and as Lucas came up, the ram handlers smashed the door open, and the armored cops went in.

Lucas was right there with Lily, and as they piled into the entryway, the team suddenly stopped, there was some milling, and the team leader called, "We got a body."

Lily and Lucas shouldered their way from behind through the crowd, with Amelia a step behind, and they turned the corner at the door that went into the studio.

Verlaine was there, staring sightlessly at one of his sculptures. His head was a bloody mess, and a semiauto pistol lay on the floor by his fingertips.

"Got some brass," Amelia said; she sounded like a professor of murder, her voice cool and analytical. Lucas saw the shell sitting by Verlaine's foot. Then Amelia turned to the entry-team leader and said, "We've got to clear the building. But just two guys on this floor, and stay out on the perimeter, away from the kill site."

The team leader nodded, and started calling names.

Lincoln pushed through the crowd in his chair, saw the body. Lily said to him, "This could solve a lot of problems."

"Yes, it could," he said. "But the statistics say that it probably won't."

"What do you mean?"

"Serial killers don't often commit suicide. They like the attention they get from us. The spree killers, who are going through a psychotic break. They'll kill themselves almost every time, if you give them a chance. It's either a problem or an opportunity," Lincoln said.

"Opportunity?"

"If he didn't kill himself, it's a problem," Lincoln said. "If he did, I might get a nice paper out of it."

•◆•

"How bad is it, Sachs?"

Looking over Verlaine's apartment, she said, "Seen worse." She was speaking to Lincoln, who was outside on the street in front of the place. They were connected via a headset and stalk mic.

Her judgment had nothing to do with the unpleasant detritus of gore and bits of bone littering the sculptor's floor near the body (in fact, head wounds produce minimal blood flow). What she meant was that the place was relatively uncontaminated. If scenes were left virgin after the crime, forensic teams would have a much easier time processing the evidence. But that rarely happened. Bystanders, souvenir hunters, looters, grieving family members would pollute the scene with trace evidence, smear fingerprints, and walk off with everything from telltale epidermal cells to the murder weapon itself. And some of the worst offenders were the first-responders. Understandably, of course; saving lives and clearing a scene of the bad guys take priority. But leads have been destroyed and suspects found not guilty because otherwise solid evidence was destroyed by tactical teams and EMTs.

Here, though, once it looked like Verlaine had offed himself, the entry team backed out and let Lily and Amelia, armed with their Glocks, clear the place. They were careful not to disturb anything.

Then Lily backed away and let the expert do her thing. Now in her crime scene unit overalls, booties, and hood, Amelia was walking carefully through the fifty-by-fifty open space.

"It's like a junkyard, Rhyme."

Workbenches were littered with tools and slabs of metal and stone and instruments, welding masks, gloves, and leather jackets so thick they seemed bulletproof. The floor was equally cluttered. Rough-hewn wooden boxes holding ingots of metal. Pallets loaded with stone and more scrap. Gas tanks filled one wall. Hand trucks and jacks. Electric saws and drill presses. Overhead, a series of rails and tracks ran throughout the space at ceiling height, about fifteen feet up. These held electric pulleys and winches for transporting loads of metal and the finished sculptures throughout the space. Rusty chains and hooks dangled.

How homey, Amelia thought.

And everywhere: Verlaine's sculptures, made of metal sheets and bars and rods, welded or soldered or bolted together. Bronze mostly, but some iron and steel and copper. It was as if he couldn't bear to have a space in his studio not presided over by one of his ladies.

And ladies in extremis.

Though the works were impressionistic, there was no doubt what each one depicted, a woman in pain, just as horrific as Lucas Davenport had described. Bent over backward, on all fours, tied down on their backs, crying in agony, pleading. Some were pierced by lengths of rebar reinforcing rods.

She forced herself to look past the disturbing sculptures and get to work. Just because Verlaine apparently killed himself, Amelia didn't search any less carefully. After all, suicide is technically a homicide. That the perp and the vic are the same simply means the investigators don't have to hump as hard as in murder. But they still have to hump.

And in this case, of course, there was a lot at stake, even after Verlaine's death. She was well aware that the sculptor might've kidnapped and stashed another victim somewhere else, chained underground, with only a few days to live before she died of thirst or bled out—if he'd been having some of his sick fun with her.

Amelia searched the hell out of the scene.

First, she processed the body, photographing and filming, then clearing and bagging the Glock he'd used, collecting the one spent nine-millimeter shell, swabbing his hands for gunshot residue and wrapping them in plastic bags as well.

She bagged his Dell laptop, along with the phone and iPad, noting that there'd been no hard copy or e-version suicide notes. She'd just run a case where a man's farewell before leaping off the Fifty-ninth Street Bridge had been tweeted.

Amelia searched the way she always did, walking the grid. This involved pacing step by step in a straight line from one end of the scene to the other and then turning around, moving slightly to the side, and returning. And then, when she was done with that, she covered the same ground again, perpendicular to the first search.

For an hour she walked the grid, taking samples of trace. She collected the necklaces and crosses in the alcove. Seeing them up close, Amelia realized that several of them looked familiar—and finally she knew why. In the pictures Verlaine had shown to her and Lily in the bar, the women he was playing his S&M games with had all been wearing necklaces like these. Yes, Lucas was right, they were trophies. Trophies not of the murder victims, but of his sexual conquests.

Then she turned to the steel door Lucas had told them about, the one leading to the basement. It had been unlocked when the team entered and she and Lily had cleared it fast. Now she searched it from the point of view of a forensic cop. The small underground chamber was brick-lined and had a raw concrete floor. The smells were of heating oil, mold, standing water, and sweat. Maybe that last scent was her imagination but she thought not.

She looked at the hooks protruding from the walls, the stains on the floor. Amelia walked down a set of rickety stairs into the thoroughly creepy place. She ran a fast fluorescein test on several of the dark patches; the results confirmed her initial hypothesis of blood. And there was no doubt about the bits of dark, elastic curls she popped into evidence bags. She knew dried flesh when she saw it.

Her gloved finger hit TRANSMIT and a moment later she heard Lincoln's impatient voice. "Sachs. Where the hell are you?"

"On the other side of the steel door. In Verlaine's basement."

"And?"

"It's almost a home run."

"That's like being nearly pregnant. But I'll forgive the sloppy metaphor just this once. Get the evidence back ASAP."

He disconnected without a good-bye.

•◆•

Lucas was staying at the Four Seasons on Fifty-seventh Street. He was lying in bed with his toenails scratching the top sheet, thinking about clipping his nails and then walking over to Madison Avenue to do a little shopping for an autumn ensemble, when his cell phone rang.

Amelia: "Get over here. Right now."

"What happened?"

"It's not good. And better not to talk about it on a cell phone."

He needed to clean up: unless there was a shootout going on at Lincoln's town house, he figured he had that much time. He was out of the hotel fifteen minutes after the call, and found a taxi outside the front door, dropping off a customer. Lucas got in the cab and gave the driver Lincoln's address, and the driver said, "Not hardly worth turning on the meter for that."

"Do what you want; I'll give you a twenty when we get there."

The driver drove with some enthusiasm, and Lucas was ringing Lincoln's doorbell twenty minutes after Amelia called.

"What happened?" he asked, when she opened the door.

"Lily's been detained by Internal Affairs. They could be coming for us next."

"What?"

"I'll let Lincoln tell you."

Lincoln smiled when Lucas came in and said, "Now things are getting interesting."

"Tell me."

The evidence that Amelia had collected under Lincoln's direction, which Lincoln conceded was "quite good, under typical circumstances," had not been taken to Lincoln's lab, but to the city laboratory.

First, they found some evidence that the dead women had been tortured and murdered in a small storage area in the basement of the sculptor's studio. Not much evidence was visible, but the small stuff—tiny spatters of blood, flakes of skin, urine samples—proved that the dead women had been there.

The gun had also been examined—and that was where the problem arose.

"Last year, we had another psycho roaming around the city, but he was not particularly clever. He was a serial shooter. Guy named Levon Pitt. Owned a junkyard here in town. That's where he had dumped the bodies. Lily ran the team that tracked him down. They had an entry team, and cracked his apartment but there was nobody home. So they set up outside the apartment to wait for him, and pretty soon, here he came, with his adult son. When the police approached him, he figured out what was about to happen, and pulled a gun, and actually tried to take his son hostage. In the scuffle, he fired the gun, once, and Lily shot him, firing three times, and he died on the way to the hospital.

"When the man had been shot, Lily froze the scene, and they brought in the crime scene crew. Among other things, they recovered seven different pistols in the man's apartment. He'd used four different weapons in the murders that the police knew about, and after testing, they found that three of the guns they'd recovered were among the four used in the crime."

Lincoln paused in his narration, and Lucas prompted, "So?"

"The gun we found yesterday, by Verlaine's hand, was the fourth gun."

"What?" Lucas was momentarily confused. "Verlaine was involved with Levon Pitt?"

"That's not what they're suggesting," Lincoln said. "For one thing, there's no apparent connection. For another, one of the shells in Verlaine's gun had Lily's fingerprint on it."

It took Lucas a moment to get it. "So they're saying, what?

That she picked up a gun at the first site, and kept it as a throw-down? And then she went into Verlaine's apartment sometime last night, killed him, and made it look like a suicide?"

"That's what they're suggesting."

"That's ridiculous," Lucas said.

"Internal Affairs doesn't think so," Amelia said. "The thing is, they can't figure out any other mechanism for getting Lily's finger-print on that shell. She never touched the gun at Verlaine's place."

"But why would she do that? Why kill Verlaine? After I went in there, we knew we had him."

"But we had no hard evidence, and that's all Internal Affairs knows. That's what Lily reported last night. We can't tell them that we did have hard evidence, because then we'd have to tell them that you illegally entered. So their theory is she knew who the killer was, but couldn't get at him, so she killed him. Got him off the street."

"Aw, man, that's not right," Lucas said.

"There's another aspect to it," Amelia said. "Lily is an opera-tor. She gets things done, but she steps on a lot of toes. That's fine, when she's got all that protection at the top. But now, with this, well, somebody leaked the lab results almost instantly. Probably some old bureaucratic enemy. It's on every TV station in New York. They're screaming for her head."

"Don't forget to tell him about what else is coming down the line," Lincoln said.

"Oh, yeah." Amelia pulled out her cell phone and looked at the time. "IA wonders if any of us had anything to do with it. We've got a couple of homicide cops on the way here. They want to talk to us. I know them. They're hard-nosed guys."

Lucas shrugged. "We leave out the burglary, leave out the evi-dence collection from last night, and tell them everything else. And we tell them that they're being taken as chumps—that Lily couldn't have done this, and that somebody is running a con on them."

"That'll piss them off," Amelia said.

"Which is what we want to do," Lucas said. "We want them on the defensive. We want them off our backs so we can figure out what actually happened. And we tell them that."

"The question," Lucas Davenport spat out, "is who's setting her up?"

Lincoln agreed. That was the *only* question. There was no doubt in the minds of Lucas, Amelia, and Lincoln that Lily was innocent.

However much of a shit Jim Bob Verlaine had been, however guilty he was of sadistic murder—and however much of a tough number Lily Rothenburg was—there was no way she'd take him out like that.

The team was back in Lincoln's town house—all of them except Lily, of course, who was still being detained.

And whose absence was glaringly obvious.

"So," Lucas repeated. "Who's behind it?"

"Somebody with a grudge?" Amelia offered.

"Could be," Lucas said. "She's made some enemies in her day. Or maybe some asshole wants to derail a case she's running."

"And what about Verlaine?" Amelia asked. "Did he kill those women? Or was he being set up, too? And what's the reason behind that?"

Lincoln's view, admittedly myopic at times, as to the questions why and who was generally best answered by how and what: that is, by the evidence. "Why waste fucking time speculating? Look at the *facts*."

"You ever in a good mood, Lincoln?" Lucas asked.

A grunt suggested that the answer might be no.

But Lucas took his point. "What do we have to prove the suicide was faked?"

Looking over Amelia's photos of the body, Mel Cooper said, "Powder burns and muzzle stamp're consistent with a close-contact gunshot."

Lucas regarded the pictures, too. "And the tissue, blood, and bone on the receiver of the piece confirm that. But it was a temple shot. That's rare in self-inflicted wounds. Usually the poor bastard bites the muzzle."

"Which means somebody could've pulled out the piece when Verlaine was turned away, come up behind or beside him, and shot. So, maybe he knew the shooter."

Cooper said, "But there was gunshot residue on Verlaine's hands."

Firing any pistol, and most rifles, results in burnt gunpowder particles and gases contaminating the hand holding the weapon.

But Lucas muttered, "Fuck, that's easy. He fired twice."

"Yes!" Lincoln said enthusiastically. "Good. Verlaine lets the perp in. He—or she—stands beside him and blows his brains out. Then the perp puts the gun in Verlaine's hand and pulls the trigger again. Bang . . . Verlaine's fingerprints're on the piece, and GSR's on his hand. Perp collects the second shell and leaves the gun on the floor."

"But where's the other slug?" Cooper asked.

Lucas, clearly pissed his friend had been set up, snapped, "Christ, just look at the pictures of the scene! The whole goddamn studio's like a gun-range bullet trap—a thousand hunks of metal. Half of his quote art looks like a monkey pounded on it with a hammer. Nobody'd spot a bullet ding."

Amelia said, "Okay, that could work. But the big issue: what about Lily's fingerprint on the shell casing fired from the murder weapon? How the hell did the perp finesse that?" She tossed her long red hair over a shoulder. Lincoln was amused to see Lucas following the sweep closely. He reflected: Just 'cause you're a faithful husband doesn't mean you are blind.

Lincoln said, "Internal Affairs is claiming that Lily picked the gun up at the scene where she shot Levon Pitt—rescuing his son. What was the name again?"

"The boy?" Mel Cooper asked, flipping through a file. "Andy."

Lucas then snapped his fingers. "Hold on. Something's wrong here. It's Levon Pitt's gun—and presumably it was loaded with Pitt's ammo. Why would Lily reload the mag with her rounds? That makes no sense. I'm not saying she'd take somebody out like that, but if she did, she wouldn't be stupid about it."

Amelia said, "Somebody stole one of her cartridges and popped it in the mag."

"Wore gloves."

"Or knuckled it," Lucas said, referring to loading a weapon by holding the bullets between your fingers, never letting the tips come in contact with the brass or slug.

Lucas nodded. "Our friend Markowitz ain't real crazy about the boys and girls from Narcotics being involved. But it's leaning that way to me."

"Well, IA's not going to take our word for it," Cooper pointed out. "How do we prove somebody copped a spent shell from Lily?"

An idea occurred to Lincoln. "Call Ballistics. Have them test fire a round from the bottom of the mag of the gun at Verlaine's suicide. I want three-D images of that shell compared with the one with Lily's prints on it. And I fucking want them now."

"Will do."

Not that fast, but it wasn't bad. A half hour later the images were on the big monitor in front of them.

Lincoln glanced toward Lucas then Amelia. "You two are the shoot-em-up mavens. What do you think?"

It took no more than a fast glance. They nodded at each other. Lucas said, "The shell with Lily's prints was machined to fit the receiver of Pitt's gun. The real perp got one of her cartridges and altered it."

"Yep," Amelia agreed. "So whoever did it knows weapons and metalwork. It's real high quality, close tolerances."

"Okay, that proves she was set up. But it doesn't get us any closer to *who's* setting Lily up," Cooper said.

Breaking a lengthy silence, Lucas said, "Maybe it does. Amelia, you know somebody in the NYPD evidence room?"

"Know somebody?" she asked, laughing. "It's my home away from home."

•◆•

Stan Markowitz stood at the podium beside the police commissioner, along with some minion from the mayor's office and a Public Affairs officer or two. They were in the Press Room in One Police Plaza.

Microphones and cameras and cell phones in video mode bristled like RPGs and machine guns, aimed the officials' way—though Markowitz, it seemed, was the preferred prey in the crosshairs, to judge from the tight shots.

"I don't think your boss's having a good day," Lincoln said to Amelia. They sat beside each other, watching on the big-screen TV in the corner of his parlor.

Lucas was elsewhere, preparing.

"Doesn't look it. And what do you think?" she mused. "Half the city's watching?"

"Half the *country*," Lincoln countered. "No good serial killers in the news lately. All the sharks want a piece of this one."

Every media outlet except CSPAN and Telemundo, it seemed, was represented.

"Ladies and gentlemen," Markowitz began reasonably, though with a tone that suggested he actually viewed them as sharks.

He was drowned out by their shouted questions.

"What was the motive for the torture?"

"Is it significant that the victims were minorities?"

"Is there a connection between this case and the Bekker case a few years ago, involving Lucas Davenport?"

"Could you fill us in about Verlaine's sex life?"

Frenzy.

Markowitz had obviously done this before and he began speaking very softly—an old trick. Suddenly the sharks realized that they weren't going to hear anything if they kept yammering away and they spontaneously, to a fish, fell silent.

The COD gave it a beat and then continued. "As you are probably aware, a thorough examination and analysis of evidence and behavioral profiling led investigators to believe that a resident of Manhattan, James Robert Verlaine, was the perpetrator in the spate of recent killings of women in the city. Mr. Verlaine appeared to take his own life as a result of said investigation. And evidence supported that supposition."

Lincoln muttered, "Ah, sooo pleased to see that they still teach courses at the academy in using ten words when one will do."

Amelia laughed and kissed his neck.

"You are probably also aware that it was believed that an NYPD detective shot and killed Mr. Verlaine and attempted to cover up the murder by making it *appear* that the death was a suicide.

"Further investigation has determined that the detective, Lily Rothenburg, was not, in fact, involved in the death of Mr. Verlaine. A person or persons intentionally planted evidence in an attempt to implicate the detective. This officer has been exonerated. It now appears, too, that Mr. Verlaine was not the perpetrator behind the murder of the women. Detective Rothenburg is once again in charge of the task force investigating the killings. We expect to have a suspect in custody soon. I have no further comments at this time."

"Does that mean, Chief of Detectives, that Verlaine was murdered by this suspect as well? . . ."

A new microphone logo popped into sight. Telemundo had arrived.

"Can you tell us what leads Detective Rothenburg is working on? . . . Can you reassure the people of New York that no one else is at risk?"

Markowitz studied the sharks for a moment and Lincoln thought he was actually going to say, "How fucking stupid do you have to be not to understand 'I have no further comments'?"

Instead: "Thank you." He turned and walked off the stage.

•◆•

Amelia made a few calls to the television stations, posing as an angry cop, and told them that Lily was at Lincoln's town house. "She's guilty, she's the one who did it, you got to get on her," she told the newsies.

Within the hour, there were six news crews and fifty rubber-neckers on the sidewalk outside of Lincoln's town house. One of them finally came up and pounded on the door, and Amelia peeked out and asked what they wanted.

They wanted Lily.

After some back-and-forth, Lily went out on the stoop, told them that she would make one statement for the record, and that would be it.

"I have some very clear ideas of how this may have happened," she began.

"Are you guilty?" somebody shouted.

"Of course I'm not guilty," Lily said. "I'm not guilty of anything except trying to track down a torture-killer. But the possibilities now are quite few: the logical possibilities. I'll knock them down one at a time, and when I'm finished, we'll have this madman. Within the next day or two. I'm confident of that."

The press conference lasted for another two or three minutes, then she said she would not talk anymore about it, and went back inside. The news crews dispersed, with the exception of a radio reporter. The rubberneckers went with them.

An hour later, Lucas stuck his head out the door. "If you're waiting for Lily, she went out the back a half hour ago."

At ten o'clock that night, Lucas and Lily headed over to the West Side, in the Thirties west of Ninth Avenue. They were tracked by two other cars, each with two cops in them, including Amelia.

Lily took a call, and then said to Lucas, "He's on the way. He'll get off at Penn Station and then walk over, unless he's going somewhere else."

"I'm worried," Lucas said. "He's nuts. If he goes off on you, I mean he could just—"

"He works at a hospital. He's unlikely to be carrying a gun. And the stuff I'm wearing is stab-resistant."

"Nothing is stab-proof, though," Lucas said. "What we really need to do is slow down."

"I disagree," Lily said. "This is hot, right now. He's got to be feeling the street. If he has too much time to think about it, he can start covering it up. If he really thinks about it, he'd know that I'd never approach him alone. We can't let him think."

Andy Pitt lived in a dark brownstone building that would take at least fifty yuppies and a couple of generations to gentrify, Lucas thought. They sat a block away, and the few people on the sidewalks either crossed the street or moved to the far edge of the sidewalk when they realized that there were people in the parked cars. A couple went by, and then a too-happy guy with a white dog.

Lily took a call on a police handset. "He's on the sidewalk. He's coming this way."

"Wire is good," Lucas said. Lily was wearing a wire over her vest, which made her look a little paunchy; but paunchy was okay, considering the alternative.

They took a call from Amelia, who was with three other cops, concealed down some cellar steps at a building on the other side of the street. "We're set here."

A minute later she took another call: "He's across Ninth, still coming on. He's got a grocery sack."

Another two minutes: "He's two blocks out."

Lily said, "Let's go."

Lily went to the stoop that led into the apartment building. The doors were locked, but the rake opened them in a moment, and Lucas stepped into the entry hall. There was a weak bare-bulb light inside, and he reached up and unscrewed it, a quarter inch at a time, because of the heat. When it went out, he unscrewed it another quarter inch, then pulled his gun, cocked it, and leaned against the wall. Lily was facing him through the glass, five inches away, and he could hear her radio. "He'll turn the corner in ten seconds. Nine. Eight."

Lily opened the door, turned off the radio, and handed it to Lucas. They were both counting. Seven. Six. Five. Four.

Andy turned the corner. Lucas was looking past Lily's head, and he said, just loud enough for her to hear, "He's seen you. Bang on the door."

She banged on the door.

Lucas said, "He's coming up. He's a hundred feet out."

Lily turned away from the door, as if giving up, then saw Andy and his bag. Andy stopped under the only nearby streetlight, and Lily walked down the steps and called, "Police. Is that you, Andy? Wait there."

If he ran, they'd have to try something different.

He didn't run. He said, "You're the cop who killed my father."

"That's right. I have a few questions for you. We're trying to find out how a piece of brass, a shell from a nine-millimeter cartridge, got into a gun that was used in another killing. You may have heard about it. After I thought about it, Andy, there's only one way, isn't there? You picked it up. We froze the crime scene, but you were right in the middle of it, with your father. What did you do, step on it? Kneel on it? You were kneeling right next to him."

Lucas, watching from the window, saw Andy do something with his left hand, his free hand; something in the pocket of his jacket. Couldn't see what, but Lily didn't seem worried; but then she might not have been able to see the move. She pushed him, still talking. "Found the kill room, and found some DNA that shouldn't have been there. Not much, a few flakes of skin, but good enough for us. So, I have a warrant. We need a DNA sample from you. It won't hurt. I have a kit, we need you to scrub a swab against your gums."

"I knelt on it," Andy said.

"What?"

"I knelt on it. The shell. I didn't try to do that, I just knelt on it by accident. When I saw what it was, I put it in my pocket."

"And you reloaded it."

"Of course. My pop and I reloaded everything. When you shoot a lot, you don't want to waste all that brass. We saved more than half, except that we shot more."

"Who killed the women? You or Verlaine?"

"Not Verlaine." Andy laughed, and dropped his grocery sack by his ankle. "We had the same interests, but he never had the guts to do anything real. He just liked to get the women in there and pose them like slave girls and make his sculptures, and then he'd go around to the S&M clubs and brag about it. But he had that room down in the basement where he kept his finished work—he had that big steel door because the metal thieves will take that bronze shit and melt it right down—but that was perfect. I'd get the girls down there and do what I wanted. What he dreamed about. You ever had a slave? There's nothing like it."

"Why'd you kill him?"

"Because of you. I didn't even know how close you were to finding him, even with all those clues I left for you. All those brass filings. But I had that shell, and a shell is a terrible thing to waste. You killed my pop. I thought they'd put you in prison, so you'd have all that time to think about it."

"Why those victims, Andy? Why those particular women?"

But he didn't answer, just stepped closer. Fist coming out of his pocket.

Lucas stepped through the door with his gun and shouted, "He's got something in his hand, Lily, he's got something."

Lily jumped back, but Andy was right with her, grabbed her by the collar and yanked her back, looking around. "Stay away. Stay away," he screamed. "I got a scalpel, I'll cut her face off."

Amelia and the other cops emerged from the stairway across the street and spread out.

"Get away. Get away or I'll cut her throat, I swear to God, I'll cut her fuckin' throat."

He yanked Lily backward, and Lily called to Lucas, "I can't reach my gun. It got stuck under the damn vest when he pulled me back."

Lucas: "Can you go down?"

"Maybe."

"Don't try anything. I just want to go away. I walk her up the block and I—"

Lily, using both hands, grabbed his knife arm and pushed it away from her, just an inch, and at the same time kicked her feet out from under herself and dropped. Amelia and Lucas fired at the same time, and Andy's head exploded.

Lily landed on her ass and rolled away from the falling body; the scalpel tinkled to the ground six feet away. "That was not optimal," she said, as she got back to her feet and turned to look down at the body.

After that, it was mostly routine: checking the tape, calling crime scene. Andy Pitt had two bullet holes in his head, one right through the forehead and out the back, and the second in one temple and out the other.

As the scene was taped off, Lucas stepped over to Amelia and asked, "You okay?"

"I'm okay. How about you?"

"I'm okay," he said. He looked her over and said, "Do you know that you smile when you pull the trigger?"

• ◆ •

They sat in Government-issue furniture and wheelchair, across from the chief of detectives. His office.

Lucas, Lily, Amelia, and Lincoln. They were here for what Lincoln joked was the post postmortem. Maybe in bad taste, but nobody was all that upset that Andy Pitt was lying in the morgue at the moment.

Markowitz was on a call (nodding subconsciously, from which Lincoln deduced he was speaking, well, most likely *listening,* to his boss, the commissioner). Lincoln looked around. He thought the office was pretty nice. Big, ordered, with nice views, though Lincoln had no use for views. His town house, for instance, offered a nice scene of Central Park. He invariably ordered Thom to close the curtains.

Distracting.

Finally, Markowitz hung up. His gaze incorporated them all. "Everybody upstairs's happy. I was worried, they were worried, well, it was a little radical what you wanted to do. But it worked out."

Lincoln shrugged—one of the few gestures he was capable of—and turned his chair slightly to face Markowitz. "The plan was logical, the execution competent," he said. Those were about his highest forms of praise.

It was Lucas who'd initially come up with the theory of who'd killed Verlaine and set Lily up.

Amelia, you know somebody in the NYPD evidence room?

He had a possible source for the shell casing with Lily's fingerprint on it: the crime scene where she'd tapped Levon Pitt. Sure enough, the evidence log from that crime reported three slugs recovered but only two spent casings. Somebody, possibly, had pocketed the third.

"Okay, the gun at Verlaine's belonged to Levon Pitt. The shell casing at Verlaine's had been Lily's, fired when Pitt was shot," Lucas had pointed out when they'd learned this. "How could they be linked? Only through the one individual who had a connection to them both: Andy Pitt, Levon's son, the kid who had—supposedly—been held hostage by his father."

But what, Lucas speculated, if he hadn't been a hostage? What if he was his father's accomplice in the serial shootings back then? And he was enraged that Lily had killed his father?

It made sense, Lincoln had agreed, and he'd pointed out that Andy might've met Verlaine through his father's junkyard, where, possibly, the sculptor bought metal for his art.

They'd found where the young man lived and worked and set up surveillance.

But no evidence implicated him. They needed more. They had to flush him, force him into making a move.

And Lincoln had come up with a plan. Using Lily as bait. They'd proved to Markowitz she was innocent and asked him to make the initial press announcement to that effect. Then Amelia contacted more reporters. Lily, too, had made her statement.

That virtually guaranteed that Andy knew Lily was getting close. He'd have to make his move.

"I can't thank you enough," Markowitz said. "I mean, you, Lucas, coming all the way from Minneapolis. That was really above and beyond the call."

"Glad to help out."

"Better get back to it." Markowitz's attention was elsewhere now. He was glancing at the notepad on which he'd jotted notes during his conversation with the commissioner. There were a lot of notes.

But nobody rose. Lincoln glanced at Lily, who was the senior law officer here. She said, "Stan, just one thing we were thinking about. One loose end, sort of."

Still distracted. "Loose end?" He was ticking off something on the paper in front of him.

"You know what occurred to us? Remember we had the idea that somebody was using Verlaine to kill those women? Well, what if it wasn't Verlaine they were using, but Andy Pitt?

"Huh? I don't get it."

Lily continued, "Sure, he had a motive to get even with me. But that doesn't mean somebody else didn't force him or hire him to kill those women, and Verlaine."

Amelia said, "Like maybe somebody from Narcotics Four, after all. Andy Pitt never got to tell us why he picked those women. Why? Maybe the women could provide good info on drug operations in the city. Maybe it was Andy who got recruited by somebody in Narc Four."

"And another thing that we were pondering," Lincoln said. "Who exactly was it doing everything he could to protect the unit? The one who insisted that the killings had to be the work of a psycho, nothing to do with any cops?"

Lily took over again. "That'd be you, Stan."

If the words didn't have Markowitz's full attention, the Glock that Lily drew and pointed more or less in his direction sealed the deal.

◆

The chief of detectives sighed. "Goddamnit."

"What's the story, Stan?" Amelia asked. Voice cold. She tossed her hair. Lucas was still looking.

There was a pause.

"All right," Markowitz muttered. "I *did* pull some strings to get the drug side of the investigation downplayed."

"Let me guess," Lily snapped. "Because the women were tortured and killed to get information on the drug player in town so Narc Four could become the shining star of the department."

"Guess again, Detective." Markowitz gave a guttural laugh. "Do you think there might've been some *other* reason why Narc Four has such a great conviction record—other than hiring a psycho to torture and kill users?"

No one replied.

"How 'bout because the fucking head of Narc Four was on the take."

"Marty Glover?"

"Yeah. Exactly. We've suspected it for six months. Sure, the team was collaring suppliers and importers and meth cookers all over the city—except for one location. A big heroin distribution operation based in Red Hook, Brooklyn." He tapped a file on his desk. "Glover was on their payroll and using Narc Four to take down their competition. The others on the team weren't in on it. All they knew was that Glover had good sources."

Markowitz waved at Lily's weapon as if it were an irritating wasp. "Could you? Do you mind?"

She holstered the Glock, but kept her hand near the grip.

The COD continued. "But the Internal Affairs Red Hook operation against Glover had nothing to do with Verlaine or Pitt, or the torture-murders. It was just a coincidence the women were druggies, the victims. But then you started *looking* for connections. Glover freaked out. I thought he was gonna rabbit, go underground and burn the evidence. So I told you to back off. That's all there was to it."

Lucas asked, "What happened with Glover?"

"I didn't want to move so fast but there was no choice. I called Candy Preston—from Narc Four—and we set up a sting to nail Glover. I had her use one of her snitches to offer him a payoff. Fifty thousand. I didn't think he'd go for it, but he couldn't resist. We got him on camera taking the bribe. It's not as righteous a collar as we'd like—I wanted some of the Red Hook scum, too. But the prosecutor'll work him over. He'll give up names if we play with the sentencing."

Lincoln gave him points for credibility. But he remained skeptical.

Lucas, too, apparently. He said, "Good story, Stan. But I think we'd all like confirmation. Who can we talk to who'll vouch for you?"

"Well, there's somebody who's been in the loop from the beginning of the Red Hook op."

"Who?"

"The mayor."

Lincoln glanced toward Lucas and said, "Works for me."

Outside, they headed toward the accessible van, where Thom sat in the driver's seat. He saw the entourage and hit the button that opened the door and lowered the ramp. Then he climbed out.

Lincoln wheeled up to the van then braked to a stop, spun around. "Anyone care to come back to the town house for an *aperitivo*? It's approaching cocktail hour."

"Bit early," the aide pointed out. Such a mother hen.

"Thom, our guests have had an extremely traumatic time. Kidnapping was involved, knives were involved, gunplay was involved. If anybody deserves a bit of refreshment, it's them."

"Love to," Lucas offered. "But I'm heading back to the family. Got a flight in an hour."

"I'm going to make sure he gets to the airport," Lily said. "Without getting into any trouble."

They shook hands. Lincoln wheeled onto the ramp and his aide fixed the chair to it with canvas straps. The criminalist said, "We should think about doing this again, Davenport."

Thom lifted his eyebrow. "Last name. Means he likes you. And he doesn't like many people."

Lincoln grumbled. "I'm not saying I like anyone. Where did that subtext come from? I'm simply saying this case didn't turn out to be the disaster it might have."

"I may not be back here soon," Lucas said, and cocked his head. "But you ever get to Minnesota?"

"Used to go quite a bit."

"You've been?" Amelia asked.

"Of course. I grew up in the Midwest, remember," Lincoln said impatiently. "I'd go fishing for muskie and pike in Swan Lake and Minnetonka."

"You *fished*?" Thom asked. He seemed astonished.

"And I've been to Hibbing. A Bob Dylan pilgrimage."

"Site of the largest open-pit iron mine in the world," Lucas said.

Lincoln nodded. "My first impression was that it'd be a great place to dispose of bodies."

"Had the same thought myself."

"Then it's settled," Rhyme muttered. "You catch any good cases up there—something *interesting*, something *challenging*, give me a call."

"Lily's been there, too, helping us out. We could get the team back together." Lucas glanced at Amelia. "We'll go out to the range, you and me. I can teach you how to shoot."

"And we can hit that highway you were mentioning. I'll give you a few tips on how to drive that toy car of yours."

"Let's go, Sachs," Lincoln called. "We've got a crime scene report to write up."

HEATHER GRAHAM

VS. F. PAUL WILSON

Infernal Night

Repairman Jack is one of fiction's most unique characters. F. Paul Wilson created him in 1984's *The Tomb*—an urban mercenary who hires himself out to fix problems the system can't or won't deal with. *The Tomb* became a huge success. Despite that, though, Paul did not write the second Repairman Jack novel until fourteen years later. Why? He says he was afraid Jack would take over his writing career. Finally, in 1998, Jack returned for what Paul said at the time was "Just one novel."

But then he did another. And another.

Twenty-two novels later it's safe to say that Repairman Jack definitely took over Paul's writing career.

But that's okay.

Both writer and character came to deeply know each other.

Heather Graham is a publishing dynamo with over one hundred novels to her credit. Romantic suspense, historical romance, vampire fiction, time travel, occult, even Christmas holiday fare. You name it, she's written it. But Heather's at her best when she blends a bit of paranormal with real, human evil. And while Heather has been best known in recent years for her Krewe of Hunter novels, her Cafferty and Quinn series has long been simmering in the back of her mind. *Let the Dead Sleep* (2013) began the first adventure for Michael Quinn and Danni Cafferty, followed by *Waking the Dead*.

Michael Quinn is a special kind of guy. College football hero, too popular for his own good—eventually an excessive lifestyle causes his death in a hospital emergency room. Brought back to life by a crew of doctors, Quinn becomes a new man, never sure of exactly what he brought back with him from the dead. After meeting up with Danni Cafferty—who's just inherited her father's unique curio shop—Quinn finds that Danni will need everything he can give her when she starts collecting on her own. Quinn is much like Paul's Repairman Jack. Not bound by any rules that conventional law enforcement agents obey. Sure, he knows where the line is drawn, he just chooses to ignore it.

So how did this collaboration start?

Heather had an idea that involved Michael Quinn and a mausoleum containing a mysterious artifact. The problem? Repairman Jack works almost exclusively in New York City, so Paul had to come up with a way to bring him south to New Orleans.

That's where Madame de Medici comes in.

Who's that?

You'll see.

Infernal Night

Jack wandered the room as they spoke.

Okay, so Jules, the last surviving member of the Chastain family, was rich. If the private Gulfstream V that had flown him down here from LaGuardia and the Maybach with the liveried driver that had picked him up at the airport weren't enough, the sprawling New Orleans mansion provided sufficient backup.

Moss-draped oaks had swayed in the breeze on either side of the house as the driver had let him out in front. "The Garden District," he'd said. Jack had no idea what that meant, but the neighborhood spoke of genteel wealth, of a time forgotten, of slow grace, and a distant era. For all Jack knew, the manor house itself might have been a plantation once. With those massive pillars lining the front porch, it reminded him a little of Tara from *Gone with the Wind*.

He'd done a little research before agreeing to come south. Jules

Chastain had acquired his wealth the old-fashioned way: he'd inherited it.

And the guy knew people. Famous people. Newspaper clippings and original photos of Chastain with George W., with Obama, with Streisand, with Little Richard—now *that* was cool—lined the walls between artifacts from all over the world. Jack had lots of artifacts around his apartment, too, but mostly from the 1930s and '40s. These were from, like, pre-pyramid days.

I could be impressed, he thought.

He'd probably be definitely impressed if this guy was talking sense.

He stopped his wandering to face Chastain where he sat in some kind of throne-of-swords chair—only this wasn't a movie prop. With his thin moustache, thick glasses, and ridiculous silk smoking jacket, he looked like Percy Dovetonsils on crack instead of martinis.

"Let me get this straight: you flew me all the way down here from New York to steal something *you* own from *your* family crypt."

"Yes," Chastain said in a quavery voice. "Exactly."

"Okay. Now, since you're not crippled in any way I can see, go over again why you can't do this yourself."

"As I explained, the artifact I seek was obtained from another collector who wants it back."

"Because you stole it."

"Mister, I never got your last name."

Jack had had dozens over the years.

"Just Jack'll do."

"Very well, Jack, I assure you I can pay for anything I desire. *Anything.*"

"Not if the other guy doesn't want to sell."

He glanced away. "Well, occasionally one runs into bull-headed stubbornness—"

"Which obliges one to steal."

He waved a dismissive hand. "Oh, very well. Yes. I appropriated it without the owner's knowledge."

"And the owner wants it back."

"Yes, she discovered the appropriation."

He seemed incapable of saying "theft."

"Oh, a she. You never mentioned that."

"Madame de Medici. You've heard of her?"

"I hadn't heard of *you* until you called me, so why should I have heard of *her*?"

"Just wondering. You're familiar with the expression 'Hell hath no fury'?"

"It's 'Heav'n has no Rage, like Love to Hatred turn'd, / Nor Hell a Fury like a Woman scorn'd.'"

Chastain's eyebrows rose. "Oh, a poetry fan."

"Not necessarily. Just like to get things right. I had the misfortune of being an English major once."

"Really? What school?"

"The name doesn't matter once you've dropped out. You were saying?"

"Well, if the true quote is 'Nor Hell a Fury like a Woman scorn'd,' then in this case we've got 'Nor Hell a Fury like a de Medici missing a piece from her collection.' When I told her I didn't have her absent artifact, she went out and hired a hit man to kill me on sight."

Jack had to laugh. "What is she? A mob wife?"

"Despite the name, she appears to be a Middle Easterner. The point is, she wants me dead."

Over the years, during the course of business, Jack had ended more than a few lives, but never on contract.

"Well, I hope you don't think I'm going to hit her, because that's not in my job description."

"No no! As I said, I just need someone to retrieve the artifact from the family mausoleum."

"And you need a guy from New York for this? Why not somebody local?"

"I was told you are—what did he call you?—an urban mercenary. Yes, an urban mercenary with a reputation for getting the job done and being a man of his word."

"Where'd you hear all this?"

"I'm not sure the individual would like me talking about him. Let's just say you've had the benefit of an enthusiastic referral and leave it at that."

Jack wondered who it might be. He didn't know anyone in New Orleans. He shrugged it off. With the Internet, the source could be anywhere.

"Still, there must be a local guy who can—"

"You also have a reputation for not being afraid of violence. That is, if attacked, you will counterattack rather than run."

"Oh, don't go there. I've done my share of running. What else have you heard about me?"

Chastain frowned. "Very little. I made numerous queries. You don't seem to have an official existence. Some sources even said you don't exist at all. That Repairman Jack is just some urban legend." The frown morphed into a smile. "Interesting nickname, that."

Jack had never liked it himself but things had progressed far past the point where he could do anything about it.

"Not my idea. Someone laid it on me and it stuck."

As for the urban legend angle, that was fine with Jack. His favorite method was to play someone and leave them with no clue they'd been played. Those people never talked about Repairman

Jack, just a terrible run of bad luck. But fixes didn't always go as planned, of course, and sometimes things got dicey. Sometimes people got violent. Sometimes people died. Those people never talked about Repairman Jack, either.

Chastain rose and stepped to a window that had to be a dozen feet high.

"Well, whatever," he said, as he stared out at the night. "The thing is, with a hit man after me, I need someone who can overcome any resistance, retrieve the artifact in question, and bring it back. Too many locals would forget about that last part."

"With a hit man after you, you shouldn't be standing at a window."

Chastain stiffened, then ducked to the side.

"I am so stupid at times," he said, drawing the curtains across the panes. "I'm not geared for this kind of situation. That's why I need you."

Jack still wasn't buying.

"But the simple solution is to call this Medici lady and say it's in the mausoleum and tell her to go get it herself."

Chastain's hands flew into the air. "I would if I could! I've tried but she's gone off the radar! Incommunicado! And I fear the longer I wait, the shorter I'll live. If I can just get the artifact back in my hands, I can eventually negotiate a settlement. But I'm afraid to set foot outside the door."

Something not right here.

Customers had tried to run games on him before. Was this another?

"How do I know you're not setting me up to steal this from her?"

Jules laughed. "It is in the Chastain mausoleum! It's got my family name on it! I'll show you a back way in—"

"Why do I need a back way in if it's yours?"

"Take the front way if you wish. It's just that I fear Madame de Medici's hit man might suspect I'll show up there and be lying in wait."

Jack pulled his Glock from the small of his back—traveling armed was a sweet perk of a private jet—and aimed it at Chastain's face. "No need to lie in wait when you had him driven in from the airport."

Chastain's eyes were fixed on the pistol as he backed away. "What? No!"

"Madame de Medici offered me twice your fee." Jack shrugged. "You got played."

"This is impossible!"

"Quite possible." Jack returned the pistol to its nylon holster. "But not true this time."

Chastain sagged against the desk. "Why would you *do* such a thing?"

"Had my reasons."

He'd wanted to see Chastain's reaction, and it hadn't been what he'd expected.

"That was cruel!" he said, dropping back into his desk chair.

"Naw. Just serving up a dose of reality. So, just what is this artifact?" Jack pointed to a huge Olmec stone head in a corner. "Not something like that, is it?"

Hysteria tinged Chastain's twittering laugh. "Oh, goodness no! It's a ring—an ancient ring. I've drawn a diagram of the interior of the mausoleum so you can find the hiding place."

Jack didn't like this, any of it. But Chastain had called while Gia and Vicky were back in Iowa visiting her folks and he felt the need for a brief change of scenery. A fat fee, round-trip transportation to New Orleans in a private jet. It had all sounded too good to be true.

And naturally that was how it was turning out.

Hit man. *Sheesh.* He hadn't bargained for that. But if he could sneak in and sneak back out of this mausoleum with no one the wiser, everything would be cool. He'd stop by the French Quarter for a fried-oyster po' boy and then be on his way.

"All right, let's get this over with. And money up-front—all of it."

"Certainly." Chastain reached for an envelope on a nearby table in the shape of an elephant. "Cash in hundreds, as agreed." Another one of those Percy Dovetonsils smiles. "I take it Uncle Sam won't be seeing any of that."

Jack said nothing as he pocketed the envelope. He wouldn't know a 1040 if it poked him in the eye.

Chastain said, "I was concerned you might not be armed, but no longer. I'll have my man drive you over to the plantation and—"

"You'll show me how to get there, then have your man drive me to where I can hail a cab."

Arrive in a silver Maybach Landaulet. Yeah, that would work.

"Very well. But be prepared for deadly force."

"Uh-huh. Got a map?"

After watching Chastain trace a path along the Mississippi to the location of the old Chastain plantation on River Road, Jack let himself out onto the front porch to wait for the car. He stood between two of the massive columns, staring out at the misty night and listening to his forebrain playing "Should I Stay or Should I Go?" by The Clash while his hindbrain blasted "Go Now."

Something definitely rotten in New Orleans. A guy with a contract out on him didn't stand at a window. He'd have all the curtains drawn and all the doors barricaded. So Jack had pulled his pistol to see how he'd react. In the context of having your name on a contract, *"This is impossible!"* was not a response that made any sense when looking down the muzzle of a gun.

But it made plenty of sense if the contract didn't exist.

Chastain was lying—probably about many things. The smart thing to do was walk away. But Jack's interest was piqued. What was the game here? He'd come a long way, the money was good, and he felt a need to see this through.

He closed his eyes and took a deep breath. The air was different here. Heavier than New York's. Manhattan was old, and he'd found ancient secrets in its hidden corners. But this place—the atmosphere was laden with the rot of dark mysteries with maybe even a touch of magic hovering on the edges. Jack had seen magic. He hated magic.

Be prepared for deadly force.

Jack was hoping to avoid that, but he'd be ready.

• ◆ •

Michael Quinn stood flat against the side of the Boudreaux vault in the family cemetery of the Chastain plantation, listening. His ears were attuned to hear the faintest rustle of movement. A sliver of moon cast meager light, but that didn't stand against him. He had learned the art of seeing by night.

The vault was filled top to bottom with decaying coffins or the sun-cremated dead, so he couldn't hide inside. Besides, the door was sealed. The Boudreaux family had long ago left the area and it was doubtful that the vault would ever be unsealed. But he had no interest in the Boudreaux family tonight.

Still, he hadn't been desperate enough to forget all sense and wait inside the Chastain mausoleum. The crumbling old Boudreaux vault was adorned with gargoyles and angels, strange mix that it might be, and a good place to wait. In the darkness, if a piece of his head showed as he watched the night, he might appear to be simply part of a gargoyle.

The Chastain mausoleum had a gate and a door and a chapel inside filled with an altar and chairs. The walls themselves were lined with coffins; two sarcophagi stood to each side of the chairs that allowed seating. While the old Chastain plantation had burned to the ground during the Civil War, the family had merely moved on into the city of New Orleans—and every decade or so, a new Chastain joined his or her ancestors.

He knew the mausoleum well; he'd come out here often enough in his misspent youth with friends. Adolescents loved to sneak out to the ruins of the Chastain plantation and into the old cemetery to tell ghost stories and try to scare themselves—and dare one another to sleep in the mausoleum. They were somewhat outside the French Quarter and the old section of the city where the timeworn buildings and Spanish and French architecture ruled in the unique and beautiful aura of faded elegance that created the atmosphere of New Orleans. Far from the jazz bands and commercial pop that emanated from the clubs on Bourbon.

Yet, here, out in the bayou area, Michael felt even more a part of the essence of Orleans Parish. Here, the cicadas were rubbing their wings; he heard the rustle of the wind through skeletal trees that scattered the graveyard. And beneath the meager glow of the moon, he felt the pervasion of death and history and something lonely and sad as well.

The cemetery was not the size of St. Louis, but was built in the true style of the "cities of the dead" that were so much a part of the South Louisiana landscape. Eerie by night, the small and large tombs did seem to make up their own city and it was easy to imagine that ghostly denizens might emerge from the wrought iron gates and different archways and openings at any minute, ready to dance beneath the sliver of moonlight.

The vigil seemed long. The tomb he leaned against seemed

cold despite the sultry weather of the night. His muscles began to tighten.

There. Movement.

Quinn saw someone in dark clothing—almost invisible in the night—moving like a wraith. He appeared to slip through the iron gate and the giant wooden doors of the structure. They must have been left ajar. How? By whom?

Quinn waited, damning the fact that his own heartbeat seemed loud in the night. He watched; he'd seen only one person. He'd begun his vigil almost two hours early to see who would come.

He didn't head across the overgrown path to the front of the vault. He knew it well. Hell, he'd slept in the damned thing. The Chastain dead were apparently not vengeful; nothing had happened to him. And, oddly enough, he could be grateful now that he did know the vault so well.

He knew of a small entrance at the back, behind the altar. Apparently, one of the Chastain founding family members had liked to enter unobserved and mourn his dead.

Quinn hurried around as quickly as he could, ever watchful of the front.

Nothing.

Coming to the rear, he took his time, barely breathing as he carefully pried open the rear iron door, praying it wouldn't screech. No one had used it in some time but the vines and weeds that should have nearly choked it had been pulled away.

Something was off here. But still, he was sure he could use this passage to get the jump on whoever was inside.

He eased the door open just wide enough to get his body through. He dropped and rolled behind the altar as quickly as he could. The rear wall offered broken stained glass windows and the weak illumination of the moon came through what remained of the colored glass in a strange purple color. The air smelled musty, but no surprise there.

A tile tilted under his left shoe. Had the intruder hidden back here? If so, where was he now? Something within Quinn wanted to investigate that tile, pry it up—

Later.

He held his breath and listened. No sound. Not even the other's breathing. Was he holding his breath, too?

No. The mausoleum *felt* empty. But how could that be? Quinn had seen him go in.

Pulling his revolver, he moved out from behind the altar and crept around, searching. The place was empty. But that was imposs—

A sudden flurry of movement stunned him—someone moving with lightning speed, hurtling toward him. Quinn spun away but something cold and metallic rammed none too gently against the base of his skull.

"Another move and your brain stem comes out your nose."

The pistol's muzzle was positioned to do just what the intruder said, so Quinn froze, cursing himself. He'd played just about every role known to man in life, from idiot hero-addict to cop and now investigator of the unusual—and he wasn't accustomed to being the one taken by surprise.

But, hell, he'd also learned how to talk and stall, how to retreat to fight again—and this seemed the right time for that.

"Okay, okay."

The other man snickered as he removed Quinn's revolver from his grasp. "Some hit man."

The words stunned Quinn. "What—what did you say?"

"You heard me."

"You called me a hit man."

"On your knees. Gotta little hog-tying to do."

"Wait just a goddamn minute. Who do you think I am?"

"That lady de Medici's boy. Now on your knees or I put your own slugs through them."

Madame de Medici? Quinn thought. *He thinks I work for her?*

"I've had no contact with the madame. Ever. I don't know where you got your information, but I was hired by the owner, Jules Chastain."

He could feel the other man stiffen behind him.

"Bullshit."

"No, *true* shit." He spoke quickly. "Reach into my jacket pocket for my ID. My name is Michael Quinn. I'm a private investigator in New Orleans."

The muzzle pressed harder against his skull as the man reached around, found the folder, and removed it.

"It's too dark to read in here anyway."

"You mean you came without a flashlight?"

"No." His tone was annoyed. "It's just that my hands are full at the moment."

He shoved Quinn toward the chairs. "Have a seat while I figure this out."

Quinn did as he was told. The guy seemed dangerous but Quinn felt no fear of him. Odd. It was occurring to him that they'd both been taken—he hoped it was occurring to the other guy, too.

A flashlight glowed and Quinn caught a glimpse of some non-descript features, then the beam shone straight into his face.

"This could be fake."

Quinn held up a hand to shield his eyes. "Yeah, it could be, but it's not."

The ID folder sailed through the light and landed in his lap.

"I don't know why I believe you, but I do. Why did Chastain hire you?"

"To protect this place from a thief he was tipped was coming. That would be you, I guess."

Quinn winced inwardly. It had seemed like a nothing job; he hadn't even told Danni about it. Chastain was rich; he and Danni often needed hefty sums in their line of work: pulling in a nice, up-front paycheck for a few hours of work while she was busy with a celebration ceremony had seemed like a damned good idea.

He should have known there'd be a catch—like nearly getting his fool self killed.

The other man barked a bitter laugh. "No, I'm no thief. Chastain hired me to retrieve a ring he'd hidden here."

"*What?*"

"Yeah. What the fuck?"

The silence lengthened between them until Quinn finally said, "Can I have my pistol back?"

"It's a revolver, and a revolver is not strictly a pistol."

Quinn had to laugh. "You mean I let a gun nerd get the drop on me?"

"Facts is facts, and no, you can't have it back. At least not yet."

"Not yet is okay. But how the hell did you get the drop on me?"

"Chastain told me about the rear door. I didn't trust him, so I went in the front and out the back, then watched the place. I saw you go in the back so I followed."

Quinn had to admit that was pretty clever, even as he kicked himself for falling for it. He'd seen how the vines at the rear had been disturbed but he'd come in anyway.

"You do realize we've been set up, right?"

Another short, sharp laugh. "Ya think? I *knew* this smelled bad."

"You don't sound like a local."

"Got that right. Chastain told me to be prepared for 'deadly force.' He'd made it sound defensive. Now I'm thinking he wanted me to use it. What's he got against you?"

"Nothing that I know of. Barely know the man. But I *do* know him better than you. I'm local. You know my name. What's yours?"

"Jack."

"'Jack' what?"

"Just Jack'll do. Seems like I was supposed to kill you."

Quinn's muscles tightened, ready to leap. He'd actually been declared 'dead' once already. He didn't fear death.

But he sure as hell didn't want to die.

"And?" he asked flatly.

A shrug. "Don't see any reason to." Jack pulled out a folded piece of paper and handed it to Quinn. "This is supposedly where Chastain hid the ring I was supposed to bring him. Suppose it's bogus, too."

Quinn looked over the diagram and the instructions.

"Don't you want a light?" Jack said.

"Don't need it." Quinn studied the diagram. "There should be a jagged little crack in the bottom of the first vault—the oldest—according to this."

He ignored the fact that the other man had a gun while he still didn't, and chanced turning his back on him to head to the rear of the vault and hunker down. He looked at the diagram again and stuck his hand into the jagged crack on the lowest shelf—that of Antioch Chastain, founder of the clan. As the diagram suggested, his hand hit a box; a wooden box. He withdrew it—along with a mass of spiderwebs and bone dust. He looked at Jack, and then opened the box.

"Empty," they announced together.

"Figures," Jack said. "The whole thing was a setup."

"But why? He wanted us both here for a reason."

"Why here? And by the way, haven't you folks heard of *graves*?"

Quinn laughed. "The water table's too high. And, actually, the cemeteries were conceived during the Spanish rule, and their design is according to the custom of the time. Good custom here— bury someone and you could find their coffin floating along in the next heavy rain."

"So you pigeonhole them in these little buildings? Doesn't it get ripe after a while? And what happens when you run out of shelves?"

"Here in Louisiana, the rule is 'a year and a day.' The heat is so great that bodies mostly cremate in that time. These tombs are like ovens. Families shovel the bits and bones of the remains of one loved one to a mutual 'holding' section at the foot of the shelf so that another family member can find his or her resting place for a year and a day—or until the shelf is needed again."

"That's gross. What country is this?"

"The United States of Louisiana. We have our own way of doing things."

"I guess you do." Jack looked around. "Great setting for a horror film, though. Hey, you think that's why he got us here—to film us fighting? Some sick YouTube snuff vid?"

"You think he's hidden a camera?"

"He didn't fly me down from New York so we could have this nice little chat. Gotta be some reason he put us both here."

Quinn didn't see a camera anywhere, but memory of the loose tile flashed through his head. "It's probably nothing, but—"

He ducked behind the altar and pried up the tile. Only dirt beneath it. But soft dirt.

He dug and struck metal within the first inch. He worked his fingers around it and came up with a bracelet made of strange metal and carved with even stranger designs. A green stone the size of a dime was embedded in its center. It looked familiar.

"I know this piece: the Cidsev Nelesso."

"Sounds like a gelato flavor," Jack said.

"It was found sealed in a sunken temple dedicated to an as yet unidentified deity in the drowned city of Heracleion."

"So what's it doing here?"

"Good question. It and part of a papyrus scroll found with it were smuggled out and sold on the black market. The buyer was purportedly Chastain."

"And you know all this how?"

Quinn hesitated. "I'm a private investigator. And I've been a cop for the City of New Orleans. But, these days—"

He held off. He was always careful, especially with strangers— and more especially, New Yorkers. But, to his great humiliation, this guy could have killed him.

And he hadn't.

"Part of what I do these days is work with a woman," he said softly. "Danni Cafferty. Her father owned a shop and I worked with him until his death. And now Danni and I . . . collect things. Unusual things. Angus Cafferty was a real scholar and, in his business, he needed to know about history and—things."

"Things?"

"Curiosities of evil," Quinn said. "Believe me or not. Objects that are cursed or that create evil in those who know how to use them or seek power through them. And I have a feeling now that we're not dealing with any film project—we're dealing with a thing that can cause evil."

Quinn waited for the other man—*Jack*—to tell him he was crazy.

230

Jack didn't say any such thing. Instead, "What about this Madame de Medici he mentioned?"

"She's another notorious collector, but the way this is going, I doubt she knows anything—just a red herring in the story Chastain concocted for you."

Jack took the bracelet and held it up, turning it this way and that in the wan moonlight filtering through the stained glass.

"Valuable?"

"'Priceless' might be a better word. It's one of a kind. Supposedly one of the Seven Infernals."

He saw Jack stiffen. "An Infernal?" He shoved it back into Quinn's hands. "Here."

"You know of the Infernals?"

"Unfortunately, yeah. Met one."

Something in his expression said it had been a harrowing encounter. Jack hadn't doubted Quinn—and Quinn didn't doubt Jack for a minute.

"But hardly anybody's even *heard* of the Infernals. Even Danni—"

"Danni—your partner who collects things?"

"Her shop is called The Cheshire Cat. It's on Royal Street. She sells art, jewelry, and *innocent* collectibles. And she has a separate collection of things in the basement which will never be sold." He hesitated. "We also destroy things when they need destroying. And when there are things out there that might cause . . . violence or havoc, people sometimes come to her—or The Cheshire Cat." He shrugged. "We work together most of the time; she had to be at a ceremony with a friend of ours, a voodoo priestess."

"So you're moonlighting on your own?"

Quinn cast Jack a sharp glance. "That's kind of what *you're* doing, isn't it?"

"This is how I make my living—just not so far from home."

Quinn continued with, "The upper half of the scroll Chastain bought with the bracelet was copied before it was stolen. That copy and the original of the bottom half of the scroll were left to Danni on consignment."

"Who left it?"

"Some weird old guy. Wouldn't leave his name. Said he'd be back after she sold it. There didn't seem to be anything—well, *not right* about it." He hesitated and then said, "We usually have a nose for things that aren't—right."

"He trusted her?"

Quinn shrugged, hiding a burst of pride. "She has a flawless reputation."

"Any buyer?"

Quinn felt a mild jolt of unease as he remembered Danni mentioning that she had sold the fragment.

And to whom she had sold it.

"Yes. Madame de Medici."

"I thought you didn't know the woman," Jack said sharply.

"I don't know her; I know *of* her. She doesn't come into the shop herself; she sends a minion."

Jack laughed. "Minion? She's got a *minion*?"

"A number of them. Anyway, she's purchased from Danni before and nothing bad has ever come of it."

"So she does figure in this."

"What the hell—maybe. But I still think Chastain is taking the two of us on some kind of a ride."

"We'll worry about Madame de Medici later," Jack said, pointing to the bracelet. "What's the deal on this thing?"

"The top half of the scroll claims the Cidsev Nelesso confers the 'gift' of knowing the thoughts of others. *'No one can hide their thoughts from the wearer.'*"

"I can see where that could come in handy during a negotiation."

"For a collector like Chastain, who's always haggling, it's invaluable."

"What's the downside?"

Quinn was surprised by the question. "Why do you think there's a downside?" He felt uneasy. They should have sensed something bad was going to go down.

"Always a downside with an Infernal."

"How can you know that?"

"Supposedly there are seven Infernals. One of them damn near took the two people who mean more to me than anything else in this world."

"How?"

"Too long a story for here and now."

"Okay. Where is it now?"

"Gone. And don't ask where because I don't know. But it didn't go alone. It took somebody with it."

From Jack's expression, Quinn knew better than to ask who.

Jack cleared his throat and said, "Enough about me. What's the bottom half of the scroll say?"

"It says the bracelet isn't of Greek or Egyptian origin—calls it 'one of the Seven Infernals from the First Age.' I obviously don't have to explain that to you. But its 'gift' is considered a curse, so maybe that's your downside."

Jack shook his head. "If you know someone's thoughts, they can't hide anything from you. The truth can be ugly, and it can hurt, but knowing what's really going down is better than getting the shaft."

Quinn couldn't disagree. The advantage in any relationship, business or personal, was obvious.

"But either way," Jack said. "Why the hell are *we* here?"

"According to the scroll, the Cidsev Nelesso, like all Seven Infernals, must be triggered to work."

Jack's expression was bleak. "Yeah, I know."

Quinn wondered just what the hell had happened to him.

He held up the bracelet. "Well, this one requires violence to activate it."

"So, there you have it. That's why we're here. Was I actually supposed to kill you?"

"The scroll says death isn't necessary. Just violence."

Jack began wandering in a tight circle, muttering. "Curse. *No one can hide their thoughts from the wearer.* Violence."

Suddenly Jack whirled and punched him in the gut. Quinn doubled over, as much in surprise as in pain.

"Are you out of your—?"

A right cross to the jaw snapped his head back.

That did it. If this son of a bitch wanted a donnybrook, he was going to get one. Quinn charged, head down, catching Jack in the midsection and slamming him back against the shelves.

"You son of a bitch!" Jack gasped in a breathless voice.

And then he grabbed Quinn's arm and flipped him on his ass.

Ah, hell! Quinn thought, rolling and leaping to his feet.

But he was smiling as he charged at Jack.

•◆•

"Is it going as you hoped?" said a soft, feminine voice behind him.

Jules Chastain whirled, then relaxed. Even in the meager light he recognized Madame de Medici. He had found a vantage point fifty yards from his family mausoleum and had settled in to see if the seeds he had planted bore violent fruit. How had she found him?

"Not quite. And why are you here?"

"As an involved party, I have a right, yes?"

He had been trying to place her accent in the years since she'd appeared in New Orleans, but it remained elusive.

"You recommended the New York mercenary, nothing more."

She said she'd heard of a so-called Repairman Jack who hired himself out to "fix" situations. She had assured Jules he was real and reliable, though known to have a violent streak. She'd even passed along his number. Jules had liked the violent-streak aspect, and had hired Michael Quinn as cannon fodder—everyone in New Orleans knew not to mess with Quinn. The two made for a combustible combination.

She focused her amber gaze on him. "But I have an interest in the Cidsev Nelesso as well. After all, I used to own it."

Those eyes. One could almost fall into them. Could almost believe she really had lived for millennia.

But Jules chose to humor her rather than challenge her. The Cidsev Nelesso had been found in Heracleion, which had sunk in the third century BC. The idea of Madame de Medici once having owned that bracelet was beyond delusional. More like psychotic.

So, never challenge a psycho.

"I hope you're not thinking of trying anything sneaky here."

"Dear Jules, the idea never crossed my mind. I will be quite happy to see it on your wrist. I lost it in a civil upheaval. Where it lands after that is up to fate."

Whatever happened to the Cidsev Nelesso, dear lady, it landed with me.

He had made up that story for Jack about stealing it from her.

Quite clever, he thought. But he had bought it fair and square on the black market. It was *his*.

God, she was beautiful. She'd emigrated from Cairo during the so-called Arab Spring and wound up in New Orleans with a trove of antiquities. She tended to dress in gauzy fabrics that covered everything and hid nothing. He'd asked her to dinner a hundred times but she'd refused. *I'm not looking for a relationship*, was her eternal excuse.

Neither am I, dear lady. I wish only one night with you.

He jumped at the sound of gunfire echoing from the mausoleum.

"Ah," he said. "*Now* I am happy."

"It should be activated now," she said, turning and sauntering away. "Don't forget: put it on right away or it will lose power."

He bit back a laugh. So convincing.

He made himself comfortable and waited until the police and the ambulance arrived. He watched the EMTs carry "Just Jack" out on a stretcher with Michael Quinn walking behind. Both alive? *Quel dommage*. He hoped death wasn't required to trigger the bracelet.

When all the intruders were gone, Jules made his way to the mausoleum and slipped through the still-open front gates. He headed to the rear of the altar and pried up the tile. A little digging and there it was: the Cidsev Nelesso.

He noted with glee that its stone had turned from green to red, confirmation that the bracelet's power had been ignited.

He sighed. "You are *such* a genius, Jules."

He slipped it over his left hand and was taken aback when it tightened itself around his wrist. But not too tight. Okay, not a problem. Custom fit wasn't a bad thing. And he had no intention of taking it off anyway. If this trinket lived up to only a fraction of its advance publicity, the world would be his oyster.

As he stepped out into the night he heard a voice.

Two bucks, two bucks, need a dollar more to get a bottle, small bottle but better'n nothin'.

He looked around and saw a wino stumbling past the Boudreaux vault. His first thought was to drive out the trespasser, but then he realized the bum wasn't talking. Jules was hearing him in his head. Hearing his *thoughts*!

Dear God, it worked. It *worked*!

Other thoughts streamed in.

Another drink and she'll be ready.

Oh, I hope I don't hurl, I'll totally die if I hurl.

A young couple out for the night? He wondered where they were. But further speculation was cut off by more voices in his head.

Shout it was over Jim greatly alarmed me from the deepest reproach as it were soon all the other company I never thought he would my convict Do you mean that? but that it was in tomorrow but this style I had best endeavors let to see him next day when living had a but he had had no time after and apparently out old chap found the file still in—

He pressed his hands to his ears but couldn't stop the voices, the thoughts from other heads streaming in from all over the city. The state. The county. The *world*. Mixing and interweaving into a mad torrent that ran straight into his consciousness.

"Stop!" he screamed.

But it didn't stop. It thickened and quickened and ran more furiously into his brain.

Turns of yours this question mais ce style que j'ai eu mieux s'efforce de laisser burns that dread serious subcutaneous sickness of musze lub

powiedzieĆ Że wiemy, Że nie ma chwili us and arms make coil must
grunt Wir wurde mit einem guten Namen sicher glücklich cutaneous
forthy takes the good wasn't myself might have a life and the muscle to
heartache if a—

He clawed at the bracelet but it wouldn't fit over his hand. He pushed at it, digging its edge into his skin, drawing blood, but it was too tight to remove, *too tight!* He had to get it off!

Jules Chastain ran screaming through the night in search of help.

•◆•

The ambulance pulled up in front of the emergency entrance at Tulane Medical Center.

Jack sat up and looked at the EMT at his side. "Thanks for the lift."

"Hey, no worries," the young man told him. "Quinn called, that's enough for me."

Good guy to know, this Michael Quinn.

As Jack exited the vehicle, a car pulled up behind it. Quinn sat behind the wheel. Jack nodded as he slipped into the passenger's seat.

Quinn rubbed his jaw before driving out into traffic. "That's one mean right hook you have."

Jack said, "You're no slouch yourself. My ribs are bruised to shit."

Quinn laughed. "I'm glad I saw that green stone turn red when it did. It's going to be hard enough explaining. Well, hell, I think we're both beat up enough."

"Seemed the right thing to do—letting Chastain get in there and take the bracelet after we 'activated' it," Jack said. "If there really is a curse, then, the man deserved to have it."

Quinn offered him a grim smile. "I hope you're right about this—right about the way the curse will work."

Jack's own experience with an Infernal had come to a tragic end, but it could have been so much worse. They weren't called Infernals for nothing.

"I'm just guessing," he said. *"No one can hide their thoughts from the wearer* could also read *Everyone's thoughts are revealed to the wearer.* And hearing literally everyone's thoughts would definitely be a curse."

"Nice touch," Quinn told him. "I mean, firing your Glock into the floor after our fight. And reburying that bracelet so that Chastain could find it once we were out."

"Not a bad deal that you're friends with half the cops and emergency techs in the city, too."

Quinn shrugged. "Well, like I told you, I was a cop once. Still work with them—with one great cop, an old partner, Larue. He doesn't want me to explain things like curses and Infernals—he just wants me to take care of them."

"I tend to avoid cops—nothing personal. It's just the less they know about me, the better."

"You have warrants out on you?"

Jack shrugged. "Need a name on a warrant, don't you?"

"Yeah, of course."

"Well, then, I guess not. As for the here and now, we should know how things pan out by tomorrow. You know a place I can bunk for the night?"

Quinn smiled, not at all grimly then. "Yeah, I know a great place. Right on Royal. And when Danni wants to know why I'm beat to hell, I can say, 'You should see the other guy'—and then show her that other guy."

Jack laughed. He could get to like this Quinn.

It didn't take long to reach the center of the French Quarter. Jack was impressed with the historic building with the sign that read THE CHESHIRE CAT.

But they didn't enter by the front. Quinn hit a button on his dash, a garage door opened, and they moved through a beautiful garden courtyard to enter by a side door.

A woman was waiting there, tall and lithe, with a giant dog by her side.

"That's just Wolf," Quinn told him, greeting the dog, who accepted Jack right away because his master suggested he do so.

Quinn seemed a little awkward as he greeted the woman.

"Danni, you're back early."

"So I am," she said, staring from Quinn to Jack and then back at Quinn again. "I guess you two should come in and get cleaned up—and patched up. And I guess you're going to tell me that I should see the other guys?"

Jack looked at Quinn. They both smiled.

Jack said, "We *are* the other guys."

"Interesting," Danni said. "I'll put on some tea and get out the whiskey. I'm looking forward to hearing all about it."

Normally Jack would be looking for a beer, but after tonight, whiskey was definitely in order.

•◆•

In the morning, Quinn tracked down Larue by phone and learned he was at the hospital. He rounded up Jack and drove him there. The front desk gave them the room number and they headed up.

No surprise to find his old friend standing next to the bed where Chastain lay heavily sedated. His left arm was thickly bandaged—and Quinn noticed with a start it was much shorter than it should be.

"Quinn," Larue said, shaking his head. "I guess I expected to see you here at some point. Damnedest thing. Chastain—he of untold riches—suddenly went mad and cut off his own hand. You know anything about that? And who's your friend?"

"Jack. Jack, this is Detective Larue."

"Jack?"

"Just Jack."

Larue studied him a moment, then shrugged. "Anything I need to worry about?" he asked Quinn.

Quinn stared at the pale, unconscious man. "He's going to make it?"

"Minus his hand and wrist."

"How did he wind up here?"

"He's lucky he's alive. Beat cop found him wandering the streets, mumbling incoherently. I was afraid we had a psycho out there somewhere, chopping on people. But according to the EMT who worked with him first, Chastain said he cut his own hand off because it had 'betrayed' him. Not sure what the hell that means—bastard wasn't even drunk or on anything. Tox reports came back clean."

"Anybody find the hand?"

Larue shook his head. "Gone. Dog might have run off with it. Or a big rat."

"How about some jewelry?" Jack said. "Like, oh, say, a bracelet?"

Larue stared at them both. "What bracelet?"

Hell. That meant the Cidsev Nelesso was still out there.

Quinn shrugged and said, "Well, I was just thinking. If you

cut your hand off at the wrist, it might have been because you had something on the wrist that you couldn't get off. You know—something that had 'betrayed' you."

"I've got cops looking in Dumpsters—no hand," Larue said. "Strange as hell, huh? Should I be looking for a bracelet?"

"If you find the hand, you'll find something with it, I would think," Quinn said.

Larue shook his head and glanced at both men. "You make sure I know if there's something I should be worrying about, Quinn. Mr.—Mr. Jack, enjoy the city."

Larue walked by them.

Quinn watched as Jack paused at Chastain's bedside. "What goes around," he murmured.

Quinn nodded. "No one dead. That works for me."

And he now realized why he'd sensed nothing wrong about the bracelet: there hadn't *been* anything wrong until it was activated.

Jack said, "Where the hell do you think the hand and bracelet could be?"

Quinn had an idea but kept it to himself.

"Need a ride to the airport?"

Jack shook his head. "The TSA and I aren't on cordial terms."

Now *that* was interesting.

"Well, I'm afraid I don't have a private jet on hand like Chastain."

"Didn't figure you did. Guess I'll rent a car."

Quinn figured that meant whatever ID Jack was carrying was bogus.

"So, your ID's good enough for Hertz but not TSA?"

Jack gave him a long look before shrugging. "It's passed TSA before but I'm not one for tempting fate."

"Long drive."

Jack sighed. "Can't say I'm looking forward to it, but I guess it's a way to see some country."

"I take it you don't leave New York much?"

Jack shrugged. "What for?"

Quinn had to laugh. He felt the same about New Orleans.

Traffic was light. Thirty minutes later Quinn dropped Jack at the airport Hertz office.

"If you're ever in New Orleans again," Quinn said.

Jack shook his hand. "Don't hold your breath."

•◆•

Madame de Medici stood without moving, admiring the Cidsev Nelesso. It remained clamped around Jules Chastain's flesh where his hand, wrist, and distal forearm lay on a metal tray in her private museum.

She had told Jules last night that she'd be quite happy to see it on his wrist, and that had been true. In fact, she would always see it there. Chastain's extremity had to be properly preserved, of course—she knew the ancient ways of curing flesh. After that, she would place the ensemble in the glass display case she had prepared for it.

She was not tempted to wear it—not in the least. She was no fool. But she was delighted to have it back in her collection.

She smoothed back a length of elegant dark hair, quite satisfied for the moment.

Chastain had wanted the Cidsev Nelesso so badly.

Now he would wear it.

Forever.

RAYMOND KHOURY
VS. LINWOOD BARCLAY

Pit Stop

R aymond Khoury's decision to use Sean Reilly for this short story was an easy one. He'd first brought the FBI agent to life when, in 1996, as a budding screenwriter, he'd written his third (unproduced) screenplay—a modern conspiracy thriller that harkened back to the days of the Crusades called *The Last Templar*.

He then experienced the euphoria of being offered a small fortune by a major New York publisher to turn his screenplay into a novel, only then to be gutted when the publisher said they'd like him to make a "small change" to the story.

Let's lose the religion. It's boring. Turn the Templars' secret into gold, jewels, a real treasure.

Raymond decided that advice was no good, so he nixed the deal.

Smart? Gutsy? Foolish?

Maybe all three.

But interest in the screenplay did trigger a screenwriting career. So, for several years, Sean Reilly remained locked away in a dormant file on Raymond's hard drive while he worked on movies and television shows. Then, in 2006, Sean Reilly was finally allowed to breathe again in *The Last Templar*. Raymond decided to write the story for himself, religion and all. The result was a global success, selling over five million copies in more than forty languages.

Which just goes to show—not all advice is good advice.

For Linwood Barclay the decision to use Glen Garber was a little trickier. Linwood hasn't had a series character since he wrote four comic thrillers (from 2004 to 2007) starring Zack Walker. Since then each of his novels has been a stand-alone with a different hero. The obsessive-compulsive, risk-averse Zack Walker would not have been the best partner for Sean Reilly. Zack would have probably fled the story after the first paragraph, leaving Reilly to carry the load. But Glen Garber, the contractor (as in home renovator, not hit man) from Linwood's *The Accident* (2011) seemed the perfect character to team with Reilly. He's a tough, no-nonsense guy. Someone who's not unfamiliar with loss, and not afraid to put himself on the line to protect those he loves. While he doesn't have the kind of training Sean Reilly possesses, he's no stranger to courage and wanting to see justice done.

This short story emerged from a single line that Linwood e-mailed to Raymond—which ultimately became the fiery incident that launches the tale. Both writers then batted the story back and forth, each writing one of the sections and seeding clues, while leaving the choice of where to go entirely to the other.

The result?

A free flow of imagination and an exhilarating ride.

Pit Stop

Glen Garber had been given his coffee, but was still waiting for an order of chicken nuggets for his daughter, Kelly, when a woman raced into the restaurant screaming that some guy was on fire in the parking lot.

They'd pulled in off the interstate at around the halfway point of their trip. Glen was being asked to bid on a farmhouse renovation about two hours out of Milford. It was Saturday, so he invited Kelly to come along for the ride. Not just because he liked her company, but because he wasn't going to leave a ten-year-old on her own for the day. Glen had been paranoid enough when his wife, Sheila, was still alive, but being a single dad had upped his anxiety levels.

He always wanted to know where Kelly was. Every minute of every day. He could just imagine how much she'd appreciate this when she was well into her teenage years.

When Kelly saw the signs for an upcoming service center, she announced that she was so hungry she thought she might die.

"We wouldn't want that," her father said. "I guess I could use a coffee. I'll make a quick pit stop."

Turned out not to be so quick. Given that it was Saturday, and the middle of summer, the lot was packed, and the lineup deep when they went into the restaurant. When they finally reached the counter, Glen placed their order. The girl ringing up the sale said the nuggets would take a few minutes, but she had his coffee to him in seconds. Glen wrapped his hand around the takeout cup and quickly let go.

"Yikes," he said. "We'll be up there before this is cool enough to drink." He put the tip of his index finger on the bottom lip, and his thumb on the edge of the plastic lid.

"Where's my nuggets?" Kelly asked.

"The girl said they'd just take a—"

That was when the woman screamed, "He's on fire! There's a man on fire!"

The first thing Glen thought was, no way! A car on fire, maybe. Wasn't unheard of for a car to overheat here along the interstate, especially when it was pushing ninety degrees out there. But a man in flames? That didn't sound right.

The second thing he thought was, he had a fire extinguisher in his pickup, a Ford F-150 with the words GARBER CONTRACTING, MILFORD plastered on the doors. Should he run out, grab the extinguisher from behind the driver's seat, and try to help this guy, assuming what this woman said was true?

Yeah, maybe. Except he wasn't about to leave Kelly all by herself in a crowded, roadside fast-food joint, where someone could grab a kid, toss her in a car, and be God knows where in ten minutes.

"Honey," he said to her, "we're going to the truck."

"What about my—?"

But by the way her dad pulled her arm, she knew something bad was going on. She hadn't only heard the woman screaming about that guy, she could feel the anxiety sweeping the room. People trying to decide what to do. Whether to stay in there, flock to the window and gawk, or run outside and get a front-row seat.

Glen guided Kelly quickly to the door, pushing past people, butting in ahead of them to get outside. Coming out of the air-conditioning, the midday heat hit them like a warm, smothering blanket.

"Over there," Kelly said, pointing.

A crowd had formed a couple of car lengths away from the pumps. Waves of heat riffled through the air. Glen let go of Kelly's arm, reached into his pocket for the remote, and hit the button to unlock his truck as they approached it.

He brought Kelly around to the passenger's side. She was more than big enough to hop in herself, but her father gave her enough of a boost that she was nearly tossed across the seat. He reached over her and placed his coffee into one of the cup holders between the seats.

Then he went around to the driver's side, opened the door, and reached behind the seat to grab the red cylinder he always kept there. Doing construction, you were just as likely to need one of these at a work site as you were to put out a car fire.

"Stay here," Glen said firmly. "Lock the doors."

"I'll die with the windows up," Kelly said. "It's a million degrees in here."

He hopped in long enough to engage the ignition, without firing up the engine, and power down the windows, leaving the key inserted in the steering column. "Keep the doors locked just the same."

Glen, extinguisher in his right hand, ran toward the commotion.

People screaming.

He pulled the pin on the extinguisher, then got his left hand under the cylinder for support, and shouldered his way through the onlookers.

Good God.

It was hard to tell with the flames, but it was, indeed, a man. In his thirties, probably, maybe two hundred and fifty pounds, dressed in sandals and a T-shirt and a pair of those cargo shorts with the oversized pockets.

Not exactly a Tibetan monk setting himself ablaze.

If the man had been flailing earlier, he'd given up by the time Glen had arrived, now down on the pavement, his body crumpling in on itself as the flames consumed him. But that didn't stop Glen from taking a few quick shots with the extinguisher.

The people who'd gathered round backed away, mouths still open in horror. But a couple of them had screamed and shifted their gaze to something else, and were looking no less shocked.

Glen managed to tear his eyes away from the dead man to see what could possibly be distracting these people from a sight as ghastly as this. It wasn't exactly every day you came upon a man on fire.

A man was staggering out of the men's room, which was off on one side of the restaurant. He had blood across his face and held one hand against his temple, and was teetering unsteadily on his feet, barely able to walk. But even from this far, Glen could make out a fierce determination in the man's face.

He didn't have too much time to dwell on it. The next thing he heard wrenched his heart out and squeezed the life out of it.

It was a sound he was well familiar with.

The starter drive of a Ford F-150.

His Ford F-150.

He snapped his gaze away from the injured man in time to see his truck charge out of its parking spot and roar off in the direction of the interstate.

•◆•

Sean Reilly couldn't see clearly.

His eyes weren't functioning properly. Not yet, not with the blood streaked across them, and the little information they were filtering in was being processed by a concussed brain.

A direct hit from a toilet tank cover usually had that effect.

He glanced around as he advanced, willing his head to clear up, trying to process whatever inputs he could pick up from the scene around him. He could make out a small crowd gathered off to his left. He could hear panicked screams and sobbing coming from them. And then the smell hit him, a horrific smell that he instantly recognized. A putrid, sickly-sweet smell that was unique and traumatizing to anyone who'd ever suffered the misfortune of coming across it. Mercifully, most people hadn't. Then again, most people weren't FBI field agents for whom the worst horrors the human mind could dream up were just part and parcel of the job.

Reilly saw the rising smoke and instantly guessed what must have happened there. He also knew who had to be responsible for it—the same man who had left him for dead in the men's toilet—and as anger spiked through him from that realization and morsels of clarity tumbled into his mind, he heard a man yelling out, "Kelly!"

He saw a man burst out from among the crowd and charge off across the lot, chucking a fire extinguisher he was carrying. Reilly's instincts shifted all his attention away from the crowd and locked onto that man, and he willed his legs to propel him faster as he chased after him.

The man stopped by a row of parked cars that were lined up outside the restaurant, and again screamed out the name, a reverberating scream that seemed to emanate from the very pit of his soul. He was glancing ahead, down the interstate, then his head darted left and right as Reilly caught up with him.

The man must have heard and sensed Reilly. He spun around to face him, one arm raised high, its fist balled offensively and ready to pummel.

"My daughter," he growled, his face burning with fear and fury. "She's gone!"

Reilly raised his hands defensively. "Wait a sec—"

"Kelly!" the man hollered again. "My girl, she was in my truck. It was right here, and now it's gone. Heading for the highway!"

Reilly understood.

First, another innocent victim burned alive. A distraction, Reilly figured, to allow the man he was after to get away.

Now this.

This guy's daughter, abducted.

All because of him.

His own fury took over.

"It was locked," the man spat out as he shot another glance down the highway. "But the key was in it. The windows were down."

Reilly held both hands in front of him, his fingers splayed open in a holding, calming gesture. "You have a phone?" he asked the girl's father.

The man seemed momentarily confused by this. "What?"

"Do you have a phone on you?"

The man nodded and patted his jacket and pants before pulling out a cell phone from a back pocket.

Reilly snatched it from him. "Is it locked?"

Uncertainly, the man said, "No. Who the hell are you?"

Reilly dodged the question, nodded, and bolted away from him. There was no time to waste. Every second counted. He scanned the forecourt and settled on a small, burgundy station wagon that was just pulling out of its parking spot, and without so much as a split-second's hesitation, he beelined for it and placed himself right in its path, intercepting it with his arms spread wide and waving to the driver to stop.

The car squealed to a halt, coming to rest less than a foot from Reilly. He didn't pause. He spun around the car and flung the driver's door open, then reached in and pulled the vehicle's sole, confused occupant—a seventies stalwart in round sunglasses and a faded Steely Dan concert T-shirt—out of the car.

"FBI, sir. I'm gonna need your car," he told him as he threw himself behind the wheel.

Without waiting for an answer, Reilly pulled the creaking door shut, threw the car into drive, and charged off—

Only to slam on his brakes as a figure stepped in front of the car, blocking his way.

The father. Standing there, staring down Reilly with an unsettling cocktail of anger and confusion.

Within seconds, he had pulled the passenger's door open and slid in next to Reilly.

Reilly studied him for a beat.

"You said FBI?" the man said.

"Yes," Reilly replied.

The man took a breath, then said, "Drive."

Reilly nodded, turned to face the open road, and did just that.

When Kristoff saw the parked truck with the little girl sitting on the passenger's side, he figured there was a chance the keys were in it. He spotted her after he'd splashed some gas on that fat guy at the pumps, tossed a match his way. *Poof!* Guy went up like a marshmallow you'd held over the campfire too long.

While everyone was running over to see the show, he scanned the lot. He figured a guy on fire would prompt some people to bail from their vehicles without taking the time to grab their keys. That was when he saw the Ford, with the kid inside.

Kristoff sprinted toward it, clutching the brushed aluminum cylinder still in his hand. He'd had to let go of it long enough to whack that FBI agent in the head with the toilet tank cover, but he had it back in his hand now. Nearly a foot long, about two inches in diameter, it looked like a common Thermos. But there was no coffee or tea in it. No, what was inside it was definitely not something you'd want to drink. Not first thing in the morning. Not ever.

But Reilly sure wanted it.

And Kristoff definitely wanted to hang on to it. Its contents were worth a great deal to him. Worth killing for.

Stealing a truck with a kid inside it, that'd be the least of his crimes by the time this was over.

When he reached the truck, he grabbed the door handle so hard he nearly ripped off a nail when he discovered it was locked. But the window was down, so all Kristoff had to do was reach in and pull the lock up.

The kid shouted, "Hey! This isn't your truck!"

Well, no kidding.

He jumped in behind the wheel, hoping the key would be in the ignition. Hallelujah, praise the Lord, there it was. He half chuckled to himself. The very notion of thanking God, when he had with him the means to destroy so much of what the Lord had created.

He stomped one foot down hard on the brake, turned the key, got the engine going. He tucked the aluminum cylinder on the seat between his thigh and the center console.

The kid wouldn't stop yammering. "Stop it!" she shouted. "This is my dad's truck! Get out!"

Threw it into drive and hit the gas.

Kristoff glanced in the mirror, saw the crowd of people gathered around that hapless traveler. It was hard to feel bad for the man. In many ways, he was lucky. He got to go first. He was spared the misery that would befall everyone later.

"Stop!" the girl screamed.

He glanced over at her. Maybe nine, ten years old. Sweet-looking kid, really. Reminded him of his niece. Best not to think of her, or any other members of his family. This wasn't the time to get sentimental.

The girl suddenly leaned over, tried to grab at the key in the steering wheel, turn it back.

Kristoff brought down his hand, fast, hitting the girl at the wrist. She yelped, withdrew her hand, pushed herself tight up against the passenger's door. She was starting to whimper.

"Shut up!" he yelled at her. "Shut up or I'll throw you out."

Which was exactly what he wanted to do, but wanting it and being able to do it were two different things. He couldn't reach all the way across and open the door and shove her out. Not at nearly eighty miles per hour, which he was now traveling, and his foot easing down even harder on the accelerator. If he wanted to ditch the kid, he'd have to pull over to the shoulder, run around to the other side, and drag her out.

Not a bad idea, actually. But he'd lose time.

There wasn't much time before he was to make the rendezvous.

But if there was no one on his tail . . .

He glanced into the rearview mirror again.

He'd already passed several cars since leaving the service station. No one else out here on the interstate was driving any faster than he was.

But there was a car coming up from behind. Growing larger in the mirror.

A burgundy car, a station wagon it looked like, judging from the roof racks. But a small car. Maybe he hadn't hit Reilly hard enough on that goddamn head of his. Maybe the son of a bitch had commandeered a car and was coming after him.

Maybe having the kid wasn't a liability after all. The kid was leverage. What was Reilly going to do? Run him off the road? Shoot out his tires? Run the risk of killing somebody's little girl?

Then again, you could never predict what Reilly would do. He was the kind of guy who saw the bigger picture. Who might figure one dead girl was better than millions.

Kristoff reached down, felt the cylinder by his thigh. Felt its power.

He turned to the girl, who was still whimpering. "Hey, come on, stop that. But you can't try to take out the key while we're moving. You could get us both killed."

The girl sniffed, wiped the tears from her cheeks. Her eyes were wide with fear.

"So, kid," he said, "what's your name?"

"Kelly," she whispered.

"Kelly. Nice name. Better do up your seat belt, Kelly. Gonna be a wild ride."

Reilly had the pedal pressed down as far as it would go, but it still wasn't enough. The car, a Chevy Vega Kammback station wagon from the seventies with wood-grain sides and a burgundy vinyl interior that had to be a health hazard in itself, was struggling to get above sixty. Still, he thought, it could have been worse. He could have commandeered an AMC Gremlin. Or a Pacer. Or pretty much anything with an AMC badge on it, for that matter.

Up ahead, the F-150 was receding alarmingly, a fact that wasn't lost on the Ford's owner, who was now sitting ramrod-straight next to Reilly, his eyes lasered on the vehicle his daughter was in.

"He's getting away," the man blurted. "Why didn't you just hijack a scooter? Would have been faster."

Reilly frowned and squeezed the pedal harder, hoping to coax an extra mile per hour or two from the Chevy's asthmatic engine. It was no use. The Vega's speedometer probably hadn't swung past the half-century mark in decades—if ever. The faint smell of pot and patchouli that impregnated its interior only served to confirm this.

"Fuel," Reilly asked. "How much have you got in your tank?"

The man's face creased as he thought for a quick moment, then said, "It's low. Less than a quarter full. I was going to fill up after we ate."

Reilly asked, "So what are we talking about, distance-wise? How far can he get?"

The man thought again for a beat, then said, "Seventy, eighty miles, maybe?"

Reilly glanced at the Vega's fuel gauge. It was almost half full. He processed this. Given the speed the F-150 was traveling at, that suggested an hour's driving time. And with the F-150 pulling away at a rate of ten or fifteen miles per hour—or more—it would soon be out of sight, despite the flat terrain and the more or less straight road they were hurtling—well, gliding—down.

He had to find a way to bridge that gap. Quickly.

"Who is this guy?" the man asked. "What the hell's going on?"

Reilly glanced across at him. The man was alarmed enough. "He's a person of interest. We need to stop him."

The man stared at him, his eyes wide with disbelief. "Seriously?" he raged. "That's it? You're going to stonewall me with some kind of 'it's classified' bullshit? That guy's got my daughter. He's got Kelly."

Reilly's guts tightened. He could understand the man's anger. He'd only recently been through something similar himself, with his now five-year-old son, Alex. He looked at the man and could just feel the fear and worry that had to be coursing through him.

"The only thing you need to know right now is that I will do everything in my power to get your daughter back," Reilly said. "That's priority one. Everything else has to follow on from that. Okay?"

Even as the words left his lips, he was twisting inside, pained by the knowledge that he was partly lying. Of course, the man's daughter would be a priority. Just not *the* priority. Of course, he'd do everything in his power to get her back safely. But ultimately— ultimately—the man Reilly only knew by his online avatar— Faustus—had the potential to unleash a lot of damage. Lethal damage. He needed to be neutralized.

Reilly hoped it would never come down to it, never reach a point where a binary decision had to be made, where it would have to be one or the other but not both. Some decisions were too horrific to contemplate. At Quantico, during training, they referred to them as Coventry moments, after the widely accepted but false story that during World War II, Churchill had allowed the city to be sacrificed and not have it evacuated so as not to let the Germans know that his men had broken the Nazis' Enigma code and knew about the devastating raid to come. It was nonsense, of course. The code-breakers hadn't known that the target was Coventry. Still, the story had become widely accepted, and the myth endured.

Reilly hoped there wasn't a Coventry moment waiting for him.

The man didn't seem convinced by Reilly's words. "You bet your ass she's priority one. I'll see to that."

Reilly held the man's gaze, and nodded. "What's your name?"

"Garber. Glen Garber. You?"

"Sean Reilly."

"That your real name, or is that also classified?"

Reilly shrugged. "It's real."

"Where's the rest of your men?" Garber asked. "Don't you at least have a partner or something? You guys work in twos, right?"

Reilly grimaced. Under normal circumstances, Garber was right. But this case had been anything but normal right from the get-go. "I've been undercover and I didn't have a phone," he told Garber. "Then things happened real quick. I had to improvise. I was hoping to connect with my people from the service center."

"But you didn't?"

Reilly shook his head. "We're on our own."

"Well, you've got a phone now," Garber told him. "Use it. Get help."

But Reilly already had another idea. "I will," he said. "But first, tell me this. Does you daughter have a cell phone on her?"

Garber's expression clouded, then morphed from confusion to concern. "Yes, she does, but—why?"

Reilly handed him back his phone. "Call her."

◆–◆–◆

Kelly couldn't take her eyes off the man.

When you're a kid, everyone tells you to be wary of strangers. She was old enough now to realize anyone could present a threat, but when she was younger, she imagined strangers as evil-looking people. Long, pointy noses, devil ears. Thick eyebrows and bad teeth.

This man just looked like an ordinary person. He could have been someone her dad worked with, one of his crew that built and fixed houses.

But there was something about the eyes. They were cold.

Worse than cold. They were dead.

When the man glanced over at her, and she looked into those eyes, she thought about when her dad took her to the Central Park Zoo on one of their trips into the city. She and her dad did everything together since her mom had died. She remembered the reptile exhibit, and how when they looked through the glass, you couldn't tell if they were really looking at you or not.

Creepy eyes.

She noticed something else about him, too. He kept touching that cylinder, the thing that looked like a narrow Thermos, that was tucked between his thigh and the center console.

Kelly was thinking about that when the sound of her own cell phone made her jump. It was in her small purse, which was on the seat beside her.

"That you?" Kristoff asked, his head snapping right.

"Yeah." She took out the phone, looked at it, saw that it was her dad. She couldn't believe it hadn't occurred to her to call him before now, but she was so scared, she wasn't thinking straight.

"Well," Kristoff said, "you better answer it."

She did. "Dad! A man stole the truck! I'm in the truck!"

Glen said, "I know, sweetheart. I'm with a . . . I'm with a policeman. We're following you. Are you okay? Has he hurt you?"

Kelly glanced at the man. "He hit my arm when I tried to take out the key. But it doesn't hurt that much."

"Honey, everything's going to be okay. We just have to figure out how—"

"Give me the phone," Kristoff said to Kelly. When she hesitated, his eyes narrowed and his voice dropped an octave. "Now."

Kelly handed it over. Kristoff put it to his ear and said, "You're the kid's dad?"

"No," said Reilly. "It was. Now it's me."

Kristoff smiled. "That's you in that little wagon behind me, isn't it? The Vega? Those things didn't run when they were new forty years ago. Unless it's got a rocket launcher on it, I think you're screwed."

"Let the kid go, Faustus. Keep the truck but let the kid out."

Kristoff chuckled. "I think when I hit you in the head you suffered some kind of brain damage."

"You pull over, and I'll pull over at the same time. There'll be half a mile between us. Let the kid out. I'll drop her dad off. Then it'll just be you and me. We don't need a whole lot of collateral damage here."

That prompted a second chuckle from Kristoff. "Seriously? The collateral damage I had in mind amounts to a lot more than one little girl." He leaned harder on the accelerator. "You're getting smaller in my rearview. You're gonna have to pedal harder."

The Ford edged up toward eighty-five. The truck cleared a stand of trees, and parked there, tucked in behind them, was a state police car.

Kelly whipped her head around to see the car as they sped past it, then said to the man, "I think he had radar. You're gonna get a ticket," with a hint of satisfaction, like he was *really* in trouble now.

"Son of a bitch," Kristoff said, tossing the phone into a tray in the console. He glanced in his mirror. The police car was shooting out of its hiding spot and hitting the highway, back tires drifting.

Siren on, lights flashing.

•◆•

In the Vega, Reilly said, "Son of a bitch."

"What?" Garber said. "He's got the cops after him. Isn't that a good thing?"

Reilly said nothing.

•◆•

"Looks like we're going to have some fun," Kristoff said.

The cruiser was one of those souped-up Crown Vics, an Interceptor. Kristoff knew he could outrun Reilly's commandeered Vega, but the cruiser was another matter.

It was gaining on him. Gaining on him fast.

He couldn't outrun it, and he couldn't outhandle it. But one thing this Ford had over the Crown Vic was bulk.

Maybe Kristoff could run it off the road. But he'd have to let it catch him first.

Kelly was twisted around in her seat, watching the cruiser close the distance.

"You better pull over," she told him. "You're gonna get a *huge* ticket. And he's going to put you in jail for stealing my dad's truck."

"Shut up."

The cruiser was coming up in the passing lane, siren continuing to wail. When it was only a car length behind, the officer behind the wheel was pointing to the shoulder, ordering Kristoff to pull over.

Kristoff hit the brakes. Once, hard.

The Interceptor was suddenly alongside.

Which was when Kristoff cranked the wheel suddenly to the left, ramming the pickup truck's front fender into the cruiser.

The Interceptor swerved over to the left shoulder, the left wheels rolling over the rounded edge. At that point, the driver couldn't right it, couldn't regain control and get the car back onto the pavement.

The cruiser barreled into the grassy median, spun around twice before coming to a halt in a spray of dirt and dust and grass.

Kristoff was looking in the driver's door mirror, smiling. "I think your dad's gonna be pissed about his fender," he said, and glanced over at Kelly.

He didn't like what he saw.

Kelly was holding the cylinder. While Kristoff had been occupied with the cruiser, she'd reached over the console and grabbed it.

Now she was clutching it in her right hand, holding it up by the open window.

"Let me out," Kelly said. "And give my dad back his truck."

• ◆ •

"Christ!"

Half a mile back, Glen Garber's heart imploded as he watched the police cruiser's high-speed tussle with his pickup truck. He watched helplessly, his fingers squeezing the armrest until all the blood had rushed out of them, as the cars collided—then he breathed out as the cruiser spun off to the side and disappeared in a cloud of dust in the median.

He glanced left at Reilly, who was also fixated on the drama up ahead. "You need to call your people and get them to back off. You can't put Kelly at risk with another face-off like that. This

263

guy—what was it you called him, Faustus?—he's not gonna give up lightly, is he?"

"I didn't expect him to."

Glen pointed angrily at the phone. "Then call your people. They need to steer clear of him. We've got a phone link into him, we can speak to him. Negotiate. I don't know, just—no more of this *Fast and Furious* bullshit. My kid's in that truck."

Reilly peeled his eyes off the receding pickup truck long enough to take in Garber's scowling face, then stared ahead again and nodded.

"I'll send out an alert. Make sure no one engages him. But we can't just let him ride off into the sunset. Even if he does let your daughter go. We need to make both things happen. We need to get her back, but we also need to grab him."

"Why?" Garber shot back. "Kelly's the only thing that matters here. Even if he gets away, you'll find him again. You guys always do."

"It's not that simple."

"It is for me. We get Kelly back. Priority one, remember? Then you use your drones and your keyword surveillance and your facial recognition software and all the other tricks you guys have these days and you go in and grab him. *After* I have my daughter back."

Reilly grimaced. He hated moments like this. He wanted to say something to get this man to understand the seriousness of the matter, the utterly unthinkable consequences that might well occur if his quarry were to get away. But he couldn't tell him everything. Not when it was that classified. Not when security protocols dictated who could know the truth and who couldn't.

Garber seemed to read his hesitation, as he pressed on. "Who is this guy? And what kind of a name is Faustus? I mean, Christ, it sounds like something Stan Lee dreamed up."

"I wish it was," Reilly said.

"So who is he?"

Reilly weighed his words carefully. "He's a guy with a grudge. A really big grudge. And right now, he's got the means to get himself some serious payback."

Garber went quiet for a second, then said, "A grudge? Against who?"

Reilly slid a glance across at him. "Everyone."

• ◆ •

Up ahead, Kristoff had to fight to yank his eyes off the canister in the girl's hands and make sure he kept the truck on the road. That damn girl—after everything he'd been through, after everything he'd done to get to where he was now, even if it was in the middle of nowhere, far from the nearest big city where he could unleash the demon he'd risked everything to get his hands on—she had it in her power to ruin it all.

He couldn't let that happen.

"Give me that canister, Kelly," he rasped. "Give it back, right now."

"No," she fired back angrily.

What the hell kind of a kid is this? he fumed inwardly. A stab of admiration cut through the rage he felt. She was a tough kid, and he liked that. Better than some sniveling, pathetic crybaby, he thought. A kid with some gusto in her. Good for her.

Still, it wouldn't distract him from doing whatever it took to get the canister back. Even if that meant snapping her neck with his bare hands.

He couldn't just reach out and grab it. She was holding it right by the open window. He couldn't risk her throwing it out of the car, which is what she was threatening to do.

The canister was supposed to be strong, able to withstand a considerable impact. But flying out of a car at eighty miles per hour, hitting the pavement, maybe getting run over by a car behind them—

No, that would not be good.

There would come a time when he'd be happy for the contents of that canister to hit the atmosphere, but not just yet.

Kristoff wouldn't mind a little time to get away first. Didn't want to be downwind and all that.

So he needed to persuade this kid, who was starting to get very annoying, to be very respectful of that canister.

"Kelly," he said, mustering as much calmness into his tone as he could, "you need to give it back to me. You want to know why?"

She scowled at him, a fierce determination radiating out of her face—but some uncertainty broke through, and after a moment, she said, "Why?"

"Well, right now, the reason I need you, the reason you're still alive, is because of that canister. You're kind of my safety net. My way of making sure the cops stay off my back and let me get to where I'm going. But if I don't have that canister you're holding in your hand, well then I don't need to go there anymore. Which means I don't need you anymore."

She thought about it for a second. "Which means you can let me go?"

"No," he replied in a measured, calm tone. "It means I can kill you." He kept his gaze on her, able to let it linger on her now that the road ahead was relatively straight and flat. "Do you understand? If you want to stay alive—if you want to give me a reason to keep you alive—you need to give it back to me."

Kelly stared at him, confusion clouding her expression.

"Do you want to die, Kelly?" he asked, his voice taking on a sharper edge. "Do you? Is that what you really want?"

He saw her lower lip quiver as the horrible realization settled into the little girl's mind. But she didn't say anything.

"Do you want to die, Kelly?" he asked again, putting more pressure on the accelerator as the interstate began a long, steady hill climb.

The flutter of her lip quickened. Then she dropped her eyes, and shook her head, slowly, from side to side. "No," she muttered. "I don't want to die."

"Then give it back to me," he said. "Give it back to me and everything will be all right."

She raised her head to meet his gaze. He nodded to her, gently, and reached out with his right hand open, tilting his head expectantly.

He saw defeat and acceptance flush through her expression, felt the tension ease out of his shoulders and neck as she brought the canister back into the car and rested it on her lap.

"Good girl," he said.

A sudden thud from behind shook the truck and shoved him off the back of his seat.

"What the—?" He glanced into his rearview mirror, his jaw dropped, then he flung his head around to look out the rear window in disbelief.

It was the police cruiser again, ramming his truck from behind.

Only, this time, it wasn't carrying any cops.

Reilly was at the wheel, with the kid's dad sitting next to him.

And he was charging forward again.

❖

"Are you out of your mind?" Garber asked when Reilly rammed the back of his pickup with the police cruiser. Because the truck sat high in relation to the car, Reilly was hitting the bumper with the top of the cruiser's grill.

"Need to get his attention," Reilly said, keeping his eyes straight ahead, his jaw set firmly.

"And get Kelly killed at the same time!" Garber said. "You run him off the road, that truck rolls, whaddya think's going to happen to her? She'll get tossed out the window."

Reilly, eyes still forward, nodded. "She's got her seat belt on."

Taking the police car had struck Garber as a pretty good idea. There was no way the Vega was going to catch his truck. When the cruiser went spinning into the median, and Reilly hit the brakes and jumped out, at first Glen thought the FBI agent was checking to see if the cop was okay.

Glen figured the cop could look after himself. It was Kelly that Reilly should be focused on.

But Garber quickly saw that Reilly's intentions were more pragmatic than compassionate. Reilly was flashing his FBI credentials as he was opening the car door. The cop was awake and reasonably coherent, but his vision was impaired by the blood draining from a gash in his forehead.

"Need your vehicle!" Reilly barked.

The cop said, "What?"

"Is the car operational?" Reilly said. The engine was still running, but the way the car went off the road the steering could be shot to hell.

The cop wiped blood from his eyes to get a look at Reilly's ID. "I'm not giving up my car to some dumbass fed who—"

Reilly reached into the car and grabbed the man by the shirt and hauled him out of the vehicle, tossing him into the weeds. The cop was going for the weapon at his belt as he fell onto his back in the brush.

"You do not want to shoot a federal officer, pal," Reilly said, getting behind the wheel as Garber ran around to the other side. "The keys are in the Vega."

Reilly dropped the transmission lever down into drive and hit the gas. The car moved, grass and stones brushing the undercarriage as he steered it back onto the interstate, tires squealing as they gripped pavement.

Once he had the car lined up he put his foot to the floor and the car moved. Garber looked up for a handle to grab on to as the car accelerated.

"He's up there, but this'll catch him," Reilly said.

"Who is this guy?" Garber asked. "What the hell do you want him for? What's he done?" Hoping, maybe, that his daughter hadn't been kidnapped by a serial killer, but some notorious, but nonviolent, embezzler. That might have made him feel, on a panic scale that went from one to ten, only fifteen instead of twenty.

Even if Reilly had believed the father deserved the truth, there was no way he would have given it to him.

Telling someone his daughter was trapped in a car with a man who had the capability to wipe out thousands upon thousands of lives; a man who'd had access to a government germ warfare research project that Washington didn't even acknowledge existed; a man who believed the best way to get attention for his cause was to start sending messages to the government, under the name "Faustus," threatening a biological Armageddon—well, telling Glen Garber his daughter was caught up with someone like that was just going to make him a tad anxious, wasn't it?

So Reilly basically repeated what he'd told the man earlier. "He's a security threat."

To which Garber said, "No shit?"

The pickup was looming larger in their windshield. Garber could just make out the top of his daughter's head through the back window.

Both the truck and the cruiser were pushing a little harder as the highway continued its slow climb.

"So once we catch up, then what?" Garber asked.

Reilly reached into his pocket for Garber's cell phone, put it to his ear, then glanced at the contractor. "We're still connected. I can hear background noise. Hey! Faustus! You there?"

He kept the phone pressed to his ear. Listened.

"What?" Garber asked.

"They're talking about the canister."

"What canister?"

Reilly shot him a look. "Shh!"

The FBI agent listened a few more seconds. "Shit," he muttered, and tossed the phone back to Garber.

He put it to his ear, shouted his daughter's name, as Reilly nudged the car up past a hundred.

The truck was right in front of them.

And then Reilly drove right into it.

Which was when Garber asked him if he was out of his mind.

Without a doubt, Reilly thought. *Without a doubt.*

•◆•

When the cop car rammed them from behind, Kelly screamed as her head was snapped back into the headrest. Before she had a chance to turn around and see what had hit them, they were hit a second time.

The canister fell from her lap, hit the floor in front of her, and rolled around on the floor mat.

Now she twisted around in her seat to see what exactly had happened. The cruiser had dropped back a car length, and there, in the passenger seat, was her dad.

"Dad!" she screamed, even though there was no way he could hear her. But she was sure he saw her mouthing the word.

Kelly waved. Her dad waved back.

"Give me that!" Kristoff shouted, pointing to the canister. "Right now!"

He had an idea how he could get Reilly to back off. He'd threaten Reilly the way the kid had been threatening him. With the canister. He'd dangle it out his window, make like he was going to drop it.

Reilly wouldn't want that to happen.

"I can't reach it," Kelly said, straining to bend over, the shoulder strap restricting her mobility.

"Undo the damn belt!"

"My dad says I'm never supposed to take off my seat belt."

Kristoff gave her a look that said, "Are you kidding me?" Kelly got the message and hit the button to retract the belt, and slid off the end of the seat to reach down for the cylinder.

And as she did this, she thought.

She thought very, very quickly.

Kelly was not like the other kids. Kelly was only ten, but she'd seen and been through some bad things in her short life. The kinds of things that girls her age shouldn't have to go through.

The big one, of course, was losing her mother. No little girl should lose her mom. And no little girl should lose her mom the way Kelly lost hers.

But that was just the beginning.

Not long after that, someone took a shot at her house. Blew out her bedroom window when she was in the room.

But it got even worse. Before that very, very bad time in her life was over, a man threatened to end her life. And not just any man, but a man she believed to be a *good* man.

And who got her out of that fix? Well, sure, her dad was there just in time, but it was Kelly herself who took action. It was Kelly who thought of a way to disable that man just long enough for the scales to tip in her favor.

In a split second, too.

Kelly wondered whether a similar opportunity existed now. Something that might give her an edge, buy her enough time for her dad and the policeman to help her out.

That was when her eyes landed on the cup of hot coffee sitting in the center console.

•◆•

"Great plan!" Garber shouted. "Ram the truck! Is that right out of the FBI playbook?"

Reilly had to admit to a level of frustration. He had no backup, and he had no weapon. (If there was any good news, he knew Faustus had no weapon, either. He'd checked him for one just before the man got the jump on him.) What he needed was a frickin' helicopter with lasers, but this wasn't James Bond.

This was real life.

What he needed now was some kind of break. For the truck to have a flat tire. For it to run out of gas, but based on what Garber'd told him, that was unlikely. A goddamn moose trying to run across the highway right about now would be a blessing.

At least the cruiser was topped up. He needed to get Garber to make some calls, try to get a roadblock established farther up the interstate, or maybe—

What the hell?

The pickup was swerving all over the road.

• ◆ •

Kelly said, "Catch."

She was perched on the front of her seat, leaning down into the footwell. She had her right hand on the canister and tossed it underhand and to the left, aiming it right toward Kristoff's face.

"Jesus!" he shouted.

He took his left hand off the wheel to catch the cylinder before it flew out his window, batted it down into his lap. Then it started to roll toward his knees. He wanted to catch it before it dropped by his legs, where it would be rolling around his feet, interfering with his operation of the pedals.

It was during this moment of distraction that Kelly pried the plastic lid off the coffee cup and wrapped her hand around it.

Her dad was right. It would have stayed hot all the way to their destination. How did anyone drink this stuff?

As she whipped it out of the cup holder, some coffee slipped over the edge and onto her fingers, scalding them. It hurt like hell, as her father would be inclined to say, but Kelly didn't have time to whine about it, because she only had about a tenth of a second to throw this too-hot-to-drink coffee in this bad man's face.

Which is exactly what she did.

The black liquid arced through the air, splashing across Kristoff's right cheek and neck and, judging by the way he was throwing his right hand over his eye, that, too.

Kristoff screamed. Not "Jesus!" this time. Just a cry of intense pain and anguish. Primal.

He tried to maintain steering with his left hand, and was still attempting to see the road with his left eye, but the truck was pitching all over the place, and the canister had hit the floor, rolling side to side in time with Kristoff's erratic steering.

Kristoff took his right hand off his face long enough to make a wild, retaliatory swing in Kelly's direction, but she had pushed herself up against the door, out of reach, and was thinking about whether to hop over the seat and hide in the narrow space behind them. But she decided against that, figuring that if the truck came to a stop, or even slowed, she needed to be by the door so she could hop out.

Indeed, the truck was slowing. Kristoff had taken his foot off the gas. And given that the truck was heading up a slight grade, it was going to lose speed even more quickly. He hadn't hit the brake yet, but he couldn't keep up his recent pace when he couldn't see where he was going.

After another couple of futile swings at Kelly, the man put his hand back to his face, but then he realized the wounds hurt too much to touch. His right eye remained closed.

He screamed: "You blinded me! You fried my eye, you little bitch!"

Kelly was probably more scared right now than she'd ever been in her life—even more than when that man threatened her a few years ago—but she also felt pretty good. For half a second, she'd wondered whether she'd get in trouble for making a man lose one of his eyes, but then thought her dad would probably be okay with it.

He could be pretty cool about things.

She glanced back through the window, saw the police car still there. Waved at her dad again as the truck lurched from left to right.

Then she heard the familiar sound of gravel under the tires. She whirled around, saw that they were veering off the pavement onto the shoulder. Kristoff had his foot on the brake. He hung his head low, moved it languidly back and forth, trying to deal with the pain.

When the truck was nearly stopped, Kelly pulled on the door handle, let the door swing wide, and jumped.

•—◆—•

"Kelly!"

Glen Garber screamed when he saw his daughter leap from the passenger's door of the nearly stopped truck. He bolted from the police cruiser before Reilly had thrown it into park.

Kelly landed in the tall grasses just beyond the shoulder. Her knees buckled, forcing her into a roll, her body tumbling out of view.

Glen ran. "Kelly! Kelly!"

Before he could get to her, her head popped up above the grass. An arm went into the air. "Here!"

Behind him, Garber heard Reilly shout at the top of his lungs: "Run!"

•—◆—•

It wasn't that Reilly didn't care about Garber and his kid, but he had a more pressing matter to deal with.

Like the man he knew as Faustus, who had thrown open the driver's door of the pickup and was stumbling out. But not before reaching for something on the floor ahead of the seat. He emerged, standing there a couple of steps in front of the open door, clutching the cylinder. Raising it above his head.

Whoa.

Reilly didn't know what the hell had happened in that truck, but half of the man's face was red and blotchy and blistered and some of the skin looked like it was ready to fall off. His right eye was shut.

Reilly told Garber and his daughter to run.

"I'll do it!" the man yelled. "I'll smash it right into the road! I'll crack this thing wide open. You want that?"

Reilly raised an unthreatening palm.

"Come on," the FBI agent said. "You'll take yourself out, too. You'll never have the fun of seeing your handiwork."

"Doesn't much matter now," he said.

Behind them, other motorists on the highway slowed. A couple honked their horns.

Reilly ignored them, instead staying focused on Faustus. He couldn't stop himself from asking, "What the hell happened to your face?"

"Hot coffee," Faustus said. "Maybe I'll sue."

Reilly noticed that the truck was moving, ever so gradually. They'd all stopped on a very slight, uphill grade, and the Ford was starting to roll back. Faustus had bailed out of it so quickly he must not have put the shift solidly into park.

By the time Faustus noticed, it was too late to react.

The open driver's door caught him on the back and threw him down onto the highway like he'd been tackled. The bottom edge of the door hit the back of his head hard enough that he did a face-plant on the pavement, arms outstretched.

He wasn't moving. Only his fingers, twitching, releasing their grip on the cylinder, which started to roll along the asphalt toward Reilly, bumping over small stones and irregularities in the surface.

Please don't have opened, please don't have opened.

Reilly bolted forward, threw his body over the cylinder, trapped it below his torso, smothering it like it was a grenade. Even though it was not going to explode, it had the potential to do more damage than a thousand grenades. The truck rolled past him to his right, the front wheels turning slightly, angling the truck's back end toward the ditch.

As it rolled by, Reilly saw Garber and his daughter a good fifty yards away, heading for a wooded area beyond the highway's edge. Garber glanced back, saw Reilly on the ground, grabbed Kelly by the elbow to stop her.

Reilly could just barely hear him tell her, "Stay here."

And then he came running.

"Are you hit?" Garber shouted.

"No!"

"What about him?"

"I'm guessing dead. That door hit him hard, and then his head hit the pavement. He hasn't moved."

"Why are you lying on—?"

"Have you got a bag in your truck? A plastic bag? A couple of them? Anything airtight?" A thought hit him. "Evidence bags in the cruiser!"

Garber stopped, ran for the police car, grabbed the keys and ran around back to pop the trunk. It took him about fifteen seconds to find what he was looking for. Clear plastic, sealable bags, like over-sized sandwich bags. He grabbed a handful and ran back to Reilly as his truck slowly backed into the ditch, the engine still running.

The agent, still keeping his body pressed to the pavement, reached up for a bag. "Give it to me."

Garber had some sense of how serious the situation was.

"Should I start running again?" he asked.

Reilly grimaced. "Probably not much point. We're either safe, or we're not. You couldn't run fast enough to save yourself."

He worked the bag under his torso, then, in one swift motion, got up on his knees, shoved the cylinder into it, and sealed the top.

Garber realized he was holding his breath.

"You've got the end of the world in that bag, don't you?"

"Pretty much," Reilly replied. "Hand me another. I'm going to double bag it. Maybe even triple."

"Did anything leak out?"

"If we're still standing a minute from now, I'd say no."

He reached out a hand to Garber, and he took it. He helped the agent to his feet, and they regarded each other for a moment. Garber kept glancing at his watch.

"Thirty seconds."

"Give it a little longer," Reilly said.

"If it happens, what, exactly, will happen?"

"You don't want to know. The good news is, it'll be quick."

Garber kept his eye on his watch. "That's a minute and a half now."

"I'd say we're going to live." Reilly smiled. "Your kid threw hot coffee in his face?"

Garber nodded.

The smile turned into a grin. "Get her over here."

Garber waved Kelly in. She arrived, nearly breathless, several seconds later. Shaken, but relieved, too.

Reilly rested his hands on her shoulders. "You are something else."

Kelly smiled weakly.

"Really, you are," Sean Reilly said. "You ever need anything, you just name it."

Kelly thought a moment. She said, "I never did get my chicken nuggets."

JOHN LESCROART
VS.   T. JEFFERSON PARKER

Silent Hunt

The genesis of this story goes all the way back to 2009 when John and Jeff discovered a shared love of fishing, while contributing a short story to an anthology called *Hook, Line & Sinister*. Then, in 2011, the two hung out together on a deepwater fly-fishing trip to East Cape and Cerralvo Island in Baja California. Every day for a week the anglers set out at dawn in *pangas* (Mexican fishing boats) seeking tuna, dorado, roosterfish, amberjack, pompano, or whatever else might be biting. Their guides were a fantastic and personable collection of skilled pilots and fishermen, mostly from one extended family who lived in the nearby village of Agua Amarga.

When they were approached with the concept for *FaceOff,* both immediately glommed on to the idea of John's Wyatt Hunt (*The Hunt Club, Treasure Hunt,* and *The Hunter*) and Jeff's Joe Trona (*Silent Joe*) teaming together. Both characters were close to the same age, athletic, and were more or less involved with law enforcement, so putting them together on a fishing trip to Baja was a no-brainer. As soon as the two characters showed up on the page together, the chemistry was clear and palpable. John and Jeff quickly discovered that if those two characters actually existed in real life, they would probably be buds. Friendship aside, though, this is a thriller anthology, so the story needed an adventure that would place the heroes in danger.

Jeff had done quite a lot of research into Mexico's *narcotraffican-tes.* Headlines from around the world attest every day that there is a serious problem with drug trafficking in that part of the world. So what could be better, fiction-wise, than to have these gangsters threaten a tightly knit extended family of hardworking fishermen? And what would poor fishermen possess that could possibly lure the local *narcotrafficantes* out to their village so that they could steal it? These good people don't do drugs. They're not political. They fish and play baseball. But there is one other little-known, and only partially explored, commodity in Baja California that would draw the attention of gangsters.

Gold.

A hidden stash that could rejuvenate a little fishing town, providing money for a new electric generator to make ice and run refrigerators, to power streetlights, and buy new motors for the *pangas.* But the *narcotrafficantes* have also heard rumors of gold.

Where it's hidden. Who's hiding it. They won't hesitate to torture and kill to get their hands on it.

What's to stop them?

Just two Americans, Wyatt Hunt and Joe Trona, down in Mexico on a fishing vacation.

Silent Hunt

Wyatt Hunt made it to his gate in the International Terminal of LAX with an hour to spare before boarding would begin for his noon connecting flight to La Paz. He was traveling light, with one brand-new light-brown-on-dark-brown carry-on duffel bag into which he'd stuffed nearly two grand's worth of new fly-fishing gear, his toilet kit, and two changes of clothes, long pants of good wicking material that with a zip converted into shorts and two long-sleeved shirts, the latter items newly purchased from REI against what was forecast to be debilitating heat— eight hours a day on the water, no shade, average temperature around 110.

It was September and his party of ten, all unknown to him, were going after dorado, roosterfish, various tuna, and the occasional marlin, sailfish, or shark. None of these fish would weigh less than ten pounds, and some might go to a hundred or more. Hunt, a lifelong fly-fisherman in streams for trout in the half-pound range, was skeptical about the ability of his new gear to handle fighting fish of this size and caliber, but he was game to try.

In any event, he was a gear freak and the new stuff—ten-weight and twelve-weight rods, reels holding over a hundred yards of sixty- and eighty-pound test backing, barbed and artistically feathered hooks the length of his fingers—was undoubtedly cool. He'd gone out with a fishing pro at San Francisco's Baker Beach four times over the past month, trying to master the casting technique known as double-hauling, essential if you wanted to reach surface targets in salt water. He was still far from expert, but at least felt he wouldn't completely embarrass himself.

With time to kill and slumping a bit after his five AM wake-up, he grabbed an open chair at the end of the bar, stuffed his duffel down under his feet, and ordered a large cup of coffee. When he'd finished about half of it, he turned to the guy next to him—a portly, pale, bald guy in a bright red and green Hawaiian shirt. "You mind watching my duffel a minute?" he asked. "I've got to hit the head."

The older gentleman, already drinking something with an umbrella in it, looked down at Hunt's duffel and broke an easy smile. "We are urged not to leave our baggage with strangers, are we not?"

"Constantly." Hunt had covered his half cup with a napkin and was already on his feet, now suddenly in a bit of a hurry. He lowered his voice. "I promise it's not a bomb. You can look if you want."

"I'm going to trust you," the gentleman said. "Go already."

On the way to the men's room, Hunt not for the first time found himself reflecting on the fact that in many ways, and despite his own demise, Osama bin Laden had basically won the first round of the War on Terror. Already that morning, Hunt not once but twice had to take off his shoes and belt, empty his pockets, and assume the position in the TSA's X-ray machine. A victim of his early-morning fatigue in San Fran, if they hadn't just changed the rules again, he'd also have donated to the cause the Swiss Army knife he'd forgotten in his pocket—which would have been the third time that had happened.

Even if he acknowledged the general reason for it, the whole thing pissed him off.

As if the geezer next to him was going to steal his duffel bag. He didn't look like he could even lift the thing. As if anybody, for that matter, in the secured area for boarding, was an actual threat to take anybody else's luggage.

Caught up in his internal rave, Hunt ran with it. Let's see: first, your potential thief needs a valid boarding pass with photo ID, then he's half stripped and X-rayed, and he's going along with this runaround because of the very off chance that some random person will leave their baggage "unattended"—Hunt loved that word!—and that he would then have an opportunity to steal it. And then what? Leave the building with his loot? When had that happened? Had it ever happened? Could it ever happen? Who thought of these things? What was the average IQ of a TSA employee anyway? Or of the goddamned director of the Department of Homeland Security, for that matter?

Room temp at best, Hunt was thinking as he exited the men's room . . .

. . . just in time to see a guy about his own age and size, in jeans, a work shirt, and a San Diego Padres baseball hat pulled down low over his eyes, strolling toward the security gates with Hunt's pretty damn distinctive duffel bag slung under his left shoulder. Jesus Christ!

"Hey!" Hunt yelled after him. "Hey! Wait up, there!"

The guy kept walking.

Hunt broke into a trot.

The other man was at least sixty feet away from Hunt and now almost to the exit. The thief moved with an easy grace, taking long strides, neither slowing down in the least nor speeding up, but moving, moving, moving. He would be at the exit within seconds.

When he had to, Hunt the athlete could move, too, and now he turned on the speed, closing the gap between them, calling out, "Stop that guy!" to no one in particular, but drawing the attention of every traveler in the terminal. He finally caught up just as the guy was arriving in front of the exit gate.

Hunt came up behind him and with a lunge grabbed at the duffel, getting a hold on it. "Hey! Hold up! What do you think you're doing?" Hunt pulled at the strap.

The guy held on, whirled, and threw an elbow that Hunt barely ducked away from. But in that one fluid movement, Hunt realized he was dealing with a strong, lightning-fast, and trained fighter. Hunt himself had a black belt in karate and this guy, even hampered by the heavy duffel, was coming on as at least his equal, in any case a force to be reckoned with. Now he had Hunt backing away, and like any experienced fighter he kept coming, dropping the duffel and coming around with a right chop that Hunt knocked away with his forearm. It felt like he'd stopped a tire iron.

Squaring up now, ready to press an attack of his own, Hunt got his first good look at the man's face, and it stopped him cold. Nearly half of it bore the scars of a serious burn injury, almost as though the skin had been melted away.

It immediately took the fight out of Hunt, though his breath was still coming hard. "What the hell are you trying to do?" he rasped out.

The other man spoke with an unnerving calm. "What am I trying to do? You just attacked me. I was defending myself."

"You were walking out with my duffel."

"That's not your duffel. It's mine. And I wasn't walking out anywhere. I was going to buy a newspaper"—he pointed—"at this shop right here."

Meanwhile, three TSA officers had broken through the ranks of onlookers and one of them—Hillyer by his name tag—advanced on them, arms spread out, asserting control. "All right, everybody. Easy. Easy now. What's going on here?"

"This guy," Hunt said, "was making off with my duffel bag."

"It's mine, sir," the scarred man replied, dead calm.

With his own first look at the man's face, Hillyer, too, took an extra beat, then came back to Hunt, who said, "That's my duffel. You can check it out. It's filled with fishing gear. I'm on my way down to Baja."

"So am I," the scarred man said. He reached into his shirt pocket and held out a boarding pass. "With your permission, sir," he said to Hillyer. Going to one knee, he pulled around the identification tag attached to the strap and held it out first to the TSA officer, then to Hunt.

"Joe Trona," he said. "That's me." He stood and reached behind him and took out his wallet, which also revealed a badge. Hillyer inspected the badge and seemed to read every word on it, twice looking from badge to man. "I'm a police officer and I promise you I did not steal this man's duffel bag."

Hillyer unzipped the duffel for a quick look. Hunt saw the neatly arranged reels and spools of fishing line, similar to his own. Hillyer looked at Trona, then to Hunt. "When did you last see your own duffel bag, sir?"

"I left it at the bar when I went to the bathroom. The man sitting next to me was watching it. But then when I came out, I saw . . ." He stopped because there was nothing more he could say. "I'm a horse's ass, Mr. Trona," he said. "I owe you an apology."

Trona looked at Hunt but said nothing.

"Let's go see if your duffel's still at the bar," Hillyer said to Hunt. "As our announcement says, many items of luggage look the same. If it's still there, let's not leave it unattended anymore. How's that sound?"

•◆•

Joe Trona stood in the shade outside the La Paz terminal, his back to the wall in the infernal Baja heat. His duct-taped quiver of rod cases lay safely along the wall, along with his duffel and a cooler. The van would be there any minute. "The horse's ass."

"Hunt sounds better."

"Apology accepted."

Hunt joined Trona in the shade and offered his hand. "Wyatt."

"Are you fishing out of Baja Joe's?"

"First time."

"Always an adventure."

Trona watched a gaggle of pretty Mexican flight attendants walk-roll past them and into the terminal. One glanced at him, trying to be furtive, then let her gaze brush off of his face and into the sky where she pretended to be interested in a descending passenger jet. Even with a hat on and the brim pulled low, Trona's scar-studded face was spectacularly *there*. By now, after living thirty-odd years with that face, Trona actually forgot about it sometimes. Of course, the reminders were always quick to come—reflections, people from adults to children, even dogs.

"You're the deputy from Orange County," said Hunt. Trona nodded and enjoyed the inevitable beat of silence. "It's been ten years since all that."

"It's good to be out of view."

"Don't I know," said Hunt.

"Those murders you worked in San Francisco were big news down south. Took you all the way back to '78 and Jonestown. Man."

"History isn't so ancient."

"No," said Trona. "Not when Richard III shows up under a parking lot. How's the PI work?"

Hunt shrugged. "I read about the cartel trouble here in La Paz. Zetas barging in on La Familia is what I heard."

"Long as they stay away from Baja Joe's," said Trona.

"All I want is six days of peace, quiet, and fishing. Maybe some bourbon."

"Let's fish together tomorrow. I'll show you what I've learned."

"Twist my arm."

The van and its six passengers bounced down the beaten two-lane asphalt that led toward the bay. Trona looked out at the cardón cactus and the elephant trees and the vultures circling precisely in the blue. He couldn't wait to get on the water. They slowed down for a Policía Preventiva officer standing by his truck, flares in an angled line behind him, belching pink smoke. He saw more vehicles up ahead. The cop talked to the driver and the driver showed ID and the cop looked at each fisherman then waved them through. When they passed the other cars Trona saw that one was a white Suburban, new and shiny, windows riddled with bullet holes and smeared with red. Two bodies slumped within. Two more lay on the road shoulder, one covered with blankets, one not. Another police officer hurried them past.

"There is very little crime in this part of Baja," said the driver, resolutely. "Very little. Occasional only."

Trona wondered what the occasion was. He looked at Hunt, who had to be thinking the same thing.

•—•

At dawn Hunt and Trona were skidding across the Sea of Cortez in a *panga*, both holding their hats in their hands, spray flying and the red paint of sunrise spread out before them. Cerralvo Island was a gray behemoth in the distance. The captain was named Israel and his *panga* was *Luna Sombrero*. He said little and regarded the anglers skeptically. Hunt shot pictures left and right, swung the camera, and before he could think, he'd shot Trona not once but twice. As Hunt slid the camera back into one of the many pockets of his fishing shirt he felt embarrassed for barging into Joe's face like that, then saw the minor joy on it, the joy that a cursed childhood could not prevent, the joy of being on the water.

Two boys raised by adoptive parents go fishing, thought Hunt. What a cool thing.

As the Yamaha screamed along, Hunt saw Israel turn to Joe, take his hands off the wheel, and swing an invisible baseball bat. Nice form. Buster Posey–ish. Beside him, Trona gave the captain a thumbs-up and a smile appeared beneath Israel's sunglasses.

"What's up?" Hunt asked.

"Baseball. The captains all play. Israel says there's a game tonight. It's quality ball if you want to go."

"Done."

The water shone pale, flat, and nacreous in the early day, the sun barely a foot off the horizon. Already Hunt could feel its heat and could only imagine what it would be like when it reached its zenith.

Suddenly Israel swung the wheel and the *panga* pitched hard left, heading into a cove along the shoreline where another small boat, now just visible, had anchored. Behind them, the other fishermen from Joe's fell in line, and within five minutes they were all floating around the bait boat. Hunt wasn't expecting bait, and with all of his new flies, why would he? But bait seemed to be part of the ritual here. Whatever its purpose, he'd soon find it out.

Once everybody had loaded up with sardines, the captains held a short conference and then they were off again away from the shore and out over the vast expanse of water. With Israel leading the way and nothing even remotely like a GPS, they were all heading toward a destination that must have been clear to them, although Hunt couldn't make out any kind of a marker or buoy.

The target, a good ten minutes and perhaps a mile out, was a white one-gallon plastic Clorox container, tied to some rope that probably had a sea anchor attached down below to keep it more or less in place. Hunt thought that Israel locating this random piece of flotsam out on the endless unbroken surface of the water a fairly impressive feat of navigation.

"Fish here?" he asked.

"Shade," Trona said. "A little goes a long way."

Meanwhile, the captain had cut the motor and now Trona grabbed his rod and stepped up, taking the more precarious position on the bow. "Showtime," he said, playing line out at his feet. At his place in the middle of the *panga*, Hunt stood and started doing the same as Israel threw a couple pieces of the bait out into the water around them.

Nothing.

They waited. There was no swell and after a minute or so the light chop of the other *pangas* had dissipated as well and it was dead-still. Hunt, tensed for action, dared a look around at the other four parties who'd killed their own engines and fallen into a semicircle behind them. Suddenly, though, Israel leaned forward and slapped a heavy palm on Hunt's shoulder. "Hey, hey!" Pointing into the well of the boat at Hunt's feet.

Hunt turned back, looked down, saw nothing. "What?" he asked. Then, over to Trona, "What's he want?"

Trona risked a quick glance over. "You're standing on your line," he said. Hunt backed up off it. Israel leaned over and tossed a five-gallon plastic bucket up to Hunt's spot. "Put your line in that," Trona said. "Keeps it out of the way. Don't let it wrap around your leg, or your hand for that matter, and especially your fingers. Hundred-pound tuna hits and your finger's wrapped with eighty-pound, it'll amputate right then."

Hunt got himself squared away. Israel threw another couple sardines out into the clear, blue, still water. Trona scanned the horizon in a wide arc.

Then, a sudden swirl at the surface out in front of Hunt, and Israel came alive. "Dorado! Dorado!"

Hunt got his rod up, pumped, cast, fed line, back cast, waiting what seemed interminably for the rod to load as he'd been taught, then let it rip again. This time the instant that his fly landed, one of the big fish struck.

He'd never really imagined anything like this kind of acceleration in any fishing context. Suddenly, just about immediately, all the line that he'd so carefully dropped into his plastic bucket—fifty or sixty feet of it—was gone and now he was on to his reel, already nearly to the backing, holding on for all he was worth with one hand as the reel spun beneath his other palm and the running fish ran off yard upon yard and then, sixty or seventy yards out, jumped once, twice, a third time.

Unable to stop himself, or even aware of it, he let out a scream. "Heee-ya!"

"You got him," Trona said. "Let him run. Stay cool. You got him."

• ━ •

After the fishing and a brief siesta back at the hotel, Joe borrowed Baja Joe's van and drove to Los Planes to see the baseball game. Over the years he'd become a fan. The boat captains were all good players, and Israel's tiny village of Aqua Amarga was pitted against mighty La Paz. Hunt rode along. As soon as the sun went down and the heat dropped slightly, the game started under sparse lights, before a big and boisterous crowd. Israel was on the mound, carefully picking his way through La Paz's heavy hitters.

Trona and Hunt drank Pacíficos and ate spicy peanuts, compared California's new austerity to the poverty they saw here. Hunt noted that either one could produce fine baseball. Joe waved to Israel's sister, Angelica, sitting just a few rows down with three of Israel's four children. No sign of Israel's wife or oldest son. Joe felt the burn on the back of his neck, something no amount of sunscreen could prevent here in Baja. But it was a good feeling and he felt his heart downshift.

Halfway through the third, a fleet of four black SUVs came tearing across the flat dusty desert from far away, hopping over the creosote bushes and dunes, converging from all the outfield directions. The field they were playing on here had no home run fence, and so nothing stood between these intruders and the players. Murmurs rose, then tense voices rippled through the crowd and some of the spectators clambered down the bleachers heading for where they had haphazardly parked.

Israel stood in an alert posture on the mound, watching. Trona saw no emblems or roof lights or radio antennae on the SUVs.

"I don't think they're fans," said Hunt.

"Oh, they're not."

"I left my bazooka at home."

Joe felt for the .45 that was not on his hip, the .40 that was not on his ankle, then finally the .44 derringer that was not in his pant pocket and thought: Mexican law is Mexican law—gringo law enforcement or not. The SUVs slid to dusty stops one by one and disgorged cumbersome, heavily armed men. Trona saw the Zetas patches on their shoulders and his heart went cold. He and Hunt had joined the crowd surging down the stands then ducked under one of the bleacher benches and like monkeys lowered themselves to the ground.

Joe peered through the scaffolding and saw Israel still on the mound, waiting for four Zetas who strode toward him from center field. Their M-16s shone dully in the lights and the outfielders stood frozen, watching them with what might have been resignation or terror. Everywhere Joe looked he saw another fire squad of Zetas closing in, nine men in all, a baseball team's worth of armed men.

Fans hustled through the dust of the parking area, children scampering out ahead, car doors opening and slamming shut. At the mound the four Zetas surrounded Israel. One of them motioned with his gun and Joe could see that Israel and the man were talking and that Israel was nodding his head in agreement. The other five Zetas came trotting in from across left field, straight in Joe's direction. He had been in a situation like this before, many years ago, and he had killed several men but failed to protect the man he had pledged his life to protect.

Something touched the back of his arm and he reeled to find Angelica and Israel's three small children behind him.

"That man is Hector," said Angelica. "He left Aqua Amarga five years ago to be a Zeta. He wants to be known for his cruelty. Now Hector has come for him."

"For Israel?"

She shook her head no. "For his son. Joaquin," she said. "Joaquin comes to the games but not to this one."

The five Zetas were nearly to second base now and still coming directly toward Trona and Hunt and Angelica and Israel's children. "Joe," said Hunt. "Time to move it."

"When they don't find Joaquin here, they go to Aqua Amarga. They know."

Joe took Angelica's hand and crouched and led her and the children away from home plate and the refreshment stand and the parking lot. Wyatt brought up the rear. Where the grandstands ended they stopped and huddled, half hidden from the stadium lights in the scaffolding.

Automatic gunfire burped from the parking lot and screams rose in the sudden silence. Some of the parking lights burst and smoked. Laughter. Then more shots, and more lights exploded.

Trona saw Israel on the mound, still and tensed, searching the bleachers for his sister and children. Three of the gunmen, the ones who'd been with Hector at the mound, had taken up positions at second base, shortstop, and first, but hadn't let go of their guns. Hector strode dramatically to home plate and set his machine gun in the on-deck circle. He lifted the bat that the last La Paz hitter had left behind and took a couple of check swings, then walked to the plate and stepped into the batter's box.

By now the five oncoming *narcotrafficantes* were methodically searching the grandstands where Angelica and the children had been sitting just moments ago.

Israel wound up and slung a slow-ball and Hector drove it into left center for a single. Hector dropped the bat and raised his hands over his head as if he'd just homered. Israel backpedaled toward the chaos, his glove and free hand raised to the Zetas in supplication. The leader yelled to his men, waving the bat at them, and Trona saw Israel disappear around the dugout.

"When they are finished having fun they will go to Aqua Amarga and find Joaquin," said Angelica. "And it will no longer be fun."

Trona looked at Hunt and Hunt looked at Trona. "Something tells me we should get there first," said Hunt.

Staying low and in the darkness, they guided Angelica and the children to the borrowed van. Trona drove through the dark without lights, blended into the cars heading for the road. They hit the highway a few minutes later.

"Why do they want Joaquin?" asked Joe. "He's only, what, fifteen?"

Angelica steadfastly ignored him. Trona asked again and she turned to him, her frightened expression lit faintly by the dash lights. "Joaquin found gold in the hills, in one of the old mines. They are everywhere and the boys are always digging and searching. The gold belongs to the village. We were going to use it to make our old *pangas* more safer, and buy a new Yamaha engine for Gordo. And to buy a truck for Luis because his old truck is dying. And we were going to send Maria Hidalgo Lucero to school in La Paz because she is a smart one. And buy a new generator and a freezer for Aqua Amarga to share, one with a very good ice maker. And then when we ran out of gold, Joaquin and the boys would go find more in this mine, and we would improve Aqua Amarga with the gold forever. But Joaquin cannot keep quiet. His words spread like a fire. Now Hector knows. He will take the gold and he will force Joaquin to expose the mine. Maybe worse."

Angelica pointed out a shortcut to Aqua Amarga and Joe slowed and steered the van off the highway and onto a narrow dirt road.

"Two of us and a few village men can't keep Hector from taking the gold," said Joe.

"I just got an idea," said Hunt. "Maybe not a full idea. Part of one."

"I did, too," said Trona.

•◆•

Like all of his neighbors' homes, Israel's was one-story white-washed stucco. Strands of rebar poked up from the roofline, announcing to the government that construction was not complete. Therefore, the house was not finished. Therefore, it couldn't yet be taxed.

The house squatted by itself at the end of a dirt road just at the edge of Aqua Amarga. Behind it a vast wasteland of cactus and shrub, laced with half a dozen or more dry arroyos, stretched to a low range of foothills off in the distance, the shape of the range clearly visible now in the light of the full moon. The house itself seemed to sit in a pale glow from the bare bulb over the front door.

The four SUVs skidded to their own ostentatious stops in front of the house, dust billowing up around them. Before much of that dust had settled, the passenger's door on the lead car opened and a man emerged, cradling a machine gun. When he pulled open the back door behind him, a body in a baseball uniform got pushed from inside and fell into the road.

Israel.

The Zeta kicked out once and the body rolled away, hands coming up over the head for protection. Israel rolled over a second time and suddenly was on his feet, facing his assailant, turning halfway to face the other Zeta just coming out of the car. But the other car doors were opening all around, other men spilling out; headlights from each of the vehicles stayed on, illuminating the scene.

Israel was surrounded with nowhere to turn when the front door of the SUV he'd come in opened and Hector got out. *"Basta!"* the leader called out, and all around the men stiffened to something like attention as he came around the front of his SUV. In Spanish, Hector continued. "Israel and I will talk. He is a reasonable man."

Israel spit at the ground.

Hector got alongside the Zeta who'd kicked at their captive and now made a command gesture. Without a word, the Zeta handed his machine gun to Hector, who paused for an instant and then fired off a quick burst of three shots into the spot near Israel's feet where he'd spit.

Israel jumped backward at the same moment as a woman's scream rent the air. The front door opened and the screen slammed up against the house and Angelica was suddenly standing under the light, holding her hands up against her chest in panic.

Hector turned around slowly, unfazed by the woman's presence or her reaction. He nodded nonchalantly at Angelica, then came back to Israel. "Where is Joaquin?" he asked in a gentle voice.

"He is inside. The gold is a lie. It is a tale told by a child. There is no gold!"

"Why don't you invite me in and we can talk? Where is your hospitality?"

"No," said Angelica.

"He will come in anyway," said Israel. "Let Joaquin tell him that the gold is a lie."

•◆•

Trona and Hunt watched from the place they'd chosen to hide—behind the abandoned chassis of an old American car that someone had dumped on the side of the road and left on Israel's street about 150 feet from the front door of his home. Their shortcut across the desert in Baja Joe's van had given them a ten- or twelve-minute edge over the Zetas who'd driven the long way around on the regular highway. It was all the time they were going to have to get the details of their plan worked out, but it was going to have to be enough.

There weren't, as it turned out, too many details to consider. There was one gun—a Colt .45 six-shooter with bullets that might or might not fire—that Israel kept hidden in a cut-out floorboard under the bed. A thirty-four-inch Louisville Slugger that one of Israel's screwballs had long ago, when he'd been a teenager, broken off in the hands of Fernando Valenzuela. A bottle of Herradura.

Now, when Hector and his #1 bodyguard disappeared into the house behind Angelica and Israel, Hunt whispered, "So far, so good."

One by one, in short order the Zetas killed their engines and their headlights, until the only light on the street, beyond the moon's, was the one above Israel's door. The seven remaining Zetas broke off into their respective cars—three, two, and two. A couple of them lit up cigarettes. All of them put their weapons down on their car seats.

Hunt gave Trona a solemn nod and the two men stood up and the solemnity vanished as they lurched drunkenly out into the street. Trona had his arm thrown over Hunt's shoulder. Hunt let out a laugh. He was using the Slugger for a cane, nearly stumbling with every step, while Trona held the tequila bottle in his free hand and Hunt broke into a slurred version of "Tequila Sunrise."

They advanced on the Zetas, a couple of drunk American idiots.

The seven congealed again out of their cars, but only two of them brought their weapons out with them. Hunt saw that nobody seemed too concerned with this interruption. It was clear to them what was going on, by no means an uncommon occurrence. Cheap tequila and gringos on vacation were a staple of the economy down here. The Zetas had business they were attending to, and these guys were an interruption, but they certainly weren't anything to worry about.

One of the Zetas gave some kind of order and the two guys who had pulled out their weapons split away from the group and started moving toward the gringos, shooing their hands in front of themselves as though they were trying to move cattle.

Shoo away, thought Hunt.

Happily drunk and oblivious, Hunt and Trona kept coming, singing along, closing to a hundred feet, seventy-five, sixty. The lead Zeta held up his weapon, stopping in the road, and said, *"Alto! Ahora, alto!"*

Hunt and Trona, swaying against each other, stopped and blinked at the apparition. Hunt laughed and Trona slurred, "Sorry, dudes. *No habla español, por favor.*"

Hunt watched the Zetas turn back to their compadres, no doubt wondering what they were supposed to do with these clowns. A couple more of the *narcos* who'd stayed back by the cars decided to come on up and help get these pests out of the way, not bothering to bring their weapons.

In front of them, Hunt pointed at the machine guns, held up a hand as if he suddenly understood. At the same moment, Trona offered a sip from his bottle of tequila, an excuse to get half a step closer, let the advancing guys get within range. "And," he said, slowly, evenly, dragging it out. "Now!"

Hunt came up with the baseball bat and drilled the nearest Zeta over the ear. At the same moment, Trona swung with the tequila bottle in one hand, cold-cocking the guy in front of him, drawing the revolver out from his belt with the other, getting the dead drop on the two backup guys. "Don't move. Hands up! Don't move!"

Hunt, never slowing down, had his hands on his guy's machine gun before he'd even hit the ground, and now charged the remaining three guards down by the SUVs, who barely had had time to get halfway to their feet, scrambling, when they were all looking at a suddenly very serious American commando who was clearly well trained in the use of the M-16 and prepared to use it.

They raised their hands signaling their surrender as Trona, now armed with his own machine gun and a good handgun, came forward with the other two captives, their arms in the air as well. The gringos' two victims lay bleeding, quiet, unmoving, both facedown in the street.

Trona stood guard as Hunt collected the rest of the weapons. Minutes later they had bound and gagged the *narcos* with duct tape and fifty-pound-test fishing line that they found in the toolbox of the van, line that would cut them deeply if they struggled.

• ◆ •

Inside, for Hector, the negotiations were not proceeding well. He'd been a villager here all his life, until a few years ago, before accepting the uniform, and the dark soul, of a Zeta. So he knew how stubborn these people could be. How superstitious. Ignorant fishermen!

Even pointing his gold-plated, Malverde-embossed .45 at Joaquin, it had taken Hector a full ten minutes to convince Israel of the futility of his—and the town's—position. If there was gold in Aqua Amarga, then it was Zeta gold, Hector's gold, *verdad*? The town was only still in existence because of the forbearance of Hector Salida! Didn't Israel realize that Hector could kill every man, woman, and child in Aqua Amarga and nothing would happen? Nobody would care. The useless and corrupt government would do nothing. To oppose Hector would be certain death. Did Israel want to see him kill Joaquin right now in front of him, or did he want to bring him the gold? It was really that simple. Hector looked down at Joaquin, a handsome young man, now curled tight on the floor, trembling like a cold dog. Hector swirled the barrel of his fancy gun through Joaquin's lush black hair.

Israel looked at his son, then at Hector, then at Angelica.

"No," she said.

"Yes," said Israel.

Hector watched Israel rise and motion to his bodyguard to follow. They went down the hallway of the small house. Hector heard a scraping sound, like furniture being moved. He smiled at Angelica. "I miss the village."

"The village does not miss you."

"I'd rather be a legend than a slave."

"You are a slave to greed."

The two men were back in a moment, the bodyguard swinging a heavy rice bag onto the table, Israel looking on with a beaten expression. Hector swung his weapon away from Joaquin and ordered him to stand. The boy stood on shaking legs and Hector pointed the barrel of his gun at the bag. Joaquin untied and upended it and the heavy treasure thundered onto the old wooden table. Hector set his gun down and pawed through his bounty—somewhere near thirty kilograms of quartz run through with thick, visible veins of gold. Five, eight, perhaps ten kilograms of the gold itself. A fortune.

Finally, thought Hector, things are going my way. "Now. Where is the mine? Which mine?"

Hector saw Joaquin hang his head and cast a look at his father.

"You have ten seconds to tell me the mine, or I shoot your mother," said Hector. He pushed the end of the barrel between Angelica's breasts. "One. Two. Three."

"Father?"

"Four. Five."

"Yes, son. Tell him!"

"Six. Seven. Eight."

"Father?"

"Tell him!"

"Nine."

"Test pit ninety-six!" said Joaquin. "On the way to San Antonio!"

"That is government property!" bellowed Hector. "How did you steal gold from the government? *How?*"

Joaquin looked at his father again, imploringly, and Israel nodded. "I have a friend in the ministry," said Joaquin. "He knows I steal. We share."

"His name?"

"If I tell you, he will kill me. If I don't, you will."

"I feel such sadness. His *name!*"

"Narcisso Rueda," muttered Joaquin. "God help me."

Someone knocked on the front door. Hector and the bodyguard swung their guns toward the sound.

Hunt stood way aside from the door, flat against the wall, and waited for the bullets to punch through. He mustered his best Spanish accent. *"Hector! Policia! Vamos!"*

The door cracked open and the bodyguard peered out. Hunt grabbed his neck and twisted him back inside just as Hector raised his gun and fired. He felt the heavy .45s thudding into the Zeta's armor, the powerful shock waves transferring from the bodyguard straight into himself. He threw the man to the floor as Israel crashed down on Hector's arms with a chair—his golden gun skidding across the floor—and Angelica walloped him over the head with a cast-iron tortilla press. Trona burst in from behind them with one of the Zeta's good semiautomatics held straight at Hector, who was back up on his knees, barely.

Hunt grabbed the golden gun, then drew his own borrowed handgun from his belt and gave the bodyguard a sharp rap to the head with it. He ordered the family to raise their hands and move back against the wall. "Now!"

Joe stepped in and herded them. Angelica raised her hands and looked at Trona. "The devil himself. Look at his face."

"How nice of you to notice," said Joe, unfailingly polite. "I've heard much worse."

"Get out of my house," said Israel.

"You gringo pigs leave us alone!" yelled Joaquin.

"Leave you alone?" asked Hunt. "After all your father's talk on the boat radio today? All that fast Spanish he thought we couldn't hear? After his endless bragging about his son finding the gold that was going to bring miracles to Aqua Amarga? Leave you *alone*?"

Hunt saw Israel's pitch-perfect expression of shame. Of foolishness confessed. Of utter defeat.

"So," said Trona. "Thanks for the tip, captain. There's no way we could pass up an opportunity to rob you. But, since this hombre beat us to it, we'll just rob him. *Le gusta? Es bueno?*"

Trona, eyes now on Hector and gun still in hand, swept the gold ore back into the rice bag and slung it over his shoulder.

"I vow to take back my gold and murder you," said Hector.

"We'd have been disappointed if you didn't," said Joe.

"Let's go, partner," said Hunt.

"Let's tie everybody up first," Trona said. "Just for the hell of it."

They had an early plane—nine AM—out of La Paz Airport, but both men felt it couldn't really be too early.

As they watched and waited for their nearly twin duffel bags to pass through the X-ray machine, Hunt said, "All I want is to get past the security gate. I don't think they'll storm the airport."

Trona shrugged. "They're still tied up. Israel not as tight as some, that's all. And Hector and his boys? Who's going to cut 'em free? The villagers?"

"I hope you're right."

"Don't get me wrong," Trona said, "I'm keeping my eyes open." He lowered his voice. "I just hope nobody notices we're not boarding with any gold. Which might make somebody wonder where it could be."

"Who's going to notice? It's not like Hector's going to go to the cops. 'Hey, those two gringos just stole the gold that I just stole.' I don't think so. Instead, we just walk on the plane and stay cool. As far as Hector's concerned, we got clean away, and the gold with us. And he'd never think—he'd never believe—that we put it back in Israel's *panga*."

304

"I know. Although he has vowed to take back his gold and kill us, remember?"

Hunt broke a smile and shook his head. "Not gonna happen. Just like he's not going to find any gold in test pit ninety-six."

With only the ten minutes or so that they'd had to go over their plan with Israel's sister, they'd had to play things by ear. When they'd arrived at Israel's home, for example, first thing they'd had to contend with was a very distrustful and hostile Joaquin and his fifteen years' worth of testosterone. Why should he believe that Hunt and Trona were going to steal the gold from Hector and then return it to Israel and the good people of Agua Amarga? How could Angelica believe or trust these two gringos whom she had just met? Who were they anyway?

It had been a close thing, Joaquin getting the Colt from its hiding place, only to hold it on Joe and Wyatt for a tense few moments until Angelica could convince him that they really had no other choice. Hector and his *narcos* would be there within minutes. If Hunt and Trona were in fact planning on stealing the gold and keeping it for themselves, there was nothing Joaquin or anyone else could do about it.

"We could kill them right now and then kill as many of Hector's men as we could before they kill us," Joaquin said.

"We know that there is more gold in the ground," Angelica had said. "No one needs to die over the gold we already have."

And in the end, only two or three minutes before Hector and his men had arrived, Joaquin had given in.

And still, there had been one element of the plan that had worried Joe—they had no provision for Hector's return to claim the rest of the gold from Joaquin's secret mine. Everyone knew that

Hector would not rest until he knew where Joaquin had found the gold, and even if Hunt and Trona were successful in keeping the town's gold from him that night, Hector would eventually cause more trouble when he came again.

"He's going to need to know where you found it," Trona had said, "and he will torture you until you tell him. So there is only one thing to do."

"What is that?"

"Tell him the wrong mine," Joe said, "and sting him."

"Sting him how?"

"That is for you and your father to figure out."

•◆•

Four days after Hunt and Trona had landed safely back in the States, Narcisso Rueda, a longtime angling customer of Israel's, sat in the bow of the *panga* about a hundred meters offshore. He was awaiting the long run-up at full power into ever more and more shallow water until Israel with perfect timing lifted the screaming, whining propeller up out of the water and killed the engine as the water became the beach and the *panga* sheared its way through the sand until it came to rest twenty or thirty feet up onto the strand, high and dry. No matter how many fish they caught, and today Narcisso had landed two dorado and two tuna, the beaching of the *pangas* always provided an adrenaline rush, a last moment of excitement and pure, simple fun.

But today, though they were in position to rush the shore, Israel kept the engine in neutral. Narcisso was, in fact, head of security for the government's gold mining operations near La Paz. He had, of course, never made any kind of gold deal with Israel's son. In fact, he was widely known as an incorruptible official. Unlike so many of Mexico's security forces, especially those dealing with the *narcotrafficantes,* Narcisso had successfully investigated and prosecuted both gold thieves from among the miners and corruption at the corporate level. No fewer than two dozen men now sat in federal prisons because of Narcisso's efforts.

After he listened to Israel's story, a smile played at the corners of his mouth. "I have heard something of this Hector Salida. A nasty piece of work. He thinks he can bribe me?"

Israel nodded. "I took him out off Cerralvo last week," he lied. He has a reckless mouth, and he has heard of gold in one of the abandoned mines. Gold that, supposedly, you don't know of."

This made Narcisso laugh. "Ah, *that* gold. And I let him mine that vein and turn the other way. For a cut. That's the idea?"

"It's what he bragged about. You might be expecting him to contact you."

"I'll look forward to the conversation, which I'll be certain to record. He is not the first one to have this idea. And our judges have found such recordings to be . . . persuasive."

"I just thought you would want to know."

Narcisso nodded. "It is always good to have knowledge. It keeps the vermin down."

STEVE BERRY

VS.   JAMES ROLLINS

The Devil's Bones

I n his 2006 thriller, *Black Order*, Jim Rollins dispatched his hero, Gray Pierce, to Denmark. While there, Pierce spent two days "visiting the dusty bookshops and antiquary establishments in the narrow backstreets of Copenhagen. He discovered the most help at a shop on Højbro Plads owned by an ex-lawyer from Georgia." No name. Just enough information that, if you were a fan of Steve Berry's hero, Cotton Malone, you'd know instantly who Pierce was talking about. Jim's purpose was to see if readers were paying attention and could discover the extent of crossover between his and Steve's work.

He learned things on both counts.

Readers definitely noticed. Jim and Steve together received several thousand e-mails (and still do to this day). When Steve reciprocated and included a reference to Sigma Force (Jim's clandestine agency where Gray Pierce works) in his next novel, people noticed again. Together, they continued the experiment for several more books. Eventually, fellow thriller writer Raymond Khoury (who's part of this anthology) joined the mix. It was fun, but it also alerted the writers to the fact that their readers wanted to see the characters together.

That wasn't possible, until the opportunity provided by this anthology.

There are a lot of similarities between Malone and Pierce. Both are ex-military. Single. With issues. They each work for a covert government agency—Pierce with Sigma, through the Defense Department—Malone, though now retired, freelances with his former employer, the Magellan Billet at Justice. And where Pierce deals more with science and a little history, Malone focuses on history, with a touch of science.

Steve came up with the broad idea of something in South America, on the Amazon. Jim took that thought and wrote a first draft of the entire story. Steve then revamped that draft, which Jim gave a final edit.

The result is about three hours in the lives of Gray Pierce and Cotton Malone.

On a riverboat, in the middle of nowhere.

Everything happens fast.

Nothing atypical for these two.

The Devil's Bones

Commander Gray Pierce stood on the balcony of his suite aboard the luxury riverboat and took stock of his surroundings.

Time to get this show on the road.

He was two days upriver from Belém, the Brazilian port city that served as the gateway to the Amazon—one hour from the boat's last stop at a bustling river village. The ship was headed for Manaus, a township deep in the rain forest, where the target was supposed to meet his buyers.

Which Pierce could not allow to happen.

The long riverboat, the MV *Fawcett,* glided along the black waterway, its surface mirroring the surrounding jungle. From the forest howler monkeys screamed at its passage. Scarlet and gold flashes fluttering through shadowy branches marked the flight of parrots and macaws. Twilight in the jungle was approaching, and fishing bats were already hunting under the overhanging bowers, diving and darting among a tangle of black roots, forcing frogs from their roosts, the soft *plops* of their bodies into the water announcing a strategic retreat.

He wondered what Seichan was doing. He'd left her in Rio de Janeiro, his last sight of her as she donned a pair of khaki shorts and a black T-shirt, not bothering with a bra. Fine by him. Less the better on her. He'd watched as she tugged on her boots, how the cascade of dark hair brushed against her cheeks and shrouded her emerald eyes. He'd found himself thinking about her more and more of late.

Which was both good and bad.

A ringing echoed throughout the boat.

Dinner bell.

He checked his watch. The meal would begin in ten minutes and usually lasted an hour. He'd have to be in and out of the room before his target finished eating. He checked the knot on the rope he'd tied to the rail and tossed the line over the side. He'd cut just enough length to reach the balcony directly below, which led into the suite belonging to his target.

Edward Trask. An ethnobotanist from Oxford University.

Pierce had been provided a full dossier. The thirty-two-year-old researcher disappeared into the Brazilian jungle three years ago, only to return five months back—sunburnt and gaunt, with a tale of adventures, deprivation, lost tribes, and enlightenment. He became an instant celebrity, his rugged face gracing the pages of *Time* and *Rolling Stone*. His British accent and charming self-deprecation seemed crafted for television and he'd appeared on a slew of national programs, from *Good Morning America* to *The Daily Show*. He quickly sold his story to a New York publisher for seven figures. But one aspect of Trask's story would never see print, a detail uncovered a week ago.

Trask was a fraud.

And a dangerous one at that.

Pierce gripped the rope and quickly shimmied down. He found the balcony below and climbed on, seizing a position to one side of the glass doors.

He peered through the parted curtain and tested the door.

Unlocked.

He eased the panel open and slipped inside the cabin. The layout was identical to his suite above. Except Trask seemed a slob. Discarded clothes were piled all over the floor. Wet towels lay scattered on an unmade bed. The remains of some meal cluttered the table. The one saving grace? It wouldn't be hard to hide his search.

First, he'd check the obvious. The room safe. But he had to be quiet, so as not to alert the guard posted outside. That security measure had necessitated his improvised point of entry.

He found the safe in the bedroom closet and slipped a keycard, wired to an electronic decoder, into the release mechanism. He'd already calibrated the unit on the safe in his cabin. The combination was found and the lock opened. But the safe contained only Trask's wallet, some cash, and a passport.

None of which he was after.

He closed the safe and began a systematic examination of the room's hidden corners and cubbies, keeping his movements slow and silent. He'd already reconnoitered his own suite in search of any place that might hide something small.

And there were many possibilities.

In the bathroom he checked the hollows beneath the sink, the underside of drawers, the service hatch beneath the whirlpool tub.

Nothing.

He lingered a moment and surveyed the tight space, making sure he didn't miss anything. The bathroom's marble vanity top seemed a collage of dried toothpaste, balled-up wet tissues, and assorted creams and gels. From his observations over the past three days he knew Trask only allowed the maid and butler into the room once a day and, even then, they were accompanied by the guard, a burly fellow with a shaved scalp and a perpetual scowl.

He left the bathroom.

The bedroom was next.

A loud *oomph* reverberated from the cabin door, which startled him.

He froze.

Was Trask back? So soon?

What sounded like something heavy slid down the door and thumped to the floor outside.

The dead bolt released and the doorknob turned.

Crap.

He had company.

•◆•

Cotton Malone crouched over the slumped guard. He held a finger to the man's thick neck and ensured the presence of a pulse. Faint, but there. He'd managed to surprise the sentry in a choke hold that took far longer than he had expected. Now that the big man was down he needed to get him out of the hallway. He'd just arrived on the boat an hour ago at its last stop, so everything was being improvised. Which was fine. He was good at making things up.

He opened the door to Trask's cabin and hauled the limp body by the armpits. He noted a shoulder holster under the guard's jacket and quickly relieved the man of his weapon. He'd not had time to secure a sidearm due to the foreshortened nature of this mission. Yesterday, he'd been attending an antiquities auction in Buenos Aires, on the hunt for some rare first editions for his Danish bookshop. Cassiopeia Vitt was with him. It was supposed to be a fun trip. Some time together in Argentina. Sun and beaches. But a call from Stephanie Nelle, his old employer at the Magellan Billet, had changed those plans.

Five months ago, Dr. Edward Trask had returned from the Brazilian rain forest, after three years missing, toting an armful of rare botanical specimens—roots, flowers, leaves, and bark—all for the pharmaceutical company that had funded his journey. He claimed his discoveries held great potential, hope for the next cancer drug, cardiac medicine, or impotency pill. He'd also returned with anecdotal stories for each of his samples, tales supposedly told to him by remote shamans and local tribespeople. Over the intervening months, though, word had seeped from the company that the samples were worthless. Most were nothing new. A researcher for the pharmaceutical firm had privately described the much publicized bounty best. *It was like the bastard just grabbed whatever he could find.* To both save face and protect the price of its stock, the company clamped a gag order on its employees and hoped the matter would just go away.

But it hadn't.

In fact, darker tales reached the U.S. government, as it seemed Trask had not come out of the forest entirely empty-handed. Folded amid his specimens—like a single wheat kernel amid much chaff—lay the real botanical jackpot. A rare flower, still unclassified, of the orchid family, that held an organic neurotoxin a hundredfold deadlier than sarin.

Talk about a jackpot.

Trask had been smart enough to both recognize and appreciate the value of his discovery. He'd analyzed and purified the toxin at a private lab, paid for out of his own pocket, his book deal and television appearances lucrative enough to fund the project. Part P. T. Barnum, part monster, last week Trask had secretly offered his discovery for auction, posting its chemical analysis, its potential, and a demonstration video of a roomful of caged chimpanzees, all bleeding from eyes and noses, gasping, then falling dead, the air clogged with a yellow vapor. The infomercial had gained the full attention of terrorist organizations around the world, along with U.S. intelligence services. Malone's old haunt, the Magellan Billet, had been tasked by the White House to stop the sale and retrieve the sample. His mistake had come when he'd mentioned to Stephanie Nelle last week, during a casual conversation between old friends, that he and Cassiopeia were headed to Argentina.

"The sale will happen in Manaus," Stephanie told him yesterday on the phone.

He knew the place.

"Trask is there with a video crew from the Discovery Channel, aboard a luxury riverboat. They're touring the neighboring rain forest and preparing for a television special about his lost years in the jungle. His real purpose for being there, though, is to sell his purified sample. We have to get it from him, and you're the closest asset there."

"I'm retired."

"I'll make it worth your while."

"How will I know if I found it?" he asked.

"It's stored in a small metal case, in vials, about the size of a deck of cards."

"I assume you want me to do this alone?"

"Preferably. This is highly classified. Tell Cassiopeia you'll only be gone a few days."

Cassiopeia did not like it, but she'd understood Stephanie's condition. *Call, if you need me,* had been her last words as he left for the airport.

He hauled the guard over the cabin threshold, closed the door, and secured the dead bolt.

Time to find those vials.

Movement disturbed the silence.

He whirled and saw a form in the dim light, raising a weapon. Trask was gone. In the dining room. He'd made sure of that before his assault on the sentry.

So who was this?

He still held the gun just retrieved from the guard, which he aimed at the threat.

"I wouldn't do that," a gruff voice flavored with a slight Texas twang said.

He knew that voice.

"Gray friggin' Pierce."

•◆•

Pierce kept his pistol firmly aimed and recognized the southern drawl. "Cotton Malone. How about that? A blast from the past."

He took stock of the former agent in the dim light. Mid-forties. Still fit. Light-brown hair with not all that much gray. He knew Malone was retired, living in Copenhagen, owning a rare bookshop. He'd even visited him there once a couple of years ago. There were stories that Malone occasionally moonlighted for his former boss Stephanie Nelle. Malone had been one of her original twelve agents at the Magellan Billet, until he opted out early. Pierce knew the unit. Highly specialized. Worked out of the Justice Department. Reported only to the attorney general and the president.

He lowered his gun. "Just what we need, a damn lawyer."

"About as bad as having Mr. Wizard on the job," Malone said, lowering his gun, too.

Pierce got the connection. Sigma Force, his employer, was part of DARPA, the Defense Advanced Research Projects Agency. Sigma comprised a clandestine group of former Special Forces soldiers, retrained in scientific disciplines, who served as field operatives. Where Sigma dealt with lots of science and a little history, the Magellan Billet handled global threats that delved more into history and little science.

"Let me guess," he said to Malone. "You know about Trask's neurotoxin?"

"That's what I'm here to get."

"Seems we have an interagency failure to communicate. The coaches sent two quarterbacks onto the field."

"Nothing new. How about I go back to Buenos Aires and you handle this?"

Pierce caught the real meaning. "Got a girl there?"

"That I do."

An explosion rocked the boat—from the stern, heaving the hull high, tossing them both against the wall. He tangled with Malone, hitting something solid, but managed to keep hold of his gun. The blast faded and screams filled the air, echoing throughout the ship.

The riverboat listed to starboard.

"That ain't good," Malone said as they both regained their balance.

"You think?"

The boat continued to list, tilting farther starboard, confirming the hull was taking on water. A glance past the balcony revealed a pall of black smoke wafting skyward.

Something was on fire.

A pounding of boots sounded from beyond the cabin door. A shotgun blast tore through the dead bolt and the door crashed open. Both he and Malone swung their guns toward the smoky threshold. Two men barged inside, dressed in paramilitary uniforms, their faces obscured by black scarves. One carried a shotgun, the other an assault rifle. Pierce shot the man with the double-barrel, while Malone took down the other.

"This is interesting," Malone muttered, as Pierce quickly checked the hallway and confirmed only the two gunmen. "Seems we're not the only ones looking for Trask's poison. Were you able to find it?"

He shook his head. "I only had a chance to search half the suite. But it shouldn't take long to—"

Gun blasts popped in the distance.

Pierce cocked an ear. "That came from the dining hall."

"Our visitors must be going after Trask," Malone said. "He could have it on him."

Which was a real possibility. He'd already considered that option, which was why he'd gone to great lengths to keep his search of the cabin under the radar. If the effort proved futile, he didn't want to alert Trask and make him extra guarded.

"Finish your search here," Malone said. "I'll get Trask."

He had no choice. Things were happening fast and off script. Lawyer or no lawyer, he needed the help.

"Do it."

•◆•

Malone raced down the canted passageway, a hand on the wall to keep his balance. He'd not seen Gray Pierce since that day in his bookshop a couple of years ago. He actually liked the guy. There were a lot of similarities between them. Both were former soldiers. Both recruited into intelligence services. Each seemed to have taken care of themselves physically. The big difference came with age; Pierce was at least ten years younger and that made a difference. Particularly in this business. The other contrast was that Pierce was still in the game, while Malone was merely an occasional player.

And he wasn't foolish enough not to realize that mattered.

He skidded to a stop as he approached the stairs that led down to the riverboat's dining hall. Take it slow from here in. Through a window he surveyed the river outside. The boat sat askew, foundering in the swift current. Past a roil of smoke he spotted a gunmetal-gray craft prowling into view. A uniformed man, whose features were obscured by a wrap of black cloth, stood at its stern, the long tube of a rocket-propelled grenade launcher resting on his shoulder.

Which was apparently how they'd scuttled the boat.

He rounded the landing and double doors appeared below. A body lay at the threshold in a pool of blood, the man dressed as a maître d'. He slowed his pace and negotiated the steps with care, approaching the door from one side, and snuck a quick peek into the room.

More bodies lay strewn among overturned tables and chairs.

At least two dozen.

A large clutch of passengers huddled to one side of the spacious room, held at gunpoint by a pair of men. Another two men stalked through bodies, searching. One held a photograph, likely looking for someone who matched Trask's face. Amid the captives Malone spotted the good doctor. Stephanie had provided him an image by e-mail. Trask kept his back to the gunmen, hunching into his dinner jacket, a hand half covering his face, trying to be one among many.

That ruse wouldn't last long.

Trask was strikingly handsome in a roguish way, with unruly auburn hair and sharp planes defining his face. Easy to see how he became a media darling. But those distinct looks should get him flushed out of the crowd and into the assault force's custody in no time.

Malone couldn't let that happen.

So he bent down and patted his palm into the maître d's blood. Not the most hygienic thing in the world, but it had to be done. He painted his face with the bloody palm, then slipped the pistol into the waistband of his pants, at the small of his back, and tugged the edge of his shirt over it.

Why he did stuff like this he'd never know.

He stumbled into view, limping, holding a bloody hand to his fouled face.

"Help me," he called out in a plaintive tone, as he wove a path deeper into the room—only to be accosted by one of the gunmen holding the passengers at bay.

Orders in Portuguese were barked at him.

He feigned surprise and confusion though he understood every word—a benefit of the eidetic memory that made languages easy for him. He allowed the man to drive him toward the clutch of passengers. He was shoved into the crowd, bouncing off a matronly woman who was held close by her husband. He shifted deeper into the mass, bobbling his way through until he reached Trask's side. Once there, he slipped the pistol out and jabbed it into the botanist's side.

"Stay nice and still," he whispered. "I'm here to save your sorry ass."

Trask flinched and it looked like he was about to speak.

"Don't talk," he breathed. "I'm your only hope of getting out of here alive. So don't look a gift horse in the mouth."

Trask stood still and asked, his lips not moving, "What do you want me to do?"

"Where's the biotoxin?"

"Get me out of here, and I'll bloody well make it worth your while."

Typical opportunist, quickly adapting.

"I'm not telling you a thing," Trask said, "until you have me somewhere safe."

Clearly the guy sensed a momentary advantage.

"I could just identify you to these gentlemen," Malone made clear.

"I have the vials on me. If even a single one breaks, it'll kill anything and everything within a hundred yards. Trust me, there's no stopping it, short of incineration." Trask threw him a glorious smile of victory. "So I suggest you hurry."

He took stock of the four gunmen. The two searchers had about completed their path through the corpses. To better the odds of success he needed them all grouped together. As he waited for that to happen, he decided to press his own advantage.

"Where did you find the orchid?"

The doctor gently shook his head.

"You'll tell me that much, or I'll shoot my way out of here and leave you to them—making sure I'm a hundred yards away fast."

Trask clenched his jaw and seemed to get the point.

They both continued to stare out at the macabre scene.

"Six months into the jungle I heard a rumor of a plant called *Huesos del Diablo*," Trask said, keeping his lips still.

Malone silently translated.

The devil's bones.

"It took another year to find a tribe that knew about it. I embedded myself in their village, apprenticed myself to the shaman. Eventually he took me to a set of ruins buried in the upper Amazon basin, revealing a vast complex of temple foundations that stretched for miles. The shaman told me that tens of thousands of people had once lived there. A vast unrecorded civilization."

Malone had heard of similar ruins, identified via satellite imaging, found deep in the hinterlands of the Amazon, where people thought no one lived. Each discovery defied the conventional wisdom that deemed the rain forest incapable of supporting civilization. Estimates put the number living there at over sixty thousand. The fate of those people remained unknown, though it was theorized starvation and disease were the main culprits of their demise.

But maybe there was another explanation.

The searchers across the dining hall checked the last of the bodies. The two armed men closest to them alternated their attention from their colleagues to their captives.

"Among the ruins I found piles of bones, many of them burned. Other bodies looked like they died where they dropped. The shaman told me the story of a great plague that killed in seconds and wilted flesh from bones. He showed me an unusual dark orchid growing nearby. I didn't know then if the orchid was the source of the plague, but the shaman claimed the plant was death itself. Even to touch it could kill. The shaman taught me how to gather it safely and how to wring the poison from its petals."

"And once you learned how to gather this toxin?"

Trask finally glanced at him. "I had to test it, of course. First on the shaman. Then, on his village."

Malone's blood went cold at the matter-of-fact admission of mass murder.

Trask turned back. "Afterward, to ensure I had the only source, I burned all pockets of the orchids I could find. So you see, my rescuer, I hold the key to it all."

He'd heard enough.

"Stick to my side," he mouthed.

He eased toward the edge of the crowd, towing Trask in his wake. Once there, he knew he had to incapacitate the four armed men as quickly as possible. There'd only be a few seconds of indecision. The men were finally gathered in a group. Seven rounds remained in his gun's magazine. Not much room for error. He eyed an overturned table with a marble top that should offer decent cover. But he needed to be away from the civilians before the shooting started.

He gripped Trask by the elbow and motioned to the table. "Come with me. On my mark."

He did a fast three count, then sprinted toward the table, swinging his gun into view—only to have the floor beneath his feet jolt, throwing him high. He flew past the table, crashing hard, losing his grip on the gun, which skittered across the floor out of reach. He rolled to see the front of the dining hall tear away, glass exploding, the walls splintering open.

Dark jungle burst inside.

Then he realized.

The boat had hit shore and run aground.

Everybody had been knocked off their feet, even the gunmen. He searched for Trask, but the botanist had been tossed into the assault team. Trask straightened up and even the blood gushing from a broken nose failed to hide his features. Surprised voices erupted from the four gunmen. Rifles were pointed and Trask lifted his arms in surrender.

Malone searched for the pistol, but it was gone.

Trask glanced in his direction, the fear and plea plain on his face. The man's thoughts clear. *Help me. Or else.* Malone shook his head and brought a finger to his lips, signaling silence, the hope being that the doctor would realize selling him out was not a good idea.

One of them had to be free to act.

Trask hesitated, was jerked to his feet, but said nothing.

A parrot screamed across the ruins of the dining hall, cawing, seemingly voicing Malone's frustration.

And he could only stare as Trask and his captors vanished into the dark bower of the jungle.

• ◆ •

Pierce stared across the ruins of the dining hall, studying what lay beyond a gash in the walls. "So you lost him."

"Not much I could do," Malone said, on his knees, searching among a tumble of chairs and tossed tables. "Especially after the boat ran aground."

Trask's cabin had come up empty. But Pierce now knew that the doctor had the sample hidden on him. He'd also listened as Malone reported everything else Trask had said.

Malone reached under a tablecloth and came up with the pistol he'd lost earlier. "Lot of good it does me now. What's our next move?"

"You don't have to stay on this. You're retired. Go back to your lady in Buenos Aires."

"I wish I could. But Stephanie Nelle would have my ass. I'm afraid you're stuck with me. I'll try, though, not to get in the way."

He caught the sarcasm.

So far, this brief partnership between Justice and Defense had proved fruitless. But with Trask on the run and captured by a guerrilla force, as much as he hated to admit it Pierce could use the help.

Malone picked his way across the dining hall to the demolished wall of the ship. Pierce watched as the former agent bent down and examined something. All of the other passengers were gone, being offloaded to other boats.

"Got a blood trail here that leads outside."

He hustled over.

"Has to be Trask," Malone said. "He broke his nose when the ship crashed. It was bleeding badly."

"Then we follow it."

"I saw a patrol boat earlier. They could have offloaded him by the river."

"I spotted that craft, too, from the cabin. But it took off shortly after we went aground. The attack, the fire, the crash—it's drawn lots of river traffic."

"You think the ground team and the boat are planning a rendezvous farther along the Amazon? Where there are fewer eyes to see them?"

"It makes sense. And that gives us a window of opportunity."

"A small one, which is shrinking fast." Malone pointed to the drops of blood, scuffed by the boot of one of the guerrillas. "Once in the jungle, it'll be hard to track in the dark."

"But they're in a hurry," Pierce said. "Not expecting anyone to follow. And they'll have to stay close to the riverbank, waiting for their ride. With four men and a prisoner in tow, they should leave an easy trail."

Which proved true.

Minutes later, slogging across the muddy bank, Pierce saw that it wasn't difficult to spot where the guerrillas had pushed into the forest. He glanced back at the beached riverboat, its bulk angled in the river, the stern still billowing black smoke into the twilight sky. Other watercraft had now come to its rescue. Passengers were being ferried away as the fires aboard spread.

He turned from the smoking ruins of the MV *Fawcett*.

The boat had surely been named after the doomed British explorer Percy Fawcett, who vanished in the Amazon searching for a mythical lost city. Pierce faced the jungle, hoping the same fate didn't await them.

"Let's go," he said, leading the way.

Less than ten feet into the dense vegetation the forest snuffed what little light remained. Night shrouded them. He limited any illumination to a single penlight, which he shone ahead, picking out boot prints in the muddy mulch and broken stems on the bushes. The trail was easy to track but hard to traverse. Every vine was armed with thorns. Branches hung low. Thickets were as convoluted as woven steel.

They forged onward, moving as quietly as possible. A growing ruckus from the night helped mask their advance. All around them were screams, buzzes, howls, and croaking. The shine of his tiny light also caught eyes staring back at them. Monkeys huddled in trees. Parrots nesting atop branches. A pair of larger pupils—like yellow marbles with black dots—glowed.

Maybe a jaguar or a panther.

After forty minutes of careful advancing, Malone whispered, "To the left. Is that a fire?"

Pierce stopped and shaded his penlight with his palm. In the blackness, he spotted a flickering crimson glow through the trees.

"They made camp?" Malone whispered.

"Maybe waiting for full night before making a break for the river and their boat."

"If it's them at all."

Only one way to find out.

He flicked his flashlight off and continued toward the glow, noting that the path they were following led in that direction, too. Twenty minutes of careful plodding were needed to close the distance. They halted in a copse of vine-laden trees that offered cover and a vantage point to spy upon the camp.

Pierce surveyed the clearing.

Mud-and-thatch huts indicated a native village. He spotted a clutch of children and a handful of men and women, including a wizened elder who cradled an injured arm. All were held at gunpoint by one of the guerrillas from the boat. The campfire must have attracted their attention, too.

He spotted Trask, on his knees, by the flames. One of the guerrillas leaned over him, clearly shouting, but the words could not be heard. Trask shook his head, then was backhanded for his stubbornness, sending the doctor sprawling across the ground. Another of the assailants came forward, balancing a small metal case on his open palm. His captors must have searched Trask and found the vials. The faint glow of LED lights could be seen on the case.

"Locked with an electronic code," Malone said.

He agreed. "Which they're trying to learn from Trask."

"And I can tell you, from our little bit of conversation, he's going to drive a hard bargain."

Pierce counted four guerrillas, each heavily armed. The odds weren't good. Two to one. And any firefight risked harming or killing the villagers.

A new group of guerrillas appeared at the village's western edge, filing out of a worn trail that likely led to the river. They numbered another six, along with a seventh who stood taller than the others and unwrapped the black cloth from his face. A deep scar ran down his left cheek, splitting his chin. He barked out orders that were instantly obeyed.

This one was in charge.

Two-to-one odds just became five to one.

The newcomers were also heavily armed with assault rifles, grenade launchers, and shotguns.

Pierce realized the futility of their situation.

But Malone seemed unaffected. "We can do this."

● ◆ ●

Malone watched as the assault force leader yanked trask to his feet and pointed west, toward the river, where the boat was likely waiting.

"We can't let them get to the water," he said. "Once they've cleared the village, we can use the jungle to our advantage."

"Guerrilla warfare against guerrillas." Pierce shrugged. "I like it. They teach you that in law school?"

"The navy."

Pierce smiled. "With any luck, maybe in the confusion we can grab Trask *and* the vials."

"I'll settle for the vials."

Their targets left the village.

They kept low, running parallel. Interesting how their quarry was making no effort to move quietly. Orders were barked in loud voices, the crunch of boots and snap of branches announcing a retreat toward the river. The entourage moved as if in total command of their surroundings—which, in a sense, they were. This was home field for them. But that didn't mean the visiting team couldn't score a few points every once in awhile.

They neared the village clearing and Malone noted two of the gunmen had remained behind, assault rifles still trained on villagers.

A problem.

It seemed they intended to leave no witnesses. He caught Pierce's attention, pantomimed what they should do, and received a nod of acknowledgment. They closed the last of the distance at a run, bursting into the clearing, appearing in an instant behind the two gunmen.

A shot to the chest and he dropped one.

Pierce killed the other.

The pistol blasts were loud, echoing into the forest.

Malone skidded on his knees and caught the assault rifle as his target collapsed. Pointing it toward the sky he strafed a fierce blast at the stars. He hoped the initial pistol shots accompanied by the rifle fire would be taken by the retreating guerrillas as the village's bloody cleanup.

Pierce motioned for the locals to stay calm and not spoil the ruse. The elder nodded, seeming to understand, and waved the others down, ensuring that mothers kept frightened children quiet, signaling the men to gather what they could in preparation to flee.

Pierce holstered his Sig Sauer and gripped one of the guerrilla's rifles. Malone followed his example. He spotted a grenade launcher resting on the ground near one of the bodies. He considered taking it, too, but it would likely only burden him in the confines of the jungle. The rifle and his pistol would have to do.

They fled toward the trail taken by the guerrillas.

Thirty yards in, the shadowy form of a guerrilla blocked their path. Someone must have been sent back to make sure the village was secure. Before they could react, the man opened fire, shredding leaves and sending them diving into the vegetation.

Malone rolled behind the bole of a tree and twisted in time to see the muzzle flash of Pierce's return fire.

Not bad. Fast response.

The guerrilla was thrown backward, his chest blown out as bullets tore into flesh.

The body thudded to the ground.

"Keep going," Pierce said. "Let's try to stay on their flanks."

Malone bit back a groan of complaint from his sore knees. Jungle warfare was definitely a younger man's game.

But he could handle it.

They plunged ahead.

• ◆ •

Pierce kept track of Malone's progress, matching the pace. What they needed was for any boat waiting for the group to be out of commission. Unfortunately, they were a little shorthanded and would have to handle the situation once there.

He continued through the forest, paralleling the path taken by the guerrilla force. He on one side of the trail, Malone on the other, out of sight. A slight wind coursed through the trees. Its direction appeared away from the river, inland. Shouts from ahead brought him to a stop. First in Portuguese, then English.

"Show yourself, or I kill your man."

He edged forward and crouched low.

A deadfall opened ahead, where one of the canopy trees had recently fallen tearing a hole in the forest. Starlight bathed the open wound, revealing the guerrilla leader. He held aloft the small steel case, its LED display still glowing. Another of the guerrillas nestled the muzzle of an assault rifle to the back of Trask's skull. Pierce cared nothing for the doctor's life. Malone had shared what he'd learned as to how Trask had obtained his prize and at what cost. All that mattered was securing the toxin before it escaped to some foreign enemy's manufacturing lab, where it could be mass-produced.

"Come out now, or I kill him," the leader shouted.

From the edge of the deadfall, another pair of gunmen appeared.

Only then did Pierce realize his mistake.

Your man.

Prodded at gunpoint, a second prisoner was thrust into view, gagged, his face bloody.

Malone.

• ◆ •

Malone kept his fingers folded atop his head. He'd been ambushed shortly after parting company with Pierce. A shadow had loomed behind him clamping a hand over his mouth, an arm around his throat. Then a second figure slammed the butt of a rifle into his gut, dropping him to the ground. Dazed, he'd been gagged with one of their face scarves and thrust forward at gunpoint. He now stared out at the dark forest, willing Pierce not to show himself.

Unfortunately his silent plea was not answered.

Twenty yards away Pierce appeared, rifle high over his head, surrendering.

One of his captors shoved Malone forward.

Pierce caught his gaze as he staggered near and mouthed, "Be ready to run."

• ◆ •

Pierce stepped past Malone and shouted, "I surrender," which gained the guerrilla leader's full attention.

He tossed the assault rifle away. As expected, all eyes followed the weapon's trajectory across the deadfall. He quickly dropped an arm to his waist, yanked out his Sig Sauer, and shot from the hip, taking out the two closest gunmen.

Now for the real prize.

He aimed at the leader and fired.

Instead of a clean kill, though, the round found the man's out-stretched hand, smacking into the steel case, then penetrating the chest. A yellowish mist burst instantly outward, swamping those nearby. He remembered Malone's relating the botanist's warning. *If even a single vial breaks, it'll kill anything within a hundred yards.*

The danger spread.

Screaming began.

He backpedaled as the breeze caught the cloud and blew it toward him. Malone, still gagged, didn't have to be told twice and bolted for the trailhead. Pierce turned to follow—only to see a fig-ure emerge from the toxic cloud.

Trask.

His face appeared parboiled, eyes weeping and blind. Another few steps and a convulsion jackknifed through every muscle, throwing the body off balance and to the ground.

Couldn't happen to a nicer guy.

Pierce turned and sprinted after Malone. The windblown dan-ger rolled after him. He glanced back at the spreading devastation. Monkeys fell from tree limbs. Birds took flight only to cartwheel to the ground. Anything that crawled, slithered, or flew seemed to in-stantly succumb. He caught up with Malone and together they fled down the last of the trail and burst into the village clearing.

Which unfortunately wasn't empty.

The locals were still there, having not yet evacuated. Children darted behind mothers' legs, frightened by their sudden reappear-ance, thinking perhaps the guerrillas had returned. Matters weren't helped by the fact that Malone was bloody and gagged. Pierce drew to a halt and swung around to face the trail. Above the can-opy, a flurry of bats spun and darted, beginning their nightly forage for insects. Then they began to drop from the sky—at first farther out, then closer in.

Death swept toward them, carried by the wind.

He turned to the villagers and saw frightened faces. None of them, himself included, would ever be able to run fast enough to escape the cloud.

His errant shot had doomed them all.

•◆•

Malone searched for their only hope, again skidding to his knees and snatching up the RPG launcher.

A quick check confirmed the weapon was loaded.

Thank God.

"What are you doing?" Pierce yelled.

No time to explain.

He hoisted the tube to his shoulder, aimed for the trailhead, and fired. The weapon jolted against his face, spitting out smoke behind him. A grenade whistled in a tight arc then blasted down the throat of the trail.

A fiery explosion lit the night.

Trees erupted in a smoldering rain of limbs and leaves.

Heat washed over him. Was it enough?

Trask's words echoed in his head. *There's no stopping it, short of incineration.*

He tugged the gag free.

Fire spread outward from the blast site. Flames danced high into the night. Smoke billowed upward, masking the stars, consuming all of the air around it, which hopefully included the toxin. He held his breath, not that it would save him if the cloud reached here. Then, from the edge of the forest, a dark shape burst into view, a shred of a living shadow.

A panther.

Yellowed claws dug deep into the dirt. Dark eyes reflected the campfire's glow. The big cat hissed, showing fangs—then burst to the side, diving back into the dark bower.

Alive.

A good omen.

He waited another minute. Then another.

Death never came.

Pierce joined him, patting his shoulder. "Nice tag team on that one. And damn quick thinking, old man."

He lowered the weapon.

"Who you callin' old?"

LEE CHILD

VS. JOSEPH FINDER

Good and Valuable Consideration

When Joseph Finder decided to try a series character, he took many cues from Lee Child's Jack Reacher. Joe named his hero Nick Heller and made him not a private eye, but a private spy. Nick works for politicians and governments and corporations, sometimes digging up secrets they'd rather keep buried. Like Jack Reacher, though, Nick's sense of justice drives him. He's a mix of blue collar and white collar, the son of a notorious Wall Street criminal, raised in immense wealth that evaporated when his father went to prison. He spent his formative years in a split-level ranch house in a working-class suburb of Boston.

By nature, Nick's a chameleon. He can blend in among the corporate elite as easily as he does among the jarheads.

And, of course, he roots for the Boston Red Sox.

Jack Reacher, on the other hand, is a Yankees fan. His background is vastly different from Nick's, but equally scattered. Reacher is an army brat, raised on military bases around the world: a man without a country, but still an American. He's a loner who avoids attachments, yet he's absolutely loyal. He suffers no fools.

Nick Heller and Jack Reacher. Chalk and cheese, as the Brits say. Couldn't be more different, yet so much the same.

Which can also be said for the two writers.

Lee and Joe are good friends. They share a love of writing, baseball, and the quest for America's best hamburger. Not a gourmet burger. Just the best plain, honest, normal burger. Lee tells the story of some years ago when they were trying a contender in a Spanish restaurant (yeah, go figure) on Twenty-second Street in New York. The talk turned to upcoming projects and Joe started riffing, thinking out loud about maybe starting a series character. He gave Lee a lengthy and penetrating analysis that covered every cost and benefit, every desirable and undesirable characteristic, every strength and weakness.

"I wish I'd had a voice recorder running. I could have sold the transcript to *Writer's Digest*. It would have become the Rosetta Stone for all such decisions," Lee recalls.

Eventually, Joe followed through on his analysis with the first Nick Heller story, *Vanished* (2009), written with his trademark blend of freewheeling imagination mixed with iron self-discipline.

Lee is not a planner. He does not outline stories. They just emerge naturally. For Joe, that's like walking on a wire without a net. So Lee came up with the premise of two guys in a bar in Boston. Reacher would be the out-of-towner, like always. Heller would be home, in the city he loves. Lee was taken by the notion of a mirror at the back of a bar—the way you can look at the reflection of the person next to you and talk with both intimacy and distance. Heller and Reacher would both end up talking to and about and around someone who's in trouble. Eventually, they'd help the guy out, because that's what they do. But that help would come in vastly different ways.

The story was written long distance. Lee sent the first chunk by e-mail and Joe immediately asked, "What do you see happening next?"

In typical Lee Child fashion he answered, "No idea. Until you've written it."

Joe coped with such improvisation just fine.

Actually, their biggest problem was who would win the Yankees-Sox game that kicks the whole thing off.

Good and Valuable Consideration

T he bar was a hundred years old, built for an ink-stained subset of the working class. Clerks, scriveners, printers, and other office-bound wretches of every kind, who had once filled the narrow streets as they quit at the ends of long days in poor conditions, seeking solace wherever they could find it. Now it was just another Boston curiosity, full of dim light and glazed oatmeal-colored tile, and brass, and mahogany, most notably on the bar itself, where a length of tight-grained wood from a massive old tree had been polished to an impossible shine by a million sleeves. The only discordant decorative note was high on the bar back itself, but it was also the only reason Reacher was there: a big flat-screen television, tuned to a live broadcast of the Yankees at Fenway Park.

Reacher paused inside the door and tried to pick his spot. His eyesight was pretty good, so he didn't need to be close, but in his experience flat-screens weren't great when viewed at an angle, so he wanted to be central. Which gave him just one practical choice, a lone unoccupied stool among five in the middle section of the bar, which was more or less directly face-on to the screen. If it had been a theater seat, it would have been expensive. Front row, center. There was a dark-haired woman on its left, her back to the room, and a fat guy on its right, and then came a lean guy with short hair and muscles in his neck and his back, and on the right-hand end of the section was another woman, a blonde, with her high heels hooked over the rail of her stool. The lizard part of Reacher's brain told him immediately the only one to either worry about or rely on was the guy with the short hair and the muscles. Not that Reacher was expecting trouble, even though he was in Boston, rooting for the Yankees.

The bar back was mirrored behind a thicket of bottles, and Reacher saw the short-haired guy spot him, just a blink of roving vigilance, automatic, which reinforced the message his lizard brain had sent. Not a cop, he thought, but some kind of a lone-wolf tough guy, very relaxed, very sure of himself. Ex-military, possibly, from the kind of shadowy unit that taught you to glance in mirrors from time to time, or suffer the consequences.

Then the fat guy on the right of the empty stool looked in the mirror, too, much more obviously. He was not relaxed. He was not sure of himself. He kept his eyes on Reacher's reflected image, all the way through the trip from the door to the empty stool. Reacher slid in beside him and rocked from side to side, to claim his space, and he put his elbows on the mahogany, and the fat guy half turned, with a hesitant but expectant look, as if unsure whether to speak or wait to be spoken to. Reacher said nothing. He rarely offered greetings to strangers. He liked to keep to himself.

Eventually the guy turned away again, but he kept his gaze on the mirror, not the screen. He had a prominent lower lip, sticking out like a pout, and then a great wattle of flesh fell away in a perfect parabola to his shirt collar, uninterrupted by any kind of bony structure. The pneumatic impression continued all the way to his dainty feet. The guy was like a balloon made of flesh-colored silk. He looked like he would be soft and dry to the touch. He had a wedding band on his left hand, deep in the fat, like a sausage with a tourniquet. He was wearing a suit made of the same material as chino pants. The waistband could have been sixty inches.

Reacher looked up at the game. The top of the first was over, no hits, no runs, one man left on base. The commercials were starting, first up being a leasing offer on a brand of automobile Reacher had never heard of. The barman finished up elsewhere and scooted over sideways and Reacher asked for a full-fat Bud in a bottle, which he got seconds later, ice cold and foaming.

The fat guy said, "I'm Jerry DeLong."

At first Reacher wasn't sure who he had been addressing, but by a process of elimination he figured it was him. He said, "Are you?"

The guy with the short hair and the muscles was watching the exchange in the mirror. Reacher glanced at his reflection, and then the fat guy's, who looked straight at him via the glass. Barroom intimacy. Eye contact, but indirect.

Reacher said, "I'm here to watch the game."

Which seemed to satisfy the guy. He looked away, as if an issue had been settled. His gaze returned to the mirror. The various angles of incidence and reflection were hard to calculate, but Reacher figured the guy was watching the door behind him. He was giving off a low-level buzz of anxiety. His eyes were pale and watery. But the rest of him was composed. His huge, pale face was immobile, and his body was still.

The commercials ended, and the broadcast returned to Fenway. The little green bandbox looked luscious under the lights. The Yankees were in the field, in road gray. Their pitcher was throwing the last of his warm-ups. He didn't look very good.

•◆•

Nick Heller had entered the bar three minutes earlier, and had immediately picked up on the after-work vibe, the frenzied high spirits, the smell of sweat and cologne and beer and unwinding anxiety. It was like walking into a party at its very peak: the disorienting cacophony of chatter, the nearly deafening babble, the whooping laughter.

It was one of Heller's favorite hometown bars because it was the real thing. You'd never find raspberry wheat craft beer here. They had Narragansett beer on tap, a beer that Bostonians were loyal to even if it was watery swill.

There were a couple of available seats at the bar, on either side of a great fat man. Interesting. Heller wondered whether the fat guy was saving them for friends. He couldn't be from the neighborhood. No one who came here did things like saving seats.

Heller sidled through the crowd toward the bar counter. One of the things he liked about this place was the mirror behind the serried ranks of bottles. A mirror like this, you could see the faces of those sitting at the bar as you approached. Or you could sit at the bar, back to the room, and see who was coming up from behind. You could talk to the guy or the woman next to you and be looking him or her in the face. In the mirror. Directly, but at the same time indirectly. Heller liked being able to relax when he went for a drink, and you never knew who might turn up.

As he neared the bar, he noticed one face in the mirror looking at him. The fat guy. He had an odd face, a receding chin with a cowl-like wattle that tucked under his collar like an apron. He reminded Heller of a trout. He was watching Heller intently. Like he'd been waiting for him. Heller had never seen the guy before, but still the fat man studied him. As if . . . well, as if he were expecting someone but didn't know what that person might look like.

As if Heller might be that guy. Strange. Heller didn't know him. Heller sat on the stool and nodded at the man.

"Howyadoin?" the guy said.

"Hey," Heller said, neither friendly nor rude.

A pause. "Jerry DeLong," the man said, sticking out his hand.

Heller didn't feel like making friends. He didn't want to chat. The Red Sox were playing the Yankees at Fenway Park. This was a major moment in Boston sports, a rite, like the gladiator games at the Roman Coliseum back in the day. And there was no better place to watch an important game like this than here.

After a brief pause, Heller shook his hand. "Nick," he said. No last name. Heller didn't like to give out his name. He immediately turned to the huge, flat TV screen, set to the Sox. Of course it was. The owner of the bar, a buddy of Nick's, was an ardent Sox fan. So was Sully, the bartender. Some nights, though, there was discord in the bar when the Sox were playing opposite the Bruins. Bostonians also loved their hockey. You even had nights when all four Boston teams—the Sox, the Bruins, the Celtics, and the Patriots—were playing on four different channels. You didn't want to be in this particular bar on a night like that. It got ugly.

"Nick," the bartender said, pulling him a Budweiser without asking.

"Sully," Heller said.

"Big night, huh?"

"Romp to victory."

"Absolutely," said Sully, setting the glass of beer in front of him, a foamy white head like a layer of cotton batting. He wagged his head as if to say, *From your mouth to God's ear.*

Then Heller sensed in his peripheral field the fat guy staring at him again.

In a neutral voice Heller said, "Do I know you?"

The guy sipped a gin and tonic. "Uh, you here to meet someone?" he said.

"I'm here to watch the Sox win," Heller said. A degree friendlier this time, but still no-nonsense.

"Sorry."

"It's cool," Heller relented.

In the bar-back mirror he noticed a large man approaching the empty seat on DeLong's left. Heller knew at once this was someone to keep a wary eye on. He was huge, way taller than most—easily six-foot-five—and at least two hundred fifty pounds. Unusually broad-shouldered. A tank. He was all muscle and had that ex-military look you couldn't miss. The thrift-shop clothes and brutalist haircut made him look a little like a drifter, or at least not someone who paid more than ten bucks at the barber shop.

But there was also a canny intelligence in the eyes, and a wariness. He had the confident look of someone who wasn't challenged physically very often and, when he was, usually won. He intimidated people and didn't mind it.

So this was who Jerry DeLong was meeting. That was a relief. Heller wasn't going to have to fend off some blab-o-maniac during the ball game.

Then he overheard Jerry DeLong introduce himself to the big guy and meet with the same puzzled reaction he'd got from Nick.

Heller put his elbow on the mahogany bar next to an ugly cigarette burn from the good old days when you could smoke in bars, and took a sip of the beer. It was crisp and cold. He never understood why the Brits liked beer at room temperature.

The Yankee pitcher was throwing the last of his warm-ups. He was dismayingly good. Graceful, and a great arm. A knuckleballer. He had a mean slider and a nasty power changeup with serious depth and fade. Most important, he wasn't wasting his stuff. He was saving it for the game. This wasn't a pitcher who'd burn out long before one hundred pitches, like so many others did.

Of course he was good: he'd been one of the Red Sox's best starters until the Yankees hired him away for money no one could turn down. The best pitching money can buy. Yankee fans used to boo him relentlessly when the Sox came to Yankee Stadium. But as soon as he started pitching no-hitters for them, they switched allegiances.

Heller wasn't a guy who switched allegiances.

The bottom of the first started and the Red Sox batter stepped up to the plate and hit a smash off the first pitch. A home run. It sailed over the Green Monster, that ridiculously high left-field wall that had turned many a surefire homer into a double. The ball probably broke a store window somewhere over on Lansdowne Street. The bar erupted in cheers, predictably.

Then Heller noticed three interesting things.

Jerry DeLong hadn't been paying attention to the game. He turned to the set searchingly, a beat too late, trying to figure out what had just happened.

And the big bruiser on his left wasn't cheering. Not even smiling. He'd been watching the game closely, but obviously wasn't a Sox fan. He winced at the home run and made a little snort. He didn't look happy. A New Yorker, then. A Yankees fan. It took a fair measure of chutzpah for a Yankees fan to watch a Sox-Yankees game in a bar like this one. Either that or not caring what other people thought. The latter, Heller decided.

Then the fat guy's cell phone rang and he took it out of his pocket and held it up to his ear, next to the pouch of flesh below his jowls. He cupped his other hand around the phone, shielding it from the clamor of the bar.

"Hey, honey," he said, easy and familiar, but also a little panicked, like husbands in bars everywhere. "No, not at all—I'm watching the game with Howie and Ken."

Which was the third interesting thing. The fat man was lying to his wife.

Men lie to their wives for a long list of reasons, infidelity being right at the top. But this was no Craigslist assignation. He wasn't here for sex. He didn't have that freshly scrubbed look of a guy on the make. He hadn't combed his hair or splashed on fresh cologne.

He looked scared.

• ◆ •

Reacher's first name was Jack, and he was pretty damn sure the guy with the muscles wasn't called either Howie or Ken. He could have been born with either moniker, obviously, but he would have abandoned it fast, in favor of something harder, if he wanted to survive the kind of world he evidently had. Which meant the fat guy was lying through his teeth. He wasn't watching the game with Howie and Ken. In fact he wasn't watching the game at all. When the lucky fly ball had left the tiny bandbox the guy had been a long beat behind. He had looked up with a blank expression because of the sudden noise. He was watching the mirror. He was watching the door. He was expecting someone he didn't know by sight. Hence the half-expectant welcome a minute earlier. *Jerry DeLong,* the guy had said, as if it might mean something.

Reacher snaked a long arm behind DeLong's immense back and poked the guy with the muscles in the shoulder. The guy leaned back, but kept his eyes on the game. As did Reacher. The guy in the two-hole for the Sox swung and missed. Strike three. Better.

Reacher said, "Who got here first, you or him?"

The guy said, "Him."

"Did you get the same thing I got?"

"Identical."

"Was he saving the seats?"

"I doubt it."

"So now he's expecting a tap on the shoulder, and then they'll go somewhere to do their business?"

"That's how I see it."

The third batter for the Sox stepped up. Reacher said, "What kind of business? Am I in the kind of place I don't want to be?"

"You from New York?"

"Not exactly."

"But you're rooting for them."

"No crime in being a sane human being."

"This place is okay. I don't know what the tub of lard wants."

Reacher said, "You could ask him."

"Or you could."

"I'm not very interested."

"Me, either. But he's worried about something."

The third Sox batter popped up, way high, in the infield. Comfortable for the Yankees' second baseman. The guy with the muscles said, "You got a name?"

Reacher said, "Everyone's got a name."

"What is it?"

"Reacher."

"I'm Heller." The guy offered his left fist. Reacher bumped it with his right, behind DeLong's back. Not the first time his knuckles had touched a Sox fan, but by far the gentlest.

The Sox cleanup hitter grounded weakly back to the pitcher, and the inning was over. One–zip Boston. Bad, but not a humiliating disaster. Yet.

Reacher said, "If we keep on talking about him like this, eventually he might clue us in."

Heller said, "Why would he?"

"He's in trouble."

"What are you, Santa Claus?"

"I don't like our pitching. I'm looking for a diversion."

"Suck it up."

"Like you did for a hundred years?"

At that point the bar was quiet. Just the natural ebb and flow, but the barman heard what Reacher said, and he stared, hard.

Reacher said, "What?"

Heller said, "It's okay, Sully."

And then Jerry DeLong looked left, looked right, and said, "I'm waiting for someone to break my legs."

•◆•

Heller gave Reacher a glance.

Reacher seemed to have an intuition about the fat guy. He knew something was off, somehow. Something was wrong. Funny, Heller'd had the same sort of intuition. Same way he realized pretty quickly that this Reacher guy was really sharp.

The fat man had blurted it out. He was genuinely terrified.

But then he said no more.

The top of the second started. Two balls, a strike, ball three. The Boston pitcher stared in. He didn't want to give up a lead-off walk.

"Changeup coming," Reacher said. "Right down the pike."

The Yankee batter knew it. He smiled like a wolf.

Not a changeup. A full-on fastball. The batter swung as the ball hit the catcher's glove.

Reacher looked away.

He said, "Maybe this guy'll tell us what's going on. With his legs and all."

"Ya think?" Heller replied.

"Or not," Reacher said.

"Not unless I want my arms broken, too," the fat man said.

Full count, and another fastball. Another whiff. One down.

Heller gave the fat guy a searching look. "Haven't seen you here before, have I?"

"I haven't been here before, no."

"But you're from here."

From here: very Boston. Bostonians always want to know if you're one of them or not. You can't always tell from the accent. But there's the language. Do you drink soda or "tonic"? Is something a "pisser"? Do you go to a liquor store or a packie? Take a U-turn or "bang a uey"? They're expert at sussing out fakes and posers. Heller was born outside New York but moved as a teenager to a town north of Boston called Melrose. A working-class place. Heller's father went to prison and his mother was left with nothing. So Heller could sound Boston if and when he wanted. Or not.

And this guy DeLong was definitely from around here.

DeLong shrugged. "Yeah."

"You work around here?"

DeLong shrugged again. "Government Center."

"Don't like the Irish pub right there?"

"Well, my office is on Cambridge Street."

DeLong was stingy with the information. For some reason he didn't want to talk about what he did or where he worked, which was, for Heller, like a blinking neon arrow. That meant he did something sensitive, or classified, or unpleasant. But he had the look of a bureaucrat, a government functionary, and Heller took a guess.

"The good old Saltonstall Building." One of the office towers in the bleak ghetto of big government buildings at the foot of Beacon Hill. "How's the asbestos?"

The Saltonstall Building, which held an assortment of state bureaucracies, had been abandoned after it was found to be contaminated with asbestos. They did some renovation and dragged the office workers back in, and some of them were mad as a wasp's nest that's been kicked.

"Yeah, that's gone."

"Uh-huh." Heller smiled. A state worker, for sure. He thought of maps of America where the states are resized by population and Rhode Island is twice the size of Wyoming. If you did a map of state employees in the Saltonstall building, the biggest state would be the Department of Revenue.

"So you're a tax man."

"Something like that," DeLong said. He didn't look happy about it. Like he was being put down somehow. But at the same time he didn't seem to want to say more.

"One of those forensic accountant types, aren't you?"

DeLong looked away uneasily, which just confirmed Heller's theory.

"What do you say, Reacher?" Heller said, reaching around DeLong and bumping Reacher's shoulder. "Someone's trying to dodge an audit by some direct means, wouldn't you say?"

"Sounds like it," Reacher said. "Wonder how often that works."

Jerry DeLong said, "It's not going to work this time." He sounded like he was trying to be brave, but without much success.

"Huh," Heller said, looking into the mirror behind the bar. He saw a blinged-out guy sitting by himself at a small table near the front. Tinted sunglasses, necklaces, and rings. A curious upright posture. The chief enforcer for the Albanian gang in Boston, Alek Dushku. Allie Boy, as he was called, was known for all sorts of colorful executions, including strangling an old man with a shoelace until his eyes popped out of his head. On the table in front of him was a grocery sack, bulky with something.

Heller said, "You're meeting Allie Boy?"

Jerry DeLong looked in the mirror and his face paled.

He said, "Is that him?"

"Sure is." Heller gestured with his head, straight at the guy. "No time like the present."

DeLong said nothing.

Reacher said, "What's in the grocery sack?"

DeLong said, "Money. A hundred grand."

"What for?"

"Me."

"So what is this? A bribe or a threat?"

"Both."

"He's going to break your legs and then give you a hundred grand?"

"Maybe the money first."

"Why?"

DeLong didn't answer.

Heller said, "It's an Albanian thing. One of them read a law book. They like to give good and valuable consideration. They think it cements the deal. And legs heal. Money never goes away. It's either in your house or your bank. It means you're theirs forever."

Reacher said, "I never heard of that before."

"You're not from here."

"Ethical gangsters?"

"Not really. Like I said, legs heal."

"But it's definitely a two-part deal?"

"All part of the culture."

The top of the second ended with a limp swing-and-miss, strike three. Still one–zip Boston. The zip didn't look likely to change. The one did. Reacher turned to the fat guy and said, "He's supposed to make contact with you, right?"

DeLong nodded yes.

"When?"

"I'm not sure. Soon, I guess. I don't really know what he's waiting for."

"Maybe he's watching the game."

"He isn't," Heller said.

"Not as dumb as he looks, then."

"You thinking what I'm thinking?"

"Depends when the audit starts, I guess."

"Tomorrow morning," DeLong said.

"And what happens if you're in the orthopedic ward?"

"Someone else does it. Less well."

The bottom of the second started. A four-pitch lead-off walk. Hopeless. Reacher rocked back and looked at Heller and said, "Do you live here?"

Heller said, "Not in this actual bar."

"But in town?"

"Shouldn't I?"

"I guess someone has to. You worried about these Albanians?"

"Altogether less hassle if Allie Boy doesn't remember my face."

"Where did you serve?"

"With General Hood."

"Did you get out in time?"

"Unscathed."

"Good for you."

"What were you?"

"MPs," Reacher said. "Hood's still in Leavenworth, as far as I know."

"Where he belongs."

"You armed, by any chance?"

"No, or I'd have shot you already. When you said a hundred years. It was less than ninety."

"Is the Albanian guy armed?"

"Probably. A Sig, most likely. In the back of his pants. See how he's sitting?"

"I don't think we can get it done during the commercials. We're going to have to give up half an inning."

"Top of the next."

Now Boston had two runners on. Reacher said, "I'm not sure our corpulent friend can wait that long."

The fat guy said, "What are you talking about?"

Reacher saw the Albanian moving in the mirror, shifting in his chair, putting his hand on the grocery sack.

Heller said, "Now."

Reacher turned back to DeLong and said, "Get up, right now, and walk out, straight line, fast, don't look back, and keep on going."

"Out?"

"To the street. Right now."

"Which way?"

"Turn left. If in doubt, always turn left. That's a rule that will serve you well."

"Left?"

"Or right. It really doesn't matter. Fast as you can."

Which wasn't lightning-quick, but it was reasonably speedy. The guy swiveled and kind of fell forward off his stool, and waited while his fat bounced and jiggled and settled, and then he set off through the crowd, surprisingly light on his dainty feet, and he was already past the blinged-out Albanian before the guy really noticed. Reacher and Heller paused a beat and slid off their stools in turn, and made up the third and fourth places in a determined little procession through the throng, first DeLong, then the Albanian with the sack, then Reacher, with Heller right behind him. DeLong had the advantage. He was cruising like a ship. People were scattering in front of him, for fear of getting run over. The Albanian guy wasn't getting the same physical deference. From a distance he wasn't imposing. Reacher and Heller didn't have that problem. People were stepping smartly aside, out of their way.

DeLong pushed through the bar door and was gone. The Albanian got there a second later. Reacher and Heller followed him out, practically close enough to touch. The street was quiet and dark and narrow. Old Boston. The fat guy had turned left. His pale bulk was twenty yards away, on the sidewalk. The Albanian had seen him. He was getting ready to hustle in pursuit.

"Here?" Reacher asked.

Heller said, "It's as good a place as any."

Reacher called, "Allie Boy?"

The guy missed a step, but kept on walking.

"Yes, you, asshole," Reacher said.

The guy glanced back.

"All those rings and chains," Reacher said. "Didn't your momma tell you it's dumb to walk around like that in a poor part of town?"

The guy stopped and turned and said, "What?"

"You could get mugged," Heller said.

The guy said, "Mugged?"

Reacher said, "Where a couple of guys take all your stuff. You don't have that in Albania?"

"You know who I am?"

"Obviously. I just used your name and said you're from Albania. This stuff ain't rocket science."

"You know what will happen to you?"

"Nobody knows what will happen to them. The future's not ours to see. But in this case I don't suppose much will happen. We might get a couple bucks for the bling. We're certainly not going to wear it. We got more taste."

"Are you kidding me?"

"Was that a comedy club we were just in?"

There was a dull roar from inside the bar. Likely a three-run homer. Reacher winced. Heller smiled. The Albanian hitched the paper sack higher to the crook of his left elbow. Which left his right hand free.

Heller stepped forward, going right, and Reacher went left. At that point the Albanian guy should have turned and run. That was the smart play. He was probably fast enough. But he didn't, inevitably. He was a tough guy. The streets were his. He went for his gun.

Which was very dumb, because it took both his hands out of the game. One was cradling his grocery sack, and the other was snaking around behind his back. Reacher hit him with a straight right, hard, in the center of his face, and after that it didn't really matter where his hands were. Command and control were temporarily unavailable. The guy dropped the sack and rocked back on rubber legs, blood already spurting, ready for a standing count.

Which he didn't get. Street-fighting's first rule: there are no rules. Heller kicked him dead-on in the nuts, hard enough to take his weight off his feet, and then the guy collapsed down to about half his size in a crouch, and Heller used the flat of his sole to tip him over on his side, and Reacher kicked him in the head, and the guy lay still.

"Was that hard enough?" Heller said.

"For amnesia? Difficult to judge. Amnesia is unpredictable."

"Best guess?"

"Better safe than sorry."

So Heller picked his spot and kicked the guy again, in the left temple, going for lateral displacement of the brain in the pan. Generally four times more effective than front-to-back. No surprise. One of General Hood's boys would have learned stuff like that pretty early. Hood wasn't all bad. Mostly, but not all.

In the far distance Jerry DeLong was watching.

Reacher picked up the grocery sack. It was full of hundred-dollar bills, all used and wrinkled, held together in bricks by orange rubber bands. Reacher had four pants pockets, two in front, two in back, so he took four bricks from the sack and stuffed one in each pocket. Then he tore off the gold chains and pulled off the rings and found the Sig and went through the Albanian's pockets and dumped out all the loot. He gave the sack to Heller.

Heller said, "The cops will come. We don't leave people on the street here. Not like New York."

Reacher said, "They'll check the bar."

"Their first stop."

"I'll go east and you go west. Pleasure working with you."

"Likewise," Heller said.

They shook hands, and melted away into the darkness, opposite directions, leaving the Albanian where he was on the sidewalk, an unfortunate victim of a mugging, his good and valuable consideration stolen before the deal with DeLong could be properly consummated. Therefore no deal existed. Their own rules said so. DeLong had no obligations, and nothing to betray. An Albanian thing. Part of the culture.

•◆•

Reacher watched the end of the game in a bar a mile away. He was sure Heller was doing the same thing a mile in the other direction. In which case they were watching two different events. Reacher was watching a limp and miserable defeat. Heller was watching a glorious and triumphant victory. But such was life. You can't win them all.

Author Biographies

DAVID BALDACCI made a splash on the literary scene with the publication of his first novel, *Absolute Power*. A major motion picture adaptation followed, with Clint Eastwood as its director and star. David has now published twenty-six novels, all of which have been national and international best sellers. His novels have been translated into more than forty-five languages and sold in more than eighty countries, with over 110 million copies in print worldwide. A lifelong Virginian, David received his bachelor's degree in political science from Virginia Commonwealth University and his law degree from the University of Virginia School of Law, after which he practiced in Washington, DC. He's also an accomplished philanthropist. With his wife, Michelle, he started Wish You Well Foundation, which supports literacy by fostering and promoting the development and expansion of literacy and educational programs. In 2008, the foundation partnered with Feeding America to launch Feeding Body & Mind, a program to address the connection between literacy, poverty, and hunger. Through Feeding Body & Mind, more than one million new and used books have been collected and distributed through area food banks nationwide. David lives with his wife and their two teenagers in Virginia. To learn more, visit davidbaldacci.com.

LINWOOD BARCLAY had written several novels by the time he was in his early twenties, but no one wanted to publish them (this may have been because, according to Linwood, they were not all that good). So he decided on a field where he could get paid to write every day. He spent twenty-seven years at Canada's largest paper, the *Toronto Star*, the last fifteen as a columnist. But in 2004, with the publication of *Bad Move*, he finally got to do what he'd always wanted. In 2008, he left the paper to write fiction full-time. Linwood has published more than a dozen novels, which have been translated into nearly thirty languages. They include the best seller *No Time for Goodbye* and *Trust Your Eyes*, which has been optioned by Warner Bros. for film. He lives near Toronto with his wife, Neetha. They have two grown children. His website is linwoodbarclay.com.

STEVE BERRY is the *New York Times* and number one internationally best-selling author of nine Cotton Malone adventures, four stand-alone thrillers, and four short story originals. His books have been translated into forty languages with more than seventeen million printed copies in fifty-one countries. History lies at the heart of all of Steve's novels. It's his passion, one he shares with his wife, Elizabeth, which led them to create History Matters, a foundation dedicated to historic preservation. Since 2009 Steve and Elizabeth have crossed the country to save endangered historic treasures, raising money via lectures, receptions, galas, luncheons, dinners, and their popular writers' workshops. He is a member of the Smithsonian

Institution Libraries Advisory Board and a founding member of International Thriller Writers—where he served three years as its copresident. For more information on Steve and History Matters, visit steveberry.org.

LEE CHILD has been a television director, union organizer, theater technician, and law student. After being fired, and on the dole, he hatched a harebrained scheme to write a novel, thus saving his family from financial ruin. *Killing Floor* (1997) was that novel and won worldwide acclaim. The hero first introduced there was Jack Reacher. Seventeen novels later Reacher is a worldwide phenomenon. Millions of copies of those books have been sold in countless languages. In 2012, Tom Cruise brought Reacher to life on the big screen. Lee himself was born in England but now lives in New York City. He likes to say that he leaves the island of Manhattan "only when required to by forces beyond his control." Visit Lee online at leechild.com.

MICHAEL CONNELLY is the author of twenty-six published novels and a book of nonfiction. He is a former journalist who covered crime and courts for the *Los Angeles Times*. Eighteen of his novels have featured LAPD detective Hieronymus "Harry" Bosch, who debuted in the mystery world in 1992 with *The Black Echo*. Michael has also written several novels featuring defense attorney Mickey Haller, who debuted in 2005's *The Lincoln Lawyer*. More than fifty million copies of his books have been sold worldwide. Two of his novels—*Blood Work* and *The Lincoln Lawyer*—have been made into films. Michael was born in Pennsylvania, raised in Florida, and spends much of his time in California where he researches his characters and books. His website is michaelconnelly.com.

JEFFERY DEAVER is a former journalist, folksinger, and lawyer. Now he's a number one internationally best-selling author, sold in 150 countries and translated into thirty-one languages, with thirty-two novels, three collections of short stories, and a nonfiction law book to his credit. His *The Bodies Left Behind* was named 2009 Novel of the Year by International Thriller Writers. He's also won the Steel Dagger and the Short Story Dagger from the British Crime Writers' Association and the Nero Wolfe. He's even entered the world of James Bond, chosen by the Ian Fleming estate to write *Carte Blanche* (2011), a huge best seller, which also received the Japanese Grand Prix award. Movies are no stranger to him, either. His book *A Maiden's Grave* was made into an HBO film starring James Garner and Marlee Matlin. *The Bone Collector* became a feature release starring Denzel Washington and Angelina Jolie. His *The Devil's Teardrop* is a Lifetime Network feature film. And, yes, the rumors are true, Jeff did appear as a corrupt reporter on his favorite soap opera, *As the World Turns.* Jeff was born outside Chicago, has a bachelor's degree in journalism from the University of Missouri, and a law degree from Fordham University. Learn more about this fascinating writer at jefferydeaver.com.

LINDA FAIRSTEIN spent thirty years as a prosecutor in the New York County District Attorney's Office. But she is now the author of fifteen *New York Times* and internationally best-selling Alex Cooper crime novels. She is also the author of a *New York Times* Notable Book of the Year, *Sexual Violence: Our War Against Rape*. Among her many honors, Linda was awarded the International Thriller Writers' 2010 Silver Bullet for her work with battered and abused women. You can find out more about Linda at lindafairstein.com.

JOSEPH FINDER is the *New York Times* best-selling author of ten novels. The *Boston Globe* called him a "master of the modern thriller."

His first novel, *The Moscow Club* (1991), was named one of the ten best spy novels of all time. In 2007, his *Killer Instinct* (2006) was tagged as Best Novel of the Year by International Thriller Writers. He's also made a successful move into theaters. A major motion picture based on his novel *Paranoia,* starring Harrison Ford, Gary Oldman, and Liam Hemsworth, was released in 2013. Previously, his novel *High Crimes* became a hit starring Morgan Freeman and Ashley Judd. Joe is a graduate of Yale College and the Harvard Russian Research Center. He is a member of the Council on Foreign Relations and the Association of Former Intelligence Officers. He lives in Boston. Check him out at josephfinder.com.

LISA GARDNER is both a number one *New York Times* best-selling author and the 2010 winner for Best Hardcover Novel (*The Neighbor*) from International Thriller Writers. She began her career in food service, but after catching her hair on fire she took the hint and focused on writing. With sixteen million copies of her books now in print, Lisa's glad she did. She lives in the mountains of New Hampshire with her race car–driving husband, speed-skiing daughter, two extremely barky dogs, and one silly puppy. For the full scoop on Lisa, check out lisagardner.com.

HEATHER GRAHAM is the *New York Times* and *USA Today* best-selling author of over one hundred novels ranging from suspense, paranormal, and historical, to mainstream Christmas fare. She lives in Miami, Florida, which makes for an easy drive down to the Keys where she can indulge her passion for diving. Travel, research, and ballroom dancing also help keep her sane. She is the CEO of Slush Pile Productions, a recording company and production house for various charitable events. Look her up at eheathergraham.com.

PETER JAMES's *Sunday Times* number one best-selling Detective Superintendent Roy Grace crime novels have been translated into thirty-six languages, with worldwide sales of over fourteen million copies. Three of his books have been filmed and two more are currently in development, as well as a stage play. All of Peter's novels reflect his deep interest in law enforcement. His research is legendary, delving into science, medicine, and the paranormal. He's also produced numerous films, including *The Merchant of Venice*, starring Al Pacino, Jeremy Irons, and Joseph Fiennes. In 2010 he was awarded an honorary doctorate by the University of Brighton. He served two terms as chair of the Crime Writers Association and is a board member of International Thriller Writers. He divides his time between his homes in Notting Hill, London, and near Brighton in Sussex. Visit Peter's website at peterjames.com.

RAYMOND KHOURY is the *New York Times* and internationally best-selling author of four Reilly and Tess adventures: *The Last Templar, The Templar Salvation, The Devil's Elixir,* and *Rasputin's Shadow*, as well as two stand-alone thrillers, *The Sanctuary* and *The Sign*. His debut novel, *The Last Templar*, spent twenty weeks on the *New York Times* best-seller list and was adapted for television by NBC. His books have been translated into over forty languages and sold over ten million copies. Raymond earned an MA in architecture and an MBA before deciding he wanted to write. His screenwriting work includes the award-winning British series *Spooks (MI-5)* and *Waking the Dead*. You can connect with him at raymondkhoury.com.

DENNIS LEHANE grew up in Boston. Before becoming a full-time writer, Dennis worked as a counselor with mentally handicapped and abused children, waited tables, parked cars, drove limos, worked in bookstores, and loaded tractor-trailers. His first novel,

A Drink Before the War, won the Shamus Award. He has published nine more novels since that have been translated into more than thirty languages, each an international best seller. Gems like *Darkness, Take My Hand; Sacred; Gone, Baby, Gone; Prayers for Rain; Mystic River; Shutter Island; The Given Day; Moonlight Mile;* and *Live by Night.* He was a staff writer on the acclaimed HBO series *The Wire* and is currently a writer-producer on the fourth season of HBO's *Boardwalk Empire.* Learn more at dennislehane.com.

JOHN LESCROART is the author of twenty-four novels, most of which have been *New York Times* best sellers. With sales of over ten million copies, his books have been translated into twenty-two languages in more than seventy-five countries. John has also endowed the perennial $5,000 Maurice Prize for excellence in long-form fiction at the University of California at Davis. Additionally, he is a member of the board of directors of Cal Humanities, an independent nonprofit partner of the National Endowment for the Humanities. Finally, and perhaps less known, John loves to cook. His original recipes have appeared in *Gourmet* magazine and in the cookbook *A Taste of Murder.* John and his wife, Lisa Sawyer, live in Northern California. His website is johnlescroart.com.

STEVE MARTINI is the author of numerous *New York Times* bestselling novels, including *Shadow of Power, Double Tap, The List, The Judge,* and *Undue Influence,* the last two of which were produced as network television miniseries on NBC and CBS. In all Steve has written fifteen novels, twelve of them in the Paul Madriani series. Once upon a time Steve worked as a newspaper reporter and California State Capitol correspondent. He also practiced law in California and served as an administrative law judge. He currently travels widely and divides his time between his home in the Pacific

Northwest and a condominium overlooking the Gulf of Siam in Thailand. To discover more about Steve's interesting life, go to stevemartini.com.

T. JEFFERSON PARKER is the author of twenty crime novels, including *Silent Joe* and *California Girl*, both of which won the Edgar Award for best mystery. His last six books are what he calls a "Border Sextet," featuring ATF task-force agent Charlie Hood, who tries to staunch the flow of illegal firearms being smuggled from the United States into Mexico. Jeff enjoys fishing, hiking, and cycling. He lives in Southern California with his family. His website is tjeffersonparker.com.

DOUGLAS PRESTON and **LINCOLN CHILD** have been a writing team for a long time. They are the creators of the number one *New York Times* and internationally best-selling series of thrillers starring Special Agent Aloysius Pendergast. Their novel *Relic* was made into a number one box-office movie by Paramount Pictures. Two of their novels, *Relic* and *The Cabinet of Curiosities*, were named as among the one hundred greatest thrillers ever written in a National Public Radio poll of avid thriller readers. When not writing together, they write alone. Lincoln is the author of five best-selling novels and was once a top editor at St. Martin's Press. He first met Doug when he edited Doug's debut novel. In addition to writing his own separate novels, Doug Preston is the author of several nonfiction books. The most recent, *The Monster of Florence*, the true story of a serial killer, is being made into a film starring George Clooney. Doug also contributes to *The New Yorker* and has taught writing at Princeton University. Lincoln lives in New Jersey and is interested in fast cars, exotic parrots, electric guitars, and the culinary arts. Doug resides in New Mexico and is more the outdoorsman. Skiing, mountain climbing, and scuba diving consume his free time. Learn more about each of these men at prestonchild.com.

IAN RANKIN is known for his Inspector Rebus series. The first Rebus novel, *Knots and Crosses,* was written in 1987 while Ian was a postgraduate student at Edinburgh University. Eighteen more novels followed and there have been several TV incarnations for the irascible, hard-drinking detective. Ian has also branched out into nonfiction work (*Rebus's Scotland: A Personal Journey*), two collections of short stories, and a series of thrillers under the pseudonym Jack Harvey. Recently, Ian began to write about an Internal Affairs cop named Malcolm Fox. Ian's books have been translated into thirty-five languages, and his many awards include the Gold and Diamond Daggers, the Edgar Award, and literary prizes in Denmark, Germany, France, Italy, and Spain. He is the recipient of five honorary degrees, plus the Order of the British Empire for Services to Literature. He lives in Edinburgh, Scotland, a city that continues to confound, mesmerize, and intrigue him, with his wife and two sons. His website is ianrankin.net.

JAMES ROLLINS is the *New York Times* best-selling author of international thrillers that are sold in over forty languages. His Sigma Force novels specialize in unveiling unseen worlds, scientific breakthroughs, and historical secrets. But Jim also pays it forward, having founded Authors United for Veterans, a group of best-selling writers dedicated to raising funds and awareness for USA Cares, a nonprofit organization that helps soldiers and their families. When Jim is not writing or touring, he can be found spelunking, scuba diving, or hiking. He shares his family with three golden retrievers, amid chew toys and a collection of paleontological treasures, in the Sierra Nevada Mountains. To learn all sorts of things about him, visit jamesrollins.com.

M. J. ROSE is the award-winning, internationally best-selling author of more than a dozen novels and three nonfiction books. The television series *Past Life* was based on her novels in the Reincarnationist series. Her 2013 novel, *Seduction*, was chosen Book of the Year by *Suspense Magazine*. In 1999, Rose broke ground when she used the Internet to self-publish an ebook and became the first author to be discovered online and picked up by a major publisher. She is currently copresident of ITW, and was one of the organization's founding members. She's also the founder of the first Internet marketing company for authors, AuthorBuzz.com, which remains one of the premier resources for writers. Before turning to fiction, Rose was a creative director at a top ad agency. She lives in Connecticut with a mysterious composer and their spoiled dog, Winka. Learn more about her at mjrose.com.

JOHN SANDFORD is the pseudonym of John Camp. John was a reporter and an editor at the *Miami Herald,* and a reporter and columnist for the *St. Paul Pioneer Press.* He won the 1986 Pulitzer Prize in journalism. John is the author of thirty-one published novels, all of which have appeared on the *New York Times* best sellers lists. He is also the author of two nonfiction books, one on plastic surgery, the other art. His books have been translated into most every language around the world. He is also the principal financial backer of the Beth-Shean Valley Archaeological Project in the Jordan River Valley in Israel. In addition to archaeology, John is deeply interested in art and photography along with hunting, fishing, canoeing, and skiing. He lives in Sante Fe, New Mexico. To get to know him better, visit johnsandford.org.

R. L. STINE is one of the best-selling children's authors in history. He's also one of the most widely published writers of all time.

His Goosebumps series for young people has sold over 300 million copies in the United States alone, and has become a publishing phenomenon in thirty-two languages around the world. His other popular children's book series include Fear Street, Mostly Ghostly, The Nightmare Room, and Rotten School. His anthology television series, *R. L. Stine's The Haunting Hour*, won an Emmy Award for Outstanding Children's Series. In 2014, Bob marked the twenty-second anniversary of Goosebumps. Many of his original readers are now in their twenties and thirties and have enjoyed his adult novels, which include *Red Rain* and *Superstitious*. Bob lives in New York City with his wife, Jane, an editor and publisher. You can find out much more at rlstine.com.

F. PAUL WILSON is the award-winning, best-selling author of fifty-plus books and nearly one hundred short stories spanning science fiction, horror, adventure, medical, and virtually everything in between. His novels regularly appear on the *New York Times* best sellers lists. *The Tomb* received the Porgie Award from the *West Coast Review of Books*. *Wheels Within Wheels* won the Prometheus Award. His novella, *Aftershock*, won a Bram Stoker Award. He was voted Grand Master by the World Horror Convention and received the Lifetime Achievement Award from the Horror Writers of America. Paul also received the prestigious San Diego Comi-Con Inkpot Award. In 1983, Paramount rendered his novel *The Keep* into a visually striking but (as Paul says) "otherwise incomprehensible movie." Hollywood continues to toy with the idea of turning Repairman Jack into a franchise character. Over nine million copies of Paul's books are in print and his work has been translated into twenty-four languages. Paul resides at the Jersey Shore and more information on him can be found at repairmanjack.com.